There's nothin...
a tiny...

MAITLAND MATERNITY: TRIPLETS, QUADS & QUINTS

You're invited to celebrate the opening of
the new McCallum Multiple Birth Wing at
the Maitland Maternity Hospital – where
romances are born, secrets are revealed and
multiple bundles of joy are delivered!

Five heart-warming stories from
five favourite authors.

We're proud to present

MILLS & BOON
SPOTLIGHT™

A chance to buy collections of bestselling novels by favourite authors every month – they're back by popular demand!

April 2010

The Ashtons: Jillian, Eli & Charlotte

Featuring

Just a Taste by Bronwyn Jameson
Awaken the Senses by Nalini Singh
Estate Affair by Sara Orwig

Maitland Maternity:
Triplets, Quads & Quints

Featuring

Triplet Secret Babies by Judy Christenberry
Quadruplets on the Doorstep
by Tina Leonard
Great Expectations by Kasey Michaels
Delivered with a Kiss by Mindy Neff
And Babies Make Seven
by Mary Anne Wilson

MAITLAND MATERNITY: TRIPLETS, QUADS & QUINTS

JUDY CHRISTENBERRY

TINA LEONARD

KASEY MICHAELS

MINDY NEFF

MARY ANNE WILSON

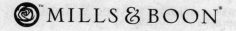 MILLS & BOON®

All the characters in this book have no existence outside the imagination of
the author, and have no relation whatsoever to anyone bearing the same name
or names. They are not even distantly inspired by any individual known or
unknown to the author, and all the incidents are pure invention.

All Rights Reserved including the right of reproduction in whole or in part
in any form. This edition is published by arrangement with Harlequin
Enterprises II B.V./S.à.r.l. The text of this publication or any part thereof may
not be reproduced or transmitted in any form or by any means, electronic or
mechanical, including photocopying, recording, storage in an information
retrieval system, or otherwise, without the written permission of the publisher.

This book is sold subject to the condition that it shall not, by way of trade or
otherwise, be lent, resold, hired out or otherwise circulated without the prior
consent of the publisher in any form of binding or cover other than that in
which it is published and without a similar condition including this condition
being imposed on the subsequent purchaser.

® and ™ are trademarks owned and used by the trademark owner and/or its
licensee. Trademarks marked with ® are registered with the United Kingdom
Patent Office and/or the Office for Harmonisation in the Internal Market and
in other countries.

MAITLAND MATERNITY: TRIPLETS, QUADS & QUINTS
© Harlequin Books S.A. 2010.

First published in Great Britain 2010
Harlequin Mills & Boon Limited,
Eton House, 18-24 Paradise Road, Richmond, Surrey TW9 1SR

The publisher acknowledges the copyright holders of the individual works, which
have already been published in the UK in single, separate volumes, as follows:

Triplet Secret Babies © Harlequin Books S.A. 2001
Quadruplets on the Doorstep © Harlequin Books S.A. 2002
Great Expectations © Harlequin Books S.A. 2002
Delivered with a Kiss © Harlequin Books S.A. 2002
And Babies Make Seven © Harlequin Books S.A. 2002

Special thanks and acknowledgement are given to Judy Christenberry, Tina
Leonard, Kasey Michaels, Mindy Neff and Mary Anne Wilson for their
contributions to the *Maitland Maternity: Triplets, Quads & Quints* series.

ISBN: 978 0 263 88035 9

64-0410

Printed and bound in Spain
by Litografia Rosés S.A., Barcelona

TRIPLET SECRET BABIES

BY
JUDY CHRISTENBERRY

Judy Christenberry has been writing romances for fifteen years because she loves happy endings as much as her readers do. A former French teacher, Judy now devotes herself to writing full time. She hopes readers have as much fun reading her stories as she does writing them. She spends her spare time reading, watching her favourite sports teams and keeping track of her two daughters. Judy's a native Texan, but now lives in Arizona.

Chapter One

Her head was beating like a bass drum during a pep rally. Briana McCallum stared at the shelf of pain relievers in the New York deli she'd found a block from the hotel, feeling lucky to have found it open after midnight.

There it was! Her favorite relief for headaches. She grabbed it and then took a soda from the refrigerated shelf nearby and hurried to the cash register.

She was digging through her purse when the clerk said, "You give me your money."

"Yes, I'm looking for it," she assured him, her head down as she dug through her bag for her billfold.

"No, all your money," he returned harshly.

She looked up to find herself staring down the barrel of a pistol pointed directly at her.

"What—" she began, confused, when the outer door opened and another customer arrived. Relief poured through her. She wasn't alone with the wacko anymore. The pistol swung away from her to the new arrival.

"You come. Give me money," the clerk ordered.

The new arrival, a handsome man in a tuxedo, his tie untied, stared in surprise. "What's going on?"

He looked at Briana for an explanation. "I think he's planning on robbing us," she said.

"I go home now. I need money," the clerk said, as if that explained everything.

"Home to—?" the man asked.

"India. My mother sick. I go home. Give me money."

After a dead silence, the man behind the counter began shifting, swinging the gun between the two of them, and Briana grew more nervous. "I—I don't have a lot of money." She pulled out about sixty dollars and laid it on the counter. "That's all I have with me."

"Now you," the clerk said, scooping up the money and looking at the man.

With reluctance, the man pulled out his wallet from his back pants pocket. He took the cash out and laid it on the counter. Then he tucked his wallet away. "That's all I've got."

It was considerably more than Briana carried with her.

But she was distracted from thinking about that. The clerk came around the counter and gestured for them to go to the back of the store. Was he going to shoot them before he left? She didn't want to die, not when her dream was just coming true. Not when she'd finally achieved—

''Go!'' the clerk shouted, becoming more agitated.

The man put his hands on her shoulders and pushed her gently in front of him, keeping himself between her and the gun. A very protective gesture. One her brother Caleb would approve of. As did she.

They reached the back of the store and the clerk shoved open a door that said Employees Only. It was dark, not a large area, and she was reluctant to go in. Suddenly the man fell into her and she fell to her knees on the concrete floor. She heard a loud slamming noise and everything went black.

She thought she'd passed out, but she was still awake. Then she realized the door behind them had been slammed shut and there was no light.

''Are you okay?'' the deep voice of the other customer asked. His hands found her shoulders again and he half lifted her to her feet.

''Yes, just bruised,'' she said softly. ''Are we—''

''Locked in.'' He turned her loose and took a step back. In the darkness she felt abandoned.

Then a bright light came on.

She stared around her before her gaze returned to her companion. He'd found the light switch by the door and turned it on. She was grateful. Nothing seemed quite so bad when there was light.

''Thank you. I'm glad we're not left in the dark.''

''I guess. But the accommodations aren't too posh.''

She couldn't argue with that assessment. They were in a small storeroom, the shelves packed with food items from floor to ceiling. The only piece of furniture was a sturdy stool, dingy white in color.

"At least we're alive," Briana pointed out. "I've heard of too many of these robberies where the witnesses were killed."

"Yeah. I guess since he's leaving the country, he doesn't think we can hurt him." The man prowled the storeroom, pacing from one end to the other. "I tried the door. I don't think I can force it open."

"Won't we be okay? I mean, someone will come in to relieve him after a while, won't they? If we just wait, he'll let us out."

The man looked at his watch. "Probably at seven, six if we're lucky. Which means we have about five and half hours in this hellhole."

She noticed his watch was a Rolex, which went well with his tux. Obviously not a man down on his luck. "Um, are you from New York?" she asked.

"No. Say, you don't happen to have a cell phone, do you?" He turned and stared at her, his blue-eyed gaze enough to convince Briana to tell him the truth and nothing but.

"Yes, but I didn't bring it with me. I didn't think I'd need it in New York City."

"Me, neither." He began pacing again. After a minute, he said, "Obviously you're not from New York, either."

"No, Texas."

"Ah. I'm from Chicago. The name's Hunter." He

stuck out a large hand with slim strong fingers, a hand almost artistic in appearance except for its size.

"Briana," she said. She tried to avoid using her last name with strangers, in case they knew of her family wealth. She'd been both pursued and rejected because of it.

"Unusual name."

"I'm part of ABC."

"I beg your pardon?" he asked, one eyebrow raised.

"I'm the second of triplets. My older brother is Adam, I'm Briana, and my younger brother is Caleb. ABC."

"Very clever."

"Not really. That's what they called us until Dad got around to naming us."

"I see," he said, but Briana knew he didn't. She'd left some information out of her explanation.

Then she thought she heard something. "Listen! Is that someone in the store?"

He came toward the door, nearer to her, and placed his ear against the wood. "I don't hear anything."

"I don't now, either. It was just a rustling sound. Or maybe it was my imagination," she admitted with a sigh. She put her fingers to her temples and massaged. Her headache was as bad as ever. Wait! The medicine she'd been about to buy. She'd stuck it and the soda in her handbag without thinking when the clerk had ordered them to the back of the store.

Her bag, large, one that could hold all kinds of

necessities, was on the floor. She grabbed it, moaning as she stood. The motion wasn't helping her headache.

"Are you all right?" Hunter asked.

"Yes, it's just my headache. That's why I was here. I didn't have any pain reliever in my room and the hotel clerk sent me here. I think I'll sue him." She smiled to let her companion know she was joking. Digging into her purse, she found the unopened medicine and the soda. "Aha!"

He stared at her. "You managed to get what you needed."

"Yes, I did," she agreed as she tore at the wrapping. "Assuming I can ever get it unwrapped."

"Here," he said, taking the package away from her and deftly ripping the box open. He removed the bottle and quickly lined up the arrows to pop the lid off. "How many do you want, one or two?"

"Three," she said distinctly, holding out her hand.

"Three? I don't think that's a good idea."

In spite of his helpfulness, she wasn't happy with his interference. "Look, unless you're a doctor—"

"I am."

That response stopped her in her tracks. She was attending a medical conference on multiple births and a number of doctors had been in attendance. That would be too much of a coincidence, wouldn't it?

"It doesn't matter. I take this medicine all the time. When a headache isn't stopped early, I need three tablets to make it go away."

Without another word, he tapped the bottle and put three tablets in her hand. She popped the lid of the soda and tossed the pills in her mouth, then swallowed some of the liquid.

"I guess I should save the rest of the soda. Did you want a drink?" she asked, remembering he was a victim, too.

He hesitated, then said, "Yeah, I'll take a sip, along with a couple of pills, if you don't mind sharing."

"Of course not. Is that why you're here, too?"

"Actually, I thought I'd get some milk to drink. My stomach needed settling."

"I don't think you're supposed to drink milk if you're queasy," she said.

"Unless you're a doctor…" he said, challenging her with his blue eyes.

Quickly, she disavowed that occupation. She'd wanted to be a doctor, but she discovered as a teenager that blood made her pass out. That rather eliminated medicine as a profession. She'd chosen the next best thing, a hospital administrator.

"Is there any milk in here?" she asked, looking around.

"No, this part has no refrigeration. There's some sodas, sports drinks, stuff like that. No milk. But I guess we won't starve to death."

"You mean we should help ourselves to their food? But wouldn't that be stealing?"

He shook his head, grinning. "Not unless you're a

purist. I think I already paid about a hundred and fifty dollars. That should cover a few Twinkies.''

''Twinkies? Do they have Twinkies?'' Normally, she restrained her junk-food urge. But stress, along with her headache, made her weak. Twinkies sounded perfect.

With a chuckle, the man reached up to a shelf behind her and drew down a box. He carefully examined the box before breaking it open.

''What were you looking for?'' she asked, puzzled.

''Just checking. Here, have one. They're individually wrapped.''

She took one and opened the cellophane, eager to taste the gooey sweetness. ''Um, thank you. I may survive after all.''

''Is the headache gone?''

''It's easing.''

''Well, you might as well be comfortable.'' He stepped away and reached for the stool, placing it in the center of the storeroom. ''Here's your chair.''

His generosity reminded her of how he'd shielded her from the gun. The man was a true gentleman. ''It wouldn't be fair for me to take the only seat.''

He looked surprised. ''You think I should sit while you stand? My mama didn't raise me that way.''

''No, but we could share,'' she assured him, smiling.

He looked even more surprised. ''It's not that big a stool.''

Realizing he thought she meant they could both

occupy the stool at once, she turned bright red. "No! No, I meant we could take turns."

A lopsided grin that only increased his sexiness was his initial response. "Darn, I was having some great images in my head."

She didn't want to think about those images. In fact, she thought the more distance she kept from this man, the better off she'd be. He was too handsome for his own good. "I'll take a turn first," she said and sat down on the stool, taking another bite of her Twinkie.

"Good decision," he said and started pacing again.

"Maybe if you leaned against the shelves, it would be easier for you," she suggested, her gaze following him as he moved. He was a big man. She wasn't short, five-seven, but he had to be over six feet tall. Though there were a few grey hairs at his temples, they blended in with his blond hair, cut short. Very businesslike.

"No, thanks," he said and continued to pace.

A big, hardheaded man. Fine, let him wear himself out pacing. She didn't care!

She finished her Twinkie, and he offered another.

"No. You didn't eat one."

"Not yet. I'm sure I will before the evening's over. My dinner was good. I had steak."

Again Briana thought of her conference. They'd served steak at the banquet tonight. "What conference were you attending?"

"It was a conference about multiple births. I specialize in obstetrics, particularly at-risk pregnancies."

"Oh." The same conference. It was a wonder she hadn't met him already. But she'd been interested in the administrative side of multiple births. Not the medical procedures being discussed.

"Not interested, even though you're a multiple? Especially when any pregnancy you might have could be multiple?"

"No."

"Have you had a pregnancy already?"

"No, I haven't. Have you?"

"I assume you mean as a father, not as a mother."

She rolled her eyes. The man thought he had a sense of humor. Ha!

"No. Me, neither. I hope to, someday."

"I don't want to be rude, but aren't you getting a little old for a first-time dad?"

"I'm under forty, by two years. Men aren't as affected by the biological clock as women. How about you? Is your clock ticking?"

"I'm thirty-one if that's what you're asking," she said, irritation in her voice. She'd thought a lot about having a baby, but she'd promised herself, no baby until she found a father, one she could love and trust. She'd been betrayed once, and she was determined that wasn't going to happen again.

He must've realized he'd upset her. With a soothing voice, he said, "You still have plenty of time."

She ducked her head. She'd been rude, and he was

trying to comfort her. "I'm sorry. That conversation was my fault, and I was rude."

"Don't worry about it. Have another Twinkie. It will sweeten you up." He presented it to her with a flourish.

She took his offering. She didn't want to be rude again. Slowly she unwrapped it and took a bite.

At the same time, he said, "What kind of conference were you attending?"

She choked. She should've been prepared, but his charm had distracted her. He came to her side and pounded on her back.

"Are you all right?" he asked.

"Fine. Please, that's enough," she added as he continued to slap her back.

"Sorry. Choking is dangerous. Maybe I should've tried the Heimlich maneuver."

"No, it just went down the wrong way. I'm fine now," she added. She hoped he'd move away from her. His distinctive male scent was enticing.

"Okay. What conference are you attending?"

She finally mumbled, "The same one."

He frowned and took a step closer instead of backing off. "What did you say?"

"I'm attending the same conference," she admitted, speaking clearly.

"You're a medical professional?"

"Not exactly."

"What do you mean by not exactly?" he demanded, his hands on his hips.

"I'm in medical administration."

"Oh. I guess that explains why I didn't meet you. The joint sessions were pretty big."

"Yes."

HUNTER CALLAGHAN stared at the beauty sitting on the old stool. She was dressed in jeans and a sweater, her light brown hair framing her delicate features and curving under as it reached her shoulders. It was the hazel eyes, however, that drew him the most.

"Suddenly you don't want to talk?" he asked, distracted by her strange attitude.

She shrugged but said nothing.

"Did you enjoy the conference?"

She shrugged again. Then she added, "Look, I came to learn all I could. I'm not very experienced."

"There's nothing wrong with that," he said, crossing his arms over his chest as he stared at her. Something was going on here, and he wanted to know what it was.

"I'm tired," she muttered, in an obvious attempt to change the subject.

"No wonder, it's almost two o'clock in the morning."

She slid down from the stool. "I think it's your turn to sit down. We should probably change every half hour."

"I don't need to sit. You go ahead."

"No, I insist. I appreciate your gentlemanly behavior, but I don't want to take advantage." Standing, she came to his shoulder. Good. He hated short women who made him feel awkward. Not that it mattered. In a few hours he wouldn't see her again.

Since she insisted, he took a seat on the stool, hooking the heels of his dress shoes over the lower rung. "Uh, Briana," he said, trying to figure out if he was going to freak her out with what he had to say. But he had to warn her.

"Yes?"

"If you walk around, stay away from that back corner," he said as casually as he could. He was hoping she wouldn't ask why.

But of course she did.

"Why?"

"Well, I think that's a rat trap. And I wouldn't want you to get caught in it. I'm not sure I could free you."

She paled and took a step closer to him, unusual on her part. He'd noticed she was more comfortable if he didn't come close.

"A—a rat trap?" she asked, her voice trembling.

"Yeah."

"That's why you examined the Twinkie box? But it's on a high shelf. Surely a rat couldn't get to it way up there?"

"It's my understanding they can climb well."

She took another step closer to him. "That's why you wouldn't lean against the shelves?" Horror had her shaking all over.

"Briana, they're not going to attack us. I just wanted you to be careful."

His words didn't calm her. She pressed against his side, her gaze swerving around the room. "Have you seen any?"

"No. Probably the trap has been efficient and we won't see any at all. I'm probably being an alarmist." In spite of the noises he'd heard. She'd heard them, too, when they'd first entered the room, and thought someone was in the store. He looped his arm around her, liking the feel of her, the smell of her.

Great. That's all he needed, to become uncomfortably aroused in addition to everything else. He was a little surprised by his response. The last few years, he'd found himself less and less attracted to the women who pursued doctors.

She broke from his hold. "I'm sorry. I'm being silly. There probably aren't any rats in here, right? I'll just stay away from that corner," she promised, her lips trembling as she stepped away from him.

For several minutes she paced around the room and he had the pleasure of watching her. Her figure was worth looking at, especially in the snug-fitting jeans. He finally closed his eyes, trying to distract his mind with thoughts of operating procedures.

But those kinds of methodical thoughts had no chance over a beautiful woman in jeans. With a sigh, he opened his eyes, trying to think of a conversational topic that would distract both of them.

Instead, the silence was broken by a terrible clang. Something had been caught in the trap.

He looked at Briana, knowing it wasn't her but wanting to make sure she was all right. He saw her just in time to catch her as she rushed to him and climbed the step stool as if it was a ladder.

She ended up in his lap, her legs wrapped around him, her arms tightening around his neck.

''Wow, why didn't I think of sharing?'' he said, a smile on his lips.

Chapter Two

Hunter sat holding a warm, trembling female, unsure what to do next. He didn't mind holding her. In fact, sitting as they were, things were getting interesting. But she might object, since she'd already been leery of him.

"I know I should get down," she muttered against his neck, sending tingling sensations through his body, "but I can't."

"Why not?"

"I have a phobia about rats."

"A phobia?"

"Yes, an unreasonable fear of something."

He chuckled. "I'm a doctor, remember? I know what a phobia is."

"Well, mine is rats. I was okay as long as I could convince myself they wouldn't really show up here, but—but is it a rat in the trap?"

"Looks like it to me," he said, staring over her shoulder. "I can't be sure until I go over there."

She squeezed him tighter. "No! No, don't go over there! He might bite you."

"How did you get a phobia about rats?" He cuddled her a little closer, liking the feel of her, her scent. "Were you raised in a slum?"

"No, not at all! We had a very nice house, but I saw a movie about a little boy and the rats—terrorized him. I screamed every night for weeks. My brothers laughed at me. Finally my father let me keep a cat in my room all night so I'd be protected."

Her voice trembled, and Hunter had an immediate picture of that little girl, wildly afraid of rats, pleading for protection. He held her more tightly against him. "It's all right. You're safe, Briana. I won't let the rats get you."

"Are you laughing at me?" she asked, her voice small.

"No. I'm not laughing. I'm understanding."

"Oh. Thank you. But we can't—I mean, we can't—this isn't seemly."

Ah. He knew what was causing her concern. "Look, Bri," he said, shortening her name, "men react to stimuli without any, uh, intent. It's not something they can control. I promise I won't take advantage."

"But it must be uncomfortable."

"If I were wearing jeans, it would be. They don't allow much wiggle room, uh, I mean, extra space." He was discovering any extra space he had was disappearing rapidly. He said, "Maybe I should go over and look. Maybe it's just a really big mouse. Would that be better?''

''I don't think you should go over there,'' she said, the trembling starting again.

''I won't get close, I promise,'' he said gently and placed his hands on her arms, deadlocked around his neck.

''Come on, Bri, turn loose. I'll come right back, I promise.''

''And I can stay on the stool?''

''Of course. You can even have another Twinkie.''

''No. Treats never help. Dad tried that.''

''I bet he did,'' Hunter muttered. Slowly he got her to lower her arms. Putting his hands on her waist, he slipped off the stool and swung her on top of it.

As he turned away, she reached out for him. ''Hunter, be careful.''

''I will, Bri, I promise.''

He walked over to the corner and stared at the dead animal. It was definitely a rat, a large one. Could he get away with telling Bri it was a big mouse? He was afraid she'd realize he was lying. He'd never been good at lying.

He came back to the stool.

She held out her arms, as if ready to resume her position in his lap. He shook his head. ''I'm going to walk around for a while, to stretch my legs.''

''And what was it?''

He hung his head. He hated to tell her. ''It was a rat. But it's definitely dead.''

She reached for him, her hold probably leaving bruises on his skin. "You'd better get back up here with me. We'll be safe here."

He wasn't going to discuss the safety of the stool. If he took that refuge away from her, she'd go to pieces. "Nope, I'll be safe enough out here in the open."

He began to pace, but thought of a question he'd wanted to ask. "You know, when you've talked about your childhood, you never mention your mother. Where was she?"

"She died when we were born."

"Why?"

"She bled to death. That's why Dad—uh, it was sad for my father, but we didn't know the difference."

"Didn't he ever remarry?"

She shook her head, but she kept her gaze fastened to the trap in the corner.

"But your dad took care of the three of you?" Somehow, he wanted to know she'd been okay.

She shrugged. "He hired someone."

Hunter was surprised by the anger mixed with sorrow he felt. "He hired someone? He didn't take care of you himself?"

"He was busy. And he doesn't seem to care for babies. Once we got old enough to talk, to understand, he began to take a little interest in us."

"Hence the cat?"

Briana shot him a rueful smile. "That was the first

time he listened to me. And then only because I was
disrupting his peace. But I believed it was because he
loved me. More than my brothers. It satisfied me for
several years. I'd tell myself the cat was there because
he loved me, even if he couldn't spend time with
me.''

''How did your brothers react?''

''They hated the cat. And teased it a couple of
times when they caught it. But then it scratched them
and they backed off.''

He'd taken a lot of psychology classes and was
fascinated with children's coping mechanisms. ''And
when did you demand more attention?''

''How do you know I did?'' She wouldn't look at
him and he grinned, stepped closer and slid his arms
around her waist. He liked holding her close.

''Just a hunch,'' he said with a grin. Her memories
seemed to relax her, and that was a good thing.

''Actually, my brothers took action first. They became little hellions. Again, my father's peace was cut
up. He demanded Grace make them behave. Grace
and her husband, Douglas, took care of us. Grace
looked him in the eye and told him if he didn't par-
ticipate in his children's lives, there wasn't anything
she could do.''

''Wise woman.''

''Yes, and brave. Dad wasn't an easy man to face
down. He'd been grieving about our mother's death
and paying attention to business. It was easier to leave
us to someone else. But to his credit, that's when he

changed. We'd started school, and he'd discovered we had minds.''

Hunter lifted one hand and cupped her soft, warm cheek. ''So then your father loved you?''

She shrugged again. ''That's when he played a part in our lives. By the time we graduated from college, I think he loved us. We've been a family the last few years.''

He pulled her against him and rubbed her back.

''What about you? Did you have the perfect childhood?''

''I suppose I did. My dad was a doctor, had a small practice in the country, handled all kinds of emergencies. My mom was always there for me and my brother. Not that we realized we had anything special. Now I do.''

She pushed away from him. ''And I suppose that's the kind of woman you'll marry for your future kids. So they'll have the same life.''

There was a bitterness in her voice that made him raise his eyebrows. ''Wouldn't everyone want the same thing? Wouldn't you have preferred to have a mother?''

''Of course I would!'' she snapped.

''Whoa, there, lady. What did I say wrong?''

''Nothing. What time is it?''

''Almost three. Are you exhausted?'' He'd give her her change of subject. Things were stressful enough for her as it was.

''Yes. I didn't get much sleep during the conference. I didn't want to miss anything,'' she said, rubbing one temple.

"Did your headache ever go away?'' he asked, taking her pulse at her neck.

"Yes, mostly.''

"Look, why don't you—I can hold you and let you sleep a little. That's probably the only thing that will give you any relief, and it will make the time pass faster. Before you know it, it will be morning and your nightmare will be over.''

"That's not fair to you,'' she said doubtfully, staring at him. "And it's—you know what happened last time.''

"I explained it's something a man can't control. But nothing happened, remember?'' He was glad she couldn't read his mind. Holding her again was becoming an obsession for him.

Finally, she slid off the stool, standing next to it. "If you're sure you don't mind. I'd give a lot to get a few minutes of sleep.''

"I don't mind.'' He climbed onto the stool and held out his arms. Slowly, unlike the last time, she responded to his invitation. She settled in his lap, but she seemed unsure where to put her hands.

"Wrap your arms around me,'' he suggested, "and lay your head on my chest.''

She did so, and he held her in place, feeling a surprising peace settle in him. He had her safe in his arms. Softly rubbing her back, he whispered, "You're safe now. Just relax.''

After several minutes, her body began to relax and grow heavy against him. She was asleep.

As Briana settled into Hunter's embrace, she knew she was being weak. But she'd reached her limit, and she didn't mind admitting it.

And she'd never met such a strong man, physically and mentally. He'd been calm and protective. It seemed all her life she'd been competing with her brothers. She loved them dearly, but being one of triplets, and the only female, made life difficult.

So, just once in her life, she was going to accept her weakness and give in to the protection this man offered. Besides, it felt so good to be in his arms. As she laid her head against his chest, his heart beat a steady rhythm that lulled her in to relaxation, and she closed her eyes.

Satisfaction filled Hunter as he realized Briana was getting the rest she so desperately needed. Apparently she'd been a lot more intense about the conference than him. He'd attended a few before. Besides, as a doctor, he'd pulled a few long nights as he came through medical school.

He checked his watch. They only had a couple more hours if the morning guy came in at six o'clock. His arms tightened around Briana as she rested against him. He'd love to be able to return to his comfortable bed in the hotel, but he wouldn't want to turn Briana loose anyway.

That thought brought him up short. What was he thinking? They'd part as soon as morning came, of course. She was from Texas. He was from Chicago. Maybe they'd see each other at future conventions and laugh about their adventure in a New York deli.

He thought again of Briana as a little girl, frightened by a movie. She'd sounded so alone as she'd told him about her phobia. She must've been adorable as a child. How could her father have ignored her?

Of course, he'd eventually responded to her fears and allowed her to keep a cat in her room. He supposed that showed the man's humanity.

But he'd want more than humanity for his children. He intended to love them and be there for them. He looked down at the brunette beauty in his arms. They'd make beautiful babies together, he decided. "Should that ever come up in the future," he quickly amended with a rumble of laughter.

She stirred in his arms, her eyes fluttering open. "Everything okay?" she muttered.

He kissed her forehead and drew her closer. "Everything's fine. You're safe. Go back to sleep," he whispered. Almost before he finished speaking, she dropped off to sleep again.

His body was responding, as it had earlier, to her closeness, but it was to be expected. He shifted a little, hoping his movement wouldn't awaken her.

He wished they'd talked longer. He'd like to know about her situation, what job she held, her personal life. Hell, he didn't even know if she had a boyfriend.

She must. She was too pretty, too dynamic, to be alone. Unless all the men in Texas were dummies, and that's not what he'd heard.

He didn't like the idea that someone else would hold her. A ridiculous thought, but he felt possessive about her. He'd saved her from the rats. She was his to protect.

He decided that kind of thinking was dangerous, so he tried to concentrate on a new theory introduced at the conference about treating at-risk pregnancies. Anything to take his mind off the woman in his arms.

AN HOUR LATER, Hunter eased off the stool. He had to stand before his rear became permanently attached to the hard surface of the stool. His arms slid beneath Briana's bottom. He was glad he worked out regularly, or he wouldn't be able to stand and hold her, too. Slowly, he maneuvered his way around the storeroom. Still another hour or two before the morning guy would arrive. He looked at the stool, not sure he could sit again.

But he wasn't sure either that he could stand with Briana in his arms until someone came. And he didn't want to wake her up.

"My choices are limited," he muttered. Finally, he pushed the stool toward the thick door. When he got the stool directly in front of the door, he shoved it a little to one side. Then he settled back onto the stool, managing to arrange Briana's sleeping form in a more comfortable position.

He'd have to give her credit. When she slept, she really slept. She hadn't shown any signs of waking up the entire time he moved around.

After she was settled, he slowly leaned his back against the door and felt relief at the support. Then he let his head rest there, too. Could he sleep at all and maintain his balance? He was kind of wedged up between the door and the edge of the shelving.

He'd just doze.

It would be all right.

SOMETHING was bothering her.

Briana shook her head, irritated by the noise that was disrupting her sleep. Then it stopped. She settled back against the mattress, the comforting throb soothing her again. This was a great bed, she decided. It held her close.

Even at the thought, arms tightened around her.

Arms? Mattresses don't have arms, do they? Briana wasn't ready to wake up, but that strange question forced her to open her eyes.

The first thing she realized was that she was upright, leaning against—a man. Suddenly she remembered where she was and what had happened. Hunter. She was leaning against Hunter.

He'd fallen asleep leaning against the door. She checked her watch. It was five after seven. "Hunter?" she whispered.

He hugged her against him, as if he thought she

was asking him to keep her safe. It did feel good, but that wasn't the point.

"Hunter, there should be someone here now," she whispered. "Shouldn't we shout or something?"

He sat upright suddenly, shifting Briana. "What?"

"It's after seven."

"After seven? Haven't you heard anyone outside?"

"I don't know. Something woke me."

He stood abruptly, and Briana found herself held in his arms.

"You—you can put me down," she insisted.

He let her slide down his body, an interesting trip to say the least, and suddenly she was standing on her feet.

"Can you stand?" he asked, still holding on to her.

"Of course. Can you, after I've used you for a bed all night?"

He smiled, but Briana noticed the strain around his eyes and the weariness. "I think so. I'm just a little stiff." He moved the stool away from the door and beat on it as he yelled.

They both heard a startled exclamation. Hunter grinned at Briana like a caveman who had found meat for his family.

"Who's in there?"

Whoever asked that question sounded more afraid of them than she was of the rats. "We're customers who got locked in last night. Please let us out."

"Oh! Yes. Yes, I will!"

When the door opened, they discovered an elderly

woman wearing an apron, a look of horror on her face. "Who locked you in?" she wanted to know.

Hunter took over. "The clerk who was working last night. He robbed us of what cash we had and put us in here before he left. He also cleaned out your cash register."

"So, it wasn't a thief?"

"No, it wasn't. Now, if you'll excuse us, we'd like to get back to our hotel," he said, gently moving the woman to one side. Then he reached out for Briana's hand.

She gladly gave him her hand. It made her feel under his protection, as she'd been all night. He pulled her toward the door.

"Aren't we going to stay and talk to the police?" she asked him in a low voice.

"Do you believe it will help them catch the guy?" he asked.

"No, of course not."

"Then what's the point? If we stay, we won't catch our planes, and I have to be back in Chicago for a special surgery in the morning."

He had a point. "Okay, we'll leave our names and addresses and they can contact us if they need to." They each wrote their information down and gave it to the owner.

They emerged into a busy world. There were car fumes, noisy taxis, people everywhere, which seemed strange after there having only been the two of them for the past few hours.

It was half a block to the conference hotel. When they reached the entrance, he wrapped his arm around her shoulders. ''They're going to think we've been out partying all night,'' he muttered. ''Hope we don't see anyone from the conference or the rumors will fly.''

She hadn't thought of that. She certainly didn't want rumors of her pulling an all-nighter with a handsome doctor. She was working too hard to prove herself. She ducked her head and both of them walked fast.

They managed to snag an elevator at once and when the doors closed, leaving them alone, they both breathed a sigh of relief.

''Glad to be alone again?'' he asked with a weary smile.

''Surprisingly, yes. This would've been awkward to explain.''

''Awkward? It would've been impossible. Is there a husband around who is going to read you the riot act?''

It was a little late to be asking that question, but Hunter had been a perfect gentleman from the beginning. She shook her head. ''No husband.''

He looped his arms around her, pulling her closer to rest against his body. ''I'm glad.''

''Any wife?''

''Nope, not even a girlfriend.''

He put a finger under her chin, and, before she realized what was going on, he kissed her.

Chapter Three

There were people waiting when the elevator door opened on her floor. Briana, who'd been enjoying the kiss as much as Hunter seemed to be, was grateful she didn't know any of them.

''Uh, out, please.'' She kept her eyes lowered. She didn't want anyone, even strangers, to see the effect of Hunter's kiss. Her lips still tingled and she felt a surprising desire to repeat their behavior.

Hunter followed her off the elevator.

''Your room is on this floor, too?'' she asked in surprise and uneasiness. She needed distance to avoid doing something unwise.

''No, I'm escorting you to your room,'' he assured her.

Always a gentleman.

''Look, Hunter, I know you must be exhausted. I certainly am. Don't worry about me. I'll be fine.''

'It's kind of become a habit,'' he said with a charming smile, ''worrying about you.''

She dug her plastic key card out of her jeans pocket

where she'd put it only a few hours ago, though it seemed like a lifetime. "This is my room," she assured him as she stopped in front of a door and inserted the key card. The small light turned from red to green and she shoved the door open.

Hunter followed her in so that when she turned to thank him for his...whatever, he was there. And his arms were around her again. And he looked as if he was about to repeat the embrace they'd shared on the elevator.

It had been an incredible kiss, one she'd felt to her very toes. Unlike any she'd ever had before. But that was probably because they'd spent so much time together, really together.

She should stop him. But curiosity, wondering if it had really been that good a kiss, welcomed him. Her arms went around his neck, her body pressed against his. Her lips, when he touched them with his, leapt to mate with him.

Three or four kisses later, Hunter, breathing heavily, managed to say "Briana."

She thought it was a good thing he could remember her name, because his kisses had scrambled her brain. All she could think about was him...and getting closer. It wasn't like her to respond so completely to a man's touch. But Hunter's touch had a magical effect on her. "Hunter," she murmured in response.

"Sweetheart," he muttered, "I need you."

Instead of bothering with words, she pulled him toward the bed. They fell on it with a sigh of relief and resumed kissing. He was the most incredible kisser.

Tuxedo studs went flying as Briana's fingers went to work. It occurred to her that later she might regret such abandon, but it felt wonderful now. As more and more of his muscular chest, with blond hairs winding their way down it, came into view, the happier she became.

Each of them removed clothing piece by piece, exposing the other. But Briana never felt awkward or uncomfortable. She was too involved in what was going on. It seemed right that, after their night of togetherness, they should be completely together.

As a lover, Hunter was as gentlemanly and considerate as he'd been all night. But there was an edge of need that made her heart beat faster. He stroked and urged her closer, his mouth consuming hers. When he entered her, she felt completely loved and cradled, protected, until an urgency began that drove her even closer.

Then there was no conscious thought, just emotions, feelings, a consuming fire that left her exhausted yet sated. Hunter fell against her as he, too, reached the zenith of feelings. She held him close.

As she sank into a drifting state of sensations, he pushed up from the bed. "Did I hurt you, Bri? Are you all right?"

"I'm wonderful, Hunter, absolutely...wonderful." She never opened her eyes. And that was the last she remembered.

HUNTER STARED DOWN at the beautiful face. It seemed most of the time he'd had with her, her eyes had been closed. But he remembered their hazel beauty. He remembered everything about her.

He'd never experienced such emotions, such sensations in making love before. It had never been so overpowering. Briana was clearly a special woman, but there'd been so little time. He truly hadn't intended to make love to her when he'd followed her into the room. All he'd wanted was one more kiss. The kiss in the elevator had been so special, so…he couldn't come up with another word to describe it.

His hand cupped her soft cheek as she slept. He didn't want to leave her, but he needed a shower and clean clothes. If he changed now, while she slept, he'd be back before she even knew he was gone. Then he'd take her to breakfast.

They had a lot to discuss. He had no intention of letting her walk away with no plans for the future. She was his to protect, to love, to cherish. That much he knew. He thought she knew it, too.

They'd plan a future. They'd compromise. Somehow they'd find a way to be together. Because Briana…he suddenly realized he didn't even know her last name. But he'd take care of that detail. Finally he'd found the one woman in the world who made his life complete. They'd find a way to be together.

After rubbing his lips over hers, he slid from the bed and searched for his clothing. He found everything but one of the studs for the tuxedo shirt. He smiled as he remembered Briana dispensing with them recklessly. He'd loved that about her. She was an enthusiastic lover, making him feel wanted, a great aphrodisiac.

Longingly, he stared once more at her sprawled under the sheet with which he'd covered her. As tired as he was, he wanted to make love to her all over again. And he suspected he'd feel that way the rest of his life.

He whispered, "I'll be back soon, sweetheart." Then he left her hotel room to climb the flight of stairs at the end of the corridor. He was on the next floor. Not far away. He hurried, unable to stand being away from her any longer than he had to.

THE BUZZING of an alarm awakened Briana from a deep sleep. She flailed at the noise and found the snooze button, she supposed, because the noise stopped. She drifted back to sleep.

Five minutes later, the noise repeated itself. This time she opened her eyes, barely, and noted the time. Eight-o-five. She sat up in bed. Her flight left La-Guardia Airport at nine-forty-five. She needed to catch a taxi by eight-thirty. She'd set the alarm last night before she ventured out of the hotel. She leapt from the bed and suddenly realized she was naked. A flood of memories held her frozen as the events of the night and, in particular, the morning hit her.

She'd made love to Hunter!

She looked around the room as if expecting him to

pop out from behind the dresser. He'd left? Disappeared? Or had she dreamed the entire thing?

She really didn't know. She was still exhausted and wasn't thinking too clearly. She moved toward the bathroom, sure a shower would help, when she winced in pain and hopped on her left foot. Bending down, she discovered a stud for a tuxedo shirt in the carpet.

So, it hadn't been a dream. Hunter had come in with her and they'd made love. Or maybe they'd just had sex. He certainly appeared to have made a fast exit. There was no note. Nothing.

Briana threw herself in the shower for a fast rinse-off. There was no time to wash her hair. She put on the sweater and jeans again, with fresh underwear, thrust the last few things in the bag and gathered her belongings.

In the meantime, her mind was searching for some kind of explanation for Hunter's behavior. He'd been such a gentleman. But leaving with no word, no pretense even of a future, almost destroyed her. Did he care nothing about her? Had she been so misled by his behavior that she'd completely misread his character?

She couldn't call his room and ask him because the only name she had was Hunter. She'd assumed that was his first name, but she didn't know.

She stared at the phone, tempted to try anyway, but she knew she didn't have time. She was going to have to chalk the bizarre night and even stranger morning to experience and go catch her plane.

As she stood in the doorway for a long moment, tears came to her eyes. She'd thought this morning she'd found something special. But like so many women, she'd been misled by a handsome face and broad shoulders. And a gentle touch and blue eyes to die for.

What a jerk!

HALF AN HOUR later, Hunter hurried down the stairs again. He was feeling much better, even though he still hadn't had much sleep. But he'd showered and shaved and changed into jeans and shirt, sports shoes, comfortable again. And he was looking forward to breakfast with Briana.

He hoped she'd gotten enough rest. It was just past eight-thirty, and he didn't want to wait too long to wake her up. His flight left at two, but he didn't know her schedule. He wanted to spend time with her before they had to be parted for however long it took for him to arrange his schedule. To work out their lives.

He shoved his hands in his pockets and started whistling as he reached her floor. It was a glorious day. When he'd arrived at the conference, he'd had a lousy attitude. He hadn't been happy lately. Now, he was on top of the world. One of the maids had her cart in the hallway near Briana's room, and Hunter greeted her cheerfully.

He passed her and reached Bri's room, and began to knock on the door. He hoped he could wake her. She slept so soundly.

"No one's there."

He whirled around, realizing it was the maid speaking.

Smiling, he explained, "No, she's there. She's a sound sleeper."

The maid shook her head. "No, they just called me from downstairs to clean the room. She checked out a few minutes ago."

The smile on his face disappeared. "No, you're wrong. She's still sleeping."

The maid shrugged her shoulders and turned away. Hunter formed a fist and beat on the door now, determined to awaken Briana.

"Here, I'll open the door."

He found the maid beside him, a look of sympathy on her face.

"Thanks. I'll wake her up."

He pushed into the room, only to find it empty. The bed with the sheets in disarray, the closet empty, nothing in the bathroom. No note.

"Where is she?" he demanded harshly, turning to the maid.

His expression must've frightened her because she backed up a step. "I told you. She checked out a few minutes ago."

"No, she wouldn't have just left! There's some mistake." He searched the room again for some minute piece of evidence that would tell him something—anything about Briana. But there was nothing.

"Sorry, sir." The maid stayed pressed against the wall, trying to keep out of his way.

"Thanks," he managed as he left the room and ran for the elevators. As soon as he reached the main floor, he hurried over to the front desk. "A woman named Briana, from room 812, just checked out?"

"Yes, sir. Miss McCallum left for the airport about twenty minutes ago." The young man behind the desk smiled, pleased to serve a customer properly.

"McCallum? Briana McCallum?"

"Yes, sir. I helped her myself."

Now why did that name sound familiar? McCallum. Then he remembered. Maitland Maternity Hospital, the famous maternity hospital in Austin, Texas, was opening a new wing, a state-of-the-art facility specializing in multiple births. The McCallum Wing, dedicated to the donor's wife, who'd died in childbirth. Administered by the donor's daughter. It had been the main gossip of the conference, heightened by questions about her competency. Most everyone figured she was a rich woman playing at being a do-gooder. He usually gave people the benefit of the doubt, but he was in too much pain.

Briana McCallum. Rich woman. Looking for a new thrill. How about a doctor? Try one for the night and then skip town if it didn't work out?

But it did work out! He raged within himself. It

did! How could she deny what had happened between them? How could she just leave?

"Sir?" The clerk said with a frown. "Is anything wrong?"

"No!" Hunter snapped. "No, nothing's wrong."

What could be wrong? He asked himself savagely. He knew his lover's name now. Briana McCallum. A rich woman—who had walked away.

But she hadn't left her name for him. She hadn't wanted him to know. She hadn't wanted any more than what she'd got.

He hoped she was satisfied.

He wasn't.

Chapter Four

Seven months later

Briana McCallum was on the first floor of the new wing of Maitland Maternity Hospital, the McCallum Wing, dedicated to her mother, talking to the head of nursing, when the phone rang. Mrs. Rodgers interrupted their conversation to take the call, then handed the phone to Briana.

"It's for you."

Bri took the phone, expecting the caller to be her assistant. She wasn't disappointed. "What is it, Lisa?"

"The new doctor's here! R. J. Maitland wants you to come meet him at once."

"I thought he wasn't supposed to arrive until two o'clock," Bri complained. She hated all the politics involved in her job.

"He got here early. Come on. I told Mr. Maitland you'd be in his office in five minutes."

"All right. I'm on my way."

She struggled up from her chair as she handed the phone back to Mrs. Rodgers. "Okay, I think I've got a grasp of the problem, Mrs. Rodgers. I'll get back to you as soon as I've worked out a solution. But the new obstetrics chief for the wing has arrived early and I've got to go be a part of the welcoming committee."

"Oh!" Mary Rodgers said with excitement. "Dr. Callaghan? That's wonderful. I'm so looking forward to meeting him!"

Bri smiled tolerantly. She'd had nothing to do with choosing the new doctor, but she'd heard plenty of praise about him. Their head doctor, Dr. Wellborn, had collapsed with a heart attack ten days before the new wing opened. He was recovering, but he'd be unable to take up his appointment. Bri had had her hands full trying to make the adjustments necessary for everything to be up and running smoothly. She'd scarcely had time to note that a committee had hurriedly formed, much less looked at the candidates. She had her own fish to fry.

Now, having survived the opening, she could turn her attention to the newcomer. She sent up a prayer that the new man would be easy to work with. He should be. He'd have the best equipment and staff that money could buy.

It suddenly occurred to her that the reception she'd planned for that afternoon might need to be moved. Instead of heading for R. J. Maitland's office, she stopped by hers.

"Lisa? Did Mr. Maitland say—'' She broke off as she realized her assistant's office was filled with people.

"Oh, here she is!'' Lisa exclaimed, drawing her attention.

R. J. Maitland, director of the Maitland Maternity complex, stepped forward. "Bri, we gave up waiting for you. Here's Dr. Hunter Callaghan, waiting to meet you.''

Bri actually felt the blood drain out of her face as she turned to look at the only man she'd ever known named Hunter.

That's the last thing she remembered.

DR. HUNTER CALLAGHAN, recently of Chicago, stared down at Briana McCallum, who'd just wilted onto the floor. Same beautiful hazel eyes, he'd noted before she'd closed them. Same silky light-brown hair framing her beautiful face. Same peaches-and-cream complexion, until all the blood had drained out of her face.

But there was a big difference between this Briana and the Briana he'd left sleeping in a hotel-room bed in New York City seven months ago.

This Briana was very definitely pregnant. Almost full-term, if he was any judge. So she'd been pregnant with another man's baby when he'd met her. She'd said she had no boyfriend, hadn't she? That she was alone? That was the impression he remembered. Obviously she was not only a wealthy woman, but a liar, too.

Dr. Abby Maitland McDermott, who was chief ob-gyn at Maitland Maternity and who had accompanied her brother R.J. and Hunter, bent over and took Bri's pulse as she chastised Lisa. "I told you to keep her from rushing around, Lisa. Having triplets carries enough pressure without adding to it."

Hunter stiffened. "She's having triplets?"

"Yeah, we're all excited that one of our first customers is our own administrator," Abby told him with a grin.

"How far along is she?" Hunter asked, a slight tremble in his voice that he hoped no one noticed.

"Help me lift her to the sofa. Everyone stand back and give her some room to breathe," Abby ordered.

Hunter stepped forward and put his hands on Briana. Lifting her shoulders, he slid his arm under her and lifted. Her head rolled over against his chest. As it had in the deli. Gently, he placed her on the sofa.

"She's seven months along and doing well. I don't know what caused today's fainting episode, but we'll check her out. Lisa, call and tell my staff I want a room for Bri."

"Oh, Doctor, she won't like that. Can't you wait until she comes to and ask her?" the assistant pleaded.

"No, I'm her doctor. I get to decide what kind of treatment she receives. Get a bed."

"Yes, ma'am," Lisa said.

"Don't get me a bed, Lisa," a faint voice Hunter had never forgotten spoke up. "I'm fine, Abby. You're right. I rushed because your brother is such a bear when he's kept waiting." Bri accompanied her words with a weak smile.

Hunter watched her, waiting to see if she remembered being introduced to him.

"I apologize for all the trouble, Dr. Callaghan. Not a particularly graceful way to welcome you to the McCallum Wing," she said in her soft voice, but Hunter noted she didn't look at him.

Swinging her feet off the sofa, she looked at R. J. Maitland. "I wanted to know if you want the reception set up for now, or leave it at two o'clock?"

"It can stay at two," the director said.

"But I'd really like to check you out, Bri," Abby said. "At twenty-eight weeks, you're doing well, but I'd like you to carry the girls a little longer."

"I intend to, Abby," she assured her, her smile sassier this time. "Now, I have a list of problems to deal with before the reception this afternoon, so if you and our new head of obstetrics will excuse me, I'll get busy." She smiled at the rest of the group, several other members of the Maitland family, and stood.

They all began to leave the office. Hunter, however, stood his ground. Finally, R. J. Maitland said, "Hunter, you coming?"

"I need a word with my new administrator," he said. A hazel-eyed gaze collided with his.

Abby stepped forward once again. "I'd rather Bri

not deal with much right now. In fact, though she said she was going to deal with problems, I'm ordering her back on the couch to rest.'' She smiled at Bri, and Hunter was filled with jealousy when Bri smiled back. Bri hadn't smiled at him that way.

"I just wanted to set up a time for a meeting with her,'' Hunter explained.

"Oh, Lisa? Does Bri have a time cleared to meet with Dr. Callaghan?'' R.J. asked.

"She set aside some time tomorrow morning. She thought he might be too busy with the welcome until then.''

"I knew Bri would have,'' R.J. said with a sigh. "She's so damned efficient it wears you out just thinking about it.''

"Fine. I'll see you then, Ms. McCallum.'' Hunter said, trying to sound impersonal. But it wasn't easy. His mind was all ajumble. She could be carrying his child—children! He could go from bachelor to father of three in the space of a few weeks—if her babies were his.

He walked out of the office with R.J. "So she's having three girls? Fraternal?'' He hoped R.J. would believe the huskiness of his voice was excitement about the new job.

"No, identical.''

"Is her husband pleased?'' He held his breath for Maitland's response.

"She's not married.''

"But surely the babies' father is participating in the pregnancy," he pressed.

"She's never named anyone as father. Refuses to do so. Says these are her babies." R.J. changed the subject to the medical equipment available, and Hunter could do nothing but go along with him. Otherwise, it would've appeared odd.

But he hadn't seen the last of Briana McCallum today. And he suspected she knew it, too.

ONCE THE DOOR had closed behind her visitors, Briana slid back down to sit on the sofa before she fell on her face. Her knees were so wobbly, she knew she couldn't walk.

"Bri?" her assistant demanded, alarm in her voice. "Are you really sick? Do you need the hospital bed Dr. Abby asked for?"

"No, Lisa. But I could use a bottle of apple juice." She kept juice and nutrition bars in the small kitchen area beside her office. Lisa scurried away at once and returned with the apple juice.

"Are the girls all right?" she asked as she handed the juice to Briana.

"The girls are fine. Where is the file on Dr. Callaghan? I meant to read it before he arrived, and his early arrival has thrown me off." She hoped that excuse made sense to Lisa. "Could you bring it to me so I can review it while I'm catching my breath?"

Lisa scurried off to Bri's office to find the file on her desk and bring it back to her. Then, clutching the file and her juice, Bri stood. "I'm going to get into my rocker and study the file."

Lisa escorted her to the rocker in her office over-looking a spectacular view of Austin, and saw her settled. Then she asked if Bri needed anything else and assured her she should just call if she didn't feel well.

Gently, Bri smiled. "I know, Lisa. Thanks for tak-ing such good care of me, but I'm fine." *Now that I've recovered from seeing the girls' daddy come through the door. What a shock.*

She'd actually thought she'd never see Hunter again. Some nights she'd prayed she'd never see him again. Others she'd prayed the opposite. The memory of their one time together still promised it would be heaven to be with him again. The anger and pain of his dismissal of her contradicted that thought.

What did he think? With any luck, he wouldn't realize he was the father. But Abby had been pretty specific about the length of her pregnancy. Maybe she could convince Hunter she'd gotten off the plane and been met by an old lover who'd begged her forgive-ness. She examined that thought from several angles. How could he dispute it?

That's what she'd tell him. As long as she denied his involvement, he'd leave her alone. And that's what she wanted, she assured herself staunchly. To be left alone.

In the seven months since she'd left the hotel in New York, she'd adjusted to the changes in her life.

She was prepared for the birth of her children, three precious little girls. Her family was supportive, though Caleb still wanted to go beat up the father, whoever he was.

Her friends, too, at the hospital, never mentioned the fact that she was to be a single mother. They were happy for her. Everything was perfect.

Most of all, she was happy about her babies. Thrilled, in fact. She had enough money to eliminate a lot of the problems most single parents had. And she knew what her babies needed that money couldn't buy: love. Her babies would know she loved them. They'd know how special they were to her. Like she would have if her mother had lived. A shiver ran over her body. Yes, her girls would be loved.

And then along came Hunter Callaghan. What was he doing here? Obviously, he hadn't known who she was, that she was here, or he wouldn't have come. Or maybe he figured he shouldn't let his personal life interfere with his career. And being head of the McCallum Wing was a definite feather in his cap. There were only two or three comparative situations in the country.

Well, she could be professional. She'd deny his involvement with her pregnancy and continue as before.

Her mind drifted back to picture Hunter, standing there in his expensive suit, looking fit and handsome. Probably all the nurses had been drooling over him already. They'd certainly talked about the fact that he wasn't married.

Which reminded her of the file in her hands. She opened the folder and read through Hunter's impressive credentials. He was certainly qualified.

But she didn't want him to have anything to do with her babies' birth. Not even as an observer. He was to keep away. He'd walked out on her, left her alone in that hotel room without even asking her if she was okay. He'd broken her heart. She wasn't going to do the same thing to the girls.

"Is she all right?" Bri heard someone ask. Before she could react, Lisa opened the door to escort in one of Bri's best friends, Annabelle Reardon, a delivery nurse at Maitland.

"Of course I'm all right," Bri answered as they came in, but she didn't rise from her chair. Her friends didn't expect that these days.

"But gossip said you fainted," Annabelle said, alarm in her voice.

"Annabelle, you're being way too dramatic. I'm fine. See for yourself," Bri said, spreading her arms wide.

Taking her at her word, Annabelle pulled a chair over to the rocker and sat down to take Bri's pulse. Bri dismissed Lisa with a nod over Annabelle's shoulder.

"You know, you're acting like my mother, and I'm ten years older than you," Bri pointed out with a grin.

"Not ten years, Bri. You're exaggerating. Your

pulse is normal,'' she said as she put Bri's wrist back on the chair.

"Of course it is, because nothing's wrong. I just rushed a little too much because the great Dr. Callaghan got here early.''

"You don't like him?''

Bri warned herself to be careful. "Of course, what little I know. I was referring to the nurses' enthusiasm for his, um, appearance.''

"You've heard the roar of appreciation?'' Annabelle asked with a grin. "Mind you, I don't think he compares to our Dr. Beaumont.''

"Of course not. You've got a crush on him.''

Annabelle's cheeks flushed bright red. "Don't be ridiculous. But I can't help but admire him.''

Bri let her get away with that white lie. She worried about her friend. Annabelle was only twenty-three and Zach Beaumont was thirty-six. But who was she to pretend to be an expert about relationships? She was going to be a single mother.

"I doubt that anyone will complain about having another single doctor around here. Especially a handsome one.''

"You think he's handsome?'' Annabelle asked, her expression alert.

Bri struggled to remain calm. "I was speaking generally, friend. No one seven months pregnant with triplets is going to get excited about a man. They cause these situations. And then walk away from them,'' she couldn't help adding.

"You've never said who—" Annabelle began and then broke off.

"No I haven't. And I won't. The man involved didn't want any future with me. These are my babies. No one else's."

"I know. I'm sorry." There was a moment of silence, as if Annabelle was remembering the past seven months. "How's Maggie?"

Bri sighed. "She's fine. Not pregnant." Her sister-in-law, Adam's wife, had been trying to get pregnant for some time. Her inability to conceive had put a real strain on her marriage. When Bri had announced her pregnancy, however, Maggie had been as supportive as a real sister. Just thinking about the courage and generosity Maggie had shown brought tears to her eyes.

"It's unfair," she whispered, closing her eyes.

"Maybe things will change soon," Annabelle said. "I didn't mean to upset you."

Bri forced her eyes open and pasted a smile on her face. "Oh, it's those hormones, Annabelle. You know how those affect us expectant mothers."

"Yeah. And anyway, Madeline's a miracle worker, so probably Maggie will have a baby before we know it."

Bri had believed that at first. Madeline Sheppard was one of the fertility experts at the McCallum Multiple Birth Wing. But so far, there were no results. Bri feared for Adam's marriage. Maggie seemed unable to think of anything else.

The door opened again and another friend, neonatal nurse April Sullivan rushed in. Instead of speaking to Bri, she looked at Annabelle. "Is she all right?"

Bri chuckled. "You'd think you'd ask me, silly," she said, reaching out for April's hand.

"She seems to be okay," Annabelle answered anyway.

"Okay, now that I've had a professional opinion, I'll ask you," April said to Bri, with a grin at Annabelle.

"Oh, you nurses! I'm fine, April. What are you doing here?"

"Well, word has flown all over the hospital that you fainted. You know how excited we all are about your babies. So I took a break to come make sure you're all right."

"Not all over the hospital?"

Both ladies nodded.

"Oh, no, that means I'll have a lot of visitors."

As if on cue, the door burst open and a handsome man, with hazel eyes just like Bri's, burst into the room. "Are you all right?" he demanded, ignoring her other guests.

Bri grinned at her younger—by three minutes— brother. "Of course I am. I just tried to hurry too much. How did you hear?"

Though he'd at least asked *her* first, Caleb now looked at the other two women. "I was running an errand for Dad. Is she telling the truth?"

"Caleb!" Bri protested, still grinning. It wouldn't

have been the first time she'd tried to con her brothers, and they both knew it.

"As far as we can tell. Abby was there, and she seemed to think everything was fine," April said.

"All right," Caleb said with a sigh.

Bri relaxed again, glad her brother was satisfied. Until he spoke again.

"I'll be back around five to take you home. I don't want you driving anymore. I'll bring you to work each day and take you home."

"You'll do no such thing. I am not an invalid. I'm pregnant, that's all. I'm perfectly capable of driving a car."

"Bri, you'll do as you're told," he ordered in his sternest voice. It wasn't the first time he'd tried to give Bri orders.

"I'll do as my doctor orders me, dear brother, and Abby assures me I should continue to lead a normal life until she says differently."

"But I did tell you to rest, didn't I?" Abby said from behind Caleb. "How can you rest with the room full of people?"

"Abby, don't tell me you've taken time to come back and check on me," Bri protested.

"Yes, and it's a good thing. Everybody out. I want my patient to rest. Lisa is going to bring you your lunch, Bri. I don't want you traipsing down to the cafeteria. In fact, I want you in that chair or on the sofa from now until two when you'll have to make an appearance at the welcoming party."

"But Abby, I'll need to make sure my directions are being carried out before it starts," Bri protested.

"Send Lisa. I mean it, Bri. Either you cooperate or I put you in that hospital bed."

Bri sighed and looked at her brother and friends. "Okay, guys, I guess you'd better go. Oh, Abby, tell Caleb I can still drive myself to work," she asked hurriedly as her brother was turning toward the door.

He paused and stared at Abby.

After looking at first Caleb and then Bri, Abby said, "For now, she can still drive herself to work."

Caleb frowned, but gave an abrupt nod and left the room. The two nurses followed, with offers to do anything for Bri thrown over their shoulders.

Finally, with only Abby in the room, the doctor moved to her side and picked up her wrist.

"Annabelle already checked my pulse."

"Good for her," Abby said mildly, continuing to watch her wristwatch.

Bri shook her head in disgust. "Well?"

"Your pulse is fine. But I do have a question for you."

"Sure. I ate breakfast, I promise, and I've taken it easy."

"I know you have. What I don't know is why you fainted at the sight of Dr. Hunter Callaghan."

Chapter Five

"I—I guess I hurried too much when Lisa called me. You know how your brother is about wanting everything to run smoothly."

"Don't give me that garbage about R.J. scaring you. I've seen you go toe-to-toe with him when you think he's wrong."

Bri thought desperately. "I have several problems I need to deal with. I guess I went on overload. I don't have as big a capacity for trouble right now."

Abby stared at her a little longer. Then she reached over and felt Bri's cheeks, as if she were a mother checking her child for fever.

"Is your back hurting?"

"No, not at all."

"Are you having any pains anywhere?"

"None, other than when one of the girls gets under my ribs and gives me a swift kick." There wasn't a lot of room for three babies, even with her stomach as big as it was.

"Hmmm." Abby continued to stare. Finally, she

said, "Okay, but if you have any pain, no matter how minor, you have Lisa page me, you hear?"

"I hear, Abby, and I will. I won't take any chances with my girls. You know that."

"I know. And that's the only reason I'm letting you stay out of a hospital bed. I want you to lead a normal life as long as you can. I believe that helps the health of the babies."

"Me, too," Bri agreed, giving Abby her best smile. "Emily, Elizabeth and Eleanor are going to be the healthiest triplets ever born."

"Okay. So follow my orders until two o'clock. You can put in a brief appearance at the welcoming party, but don't stay long."

"I won't. I promise." Relieved that she'd have a good excuse to exit early, her smile grew even brighter.

"Then I'll see you there. And eat all your lunch!"

"Yes, ma'am." Bri even added a mock salute as Abby left her office.

Alone once again, Bri released a big sigh. She hadn't even gotten around to worrying about the welcoming party. Before she could, Abby had given her an out. She'd go for the initial introduction, shake Hunter's hand...dear heavens, she didn't want to touch him.

"You're being ridiculous!" she exclaimed to herself. Their brief acquaintance had happened seven months ago. She'd simply exaggerated the effect he had on her. That was all, a silly exaggeration. She could shake his hand, as if they were two business acquaintances, without feeling anything. Nothing to it.

She drew a deep breath.

"Did you call me?" Lisa asked from the door.

"Uh, no, I hate to admit it, but I was talking out loud to the girls. Sorry."

"No problem. I think that's so sweet. They're lucky girls to have you for a mom."

Bri smiled at her assistant. "Thanks, Lisa. You always make me feel better."

"I'm going down now to get your lunch. I've switched the phones to voice mail, so don't bother answering them. Just stay in your rocker and rest."

"I promise to follow orders," she agreed, and Lisa nodded, disappearing from view.

And the best thing she could do for herself and her girls was not to think about the new obstetrics chief for the McCallum Wing. Ever. She didn't want her girls feeling any connection to the man.

They were her daughters. Three little miracles who belonged to no one else. That was her story and she was sticking to it!

HUNTER FOLLOWED R. J. Maitland through the wing, impressed with the facilities and the friendliness of the staff. He wouldn't find out about their skills until he saw them in action.

"You're cutting a wide swath through our nursing staff," R.J. muttered as they left yet another area.

Hunter frowned. "What do you mean?"

"You haven't noticed all the younger nurses fainting at your feet? Even some of the older ones are swooning."

Hunter continued to stare at him, wondering what he was talking about.

"Man, the nurses are interested. Surely you noticed?"

"Look, Maitland, all I've seen are a lot of friendly faces, which I appreciate. I think you're exaggerating."

"I thought you were single."

"I am. Very."

"Not looking?"

Hunter ground his teeth together, wondering what the man would say if he told him he'd learned his lesson about women at his administrator's hands. Instead, he said simply, "No, I'm not looking." Then, before the man could speak, he added, "And, before you ask, I'm not gay. I'm just intent on my work."

"Good enough. I hope if you do decide to, uh, change your status, you'll look outside the hospital. I'm sure local Austin society will make you feel welcome. Some of our Texas ladies are real lookers."

Hunter smiled. He'd already heard stories about Maitland Maternity's past history. "Like you looked outside the hospital?"

R. J. Maitland's cheeks turned bright red. He cleared his throat. "Well, uh, I guess you know I didn't.'' R.J. had married his secretary Dana Dillinger.

''Yeah, I know. But I didn't let it sway my decision to come here. I don't think personal relationships affect a man's work that much.''

''Okay. Let me take you to your office now. You already have an assistant, Mrs. Helen Robb. If you don't think you can work with her, let me know. I'll find another place for her and you can hire your own assistant.''

''Thanks. I'll let you know.'' Hunter hoped he could work with the woman, but if she was young and followed him around all day long, he'd take R.J. up on his offer. He wanted nothing to do with romance or women.

But he did want to talk to Briana.

Not because he was still attracted to her. He'd explained away his attraction a million times. When he'd let down his guard over the past seven months and found himself yearning for her, he'd immediately reminded himself that she was a wealthy woman, looking for kicks, taking a title to make herself feel important.

Not the woman for him.

But for those few hours when he'd held her, when he'd made love to her, she'd been his dream, his future, his love. He was fortunate, really, that she'd slapped him in the face with reality so quickly. If he'd spent a month or two believing in that fantasy, he might not be able to dismiss those thoughts so easily.

He ignored the sarcastic laughter those thoughts earned from his mind. He was beginning to think he'd misjudged Briana because he was afraid of being hurt. He'd sought ways to dismiss the magic of their time together to make it easier to forget her.

"Hunter? Allow me to introduce Mrs. Helen Robb," R.J. said, jolting him from his thoughts. Apparently they'd reached his office while he was thinking. He had no idea how they'd gotten here.

"Welcome to Maitland Maternity, and McCallum Wing in particular, Dr. Callaghan."

Hunter stared at the trim, gray-haired woman. Her voice was serene and soothing. Now, if she had brains, he was in luck.

"Thank you, Mrs. Robb."

"Please, call me Helen. Everyone does." She turned and led the way into his office. "I arranged the furniture to my liking. If there's anything you want changed, don't hesitate to tell me. I'll call maintenance and get someone up here at once."

His office was large. "I like the arrangement very much. It looks efficient and soothing." The decor was done in blue and beige with an occasional touch of yellow.

"I left room on the wall by the windows for your degrees and certificates. If you'll give them to me when you've unpacked, I'll see that they are hung in place."

"Perfect. Have you worked at the hospital long?"

"Yes, almost since the beginning. I was Mr. William Maitland's secretary until he died. Then I've worked in different departments, so I feel I know the hospital well.''

Hunter looked at R.J. and nodded before he responded to her words. ''Good. You'll be a big help to me as I try to learn everyone's name and position. Thank you, Helen.''

She smiled and disappeared into the outer office.

''She seems perfect, R.J. Thanks.''

''She's one of the best. But if a problem arises, let me know. Now, do you want to go to lunch at a nearby restaurant, eat in the cafeteria, skip lunch while you settle in, have Helen bring you something, or—''

''I'd love for Helen to bring me something while I get settled in, if that wouldn't be rude of me. I'm anxious to find my footing. Everything happened so quickly, I need some time. It's only been ten days since I first interviewed.''

''Of course, and Helen will be glad to do so. She'll start you a tab in the cafeteria. You don't pay until after you've run up a hundred dollars a month, so you don't have to give her any money,'' he added as Hunter reached for his wallet. ''It's part of your contract.''

''Maybe the first thing I'd better do is read the details on that contract,'' Hunter said with a laugh. ''I'd forgotten that little benefit.''

R.J. smiled in return. ''I'm just glad you signed it. You could've stayed in Chicago and received the

same promotion within another year. We feel fortunate you felt like a change of venue. Any particular
reason?''

Hunter avoided the other man's gaze. With a shrug
of his shoulders, he said, ''You know, sometimes you
just feel the need to move on. And Maitland Maternity Hospital, even without the new wing, has a great
reputation.''

''True. Well, welcome one more time. I'll stop by
at two and pick you up for your welcoming party.''

''Thanks,'' Hunter said again. Once R. J. Maitland,
whom Hunter liked so far, had disappeared he
breathed a sigh of relief. No more questions about his
acceptance of the job. He didn't want his reasons examined too closely. He didn't even want to think
about them. After telling himself he didn't ever want
to see her again, he'd jumped at the chance to work
with her. The job was a good one, but Briana had
been the deciding factor.

When Helen appeared at his door after he called
her name, he asked her to fetch him lunch. She gave
him a succinct summation of what they offered, and
he chose randomly and sent her on her way.

Now he was really alone.

No one watching, no one talking, no one guessing
about him.

Now he could replay his meeting with a very pregnant Briana McCallum. Pregnant with his children.
He was going to be a father of three identical little
girls. At least he thought so. He'd dreamed of having

a family—one day. When he'd found Briana seven months ago, he'd dreamed of the family they would have. But then reality had slapped him in the face. He wasn't married, making a future.

Reality. What would she expect of him? Now that she knew how to find him, would she insist on marriage?

His heart sped up as he again remembered the sensations he'd felt when he'd held her in his arms. Sensations he'd dismissed for seven months. They weren't so easily dismissed now.

But he didn't dare give in to those thoughts. He still had no proof that Briana was anything but a rich uncaring woman. She probably had no intention of raising her children. Maybe she was like her father, not interested in babies.

Even he couldn't believe that fantasy. She might have left him high and dry. She might not have been interested in a future with him. But he'd seen nothing in their brief time together that said she would ignore her—their daughters.

And he intended to play a role in his daughters' lives, so if she insisted on marriage, then he'd marry her. He didn't want anyone calling his daughters illegitimate. He'd punch their lights out if they dared.

So, a marriage of convenience?

That was probably what she'd want. He could handle that. Of course he could. He began massaging his temples at the thought of living in the same house with Briana and never touching her. Never.

"Dr. Callaghan? Do you have a headache?" Helen asked. She'd entered his office quietly while his eyes were closed.

"No! No, not at all. I was thinking. That was fast, Helen. I promise I won't ask you to wait on me all the time. I just needed a little time to myself."

"I don't mind at all."

"Have you eaten?"

"I picked myself up some lunch while I was there."

"Why don't you bring it in here and we can talk while we eat. Unless you would be uncomfortable?"

"Not at all."

Hunter wondered how long it would take him to lead the conversation to Briana McCallum without being obvious. Because she was the only part of the hospital he was interested in right now.

AT FIVE UNTIL TWO, Briana touched up her makeup, determined not to look washed out, combed her hair, smoothed any wrinkles out of her navy blue two-piece maternity suit, and started out of her office for the welcoming party in the cafeteria.

"Are you ready to go, Bri?" Lisa asked, jumping up from her desk. "Dr. Abby said I was to go with you, in case you felt faint."

Bri sighed. She was paying a heavy price for her silly fainting spell. But it wouldn't happen again. Because she wasn't going to be surprised again. "Fine, Lisa." She waited patiently for Lisa to reach her side.

''The new doctor sure is a looker. Everyone's talking about how handsome he is. You should hear all the nurses.''

Bri sank her teeth into her bottom lip. It shouldn't bother her. She already knew he was handsome. But she also knew he was one of those men who took his pleasure and avoided the consequences. He was a jerk, plain and simple.

''Really? I guess I didn't notice his appearance all that much.''

Lisa giggled. ''I guess not. You were too busy fainting.'' Then she covered her lips with her free hand. ''Oops, sorry, Bri.''

''Nothing to be sorry about. That about sums it up. So, did you think he was that handsome?''

''Wow, yeah! I mean, I guess he's too old for me, but he's very handsome. And he has just a few grey hairs at his temples. They blend in with his blond hair, but still, they make him look distinguished. I'd trust him with my life,'' she added, a dreamy expression on her face.

''Good looks aren't a lot of help in a medical emergency, Lisa,'' Bri pointed out, sarcasm in her voice.

''I know, but what I meant is he looks trustworthy.''

''Even jerks can look trustworthy. That's why they get the opportunity to be a jerk. No one trusts an ugly man.''

''That's not true. I trust Benny, and he's not handsome.''

"I trust Benny, too, and I think he's kind of cute."
Lisa giggled. "Yeah, so do I."

Benny was a paramedic who made deliveries to the hospital. Sometimes he and his partner would go to the cafeteria and have a cup of coffee. His nose looked as if it had been broken, and he could use a good dentist, but he had a heart of gold.

They'd arrived at the cafeteria, and Briana immediately began checking to see if everything had been done as she'd asked. The cafeteria supervisor appeared at her side to see if there was anything else to be done.

"It looks wonderful, Mrs. C.," Bri said at once.

Joanna Carpenter beamed at her. "Oh, thanks, Bri. I think I did everything you asked. Come have a look at the cake. Sam did a great job decorating it. He's getting very good."

Bri looked at the cake and offered praise for Sam, the baker in their cafeteria. It hadn't been an easy task writing Welcome Dr. Callaghan on the cake.

Members of the staff began filling the cafeteria, many of them checking on Bri before they drifted off to chat with friends.

When the new arrival entered with R. J. Maitland, a cheer went up from everyone gathered, and helium balloons were released from bags in several corners of the room. Of course, they didn't have far to go but soon the strings tied on them were hanging down, allowing those present to take one of them as a souvenir. And they did add a lot of color.

R. J. Maitland raised one hand for silence and again welcomed Hunter Callaghan, obstetrician extraordinaire to the staff, adding an impressive list of qualifications. Everyone cheered again when he'd finished and began shouting for Dr. Callaghan to speak.

Hunter nodded, smiled and held his hand up in appreciation for their welcome. When they quieted, he made a gracious speech about how much he was looking forward to working with them and how much he appreciated the warmth of their welcome.

Bri tried to ignore the warm tendrils of remembrance that curled around her heart as she listened to his voice. How calming that voice had been when they were stuck in the storeroom. How exciting it had been when he'd held her in his arms and made love to her.

Now it meant nothing to her, she assured herself. Nothing at all. But she didn't approach him at once to excuse herself. She had to have time to regain control, because touching him could be even worse than hearing his voice.

Finally, she approached the table where he was eating his piece of cake and assuring Sam it was the best cake he'd ever had. Sam, beaming, backed away from the table and Bri just barely managed to sidestep him in time.

"Oh, Bri! I'm so sorry! I didn't hurt you, did I?"

"No, Sam, not at all."

"Did you get a piece of cake?"

"I'd love one, but my doctor said I had to give up all that sugar for a while."

"Oh, of course. When you can eat cake again, I'll bake you a special one."

"I'll hold you to that."

Sam kissed her cheek and hurried off to the kitchen where he could repeat Hunter's appreciative remarks to his friends.

Dr. Callaghan, as she was determined to think of him, had risen to his feet and stood waiting.

Bri kept about three feet of distance between her and the table. "Sorry to interrupt, R.J., Dr. Callaghan. I wanted to welcome you again to our wing, Dr. Callaghan. And to excuse myself. Abby insisted I only stay a couple of minutes."

R.J. stood and crossed the three feet and kissed her on the cheek. "You did a bang-up job, Bri. Now go take care of those girls. I'm sure Hunter agrees that their well-being takes precedence over any party."

"Thanks, R.J." She immediately turned to head for the door, but she couldn't escape quite so quickly.

"Ms. McCallum," Hunter said, stopping her in her tracks. "Thanks for arranging such a nice party."

"You're welcome," she said, backing up.

"And I believe you said you'd set aside some time in the morning for us to talk?"

Her gaze flickered to his blue eyes and hurriedly looked away. There was an edge to his words, almost threatening. "Yes, at nine in the morning, but only if you want to talk then. If you have more important things to do, we can make it when it's more convenient for you.''

''More convenient for me? Hmm, I'll let you know in the morning. Is that all right with you?''

''Yes, of course. Just let Lisa know.''

She hesitated, wanting to leave but not wanting to appear rude. That would start all kinds of rumors flying through the hospital. And endless questions.

Though she kept her gaze down, she couldn't help but see the hand he held out. Oh, my. She was going to have to shake his hand after all. Maybe she could claim to have poison ivy! Or the measles. Or—or— nothing else occurred to her. And none of her ideas would work. Abby would be all over her if she heard her say any of those silly things.

Come on, Briana, where's your courage? Just shake his hand and get out of here! She drew a deep breath and reached out to receive his offer of a handshake. It had to be her nerves that caused the trembling, not his flesh. But something happened. She felt like static electricity had shot through her.

With a gasp, she jerked her hand away and fled from Dr. Hunter Callaghan's presence. She'd think up a good excuse later...if anyone bothered to ask.

Chapter Six

When five o'clock rolled around, Lisa stuck her head through the door. "It's time to go home, Bri. Are you ready?"

"Not today, Lisa. It's been such a strange day, I need a few more minutes to work before I can leave."

"But Dr. Abby said—"

"I know. But she said my life should go on as normal for as long as I can manage it. And I definitely wouldn't leave all this paperwork for tomorrow. Besides, I'm just going to sit here, no strain. I promise." She gave Lisa her best smile. After all, she was the boss.

"Okay, but maybe you should sleep in in the morning and come in late."

"And keep Dr. Callaghan waiting? Not a good career move." Bri would prefer to do as Lisa said, but she knew she couldn't.

"Oh, I'd forgotten. Okay, but don't stay late."

"I won't." She looked down at the papers on her desk, hoping Lisa would take the hint and leave without more warnings. She appreciated all the concern from her colleagues, but she didn't need a hundred mother hens.

"'Night," Lisa called, and then there was silence.

She was alone at last. No more questions about her reaction to Dr. Callaghan's handshake. As she'd figured, there had been a few. She'd told them all it was carpet shock or something. Amazingly enough, they'd believed her. Or appeared to, even Abby, who'd dropped by around three to check on her.

Now, she'd passed all the tests and would probably only see the man at rare intervals. They could handle most of their business over the phone. She'd just have to deal with his voice.

She turned her attention back to her work. She only had a few minutes worth, but she wanted to make sure she didn't run into the good doctor as he left the building. She figured he'd be gone soon. After all, it was his first day. He couldn't be behind so quickly.

After she finished the last of her chores, she cleared her desk and made a list of what she needed to deal with when she first arrived in the morning. It was best not to be caught unawares.

A noise in Lisa's office caught her attention. "Is someone out there?" Briana called through the open door.

"Oh," Dr. Hunter Callaghan said as he appeared in the doorway. "You're still here. Good." He entered her office and closed the door behind him. "I thought we should have a little talk."

Briana struggled to control the panic welling up in her. "I was about to go home, Dr. Callaghan."

"Don't be so formal, Bri. Make it Hunter."

"I realize I said we'd talk at your convenience, Dr. Callaghan," she began, ignoring his offer of informality, "but I really think tomorrow morning would be better."

"Oh, we'll talk tomorrow morning. But that will be a business meeting. Right now I think we need to have a personal meeting."

He wasn't going to play the game. Pretend they'd never met. Okay, she'd take the gloves off. "Why? It's a little late to explain why you dumped me."

"Why I what?"

She lifted her chin, not about to be intimidated by his behavior. "Why you left me asleep and disappeared, no note, no nothing."

"Lady, I went to my room to shower and change. Then I came back down to take you to breakfast."

She sneered at him. "Easy to say, now, isn't it? Look, doctor, I prefer that we forget what happened in the past and simply work together as business colleagues, nothing more, nothing less." She shoved back her chair. "If you'll excuse me, now that we've got that straight, I'll be on my way."

"There's one problem with your suggestion," he said softly, glaring at her.

"What?"

"You're having my children." His blue eyes were

piercing, leaving her no—what had he called it?—wiggle room.

But she'd prepared for this moment. "You're wrong. I'm not having your children."

"Abby said you're twenty-eight weeks. That's exactly how long it's been since I made love to you in New York City."

She cleared her throat. "I realized it might seem that way to you, but then you don't know what happened when I got off the plane." She held her gaze steady, determined to do the best acting job of her life.

"What happened?"

"My ex-boyfriend met my plane. He convinced me that he was ready for commitment, which was what we argued over. I gave him a second chance. We were together about six weeks when I took a pregnancy test. Abby told me I was four weeks pregnant, she thought. You know how inexact these things can be."

"So where is he?"

"He panicked and ran. He wasn't ready after all." She sat silently, watching him, hoping and praying she'd convinced him.

"Have you told him about the girls?"

"No."

"Are you going to?"

"Why would I? He doesn't want any children. Why would we want him?"

"What's his name?"

She was tempted to make up a name, but she refrained. "I don't think that's any of your business, Dr. Callaghan. I haven't told anyone his name, and I don't intend to start now."

He stared at her and she fought to keep her gaze level to his.

"I'm prepared to marry you," he said abruptly, leaving her without anything to say.

When she didn't respond, he said, "I assumed that's what you would want, now that you know how to locate me."

She leaned back in her chair and lifted her chin another inch. "You're wrong, Dr. Callaghan. I'm not carrying your children, and I don't require such a sacrifice of you. You made your feelings toward me and any commitment quite clear that day in New York City when you disappeared."

"I told you, I was coming back. Of course, then I thought you were a working stiff, like me. Not the incredibly wealthy Ms. McCallum, hiding behind a title."

Bri tried to remember the need to keep her blood pressure down. Drawing several deep breaths, she counted to ten. Several times. Finally, she said, "You may not care for me personally, Dr. Callaghan, but I will not accept such disparaging remarks about my work."

"So I've heard. All people have done is praise your work. They always mention how hard you work, how efficient you are. I figured you shoveled all of it to your assistant's shoulders. They've assured me that's not true.''

She gave silent thanks for the support she'd received. She'd worked hard to ensure that no one thought she was taking an easy ride because of her name. ''I hope you're satisfied, then.'' She'd discovered the hard way that people assumed wealth meant no work on her part. That she would snap her fingers and get what she wanted.

''Not yet. I like to see things for myself.''

''I understand. And if I don't meet your standards, I'll expect you to let me know.''

''You can be sure of that. Are these my babies?''

She stared at the sudden switch of topic again. ''No, these are *my* babies, no one else's. Now, if you've finished with your questioning, I'd like to go home and rest.'' She'd like to get away from him, so she could relax. The tension was getting to her.

He stood, but instead of leaving, he came around the desk and began taking her pulse.

''What are you doing? You're not my doctor. I don't want you—''

''It's high. Are you on any medication for high blood pressure?''

''No! And my blood pressure will go down as soon as you leave!''

''How far away do you live?''

''That's none of your business. Go away!''

He smiled, which, seven months ago, would've

melted all her resistance. She was made of sterner stuff now.

"I can't let you drive with such high blood pressure. I'll drive you home." He took hold of her arm as if he intended to pull her to her feet.

"Turn me loose. I can stand by myself."

He lifted his hands, as if surrendering, and stood silently watching her.

Just what she wanted. Her ex-lover to see how awkward she was. "When you leave."

"I beg your pardon?"

"I'll stand when you leave." She sat in her chair, glaring at him.

"I'm afraid that's not acceptable. I can carry you, I can call an ambulance, or I can call your doctor. You may choose which option you prefer. Or you can stand now and we can walk out to my car."

She felt herself begin to shake, knowing she was pushing her limits. It was time for her to eat, too. Abby had explained the importance of eating regularly. Without saying anything, she stood. Then she bent over to pick up her bag. As she walked to the office door, she was aware of him following her, his tall form leaning protectively toward her.

Even on the nights when she'd hated him, she hadn't forgotten how protective he'd been—until he walked out on her. She made it to the elevator without him touching her, which was a major accomplishment. But it took a lot of energy to control her reaction.

It didn't take long to go down one floor. When the door opened, Hunter took one of her arms.

"You're trembling!" he exclaimed. "Are you all right?"

"It's time for me to eat. I'll fix something as soon as I drive home."

"You're not driving home. I'm driving you. But there's a café right here. Let's grab some dinner there before I take you home."

Bri debated her choices. If she ate, she should be able to drive home by herself. That would be better than this man taking her home. She opted for the Austin Eats Café, a favorite place of hers. "I'll go eat at the café. You don't have to join me. After I eat I'll be okay."

"We'll see," he said mildly, keeping hold of her arm. "Besides, I don't like to eat alone."

"Dr. Callaghan, you're being outrageous," she protested.

He pulled open the door to the restaurant. She saw several people she knew, since many of the staff at Maitland Maternity hung out at the diner. She could protest and they'd come to her aid, but how would that look? If she acquiesced to his company, everyone would think she was welcoming the new obstetrics chief.

"A lot of hospital people eat here. Unless you want to start rumors, we'd better pretend to be friendly."

"Why, Bri, we *are* friendly," he assured her with that lopsided smile, one that she'd never forgotten.

"Bri, how are you?" one of the waitresses called as she saw her enter. "Come on in. We've got a vacant booth back here."

Bri cringed as she knew what was coming next. She'd dined in here just recently.

The waitress pulled the table between the two bench seats all the way to one side. Then she looked at Hunter. "You don't mind sharing the same side with Bri, do you? She needs more room than most people these days."

"I'd be delighted to sit beside her," he said with a smile that had the waitress fluffing her hair. "Thank you."

"Glad to be of service. What can I bring you to drink while you're reading the menu?"

"I'll have ice water, please," Bri said before the waitress forgot she even existed. Hunter had that effect on women.

"Coffee for me," he said, then added, "Decaf if you have it."

"Sure do. I'll be right back."

After the waitress hurried away, Hunter leaned back and surveyed the diner. "Nice place. Very attentive service."

Bri rolled her eyes. "Duh. I wonder why?"

"Because you look like you're about to give birth at any minute?" he said, smiling down at her.

She looked away. "No. Because the waitress can't resist your smile."

"Some women manage."

It was on the tip of her tongue to point out that if she'd been able to do so, she wouldn't look like a blimp ready to pop. But then she remembered that he would realize she was carrying his children. And she didn't want that. She wasn't going to let a heartless man into her life. He might hurt her babies.

She flipped open the menu, though she practically knew it by heart. Not that she could order her favorite things right now. The girls didn't like the chili or the enchiladas she loved.

"What's good?" Hunter asked.

She pointed out several of her favorites, but when the waitress came to take their orders, she asked for baked chicken breast and steamed vegetables. Hunter asked for chicken-fried steak and french fries, preceded by a salad.

"You're a medical professional and you're going to eat those unhealthy things?" she prodded, irritated that he could and she couldn't.

He understood completely. "Don't worry. Not much longer and you can eat them, too."

She sighed and was so tempted to lean her head on his strong shoulders that she stiffened.

"So, how long are you planning on working?"

She looked up in surprise. "I'm going home. I said I would."

"No, I mean, how long before you go on maternity leave?"

"I'm going on maternity leave when I go into labor.'' Her voice was crisp, as if there was no room for discussion.

He frowned at her. ''Are you sure that's wise?''

''My doctor and I have discussed my decision and she agrees with me. And it's none of your business.'' He acted as though he should have a vote in her decision. She hadn't seen the man in seven months. Even then she'd only spent seven or eight hours with him.

''Maybe not, but as a medical professional—''

''Don't expect me to bow down. I work with medical professionals every day. While I respect your work, that does not make you God!''

The waitress returned with their food. She also brought a glass of milk. ''I forgot, Dr. Abby said for you to drink milk at every meal. Remember? Shelby says it's on the house,'' she added with a smile before heading back to the kitchen.

''Nice place,'' Hunter said without actually commenting on the milk. ''Who is Shelby?''

Briana took another deep breath. She'd planned to have her glass of milk at bedtime, but she guessed she'd have it now. Sometimes she thought everyone in Austin intended to supervise her babies' arrival. ''She's the owner of the diner, and sort of family to the Maitlands.''

''Sort of?''

''They're like cousins.''

''Okay.'' Then, as if they were really friends, he began telling her about his day, very innocuous stories that began to soothe her without her even realizing it. If anyone had said she'd share dinner with Hunter Callaghan and enjoy it, she'd have laughed in their faces. Especially about ten o'clock this morning.

By the time she'd finished her milk, vegetables and chicken, Hunter had cleaned his plate. "Very good food. I can tell I'll be eating here often," he said with a smile.

"Not much of a cook?"

"I can manage, but usually I put in long hours and I'm just too tired to want to cook. I suspect that happens to you, too. Everyone I talked to today mentioned what long hours you worked."

"Not lately. Abby's pretty strict with me."

"Good. I want my girls taken care of."

He said those words so casually, as if they both knew these babies were his. But she'd told him they weren't. "These are not your girls! They're mine. All mine."

"You shouldn't be so greedy, Bri. You're getting three. Surely you can share." His smile had a teasing tilt to it, but Bri didn't see anything to laugh about.

"I told you you're not the father!"

"A little louder and the rumors will be flying tomorrow."

He was right. She had forgotten where she was. And she was letting him upset her again. She drew another deep breath. "I need to go home now."

"As soon as I pay, we can go."

"I can pay for my meal, Doctor. And I don't need you to see me home. I'm perfectly fine now."

He gave her a steady look before saying, "Okay, you can drive home. I'll just follow you to be sure you get there all right."

"Ohhh! You're worse than Caleb!"

"Who's Caleb?" he demanded sharply.

"My baby brother. He thought he should start driving me back and forth from work. But Abby assured him I could manage a while longer."

The waitress came over to offer dessert, but Hunter gave her his credit card instead, saying they needed to go.

She rushed away, anxious to impress the doctor with her efficiency before Bri even protested.

She pulled a ten-dollar bill out of her purse and shoved it at him. "I said I'd pay for my meal."

To her surprise, he accepted the ten and folded it, stuffing it in his dress shirt pocket. "Okay, Miss Independent. Ready?" he asked as the waitress had him sign the receipt. Then he slid out of the booth and offered her a hand.

She started to refuse his help just to be rude, but it wasn't easy to slide out of the booth with both her and the girls, so she let him help her.

She was startled, however, when he wrapped an arm around her shoulders. "What do you think you're doing?" she whispered urgently.

"Escorting you home, just as I said," he responded, as if his behavior was normal.

"Take your arm down!" she urged, still whispering, not wanting to make a scene in front of people she knew.

"I just thought you could use a little support." He immediately did as she requested, however, which pacified her.

When they got outside, she said, "I didn't mean to be rude, but tomorrow there will already be a lot of talk about us eating together. If you appear too friendly, they'll think—never mind. Let's just keep our dealings on a business level."

"Yes, ma'am."

"Well, thank you for—for having dinner with me. I'll see you around nine, when it's convenient."

"Right."

She started off in the direction of her car, but he didn't move away. Instead, he fell into step beside her.

"What are you doing?" she demanded.

"Walking you to your car."

"I told you that's not necessary."

"Honey, even if you weren't pregnant with triplets, my mother would disagree with you. She was very strict about how we treated women, my brother and me. I have no choice, or she'll never let me sleep tonight."

She remembered him mentioning his mother when she'd suggested he sit and she stand in the storeroom. "Well, I certainly wouldn't want your sleep to be interrupted tonight!" she snapped.

"I knew you wouldn't," he agreed with a smile. "Do your feet swell these days?"

She considered telling him it was none of his business, but it seemed simpler to just say, "Yes."

"When we get to your place, I'll give you a foot massage. I'm pretty good at those."

As heavenly as that sounded, and only a very pregnant woman would appreciate the sacrifice she now made, she refused his offer.

"Don't worry," he said, as if she hadn't spoken, "I enjoy giving foot massages. Maybe I have a foot fetish. You can give me your opinion afterward."

He was teasing her and she knew it. She wanted to laugh and tease him back, but the last time she'd decided to quit trying to be strong and lean on Hunter, she'd ended up pregnant. Not something she wanted to try a second time. He'd broken her heart once. She wasn't going to risk her heart—or her girls—again. She'd been raised to be strong, to compete with her brothers. She mustn't forget.

When they reached her car, she said, "Thanks again for the escort. I'll see you in the morning."

"Now, honey, quit trying to ignore the foot thing. My car just happens to be right over there. If you'll wait just a minute, I'll be right behind you. We'll soon have you with happy feet, I promise."

Bri gave him a sweet smile, unlocked her car door and slid behind the wheel, grateful for her long legs that allowed her to still reach the pedals with the seat pushed all the way back. She smiled again as Hunter waved and headed toward his car.

Then she started the engine, threw her car in reverse and backed out of the parking spot. Putting the car in drive, she peeled rubber out of the parking lot, determined that the hardheaded man who'd been her shadow for the past hour wouldn't be able to follow her home.

Chapter Seven

Hunter stood in the parking lot, staring as Bri drove away.

He was an idiot. He'd offered to marry the woman, and she'd refused. So why did he still feel protective, concerned, mesmerized by her? He'd intended to keep his distance, not to risk his heart. But two minutes alone with her and he wanted to give her a foot rub.

He was crazy. But he wasn't going to walk away from his children. The girls, as Bri called them, would know their father. Briana might refuse to marry him, but he would claim his children. He'd have DNA tests run after their births if he had to. He would have his family with or without Briana.

Okay, so she wasn't a useless woman, wanting the glory without the work. Everyone had praised her work ethic. The McCallum Wing was functioning well. And that didn't happen without a good administrator. But a good work ethic didn't mean she was honorable in her dealings with men. Maybe she got her kicks by luring men in and then dumping them.

He didn't believe her story about the ex-boyfriend, though. With a frown, he crossed to his car. If she didn't tell anyone about the boyfriend, then how could he check it out? But that fact was also why he didn't believe it.

Caleb. Her brother would know, if no one else would. It was time he bought the guy a beer, did a little talking.

An hour later, after a few phone calls, he arrived at Lone Star, a steak place down the street from the hospital. But instead of heading into the restaurant, he grabbed a seat at the bar and watched for Caleb's arrival.

"Dr. Callaghan," Caleb McCallum said with a friendly smile. "Hope I haven't kept you waiting."

"Not at all, Caleb, and call me Hunter. What'll you have to drink?" Caleb had obviously seen his photo to identify him. But Hunter hadn't needed a photo. Caleb resembled his sister, only he didn't look soft, sweet, feminine.

"What you're having will do," Caleb said, nodding toward the draft beer Hunter had hardly touched. Hunter waved to the bartender. Then he debated his approach. Caleb took the lead however.

"R.J. said you had some questions about the security at the hospital. I'm a consultant for them, not actually in charge of security, but maybe I can answer your questions. What do you need to know?"

"No specific questions. More general things, like what's the crime in this area? Are there crimes in particular we need to be aware of? Have we had problems?''

The bartender delivered his beer, and Caleb took a sip before he answered. ''Maitland Maternity is in a safe neighborhood. However, in the past year, they've had a few problems. Mostly connected to the Maitlands themselves, rather than their patients.''

''Problems?''

Caleb grinned, ''Things like the day-care center being held hostage.''

Hunter had been looking for info about Bri. He'd never suspected there had been real problems. ''You're kidding.''

''Nope. But it was taken care of. Since the Mc-Callum Wing opened, there hasn't been anything.''

''Is your sister going to put her babies in the day-care center?'' Hunter realized he'd been less than subtle when Caleb's eyes narrowed, eyes just like his sister's.

''Why do you want to know?''

Hunter drew a deep breath. He had a choice—continue to try to outfox this man, and Caleb appeared to be pretty sharp, or come clean. He looked at Caleb and made his decision. ''Because I think I'm the father of her babies.''

Caleb came off his stool, his hands forming tight fists.

''Wait a minute before you beat me to a pulp,'' Hunter asked, still calm. He wasn't surprised by Bri's brother's response. He would've been disappointed if he hadn't shown anger.

"Why would I wait?" Caleb growled.

"Because she says I'm not."

Caleb slowly sat back down. "Explain."

"It's a long story," Hunter warned. Caleb nodded, and Hunter began his tale, starting seven months ago....

"And you didn't know where to reach her?"

Hunter sighed. "I knew. But would you pursue a woman who walked out on you after you thought you'd found the one woman in the world perfect for you?"

"So it was coincidence that you wound up here?"

"No. When word got out about the opening, I leapt at the chance to come here. I'd told myself Bri was a wealthy woman, playing games, not worth my time, but when I got the opportunity, I took it."

"But you've left her here alone for seven months!" Caleb exclaimed.

"Yeah, but I didn't know she was pregnant. I was shocked when she walked into the office."

"And when you asked her about the babies?"

"She told me they weren't mine. That her old boyfriend met her at the airport and told her he was ready to commit now. Then, six weeks later, when her pregnancy was discovered, he split." Hunter watched Caleb closely.

"I don't remember any old boyfriend. I mean, there was a man she was crazy about in college. Then she overheard some gossip that he only wanted her money. She had me play a role in a little drama, pretending our dad's company had gone bankrupt, and we'd lost all our money. He started backing out of the relationship at once.''

''So she's had acting experience?''

''Not professionally,'' Caleb assured him with a grin.

''I didn't believe her story, but she was pretty good when she told it.''

''So what are you going to do?''

''What do you suggest?''

Caleb rubbed his chin, staring into space. ''I don't know. She's stubborn.''

''Yeah. I think I'll try to be supportive, try to convince her I'm sincere, until after the babies are born. I don't want to put any stress on her now. Then, afterward, I'm going to insist on my parental rights.''

He stared at Caleb, his jaw firm. He wanted to know now if he was going to have a problem with her family.

''I don't blame you. But fight fair.''

''I always do,'' he assured him.

''Will you offer marriage as an alternative?''

Hunter's immediate response was yes, but he didn't say it. He'd offered marriage already. She had two months of pregnancy left, if she went to full term. Maybe he should get to know her better. Then he could make his decision. ''I'm not sure. I'll wait and see.''

Caleb seemed to be a reasonable man. "I understand. Shall I talk to my father, or my brother Adam?"

"No. I'll explain myself when the time comes. I'd appreciate you keeping what I've told you quiet."

"Okay. Just—just don't hurt her."

"No, but I won't give up my children."

FIRST THING the next morning, Hunter asked Helen to get the files on all the multiple birth patients from the various doctors on the staff. He wanted to review all the cases. "And in the future, Helen, tell the doctors I'll expect an update after each contact with the patient."

Helen nodded and excused herself.

Hunter hoped everyone else's reaction was as accepting as Helen's. But he wanted to be on top of the situation if they had difficulty with any patient. In particular, with Briana McCallum.

Helen returned a few minutes later and assured him all the doctors would send the files as soon as they could get them copied.

"Good. And after the files arrive, we'll need to schedule a visit with each doctor to go over the cases. Now, call Ms. McCallum and tell her I'm ready to go over some things with her as soon as she's free. And when she comes, I'd like you to bring in some milk and a muffin for her and coffee for me."

"Yes, sir."

He wanted to make sure she was eating properly.

He'd decided last night, lying in his bed, staring at the ceiling, that he wasn't going to risk his heart. But he was going to take care of his babies.

Only minutes later, Helen buzzed him to say Briana had arrived. He rose from his chair as the door opened and the mother of his daughters entered. Today she was wearing black slacks and a rose-colored top that matched her cheeks.

"Good morning," he said and gestured toward a large, comfortable chair in front of his desk. As she sat down, he found a low table near another chair, cleared everything off it and put it in front of Bri's chair. Then he lifted her feet to rest on the table.

"What—what are you doing?"

"It's better for pregnant women to keep their feet up."

"But I'm at work. I can't—"

"You're also one of our patients. Did you get a good night's sleep?" He didn't think so. She looked a little fragile this morning.

"Yes," she replied, her voice crisp. "I brought you a list of the problems we've dealt with in the past month. I've also set up a rotating checklist to stay on top of possible problems, and a contact sheet of people to call, depending on the specific problem. Other than me, of course. I'm supposed to be called when anything goes wrong."

"How very efficient of you. That will come in handy when you're on maternity leave. Have you thought about working half days now until you deliver?''

She glared at him. ''No, I haven't!''

''Hmmm. Well, we'll talk about that later, after I review your file.''

''After you what?''

He had been scanning the sheets of paper she'd given him. When he looked up in surprise, he discovered her leaning forward, stress on her features.

''I said, after I look at your file. I'm reviewing all the cases we're currently handling. I want to be familiar with all our patients before we have a surprise.''

''I don't want you to look at my file!'' She drew a deep breath, an obvious effort to calm down, but her gaze remained firmly on him. ''I'm going to ask Abby to keep my file private.''

''If she does, she'll have to operate at some other hospital,'' he said calmly.

She was sputtering, unable to get a coherent word out as Helen walked in carrying a tray.

''Ah, thanks, Helen. I think my guest is ready for a break.''

Helen smiled back and then looked at Briana. ''My dear, are you all right? Do I need to call Abby?'' She shot Hunter a suspicious look, as if he were responsible for Bri's distress.

''Maybe you should ask Abby to visit with us as soon as she can, Helen. Bri and I are having a difference of opinion.''

After another close look at Briana, Helen moved quickly to the door.

When it closed behind her, Bri found her voice. "You can't threaten to throw Abby out of her own family's hospital! You'll be out the door if you try such a thing!"

He smiled. "I won't have to threaten such a thing, Bri. Abby won't refuse to give me her files. It's my job to be on top of each situation. She knows that."

"No! You have nothing to do with my pregnancy. I told you that. I don't want strangers going through my file!"

"Stranger? You're calling me a stranger?"

"We're business acquaintances. It will be awkward to know that you've—you've read my files. And it's unnecessary. I'm perfectly healthy. Abby will tell you."

Hunter noted that her hands and lips were trembling. "Drink some milk and eat your muffin. It's good for the girls. Have you named them yet?" He'd thought about that last night.

"Yes."

"Well? Are their names secret, too?"

"No, of course not. I'm naming them Emily, Eleanor and Elizabeth. Emily was my mother's name."

"Elizabeth was *my* mother's name." He was amazed at how much that meant to him. He liked all three names, but Elizabeth was special to him.

"I didn't know that!"

He cocked one eyebrow. "I know."

Helen buzzed him again. "Abby is here."

Hunter stood again as Abby entered his office. "Good morning, doctor. Hope we didn't interrupt your busy schedule?"

"I don't start appointments until ten," Abby said with a smile, but her gaze was focused on Briana. "Hey, Bri, are you doing all right?"

"Fine," Bri said, but she didn't sound like it.

"Glad you're drinking milk. Mmm, that muffin looks good, too." Just as Abby finished, Helen came in with another coffee cup and saucer and poured her a cup of coffee from the pot already on the tray. "Oh, thank you, Helen."

Hunter slid the plate of muffins toward Abby. "Help yourself."

"Thanks. I missed breakfast this morning." She selected a muffin and bit into it, a look of pleasure on her face.

Hunter gave her a couple of minutes to enjoy the muffin. Then he cleared his throat. "Bri and I were having a difference of opinion and she was getting stressed. I thought it might smooth things out if you explained the necessity to her."

Abby looked first at Bri and then Hunter. "Of course, I'll try, though Bri's pretty savvy about things around here."

Bri wasn't looking at anyone, just staring into the glass of milk.

"I explained to her that I would be reviewing her

file, as I will all our patients. She would prefer that you keep her file to yourself.''

Abby stared at Bri. "I can't do that, Bri. Dr. Callaghan is the head of obstetrics for the multiple birth wing. Of course he'll review the files. He's more experienced in multiple births than me."

BRI KNEW when she'd lost a battle. And she also knew Dr. Hunter Callaghan's office was not the place to embark on her next battle. She'd talk privately to Abby about not having the man in the delivery room when it came time for her girls to arrive.

She carefully set the glass of milk, scarcely touched, back on the tray. "I'm sorry. I should never have objected. It's just that I hadn't realized—he took me by surprise. Of course he'll need to review my file. But, as I told him, I'm in perfect health. I won't take up much of his time," she added with a smile at Abby. "I'm sorry I interrupted your busy morning." She pushed herself up from the chair. "Be sure to call if you need anything, Dr. Callaghan."

"I need you to drink your milk."

His calm words acted like a brick wall. An awkward silence filled the room. Drawing a deep breath, she said, "Of course." Picking up the glass, she added, "I'll take it with me and drink it while I'm working."

"I'd rather you drink it here while you finish the muffin. I want to be sure that the girls get their nourishment."

Bri shot a frantic look at Abby, but her doctor and friend nodded in agreement with him.

"I think Hunter's right, Bri. You look like you need to take a break."

Feeling trapped, Bri sank back into the chair and closed her eyes.

"I don't think she slept well last night," Hunter murmured to Abby, as if Bri suddenly couldn't hear.

"I'm still here," she said without opening her eyes. "I haven't left the building."

"Did you have a bad night?" Abby asked.

Bri licked her suddenly dry lips. "Yesterday was a little stressful."

Abby said, "I still think we should run some tests, put you in a hospital bed for a couple of days."

Bri's eyes popped open. "No, I'm fine!"

"Multiple-birth mothers frequently can't sleep well for long periods of time. Naps are necessary. That's why I suggested Bri start working half days. Then she could go home and take a nap," Hunter said.

"That's not a bad idea," Abby murmured.

Bri drew another deep breath to calm herself. "I appreciate your concern, and possibly I will do so before my delivery date, but I'd prefer to keep going as long as I can." She shot a pleading look at Abby.

"I think you can do so for a while longer without endangering the girls," Abby agreed.

"Good. Then I'll get back to work," Bri said and started to rise.

"The milk and muffin," Hunter reminded her, his blue eyes keeping her seated.

She struggled to hold on to her temper. "I'm not hungry!"

"I'll bet the girls are." He continued to stare at her, waiting for her to comply with his orders.

Finally, Bri grabbed the muffin and tore off a big bite, shoving it in her mouth. As soon as she'd chewed it, she took a long drink of milk. She repeated the process several more times until the muffin and milk had disappeared.

"Anything else, Dr. Callaghan?" she snapped, glaring at him.

"Not right this minute, Ms. McCallum. I'll let you know, probably around lunchtime." He smiled as if he were pleased with himself.

He might as well have waved a red flag in front of a bull. Bri felt her blood pressure rise, but she fought any response. "Then I'll return to my office. Thanks for stopping by, Abby." She hurried from the office before she lost the battle with her temper.

"I DON'T THINK there's a problem with Bri, except maybe her blood pressure," Abby said in a considering manner as she stared at Hunter.

He felt guilty. He knew he'd upset Bri and caused her blood pressure to go up. "You're right. I shouldn't have pressed her as much as I did, but I could tell she hadn't slept well last night. I was concerned."

"I'm sure Bri will appreciate that concern when she calms down. I'll check on her later today. If anything, she has too many people concerned about her. Even the mail boy checks on her when he delivers the mail. Everyone's kind of adopted her as our poster patient."

"Yes, I've noticed. I had no idea it would upset her so much for me to read her file. Good thing I didn't mention that I would observe her delivery." He was already determined to be there when his daughters entered the world. Emily, Eleanor and Elizabeth.

"You're right. I'm glad you didn't mention that. It might make it hard for Bri to face you after that." Abby stood, but she didn't start toward the door. Her gaze remained fixed on him.

Hunter stood also. "I appreciate your coming so quickly."

"No problem. Uh, did you and Bri know each other before you accepted the job?"

Hunter stood frozen, not sure what to say. He knew he didn't lie well, but how could he tell Abby the truth? It wouldn't take much to put together the time of the conference and seven months later.

"If I'd met Bri before, I can assure you I'd remember," he finally said. "She's a beautiful woman."

"True. She's special, too, warm and giving, which is why so many of us want her pregnancy to be a great success. She deserves happiness." With a nod and a smile, Abby left the office.

Hunter fell back into his chair, giving thanks that he'd found a way to answer Abby's question. Bri would be furious that he hadn't believed her story about her old boyfriend fathering the triplets. She'd definitely explode if she found out he'd shared his belief that the babies were his, with anyone.

Like everyone else in the building, he wanted Bri's pregnancy to have a happy ending. That's why he'd drop by her office about lunchtime to check on her.

Chapter Eight

"Bri, do you want me to bring you some lunch?" Lisa asked, interrupting Bri's concentration.

"No, thanks, Lisa. My dad is taking me to lunch."

"Okay, I'll switch the phones to voice mail until I get back."

Bri muttered "Okay" without looking up. She was trying to find a solution to the head nurse's rotation problem. It looked like it was going to cost more money and the budget was already tight.

Several minutes later, someone knocked on her open door. "Just a minute, Dad," she said, again not looking up.

"I didn't know we were that friendly, Bri. Besides, I'm older than you, but not all that much."

She looked up to find Hunter standing at her door.

"What are you doing here?" Not exactly a gracious response, but he made her nervous.

"Wondering what you were doing for lunch. Surely you weren't planning on skipping it?"

"No, my father—oh, hi, Dad," she said as her father appeared behind Hunter.

Hunter turned around and extended his hand. "Mr. McCallum, I was hoping to meet you soon. I'm Dr. Hunter Callaghan, the new head of obstetrics for the McCallum Wing. It's a fine facility."

"Dr. Callaghan! I'm glad to run into you. I apologize for missing the party yesterday, but I had an emergency come up at my company and couldn't get away."

Bri watched the two men uneasily. She didn't want her father getting too chummy with Hunter. "Are you ready, Dad? I can go now." The sooner the better.

"You're taking your daughter to lunch?" Hunter asked, an easy smile on his face. "I was just checking to see if she'd share lunch with me. I don't know too many people yet."

Bri froze. He managed to inject a lost-puppy tone in his voice, and she knew what was coming next.

"Well, feel free to join us. I'd love to have a chance to visit with you. You don't mind, do you, Bri?"

Oh, she minded. But it would make her father suspicious if she insulted her new boss.

"Um, why don't the two of you go ahead, and I'll take a rain check, Dad? I have a lot to do."

"No way," Hunter said. "I'm not going to ruin your lunch. I'll—I'll go down to the cafeteria."

She wanted to tell him to quit acting. But her father

immediately insisted they all three go, leaving her no choice.

"I've noticed Bri works too hard. I'm trying to talk her into working half days until the babies are born," Hunter said with a smile, as if he was only concerned with her health.

Of course, she couldn't think of another reason why he'd want her to work half days, but there had to be one.

"Not a bad idea. Come on, Briana. I'm hungry for a juicy steak," Jackson McCallum said, motioning for her to join them at the door.

"Hmm, I like your taste, Jackson. A steak sounds perfect. For Bri, too. She needs protein."

"We think alike, Hunter. I'm going to feel a lot better about Bri continuing to work knowing you're keeping an eye on her." Jackson beamed at the other man, and Bri ground her teeth.

"Dad! You know I can take care of myself!"

"I know, sweetheart. Come along now."

Jackson had a driver and a limo waiting downstairs to drive them the block and half to Lone Star. The hostess seated them in a circular booth, roomy for three, but Bri, seated between the two men, thought it was too small.

Once they'd ordered, Hunter began a flattering conversation about the wing Jackson had paid for, and the good it would do.

Jackson liked hearing all the praise. And it left Bri completely out of the conversation. She was glad about that. She was afraid her father might notice her antagonism if she was forced to converse with Hunter.

"And how do you feel about having triplet grand-daughters?" Hunter asked, suddenly claiming Bri's attention.

"Wonderful!" Jackson said, beaming at Hunter. "I didn't spend much time with my children when they were babies." He frowned. "I was too busy mourning their mother's death."

Hunter murmured a sympathetic phrase.

"But I'm going to take more time for these babies. Bri is going to name the firstborn after her mother. I'm pleased about that. And it's perfect timing. Adam is doing well with the company. We made all our money in oil well supplies. But times are changing. Adam is prepared. I'm not. So I'm retiring and play-ing with the girls."

"And she's naming one of the others after my mother," Hunter added.

Jackson stiffened. "Why?"

"It's purely accidental, Dad. When I chose the names, I didn't even know Hunter's mother's name."

Jackson stared at his daughter. "You didn't even know Hunter, I assume. Or is there something you're not telling me?"

Bri wanted to bury her face in her hands and curse Hunter Callaghan. But that would make her father even more suspicious. "Don't be silly, Dad. He just got here yesterday."

"He seems to have covered a lot of territory in two days," Jackson pointed out.

Hunter still seemed relaxed, unconcerned. "Of course I have. I asked for all the files on our multiple-birth patients at once so I could get up to speed. But I'll admit, I've given a little more attention to Bri than the others. That's because she's the favorite of the entire staff."

Jackson relaxed a little. "Yes, I've noticed that. They all check on her all the time."

"That's because she works too hard. They all know she pushes herself."

"I am still sitting here," she said sharply. "I'd appreciate it if you wouldn't talk about me as if I weren't."

"Sorry, sweetheart. Do you have children, Hunter?" Jackson asked.

Bri froze again. She wasn't sure Hunter had believed her lie. What would he answer?

With a laugh, as if he were telling a joke, Hunter said, "Not that I know of."

She slowly let out her breath. Hunter went on to explain that he hadn't found the woman he wanted to spend the rest of his life with.

Bri picked up her glass of water and sipped. After he'd made love to her, she'd thought for sure she had finally found the man of her dreams. Too bad he hadn't felt the same way.

"I guess Bri hasn't, either," Jackson said with a sigh. "We've tried to get her to tell us who the father is, but you've probably discovered she's pretty stubborn.''

''Dad!'' she protested.

Jackson ignored her. ''I have three children, and only one has married.'' He frowned. ''And I hope that marriage holds together.''

Bri reached over to take his hand as it rested on the table. ''It will, Dad. Adam and Maggie will get past the problems.''

''Sure. Of course, you're right. But it's ironic. My daughter-in-law wants a baby more than anything, and here Bri is, unmarried, but having three.''

The waitress brought their steaks. Bri had such a nervous stomach, she didn't think she could take a single bite.

Jackson cut his steak and put a piece in his mouth. After chewing, he added, ''Caleb, my third child, I don't think will ever marry. He keeps to himself.''

''Dad, I'm sure Dr. Callaghan isn't interested in our family.''

''Nonsense, Bri. I find it fascinating,'' Hunter assured her, a grin on his face.

''Then you should reciprocate. What kind of family do you have?'' Bri hoped to irritate him, but he seemed pleased by her question.

''My mother passed away about three years ago. My dad is a retired doctor, my brother a corporate attorney. We all lived in Chicago until I moved.''

''Did the move upset your father?'' Jackson asked.

''Somewhat, but my brother is married with a couple of kids. Dad wants to stay close to his grandchildren. But he'll be coming to visit soon.''

"Let me know when he comes, Hunter, and we'll have a family dinner. Two old bachelors can compare notes.'' Jackson grinned, obviously looking forward to entertaining Hunter's father.

"Great. I'll do that. Dad would enjoy meeting—" he paused and looked at Bri.

She froze again. He wouldn't! Surely he wouldn't!

"—some of the people I work with, and another bachelor with grandchildren.''

Bri slumped back against the booth.

"Sweetheart, you haven't eaten your steak. Don't forget the good doctor said you need the protein.''

Without looking at either man, she took a bite of potato. Then she cut a small piece of steak and valiantly chewed it. She only hoped the lunch would end soon, before she lost everything she managed to get down.

WHEN BRI GOT BACK to the office, she made a few quick decisions. Then she loaded up her briefcase with other problems to solve and moved to Lisa's desk. "Lisa, I'm a little stressed today, so I'm taking half a day of vacation and I'm going home. If anything comes up that can't wait, call me at home. Otherwise I'll see you in the morning.''

"Can you drive yourself home?" Lisa asked, standing, an anxious expression on her face.

"Lisa, I'm going home to put my feet up. Don't worry about me."

"Should I call Dr. Abby or Dr. Callaghan?"

"No!" Bri took a deep breath. "Just let me take the afternoon off without any complications, Lisa. That's all I want."

She hurried out of the office to get away from any more questions or suggestions. She appreciated everyone's concern for her and her babies, but sometimes she wished she'd moved to a town where no one knew her.

Half an hour later, she was feeling much better. As soon as she got home, she'd stripped and filled the tub with warm water and bubble bath. She stretched out in the oversized tub and breathed deeply, trying to forget about the stressful lunch. It had lasted forever because neither man would leave until she'd finished every bite of her steak and potato.

She wanted to murder Hunter Callaghan. He'd known what he was doing with each teasing response. He'd even known she was upset. What a jerk!

"You should've known better. That was what you thought he was seven months ago. People don't change."

She shook her head. "And now I'm talking to myself. What am I going to do?"

She slid a little lower into the water, trying to clear her mind. She didn't want to think about a future with Hunter Callaghan around.

The phone rang. She considered getting out of the

tub, but with her bulky shape right now, she'd never get to the phone in time to answer it. Besides, she had her answering machine on.

She could vaguely hear a man's voice, but not loud enough to recognize it. She'd check the message when she got out.

Ten minutes later, when her skin felt as though it was shriveling, she began the laborious task of getting out of the tub. Once she was upright, she wrapped her body in a big bath towel, thinking she looked like a house moving down the road. All she lacked was a tow truck.

The doorbell rang, and she frowned. No one should expect her to be home, so who could it be? She decided not to answer it and continued down the hall to her bedroom.

But she stopped because the caller abandoned the doorbell and began beating on the door itself, yelling her name. Afraid a neighbor might call the police, she rushed to the door. "Who is it?"

"Bri? Open the door!"

Recognizing the caller as Dr. Hunter Callaghan, Bri wasn't inclined to follow his order. "What's wrong?"

"I want to make sure you're all right!"

"I'm fine. Go away!"

"I'm calling an ambulance and the police if you don't open the door in one minute."

"Why?"

"I have to check your blood pressure!" Then he began pounding the door again.

With a sigh, she opened the door. "Stop that! You're going to upset my neighbors!"

Hunter stared at her, reminding her she was wrapped in a bath towel. She began shoving the door closed, but he stuck his foot in it.

"I'm coming in, Bri. I want to check your blood pressure," Hunter insisted.

"Fine! I have to go get dressed." She gave up the battle with the door and stomped out of her living room. She came back a few minutes later, wearing a muumuu she'd bought in Hawaii several years ago. It was the easiest thing to wear when she was relaxing.

Hunter was pacing the room, checking his watch every few seconds.

"Don't let me keep you if you've got an appointment," she said, her chin in the air.

He immediately opened his medical bag. "Sit down. I want to check your blood pressure. I noticed you were stressed at lunch."

"Of course I was stressed!" Bri yelled at him. "You were upsetting me on purpose."

"What?" Hunter responded, shock on his face. "I did not do that! I was visiting with your father, that's all."

She still stood, staring at him, when he reached out. "You're weaving. Sit down before you fall down."

She sank into the nearest chair and leaned back. "Look, just go back to the hospital and leave me alone. I'll be fine if I get some time alone."

Her phone rang again.

She stared at it, amazed that she was getting all these calls when she should've been at work.

Without asking permission, Hunter snatched up the receiver. "She's okay, Lisa. I don't know—why didn't you answer the phone?" he asked Bri.

"Because I was taking a bubble bath to relax— until someone began pounding on my door."

He only repeated the first part of her sentence. "Yeah, I'll stay with her a little while until I'm sure she's okay. Yeah." He hung up the phone.

"Don't mind me," she muttered.

"Sorry, I should've asked permission, but I was sure it was Lisa. When I called and couldn't get an answer, we both panicked."

She closed her eyes. "I didn't think you knew where I lived," she muttered.

"Lisa gave me directions."

She opened her eyes when he put the blood pressure cuff on her arm.

"Just lie back and relax," he said softly.

The problem was she knew her blood pressure was high. She didn't want him to order her to the hospital.

When he released the pressure and took the cuff off without saying a word, she prompted him. "Well?"

"It's a little high, but I know you don't want to go to the hospital. I'll agree to that if you'll let me treat you here."

"What kind of treatment?"

"Remember when I told you I gave great foot massages?"

"Yes." He couldn't mean what he was implying.

"I'm going to give you a foot massage."

"Don't be ridiculous. I'm fine."

"Stay calm. It won't hurt."

"I don't want you touching me." She was afraid it would remind her too much of making love with the man.

"Bri, either you let me rub your feet and calm you down, or you *will* have to go to the hospital."

"No, I— Okay. A foot massage," she rapidly agreed. Even if she protested going to the hospital, it would only take one call to Abby or her father for Dr. Callaghan to make it impossible for her to stay home.

"Let's go to your bedroom."

"No! I can sit on the couch."

"We'll be more comfortable on the bed. Do you have any foot cream?"

"Yes. It's in the bathroom. It's pink, scented peppermint. I'll—"

"Go on to your bedroom and pile up lots of pillows behind you. I'll get the cream."

He entered the room only a couple of minutes later while she was still piling up pillows on the bed.

"I found the cream and a towel. Now, do you have a book to read, something you enjoy?"

She nodded. "I—I started a book last night, but I fell asleep."

"Get it while I pour you a glass of milk."

"But I just ate!"

He ignored her and headed for the kitchen.

"Fine. Bring me milk. If it will get rid of you, I'll even drink it!" she muttered. Then she grabbed her book, turned on the bedside lamp and crawled up in the middle of the bed.

Hunter put a glass of milk beside her on the lamp table. "I'll have to turn my back to you to do a good job, so just relax and read, drink a little milk."

Somehow, having his back to her made everything easier. He pulled her muumuu up to her knees, but no higher. Then he poured cream into his hands, holding it there for it to warm. He took her right foot into his large, warm palms and began to rub in the cream. His strong fingers kneaded the sole of her foot and she sighed.

"I'm not hurting you, am I?" he asked.

"No. No, it feels—good." She hated to admit it, but it did feel great. She hadn't seen her feet often in the last couple of months. Though she wore sensible shoes, as her weight increased, her feet grew more stressed.

Her left foot edged toward her right one, as if making its own plea not to be ignored.

Half an hour later, Bri lay back against the pillows, the milk glass empty and her eyes closed. She hadn't read a single page of the romance novel. She'd been too busy indulging in her own fantasy.

WHEN HUNTER finally felt he'd done all he could, he peeped over his shoulder to discover a relaxed Bri, her eyes closed, breathing deeply. He rose from the bed and moved around to the side, putting his fingers on her pulse.

She was doing much better. When he called her name, she didn't respond, and he realized she'd gone to sleep.

Excellent. He'd felt so guilty when he'd reached her office, and Lisa had said she'd gone home because of stress. He hadn't intentionally teased her about the babies being his. Well, maybe a little. But he hadn't realized how fragile she was.

And they *were* his babies. He felt sure of that now. Otherwise, why would she be so worried about him talking to her father? She'd denied his fatherhood and lied about an ex-boyfriend. That wasn't fair.

But he couldn't put any pressure on her. Just hinting that she might have lied could've brought on early labor. He was going to have to be very careful until she went into labor.

No offer of marriage.

No claim of fatherhood.

No seducing her.

It was amazing that he still found her sexy when she was seven months pregnant with triplets. But he did. He'd like to kiss her, just to be sure the magic was still there, but he felt sure that would bring on more stress.

He wanted to cup her cheek as she lay sleeping, but he couldn't even do that.

With a sigh, he pulled the cover over her so she wouldn't get chilled. Then he left the bedroom. Picking up the phone, he called Lisa. "She's gone to sleep. I need to know the best place to order her a decent dinner. Someone who delivers."

"Well, mostly fast food does the deliveries. I could get her some supper from Austin Eats and take it by there after work, if you'd like."

"That would be great, Lisa. I'm on my way back to the office. I'll stop by and give you some money."

"Oh, that's okay, I'll—"

"I'll be there in a minute."

Now he'd know she would eat a good dinner and then go back to sleep. And while he knew she had plenty of money to pay for her meals, it pleased him to pay for it himself. After all, she was the mother of his children—whether she admitted it or not.

Chapter Nine

Bri was feeling better than she had in days when she reached the office the next morning—except for the guilt she felt about the mean things she'd thought about Hunter.

Because he'd been wonderful.

Knowing she didn't want to go to the hospital, he'd spent a lot of time calming her down—with a foot rub. He'd actually put her to sleep. Then he'd made sure she hadn't had to cook a meal. Lisa had arrived with a nutritious meal, including milk, from Austin Eats.

She'd immediately explained that Dr. Callaghan had insisted on giving her money for dinner for both of them. ''He was so sweet, Bri, so concerned for you. I know he's a doctor, but he's only known you a couple of days.''

Bri had agreed that Dr. Hunter Callaghan was very sweet, outstandingly so. Which irritated her. Which made her angry again. Which made her think bad thoughts about Dr. Hunter Callaghan!

She knew she'd have to thank him this morning for his consideration. And that thought made her blood pressure rise again.

"Okay, has my schedule changed this morning?" she asked, hoping to discuss business rather than the sainthood of Dr. Callaghan.

"Oh, yes. Dr. Callaghan's having a department heads' meeting at nine o'clock and wants you to attend." Lisa pulled out Bri's calendar and showed her how she'd cleared her schedule by moving several appointments to the afternoon. "But if you want to go home at noon, I can transfer the appointments to tomorrow morning."

Bri suspected the idea of her going home at noon came from Hunter, which irritated her. She'd remembered how he'd said his mother stayed home with her children. How he hoped to give his children the same kind of home life.

That, of course, was before she'd realized she was going to be carrying his children. She'd spent her entire life preparing for this job as hospital administrator. She'd wanted to contribute in some way, to others, so they wouldn't die as her mother had. And she was good at it. She should give that up? Abandon her life's dream? She could provide for her children and love them. She knew about the love children needed. Besides, these were her babies, not Hunter's. He had nothing to say about it.

"Do you need anything else, Bri?"

"No, Lisa, thank you. You've taken care of everything.'' And obviously followed Hunter's lead. She liked Lisa, and she was a good worker. Bri hoped she didn't have to have her transferred.

She went to her desk and removed her shoes. She kept a stool under the desk to rest her feet on. She certainly wasn't going to a meeting in Hunter's office with her feet all swollen.

She arrived at Hunter's office at exactly nine o'clock. Helen waved her through to his office. She hadn't wanted to be late, but she also hadn't wanted to arrive before anyone else got there.

When she opened the door, it appeared she was the last to enter. All the department heads were gathered around Hunter's desk. Some were seated in folding chairs, clearly brought in for the meeting. The unusual thing was the leather wing chair she'd occupied before, the most comfortable chair in the room except for Hunter's, was empty.

Joanna, the head of the cafeteria, leapt to her feet and gestured to the big chair. ''Dr. Callaghan reserved this chair for you, Bri, so you'd be comfortable,'' she announced with a smile. Though she first smiled at Bri, Bri noticed how it slid to Hunter's face, filled with admiration for him.

''How kind of him. But totally unnecessary. Does someone else want the honor?''

No one would take the chair, of course. Not when Dr. Callaghan had designated it for her.

She felt like an ungrateful jerk, but she wanted to

walk out on the meeting. She hated being the center of attention. She had no choice, so she sat down.

Hunter immediately stood, as did Joanna. He said, "I asked Joanna to provide us with a few snacks. A reward for the good work you people have been doing."

While Joanna uncovered trays on the big coffee table before the sofa, Hunter leaned down and pulled out a padded footstool for Bri. She stared at it, sure it hadn't been in his office before.

"Where did that come from?" she whispered fiercely.

"It's a gift from one of our donors. I thought it would come in handy for you." He smiled after putting her feet on the stool, but he kept his eye on her, as if he thought she might kick him while he was squatting in front of her.

Not a bad idea.

Joanna came over, carrying a small tray holding a glass of milk and several pieces of banana nut bread. "Sam baked the banana nut bread special for you, Bri, 'cause he knew you'd be here this morning."

Bri pasted on a smile. "Tell Sam thank you for me."

"Here, Joanna, put it on the corner of my desk. I think Bri can reach everything from there," Hunter suggested.

Oh, yes, she could reach it, but it would be in plain sight of everyone, so they could monitor her appreciation of Sam's special treat. She glared at Hunter, but he ignored her response.

"Well now, first of all, I want to congratulate you on the state of our wing. I've never seen a special unit function as well as this one does. It's a pleasure to come to work here each morning."

Bri knew she was being difficult. No one could find anything wrong with Hunter's opening. But she did! Butter wouldn't melt in his mouth. When was the other shoe going to drop? And if he talked long enough, she'd think up some more appropriate clichés!

But no matter how long she listened, he said nothing she could hold against him. Except for preparing her team for when she was on maternity leave, however, he made it clear he expected her to return to her job.

Liar! She knew that wasn't what he wanted.

Of course, he did pause occasionally to remind her to eat the special bread Sam made for her. And to drink her milk for the babies' sake.

Then he stopped talking and asked them to tell him what they needed and what problems they were having.

It was a management technique Bri had used, but she hadn't expected such consideration from Hunter. He didn't hurry the staff, and never denounced their ideas. Occasionally, he complimented some suggestions but explained that they had limited funds.

She'd expected her team to ask for everything possible, thinking Bri could strong-arm the money out of her father's pocket. Hunter pointed out the generosity of their benefactor, her father, and the need to stay within budget unless what was needed would save lives.

And dammit! They listened to him.

When he dismissed her team, Bri could read the satisfaction in their faces. She began the struggle to rise.

"Stay seated, Bri. I have a couple of other things to go over," he added softly before he escorted the others out. Everyone turned and stared at her, smiles on all their faces.

As if they thought Hunter was flirting with her!

That realization sent her blood pressure over the roof. How idiotic! They were both professionals. How could her people think that she was interested in romance at a time like this?

It was Hunter's fault! He was paying her too much attention because he thought her babies were his, too. Well, she'd set him straight about that. Right now!

He closed the door and walked back toward her.

"These are not your babies!" she snarled as he got closer.

"Why are you bringing that issue up now?" he asked calmly.

"Did you see their faces? They think we're—we're interested in each other! You've got to stop paying me special attention!"

"But I *am* interested in you, Bri," he said, his gaze fixed on her. Those damned blue eyes.

"Only because you think these babies have something to do with you. And they don't!"

He sat in the chair next to her, the one earlier occupied by Joanna, and reached for her wrist. "I think you're getting upset again. You've got to stop that, or I'll have to put you in the hospital. It's bad for the girls."

She closed her eyes and leaned her head against the back of the chair. "It's your fault."

"I know. I warned you I gave good foot massages, but I didn't expect you to beg for another one so soon," he said, a grin on his handsome face.

She groaned. Then she sat up. Before she could start to rise, however, he reached for her feet. "I don't have any lotion here, but I can do a quick massage while we talk."

"No! No, you can't. What if—" Then she groaned again as his magic fingers pressed into her flesh.

And Helen entered the office.

Bri tried to jerk her feet out of his hands, but he held on. "Yes, Helen?"

"I have all the doctors' files for you to review, Hunter. Oh, Bri, you lucky girl. When I was pregnant, I would've done anything for a foot rub. My husband refused to give me one." She sighed. "Is there anything else, Hunter?"

"No, Helen, thank you." And he continued to massage Bri's feet.

Bri covered her face with her hands. "Hunter, please stop. The entire hospital is going to be talking about us if you don't." She realized her voice had descended to the level of pleading, but she didn't know how else to get him to stop.

"Honey, I'm just trying to make things easier for you, that's all. I'll explain it to anyone who says differently. Indirectly, you're my patient. I know what's good for pregnant ladies."

"I—I have to go. I have a job to do. It's very important that I do my job."

"I know. Have you arranged for some help after the babies are born?"

"Grace says she knows of someone," she muttered.

"Grace? Oh, I remember. The lady who took care of you and your brothers. She can't come?"

"She's too old to take on three babies. And I'll need help with the cooking and housecleaning. I've even been thinking about hiring someone now. I don't have a big place, but it can get dirty fast. And sometimes I don't feel up to doing laundry and the dishes."

She hadn't meant to tell him that, but it seemed once she started talking about it, she couldn't stop. She didn't want to complain at the hospital. And she couldn't talk to her father about such things. He'd move an army into her house and she'd lose her privacy.

"Why don't you call Grace today and talk to her about it? And be sure it's someone who can cook.

You shouldn't have to cook dinner after working all day.''

"Oh,'' she said with a big sigh. "That would be heavenly, wouldn't it?''

"Yeah. Will you call Grace?''

"I shouldn't. I can manage until the girls get here. I'll just get lazy if I don't keep moving.''

His blue eyes darkened, but his face remained calm. Suddenly he leaned forward and kissed her— on the lips. It happened again. Even though the kiss was almost brotherly, her response wasn't. The magic she'd felt the first time was mild compared to what she felt today with just the touch of his lips. Had she lost her mind? She wanted more and almost reached out for him. Fortunately, his phone rang before she could actually make such a disastrous mistake.

"Go back to your office, honey. I'll check on you later.''

"Yes, uh, but you shouldn't call me honey. We're professionals,'' she reminded him as she closed the door behind her.

At least she hoped she was.

DR. ZACH BEAUMOUNT was on the phone Helen told him. Hunter had met the obstetrician and liked him. He reached for the stack of files, finding the ones belonging to Beaumont as Helen put the call through.

"Zach? Hunter here. How can I help you?''

"Did you get my files?''

"Just got them. I haven't had a chance to go over them yet. Is there a problem?"

"Not with those cases. But I saw a new patient today."

Hunter waited for him to come to the point. Multiple births could show themselves very early.

"She's about five and a half months pregnant...and carrying four babies, two sets of identical twins."

"What's her history?"

"I'm the first doctor she's seen."

"Damn! Any problems?"

"The babies are undersized. I made sure she got a supply of vitamin tablets. I don't think she has any money. I want to put her on our charity list."

"Of course. Do you have an address or phone number?"

"She's staying at a boardinghouse. Says she's a widow, but she's only seventeen. Her landlady convinced her to come see me."

"Okay, I'll authorize putting her on the charity list and I'll send our social worker to visit with her and take information. Do you think she'll be able to carry them long?"

"I doubt it. She's small. I don't think she's eating well. I'd like to put her in the hospital as soon as I can talk her into it."

"That's probably a good idea. We'll get the ball moving from this end. Thanks for letting me know, and send a copy of her file to Helen."

"Right away. Thanks for supporting me on this case."

Hunter smiled. "That's what I'm here for."

He knew everyone would want to test him out, to see how cooperative he'd be. They'd soon learn that babies' lives were his first priority. If he had to go out and solicit funds himself, he didn't want any multiple birth to occur in less than exemplary conditions so that the children had the best chance of survival.

He rang for Helen, and she hurried in, a steno pad in her hand. He immediately gave her orders. Her concern for the young woman, even though she didn't know her, came through loud and clear. Hunter was pleased.

"Let me know when the file gets here and when everything has been taken care of."

"Yes, doctor, at once."

As she got up to go to her desk, he stopped her. "Do you happen to have Caleb McCallum's work number? Or could you get it for me?"

"Of course. Is there a problem with security?"

"I just have a question for him," Hunter assured her. He wasn't about to tell her that he was going to interfere with Briana's personal life. But he was.

Within minutes, he got Caleb on the line.

"Hey, doc, what's up?"

"Caleb, I need Grace's phone number."

"Grace?" he repeated, as if he'd never heard the name before.

"Yeah, you know, the lady who took care of you when you were little."

"Yeah, I know, but how do you know? And what do you want her number for? She's retired."

Caleb, it appeared, didn't take anyone on trust right away. With a sigh, Hunter said, "Grace is going to recommend someone to take care of Bri and the babies. Bri is determined to make it on her own until the babies are born, but I think she needs help now. Someone to cook and clean, to make sure she eats properly."

"Oh. Did you discuss it with Bri?"

"Yes, I did, but she's stubborn. She admitted it sounded wonderful to have some help, but she's afraid everyone will think she's lazy, which is ridiculous."

"Yeah, it is. Okay, here's Grace's number, but you do realize Bri is going to be furious that you're interfering, don't you?"

"Yeah, but I'm going to try to get Grace on my side. So keep our conversation to yourself."

"You got it, doc."

Hunter wrote down the number.

When he dialed the number, a sweet feminine voice answered.

"Is this Grace?"

"Yes. Who's speaking?"

"You don't know me. I'm the new obstetrics head at the McCallum Wing."

"Dr. Callaghan? Of course I know who you are. Is

there a problem with my volunteering? I do love it
so. I hope I'm—''

''I didn't know you volunteered.''

''I usually volunteer in the preemie nursery in
Maitland, but when you get babies in your nursery,
I'm transferring over there. I'm coming in today for
a tour.''

''You are? What time?''

''My tour is at one.''

''Come at eleven and I'll explain why I need your
help. Then we'll both go take Bri to lunch. Is it a
deal?''

''It's a deal. I'm very interested. Everything's
okay, isn't it? I mean the babies and all?''

''I'm trying to make sure of that. But you know
how stubborn Briana is.''

''Oh, yes. I'll be there at eleven.''

Then he buzzed Helen. ''I want you to call Bri and
tell her that I expect her to join me for lunch today.
I have a special guest I want her to entertain. And
don't take no for an answer. Tell her we'll drop by
her office at noon to pick her up. We'll eat in the
cafeteria.''

''What if she refuses?'' Helen asked, frowning.

''It's your job to make sure she doesn't, Helen.''

She stared at him. ''I don't want to upset her.''

''Helen, Briana's former nanny is coming to lunch
today. She's going to volunteer in the nursery as soon
as we have some customers. Her presence is a sur-

prise for Bri, so keep it a secret, but it's a surprise Bri will enjoy.''

After Helen withdrew, Hunter sighed. His secretary thought he was a bully. That was a fine state of affairs. And he was trying to be so tactful.

Right on time, Grace arrived at his office. She was elderly, he'd guess in her seventies, but she looked healthy and had the most serene expression on her face he'd ever seen.

''Dr. Callaghan, I'm anxious to hear what you want to discuss with me.''

''Bri mentioned that you were going to recommend someone to help her with the babies.''

''Why, yes, a very nice, experienced woman.''

''Is the woman prepared to do housecleaning and cooking, also?''

''Of course,'' Grace replied, a puzzled look on her face.

''Well, I'd like Briana to go ahead and hire the woman now. She goes home exhausted. I'm worried she's not eating properly because she's too tired to cook. She admitted she's too tired to do housecleaning, and she worries that if she hires someone now, everyone will think she's lazy.''

''That's ridiculous! The poor child is carrying three babies. After what happened to her mother, I worry about her all the time.''

''Could you convince her she should go ahead and hire the woman so they can get to know each other before the babies come? Tell her she'll be happier if she knows who's taking care of her babies from the word go?''

''That's a very good idea, Dr. Callaghan,'' Grace assured him with a smile. ''Of course I can do that.''

''Good,'' he said, smiling.

''And with you recommending it, I don't see how she can resist.''

''No! Don't mention me!''

Chapter Ten

Bri sat hunched over her desk, irritation coursing through her. A special guest! Hunter needed her to entertain the person! Right! All he was doing was supervising her eating habits. Dr. Hunter Callaghan was an interfering, bossy man. How were they going to stop the gossip if he didn't stop this silliness?

It was almost twelve. Helen had made it clear in her phone call that the invitation wasn't one Briana could refuse. So, where was the big man? He seemed to think he could order her life around. The least he could do was be on time!

Just as the hands on her watch reached straight-up twelve, a soft knock sounded on her door. She called, "Come in," ready to be difficult.

The door opened and Grace, her darling Grace, appeared. Bri struggled to her feet and went to the door to wrap her arms around her true mother. "Grace! What are you doing here? Is everything all right? Oh, I have to go to lunch with someone, or I'd take you—"

"Calm down, child. You're going to lunch with me. Hunter arranged it all. Isn't he a darling man?"

Bri tried to stifle her groan. Another person singing his praises? She didn't think she could stand it. "Yes, fabulous," she said, trying to dredge up enthusiasm. "Why are you here?"

"I'm taking a tour of the nursery. Once you start having babies there, I'm going to volunteer. I've had experience with multiple-birth babies, you know," she added with a beaming smile.

Bri hugged her again. "I know you have. And you're a terrific mother substitute."

"Bless you, child," Grace responded, tears in her eyes. Then she stepped back from Bri. "Now, how are you managing? Let me look at you. My, you've gotten quite a bit bigger since the last time I saw you."

"Yes," Bri agreed with a sigh.

"That's good, child. You want these babies to grow so when they're born, they'll be okay."

"Of course," Bri agreed, smiling.

Grace frowned. "But you also need to take care of yourself. How are you managing?"

"You two ladies ready for lunch?" Hunter called. He'd stopped at Lisa's desk and talked to her. Now he stepped to the door of Bri's office.

Bri stared at him. "Yes, of course, but we don't want to take up your valuable time. I'll take care of Grace."

"Oh, no, you don't. Grace is my date. I'm just

being nice, letting you come along. Let's go. We don't want to be at the back of the cafeteria line. They've got chocolate pie today.''

Grace took her hand and pulled her toward Hunter. Before Bri knew it, they were in the elevator. She was going to share lunch again with Hunter. With another family member. Grace might not be a blood relative, but she certainly was part of Bri's family.

It seemed to Bri that everyone in the cafeteria was staring at them as they went through the line. Hunter and Grace kept up a rambling conversation about their food selections. Grace added several vegetables to Bri's tray. When Hunter added the chocolate pie, Bri finally protested, but he ignored her. He was too busy waving to the cashier to charge all three meals to his account.

Oh, good, that wouldn't cause any talk!

''Hunter,'' she whispered. ''Let me pay for me and Grace. It will cause less talk.''

''Honey, you've got to quit worrying about gossip. It's not important.'' Then he raised his voice. ''Pick wherever you want to sit, Grace. We'll follow.''

Grace selected a table for four right in the middle of the room where everyone would see them.

Bri took a seat next to Grace, hoping Hunter would sit down on the older woman's other side, which would give her a little breathing room. She should've known better. He, of course, sat down next to her.

''How did you know Grace was coming today?'' Bri suddenly asked.

''She knows Helen and called to ask her to lunch. When Helen told me who she was, I included the two of us.''

Bri turned and looked at Grace. ''I didn't know you knew Helen that well. Weren't you going to at least come see *me?*''

''Of course I was. But I knew how busy you'd been with the opening; I didn't want to cause you any stress. But I'm glad I did see you. Without what we added to your tray, you wouldn't have had much to eat. Aren't you taking care of yourself and the girls?''

''Sure I am. But I already had a snack today. Lately it seems I'm eating constantly.'' She slanted a glare toward Hunter. ''And where is Helen?''

Hunter's face grew serious. ''Zach Beaumont got a new patient today. We're anxious to get her in the hospital and Helen volunteered to stay at work to speed everything up.'' He smiled at her before taking a bite of meat loaf. ''But you're coming along nicely. I looked at the latest ultrasound this morning. The girls are a nice size. But I do worry about you not getting enough rest.''

Grace immediately picked up that point. ''Are you trying to do too much, darling?''

''Of course not!'' Bri protested. ''My place is even a little messy, because I'm really not doing too much. Really, Grace, I'm doing fine.''

''Well, I was thinking it might be a good idea for Alice to start working for you *before* the babies come. Then you'll feel more comfortable, turning the children over to her while you get some rest. And it wouldn't hurt for her to cook and clean a little now.''

Bri carefully put down her silverware and turned to Hunter. ''You need to keep your nose out of my business!''

He tried to look innocent, but she had no doubt that he had put Grace up to this sudden idea. She started to rise and he clamped his hand on her arm, keeping her seated.

''Really, Bri, I'm sure I taught you better manners than that. The man is just trying to take care of you,'' Grace insisted, frowning. ''I'm thankful he contacted me. I had no idea you were ready for help. Why hadn't you called me? I could at least come by every other day or so and do some laundry or something.''

''Grace, I wouldn't ask that of you!''

''Well, thankfully, it's not necessary. I talked to Alice this morning. We thought it would be good if she came in for half a day. She could do laundry, change the bed linens, things like that, in the afternoon and then have dinner ready for you when you got home.''

''That sounds lovely, but it's totally unnecessary, Grace. I can take care of myself,'' Bri assured her.

''Of course you can, but this would be for the girls. They need their rest so they can grow. Please do this for me, darling Bri, so I won't have to worry about you so much.''

Hunter sat back and watched Grace at work. She'd outflanked Bri at every turn. He could use her on his staff. Most important of all, she was getting Bri to do the right thing.

"In fact," Grace added, "it will be good for Alice, too. She's a widow, you know, and she spends too much time alone. She'll get to know your kitchen and how you like things done, instead of having to learn all that with the complication of three babies."

Hunter grinned. Now she was telling Bri she was being selfish not giving Alice a job at once. When Bri turned to glare at him, as if she'd been able to read his thoughts, he wiped away the grin. "That's good thinking, Grace."

"Of course you would think so. Where did you get Grace's number? I didn't tell you her last name," Bri said.

"I never reveal my sources," he said with a smile.

"Darling Bri, you should've let me know you were struggling," Grace said, patting her hand. "And I should've checked on you more often. I'm afraid I'm spoiling Douglas, centering my world around him. Tsk!"

"Grace, you've always spoiled all of us. That's why we love you so much," Bri said with a gentle smile. "Tell Alice I'd love for her to start part-time to get adjusted. I'd appreciate her help."

"Wonderful, dear. I'll give her my key to your place and I'm sure she'll come in about one today. She promised she'd cook a healthy meal for you."

"I don't know if I have anything there to cook."

Bri frantically tried to go through her pantry in her head.

"I knew it. You've been neglecting yourself."

'It's just so hard to carry in groceries right now, Grace,'' Bri protested.

"Alice will do whatever grocery shopping is necessary. She'll save the receipt and you can reimburse her." Grace turned to Hunter. "I'm so glad you called me, Hunter. Bri will be feeling much better with the proper care."

Though Bri glared at him again, Hunter felt like celebrating. He'd succeeded, thanks to Grace. "Eat your pie, Bri," was his only comment, however.

"Aren't you worried about the calories I'm consuming? I'm surprised you don't have a calculator out counting each one!" she exclaimed.

"If anything, you're too thin. I want a little baby fat on the girls when they're born," he assured her.

"You should see my Bri when she's not pregnant," Grace said. "She's a beautiful woman!"

Hunter smiled at Bri. "Yes, I'm sure she is." He could remember her in that storeroom, wrapped around his body, her scent filling his nostrils, her warmth heating up his own.

"Are you married?" Grace asked, looking from him to Bri and back again.

"Grace!" Bri protested.

"No, I'm not. Want to do some matchmaking? I'm not against it," he said, his smile widening, knowing it would infuriate Bri.

"Well, it's a thought. But I suppose we should wait until after the girls are born. You're not one of those men who only like boy babies, are you?"

"Not at all. Three identical little girls, looking like their mama, couldn't make a more beautiful picture."

"Exactly!" Grace replied, almost clapping her hands in approval. "I'll bring some baby pictures of Bri and her brothers the next time I come."

"I'll look forward to it," he assured her, seeing the babies in his mind's eye. Maybe they'd have blue eyes like his. But Bri's hazel eyes were so beautiful.

Grace interrupted his thoughts. "The main thing is to get them here safely."

"You're so right," he agreed. "That's my number-one concern, too."

"I'm still here," Bri reminded them. "You've re-arranged my life. The least you can do is talk to me as though I'm a real person."

"Being pregnant makes her a little testy. She normally has a wonderful personality," Grace assured him.

"I feel like an old maid someone is trying to auction off. Please, Grace, I'm fine. I don't need a husband."

April Sullivan stopped by their table, holding her full tray. "You looking for a husband, Bri?" she asked, obviously having overheard Bri's last words.

"No! But some of my family seem to think I can't manage alone," Bri told her friend, disgust in her voice. "Have you met Grace? She and her husband took care of my brothers and I when we were babies. She's going to be volunteering in the nursery as soon as we get babies," she added.

"Then I hope you're ready soon. We've got twins that I think will arrive within the week."

"Excellent!" Grace said, beaming. "I love babies."

"Well, you must be good if you took care of Bri and her brothers," April said with a smile.

"We'd ask you to join us," Hunter said, "but I think we're finished. I know I have to get back so I can review the files. What's the name of the patient soon to deliver?"

April gave him the woman's name. He pulled out a piece of paper from his pocket and scribbled down the last name. "Ready, ladies?"

"You go ahead. Grace and I want to visit with April for a while, if you don't mind."

"Not at all," he agreed. He stood and held out the chair for April to sit down. "I enjoyed the company, ladies. And, Grace, thanks for your help." He bent over and kissed the older woman's cheek. Then he did the same to Bri. "Didn't want to leave you out, honey. See you later."

"NOT IF I see you first," Bri muttered, horrified that he'd kissed her cheek in front of half the hospital. When she dared look at April, she found her friend staring. "That meant nothing," she hurriedly said.

"He is such a sweet boy, isn't he, Bri?" Grace said, still smiling.

Bri couldn't think of what to say.

"Everyone likes him," April offered. "I've only heard praise since he got here." But she still kept her gaze on Bri, as if she expected Bri to make a major announcement at any moment.

"April, don't pay any attention to anything he does. He's intent on teasing me."

"But he just met you," April pointed out, a puzzled look on her face.

Bri felt she had to come up with something, some reason for his familiarity, or everyone was going to be convinced she and Dr. Callaghan had something going. Which was utterly ridiculous. "Uh, I met him once at a conference."

"Really? Did you keep in touch?"

"Not exactly. We have mutual acquaintances. It's nothing." Definitely nothing. She hoped if she downplayed it, no one would try to figure out which conference. She'd gone to three different ones before the wing opened.

"Oh, I guess that explains it. But you might keep him in mind for, you know, later on, after the girls are born."

"Exactly what I say," Grace agreed enthusiastically.

"I can't believe the two of you. Look at me! Do I look like I'd be thinking anything about romance? I'm like a beached whale at this point. And I don't feel friendly toward the sex that got me this way!''

April grinned. ''That will pass. I know you love your girls already.''

''Yes, and I'm concentrating on them and no one else right now.''

A FEW HOURS later, when Briana opened her condo's front door and smelled lemon-fresh polish combined with the fragrant odor of a homemade dinner, her thoughts weren't on her baby girls. She was thinking about Hunter and his trickery.

She was still angry with him, but the thought of a great meal and a clean place was nice.

''Alice?'' she called.

The lady Grace had introduced her to several months ago came out of the kitchen. ''Ms. McCallum. You're home. I hope you're hungry.''

''I'm starved, and something smells delicious. I hope coming so soon didn't cause you any problems?''

''No, ma'am. Frankly, I was ready for some company.'' The woman beamed at her.

''Why don't you join me for dinner and we'll talk? You might've had some trouble familiarizing yourself with my place.''

''Oh, I only fixed enough for one. You need to eat it all.''

Bri stepped into the kitchen and watched as Alice filled the table with food. She gulped, then said, ''Alice, when I said I was starving, I didn't mean I'd have this big an appetite. There will be plenty for both of us. In fact, I think you should eat dinner with me every evening before you go home. Unless you wouldn't like it. But some conversation would be nice, and there's no reason for you to cook twice."

"I'd love it, if you don't mind. I'll pay for half the food," Alice assured her, her eyes big.

Bri laughed. "As long as I don't have to fix it, I'll gladly pay for it." She pulled out a chair and sat down.

Alice joined her. After a few questions about how Briana liked her laundry done, Alice began asking her questions about her job and life at the hospital.

Before Bri knew it, they'd finished the meal, and she was completely relaxed. "Alice, that was wonderful. I'm feeling more relaxed than I have in weeks. Thank you."

"I'm glad you liked it. I enjoyed myself, too. Hearing about your job is like listening to a real live soap opera. Now, you go take your bath and get dressed for bed while I do the dishes. Then I can go home knowing that you're all settled in for the night."

Obviously, Alice had been taking lessons from Grace, but Bri didn't complain. She only resisted when the orders came from Hunter. She had to resist the strong pull she felt from him. Being in his arms overpowered all her common sense.

"I could help with the dishes."

"You've already worked all day. I'll take care of these."

Bri left the kitchen and went to soak in the tub. Afterward, she dressed in a long flannel gown. It was December, not cold, in Austin, but not warm, either. She pulled socks onto her feet and wandered back into the living room. One of her favorite shows was coming on. She settled among the cushions just as Alice brought her a cup of hot tea.

"Thank you, Alice. I love hot tea."

"That's what Grace said. This tea doesn't have any caffeine, so you can sleep well tonight. I'm going on home now unless there's anything else you want me to do."

"Oh, no, you've been wonderful. If you only want to come every other day, I'll be fine."

"I'd like to come back tomorrow, if you don't mind. I thought I'd bake some chicken for tomorrow's dinner. It's so nice to have someone to cook for."

"Fine with me," she agreed with a smile and bid the woman good-night. When Bri slid between clean sheets at ten o'clock, she sighed with pleasure. And Alice was coming every day. She sighed again.

She guessed she owed Hunter a thank-you for Alice, too, but she was getting tired of having to thank him all the time. Though she hadn't really gotten around to thanking him today.

Oh, well, she'd thank him tomorrow. If he didn't irritate her first.

THE HOSPITAL was abuzz the next morning. The first multiple births had occurred at 3:00 a.m. that morning. Twin boys were sleeping in the nursery, and most of the staff had taken time for a visit to look at the two small babies. They'd weighed in at 5 lbs. 9 oz. and 5 lbs. 4 oz.

As soon as Lisa told Bri about their arrival, Bri hurried to the first floor, where the nursery was located, to see them.

"Aren't they darling?" she asked without even looking to see who had come up beside her.

"Yes, they are," Maggie McCallum agreed, sadness in her voice.

"Maggie! I didn't even realize that was you. How are you doing?" Bri knew her sister-in-law wanted a baby badly.

"The same as ever," she said, offering a smile that wasn't very sincere.

Bri hugged her. "Dr. Sheppard is very good at her job. I'm sure if you give it time, you'll be all right."

"She says we will...if Adam cooperates."

Bri gave Maggie all her attention. "Is that brother of mine being difficult?" She knew Adam could be stubborn.

"He has to be tested and...you know how men are about that macho stuff." Maggie's cheeks turned pink. "I've tried to tell him it's probably all my fault but—"

"Maggie McCallum, don't you let him push you around. It's not either of your faults. Neither of you would keep from having a baby on purpose. Let Dr. Sheppard help you and soon you'll have one—or more—of your own.''

Maggie's eyes filled with tears. "I hope so," she whispered.

"Admiring our new residents?" Hunter asked as he stepped to Bri's side.

"Yes, of course," she said, hoping he wouldn't notice Maggie's distress.

He stuck his hand out and introduced himself.

Maggie took his hand and explained that she was Adam McCallum's wife.

"I haven't met Adam, yet, though I've had a couple of conversations with Caleb," Hunter explained.

Bri turned to stare at him. "Oh, really? A couple? When were they?"

She knew she'd just discovered his source for Grace's telephone number, but she didn't know what his other conversation with Caleb had been about. And she wanted to know.

"Um, just, er, casual conversations. He's a security consultant for the hospital, you know." Hunter tried a smile, then he turned to Maggie. "Do you work here, too?"

"No. I have an appointment with Dr. Sheppard."

"Great. She's a good doctor."

"You're not changing the subject, Dr. Callaghan," Bri said. "What else did you talk to Caleb about besides Grace's telephone number?"

Hunter replied, "Just this and that. How long have you been married, Maggie?"

A man stepped forward, one with hazel eyes and brown hair. "Long enough to know better than to flirt with strangers." His tone of voice told everyone he wasn't happy.

"Adam," Maggie said hurriedly. "This is Dr. Callaghan, the new head of obstetrics. Dr. Callaghan, this is my husband, Adam McCallum. He and Bri were just talking about his conversations with Caleb."

Though he still frowned, Adam seemed a little friendlier. "You had lunch with Dad and Bri the day before yesterday, too."

"Yes, I did. A nice lunch."

"So what have you been talking to my brother about?"

"Just what I want to know, too," Bri said, her arms crossed.

Chapter Eleven

Hunter took his time giving an answer. "I like to talk to adult members of a multiple birth. I think it helps give me perspective. After meeting Bri and Caleb, I'm really glad I finally get to meet you."

"You think there's something wrong with people of multiple births?" Adam demanded.

"Not at all. In fact, sometimes I envy the bonding that children do in the womb. It seems to last a life-time." He kept his gaze on Adam, but he could feel Bri bristling beside him. "Bri, for instance, is fiercely independent, but very close to both her brothers."

"That's true," Adam agreed. "How you doing, sis? Are the babies all right?"

"They're fine."

"Is Dr. Callaghan going to handle the delivery?" Maggie asked.

"Yes," Hunter said calmly.

"No!" Bri screamed at the same time. Adam and Maggie stared, and she hurriedly added, "Abby is my doctor. She'll handle the delivery."

Hunter smiled at her. "But I'll be there, too. I intend to attend all the multiple births until I become very familiar with my staff."

"You don't have to worry about Abby. She's the best."

"I'm sure she is," Hunter replied.

"I might have them at an inconvenient time," she added, realizing she hadn't convinced him.

"More inconvenient than three in the morning?" he asked, grinning. "That's when these guys put in an appearance."

"Who delivered them?" Bri asked.

"Dr. Beaumont. And he did a great job."

"Didn't he resent being watched?"

"I don't think so. We had breakfast together afterward."

"Bri," Adam added, his voice calm and reasonable, which only aggravated Bri more, "I'm sure Dr. Beaumont understood. After all, Dr. Callaghan has a job to do."

"You're just siding with him because you're a man! You and Caleb always did that!"

"Watch your blood pressure, honey," Hunter said softly.

But not softly enough.

"Honey?" Adam asked, frowning again.

"I have to go," Bri announced abruptly and left them all standing there, staring at her as she walked away.

When she reached her office, Lisa greeted her. "Hi,

Bri. I didn't know you'd met Dr. Callaghan before he arrived. Why didn't you say so?''

Bri's hands flew to her temples to massage the headache beginning to make itself felt. ''We didn't become good friends. We just met, that's all. No big deal.''

''But I guess that's why he's so friendly with you. After all, you're the only one he knew before he got here,'' Lisa said, beaming at Bri. ''So, I guess you've got the inside track.''

Bri stared at her. ''The inside track for what?''

''Dr. Callaghan. Half the staff wants to marry him. But when they hear you knew him before, they may all give up.''

Bri took a deep breath. ''Tell them not to give up, because I'm abandoning the track right now. I'm not exactly the shape for long-distance running.''

Bri started to walk past her, but Lisa raised her eyebrows and said, ''The question isn't your behavior but Dr. Callaghan's. He already acts like he's hooked.''

Bri rubbed her temples again. ''Lisa, I don't want to discuss this subject ever again. And do what you can to discourage anyone else from doing so. There is *nothing* between me and Dr. Callaghan. Okay?'' Then she stomped into her office.

''Okay,'' she heard Lisa say. She hoped Lisa meant that answer as a promise to help curtail the speculation about a romance. But Bri was afraid her agitated reaction might cause even more speculation.

And darn it! She still hadn't thanked the man!

E-mail! She was going to deal with him through e-mail. She could be calm and reasonable when she didn't have to talk to him.

She immediately wrote a gracious—well, not too gracious—note thanking him for keeping an eye on her. She reminded him that she was a professional and hoped he would treat her as one.

Then she lay back in her chair, taking deep breaths and closing her eyes. Her checkup with Abby was in half an hour. She didn't want her blood pressure to alarm Abby.

"ABBY? This is Hunter. I'm planning on sitting in on Bri's checkup. Helen told you, didn't she?"

"Yes, of course, Hunter."

"Look, don't be alarmed about Bri's blood pressure. And take it before you tell her I'm coming. I'm going to wait outside until she's on the table, prepped for the ultrasound."

"Is something wrong?" Abby asked cautiously.

"She got upset this morning. She felt her brother sided with me on something and it upset her."

"She seems particularly sensitive to—well, to you."

Hunter couldn't think of what to say.

"I heard she met you at a conference."

It was Hunter's turn to be silent. He hadn't realized she'd told anyone that. "Uh, yes, briefly. We didn't really get to know each other."

"Which conference did you meet at?"

"I don't know. I'd have to check my calendar. Does it matter?" He didn't give her a chance to answer. "Look, she's embarrassed to have me observe the checkup because we're acquaintances. It'd be like having your brother-in-law watch you undress. We just need to keep her calm. When you're ready to start the sonogram, knock on the door. I'll be waiting just outside."

"All right, fine."

He waited until five minutes after Bri's appointment time before he slipped into Abby's outer office in the main hospital. Bri wasn't in the waiting room.

The receptionist assured him Bri was already in an exam room, so he asked to talk to Abby's nurse. As he'd hoped, Abby had left instructions.

"She said you were going to wait outside the door. Peggy, the other nurse, is with the two of them."

"Just show me which room they're in," he said softly.

He felt sure Abby had planned the ultrasound for the last part of the checkup. He was eager to see his daughters.

He stood at the door for several minutes, hearing the murmur of feminine voices. Then a soft knock informed him he could enter.

Stepping into the room, he nodded to Abby and walked to the head of the table. Bri was staring at the monitor, probably assuming he was another nurse. But something must have alerted her to his presence, and she shrieked and dove for the sheet, trying to cover her stomach.

"What are you doing here?" she demanded in a hoarse whisper.

"I want to see the ultrasound, both to check the babies and to evaluate the quality of the machine. Abby agreed."

"Well, someone should've asked me. I don't want you here." She turned to Abby. "Please, Abby, make him leave!"

Abby stepped forward and took her hand. "Bri, you're all covered up except for your stomach, and I'm sure Dr. Callaghan has seen pregnant stomachs before. Just relax before your blood pressure gets too high. Your babies need more time in the womb. Take deep breaths."

Hunter spoke softly to the nurse and she left the room.

"Do you need something?" Abby asked, frowning.

"Yeah, something to bring down the blood pressure," Hunter said.

"I don't think medication—" Abby began as the nurse came back into the room carrying a towel and a bottle of lotion.

"Of course not. But a foot rub will do the trick," he said, pouring cream into his hand.

"What did he say? What's he doing?" Bri asked, trying to raise her head high enough to see over her stomach. Then she sighed as he began rubbing cream on her feet. After a moment, she remembered to protest. "Hunter, you shouldn't—"

"Relax, Bri. Abby's going to show us those three little girls. Let's have a look-see." Then he nodded to Abby as he continued to massage Bri's feet.

He only stopped once, when the picture first clearly showed his three little girls. "They're beautiful," he murmured, and received an enthusiastic agreement from Abby.

Bri, lying more relaxed on the table, blinked away tears, but her gaze was focused on the screen that showed three squirmy babies jockeying for position in their limited space.

After a quick look at Bri, Hunter began massaging her feet again, silently giving thanks that Bri had decided to keep their children and try to manage on her own. She was a courageous woman. Even if she wanted nothing to do with him after the babies were born, he felt sure she wouldn't stop him from seeing the girls.

"Everything's all right?" Bri asked Abby, sniffing away the tears.

"Oh, they're doing beautifully, Bri. And if you give birth now, they'll make it just fine. But the longer you carry them, the faster they'll go home from the hospital."

"I'm being careful." Then, she flashed her gaze to Hunter and back to Abby. "I've already hired a lady to help at home, so I can get plenty of rest."

"Oh, good. I'd been worrying about how much you were trying to do. Good decision."

Bri's gaze returned to Hunter. "Yes. I appreciated the concern that—I got some good advice."

Slowly, he grinned, knowing that was her way of thanking him. Pretty magnanimous, since he'd been interfering where he had no right to interfere. Maybe she would accept his protection a little more readily in the future.

Even as he was thinking such pleasant thoughts, her jaw firmed and her lips were pressed together. "But I'm an adult, and I can manage my affairs by myself."

He had no intention of letting her try—no matter what she said!

THAT EVENING was again delightful. Alice joined Bri for dinner, and everything in her house was sparkling and fresh.

"You're going to have to mess up more things, young lady, so I'll have enough to do."

"Oh, Alice, you shouldn't be working so hard."

"Well, I wanted to ask you about cooking ahead. Most things are good for six months, I think. I thought I'd bake some lasagna and freeze it. Maybe a cake or two, because you'll probably have several visitors after the babies are born. We'll need something to feed them when they visit."

"That's a wonderful idea, Alice, if you don't mind the extra work."

"Well, I have the time now. If you don't mind the added expense."

Bri quickly assured her she didn't. After dinner she took a shower. Abby had suggested it might be best to have showers now. Then she settled among the cushions on the sofa, turned on the television and relaxed. Alice brought her a cup of tea and some cookies.

"I'm not sure I should eat the cookies."

"Dr. Callaghan said you need to fatten up a little so your babies won't be too skinny."

Bri froze. "When did Dr. Callaghan say that?"

"He told me today when he called to tell me your checkup went well. He knew I'd be worried and he was afraid you wouldn't want to talk about it."

Though she was fuming inside, Bri tried to make her voice calm. "I'm sorry, I didn't think to tell you. But everyone's fine."

"I know," Alice said with a smile. "Now eat your cookies and drink your tea. I put in cream instead of milk. It makes it taste wonderful."

Alice was so pleased with her behavior, Bri couldn't be mad at her. But she could be mad at Dr. Hunter Callaghan.

As soon as Alice left, she grabbed the phone. She wasn't calling Hunter. Not yet. She had some other calls to make.

"Dad? Just wanted to let you know that my checkup went well."

"Yes, I'm so glad. Hunter said the girls looked

great. He thinks you may make it almost to term. I really appreciated his letting me know. I've been worrying about you.''

''So why didn't you call me?''

After a moment of heavy silence, Jackson said, ''I was afraid you'd get scared because I was worried. After what happened to your mother, you know.''

Tears filled her eyes. ''I know, Dad. But it's all right. We have better doctors and better equipment, thanks to you. Everything is going to be fine.''

''Yeah, Hunter assured me he'd take care of you and the girls.'' He actually sniffed into the phone, as if he were hiding tears, as she had in the doctor's office. ''Hey, how about lunch again tomorrow?''

''Thanks, Dad, but with the appointment today, I lost a lot of work time, so I can't go out for lunch. I'll just have my assistant bring me something. I'll take a rain check if you don't mind.''

''Okay, but you let me know if there's anything you need.''

''I will, Dad.''

When she'd disconnected, she began dialing Caleb's number, but a knock on her door stopped her. She moved to the door to peek through the peephole. Dr. Hunter Callaghan, bossy doctor, stood there.

She was wearing her Hawaiian muumuu, so she swung open the door, a big glare on her face.

''Hmm, welcome as usual,'' he said with a grin.

''How dare you!''

''I don't know how I dare, since I don't know

what's got you steamed this time. Unless it's my sitting in on your checkup.''

''No! I've accepted that you have a right to do that, though I don't like it.'' She folded her arms across her chest, though they actually rested on top of her stomach. ''But you don't have a right to interfere in my personal life.''

He nudged her backward and stepped inside, closing the door. She was so wrapped up in her anger, she didn't realize what he'd done for several minutes. ''I didn't invite you in!''

''But you should have. Grace would be appalled at your manners,'' he assured her, still smiling.

''You think you're so smart, but you wouldn't be so popular if I told everyone you abandoned me after getting me pregnant!''

She immediately realized what she'd done when his eyes brightened and he took a step closer. ''I didn't mean *you* really—I meant what if I told them that! That's what I meant. What if I lied to them?''

Somewhere during that speech, he'd switched to doctor mode, instead of father-to-be mode. ''Your blood pressure is rising again. Come sit down. I'll make you some more tea.''

''How do you know I want tea? Maybe I want a slug of whiskey, or a soda, or Kool-Aid! You don't know me—or what I want.''

''I know you don't want to hurt your babies. Come sit down, Bri.''

He arranged cushions behind her back. Then he

picked up her cup and took it to the kitchen. In no time he was back with a fresh cup of tea, with cream added, much as Alice had made.

"Do you still have cookies to eat?" he asked.

She glared at him and didn't answer.

"Honey, we need to talk about what's upset you so it won't make your blood pressure go up. I promise I haven't deliberately tried to rile you." He sat on the couch, pressing against her legs as she lay there. "Now, tell me what I did this time."

"You told Alice, my dad, and probably Adam, Caleb and Grace about my checkup." She doubled up her fist and hit him in the arm, knowing it wouldn't hurt him, but maybe it would let him know how angry she was. "Alice told me I needed to eat the cookies because you told her I needed calories."

"Who else but your cook should I have told? And I had to tell her about seeing the babies, so she'd believe me."

"And my father?"

"Well, I could tell, when we talked at lunch, he was putting up a front about everything being all right. He was scared to death you were going to die just as your mother did. I wanted to reassure him."

Her eyes filled with tears, and she bit her bottom lip. "And my brothers?"

"Your father asked me to call and reassure them because they were worried sick about you, too. You're the only female in the group. They don't know if you're just trying to reassure them, or if maybe you don't know what's going to happen.''

''And they believe you because you're a man!''

''No, they believe me because I'm a medical professional who's delivered a lot of babies.''

''Did you call Grace, too?''

''Yes, because she asked me to. She said she didn't like to ask you because she was afraid it would make you worry.''

She sniffed. She'd been sure the man had overstepped his mark, but there he was, explaining it all away, making her look like a hysterical woman. ''I— I still think you should've at least told me you were going to—to interfere in my life.''

He leaned forward to pick up the cup of tea and then held it to her lips. ''Take a sip.''

She did so, trying to ignore his body pressed against her stomach. His touch drove her crazy. It apparently affected the girls, too, because they suddenly began jumping around like five-year-olds playing soccer, running in all directions and kicking anything that moved.

After he set the cup back on the table, he looked at her and whispered, ''May I?''

She didn't have to ask what he wanted. She knew he wanted to feel her babies move. She nodded.

His big warm hands spread out over her stomach, acting like a lightning rod for the movement. One lump in particular caught his attention. ''I think one of the girls is standing on her head.'' He rubbed the lump and it shifted.

''They move around a lot, especially at night.''

''Bri, I want to thank you for having the courage not to terminate the pregnancy.''

''You're wel—I mean, it has nothing to do with you! Nothing at all.''

With his hands still on her stomach, he stared at her, challenging her words.

''These are my girls, and no one, not their father or anyone, is going to hurt my girls.''

''Why would you think their father would want to hurt them?'' he asked softly.

''Because he hurt me! He left me alone, wanting—wanting his love and—and my children are better off just belonging to me. I won't hurt them.''

''Are we talking about the mythical boyfriend who split? Or are we talking about me?''

She looked away, refusing to give him an answer. ''I'm tired. I want to go to sleep.''

He sighed. ''Okay. Do you need a foot rub?''

''No! I can manage.''

''All right, but you need to understand, Bri, that I'm going to watch over you, try to care for you and the girls. I'm not trying to hurt you or trap you into anything, okay?''

''Fine.''

''Okay, I'm going to go turn down the covers. Take my arm while I walk you to your bedroom.''

''I can—''

"I know you can. Just let me help. Then I'll lock the door as I leave."

"Fine!"

They walked to her bedroom in silence. He pulled down the covers, then covered her up as she settled in the bed. As he turned away, she saw him pause by her dresser.

"What is it?" she demanded as he picked something up and looked at it. Frantically, she tried to think what he could've found. Whatever it was, he put it back in the ceramic bowl where he'd found it and told her good-night. The minute he'd left her bedroom, she knew what he'd found.

A black stud from a tuxedo—ripped from Hunter the night they'd made love. The one thing she'd found of Hunter's the next morning.

And treasured. The one sign that what she'd experienced hadn't been a figment of her imagination.

Even if he *had* left her.

Chapter Twelve

Hunter left Bri's condo with a smile on his face. For the first time, Bri had admitted the girls were his daughters. She'd given it away when she'd threatened to tell everyone he'd abandoned her.

He was coming to know Bri better, and he was pretty sure she told the truth. Except to him.

When he'd seen the tuxedo stud, he knew it was the one he'd been unable to find the morning he'd left her room. And she'd kept it. And she'd said the father of her babies had abandoned her when she'd wanted him to love her.

She wanted him to love her.

He was willing. But he was pretty sure she couldn't handle any pressure about her life right now. It was taking a lot of work on his part to keep her blood pressure from rising too high. The best thing he could do now was to take care of her and the girls. Later, when they were safely born, he'd woo her, convince her he hadn't left her.

The last thing he'd wanted was to lose her. He

climbed into his SUV and looked up at her windows, dark now so she could sleep. If he was lucky, he'd get his cake and eat it, too. He'd have Bri to love and three little girls to complete his life.

All he had to do was wait.

THE NEXT MORNING, the tenth of December, Bri got to work early. The hospital opening had occurred before Hunter had arrived. She hadn't wanted Christmas decorations up until after the opening.

Today they would be hanging two angels in maroon robes with golden halos on their heads, playing their horns, in the huge windows of the lobby. The angels would be seen both from inside and outside the hospital.

At the other end of the lobby, there would be a huge Christmas tree, a real one. The fragrant scent of pine would fill the air. Twinkling white lights would cover the tree, as well as oversized ornaments.

All the departments would get a regular-sized artificial tree. Though Bri hated to use the artificial ones, she did because some patients might be allergic to the smell of real evergreens. The staff members would decorate their trees. Overnight, the entire hospital was going to be festive.

She loved Christmas.

"Bri, nice job," April called as she crossed the lobby at eight. "I wondered when we would have decorations."

"I wanted to wait until after the opening. By then it was hard to get on the schedule," Bri explained.

"This is perfect. We'll have at least a couple of weeks to enjoy them. How'd your checkup go yesterday?"

"Fine," Bri said, thinking that at least here was one person Hunter hadn't called. "Abby says the girls are in good shape if we have to deliver any time soon, but late January is still the expected delivery."

"Great. I heard we got several more patients in the hospital last night. Let's go to the cafeteria and have some breakfast, and I'll tell you all about it."

"Did Hunter put you up to this?"

She regretted her question when April looked at her with surprise.

"No. I didn't eat breakfast. All I could think about all the way here were those cinnamon rolls Sam makes. Don't you love them?"

With a sigh, Bri agreed. "Yeah. Let me tell the guys where I'll be if they run into any problems." She consulted the workers and then followed April to the cafeteria.

Soon she was indulging in a cup of hot tea and a big cinnamon bun, warmed to just the right temperature. "I'd worry about the calories, but Hunter is encouraging me to eat more."

"Wow! That's my kind of doctor. I thought Abby was your ob-gyn, though."

"Uh, yeah. Dr. Callaghan is a hands-on supervisor."

"I see." After taking a bite, April looked at her friend. "There are a lot of rumors circling the wing."

"About what?" Bri asked cautiously.

"About you and Dr. Callaghan."

Bri chewed deliberately on her bite of cinnamon bun, giving herself time to answer. "Don't believe anything you hear. People make things up," she said with a big smile.

The level of noise in the room mounted, and they both turned around to see what had caused the uproar. Two men brought in big boxes and began putting together the artificial Christmas tree for the cafeteria. It was bigger than most of the trees because the room was so large.

"I guess everyone's pleased about the decorations," Bri said, delighted to change the conversational topic.

"Yeah, some of them thought we wouldn't have Christmas decorations this first year, since we had the big opening."

"Oh, no! I should've said something. That didn't occur to me. I just didn't want them up until after the opening, that's all."

"I know. But it's going to lift the spirits of everyone. And having the new patients will, too."

"You haven't told me about them."

"One lady is having twins, but her blood pressure got too high. Her doctor thought she would carry them longer if she remained in bed."

"Oh," Bri groaned. She hoped that didn't happen to her.

"The other is a teenager. She'd been living at a boardinghouse nearby. Dr. Beaumont got her on the approved list for a charity case and they moved her in last night. She's only a little over six months and she's carrying quadruplets. I've heard they're small. She didn't get any prenatal care until she saw Dr. Beaumont a couple of days ago."

Bri shuddered. "That's terrible. I hope the babies make it."

"Yeah, I think they said she's twenty-six weeks, so she's three or four weeks behind you."

"Well, I'd better finish my breakfast and get upstairs. I'll want to be sure they have everything they need for both patients. But I'll stop and check on the twins we already have in the nursery. Aren't they sweet?" Bri asked.

"They're terrific, and already gaining weight. I think they and their mom will go home tomorrow," April said. "Our first successful multiple birth for the wing."

"Okay. I'll see you later."

After checking on the twins and stopping in their mother's room to see if she had any complaints, Bri went back to the lobby to make sure everything was progressing as it should.

The foreman came over to speak with her. "Ms. McCallum, the new head doctor wanted us to add a banner that says Peace on Earth beneath the angels.

We have a really nice one with gold-leaf trim that looks as if it's on a roll, but it will cost an extra five hundred. He said to ask you about the expense.''

The budget was tight, but she decided to grant Hunter's request. Everyone was so excited about the decorations. It made her feel guilty that she hadn't let them know they would have Christmas decorations before now.

''All right, that will be fine. Just add it to our bill.''

''Great. It will look real nice.''

''I'm sure it will.''

On the way to her office, she was humming ''Silent Night'' beneath her breath. She stopped by Hunter's office and told Helen to assure Dr. Callaghan they were adding Peace on Earth. ''He'll know what I mean, Helen.''

''Is that Bri?'' Hunter called from his office.

''Maybe you'd better tell him yourself, Bri. He'll be upset if you try to avoid him.''

Bri raised her eyebrows, unused to not being obeyed by the employees, but she guessed Helen didn't want to be caught between the two of them. She crossed over to Hunter's door. ''Yes, it's me. I just wanted to tell you that we're adding Peace on Earth.''

''Good. I think that will be a nice touch.''

''Thank you for leaving the decision up to me.''

He grinned. ''No problem. You heard about our two new patients?''

''Yes, I'm checking with their doctors to see if they

have everything they need. I suspect the teenager might need a few things.''

"Can we provide them?"

"It will get done," she said, not mentioning that the money might come out of her own pocket. She was fortunate to have the funds to live as she wanted. She liked to help those who couldn't.

"If you need a donation, let me know."

"Okay, thanks."

"Oh, and Bri? Nice working with you."

He was right. This was the first time they'd both wanted the same thing. And it was nice. She gave him a smile and slipped away.

After calls to the two doctors of the new patients, Bri went back downstairs to visit with the teenager, Jenny Barrows. As she'd expected, the girl had almost nothing in the way of personal supplies. Afterward, Bri talked to the nurses.

"She didn't bring much with her. We put her in a hospital gown because she didn't have anything but a T-shirt."

"And she has no family," the second nurse added.

"All right. We'll see if we can help her out a little," Bri said.

Both nurses relaxed. "Thanks, Bri. That's great."

She returned to her office. "Lisa, we're going shopping. Switch the phones to voice mail because we'll be gone a while."

An hour later, they returned from one of the large economy stores, with several bags. "Why don't you take off the price tags and go introduce yourself to Jenny, our new patient, and tell her these things are hers to keep.''

"But Bri, you should take them. You bought them."

"The charity fund bought them. I'll fill in an expense-account form for the money. Besides, I need to check all the departments to be sure the trees are taken care of.''

"But I could do that and save you some—''

"Just do as I ask, Lisa," she said quietly. "I'm going to eat lunch before I check the departments, so it will be a while before I get back.''

"Yes, ma'am. I'll switch the phones back on as soon as I return.''

"Good.''

After Lisa left, Bri drew a deep breath, then headed to the cafeteria. She was tired from the shopping expedition, which probably explained why she didn't shop anymore.

After she'd chosen her meal, she turned around to look for an empty table. She found one near the windows and sat down with a sigh. No question about her appetite today.

"Mind if I join you?" a male voice asked.

"Uh, I don't mind, but it would be better if you don't. There's a lot of gossip already," she told Hunter, giving him a quick glance and then staring at her plate.

"I told you not to pay any attention to gossip," he said lightly, sliding his tray onto the table beside her.

Bri was concerned about the thrill that seemed to flow through her. She mustn't let her hormones dictate her behavior. She had to think of the girls. And her weak resistance when it came to Hunter. She was as hard as whipped cream when it came to Hunter. Then she caught sight of Annabelle just leaving the cash register. She waved to get her friend's attention.

"You don't mind if my friend joins us, do you?" Bri asked, staring at Hunter.

"Of course not. I'm hoping to get familiar with all the staff."

Annabelle reached the table.

"Join us, Annabelle," Bri said at once, pleading with her eyes.

"Of course, if Dr. Callaghan doesn't mind." Annabelle kept looking from one to the other as she sat down after Hunter's assurance that she was welcome.

"Dr. Callaghan, this is Annabelle Reardon. She's one of our delivery nurses."

"Of course, that's where I've seen you. You were there when the twins were delivered."

"Yes, that's right."

"Good job. You work with Dr. Beaumont a lot?"

"When I can. He's a good doctor."

The two of them continued to chat, and Bri found it easier to eat her food. She could see Hunter watching her to see if she ate, but she could ignore that.

"Oh, Bri, the Christmas decorations are so wonderful. We weren't sure—"

"I should have explained to everyone. As soon as I can, I'm going to put out a weekly newsletter that will keep everyone posted on what's going on."

"Good idea," Hunter said, and Bri was pleased.

"It won't happen any time soon, what with the babies coming."

"Why not ask the public relations department?" Hunter asked. "You can provide any information you want in the newsletters to them, but they could add birthdays, events in the lives of the staff, things everyone would be interested in."

"Do you think they'd have time?" Bri asked, pondering his idea."

"More than you. Besides, that falls under their expertise."

"That's a good idea," Annabelle said, beaming at Hunter.

Bri suddenly wondered if her friend was one of those members of the staff who was interested in Hunter. Not that she minded. Of course not.

"Annabelle's right about the decorations. You did a fine job, Bri. Have you already decorated at home?"

Bri ducked her head. "No. I probably won't this Christmas. It's a lot of work." She couldn't keep the longing out of her voice, but she figured the other two wouldn't notice.

Since she'd been eating while the other two talked, she finished her meal before them. "I hope you don't mind, but I need to check the Christmas trees in each department.''

''Can't someone else do that?'' Hunter asked, frowning.

''There's no need for someone else. I need to talk to the staff a little and apologize for not letting them know we were decorating,'' Bri said, then she slipped away.

HUNTER WATCHED Bri hurry away. They'd got along better today, and it had been nice. But she was still working too hard.

''Dr. Callaghan?''

''Yes, Annabelle, and make it Hunter. No need to be formal when it's just staff.''

''Oh, thank you. I need to ask you something. You sat in on Bri's last examination, didn't you?''

''Yes.'' He wondered what she wanted to know and whether Bri would get upset.

''I was going to ask Abby, but since you're here— You see, we're going to give Bri a shower. Well, April is, but several of us are helping her. We want to wait until January because Christmas is such a busy time, but we're worried she won't carry the babies that long. What do you think?''

Hunter smiled at the young woman. ''That's a tough call, but I don't think she'll go full term. I'm hoping we can get her through New Year's.''

''Oh! Then we'd better have it right away. Thanks for the advice.'' She picked up her tray and stood.

"I've got to check in with Dr. Beaumont. He's going to look at Jenny Barrows again. He doesn't think she'll go much longer." She started to leave, then added, "I forgot to tell Bri how sweet it was that she went shopping for Jenny. The poor child has nothing."

"Bri's a generous woman."

"She's the best," Annabelle said with emphasis. Then she, too, abandoned him.

Bri had gone shopping this morning and now was touring the entire wing. She was going to be very tired tonight. He could call Alice and tell her to put Bri to bed at once, serving her dinner there. But Bri would get irritated again, and being in an almost civil relationship was quite pleasant. And gave him hope for later.

He remembered the longing in her voice for Christmas decorations. He didn't believe she could decorate even if she wanted to. Especially not after today's demands.

Maybe tomorrow would be easier. And she could sleep late on Saturday. If he carried everything to her apartment—then she might do a favor for him.

A smile settled on his face.

BRI WAS RELIEVED when she left the hospital Friday afternoon. Two days ahead of her of doing nothing but taking naps. Then she'd be able to face her job again on Monday. But it was getting more difficult to last through the week. She might have to admit that she needed to cut back.

Alice had certainly helped, but the days seemed longer recently.

Alice had fried chicken waiting when Bri arrived home. "Fried chicken? Doesn't that have too much fat and cholesterol?" she asked.

"It's not fried. It just looks and tastes that way. It's a special coating I put on it. My husband had high cholesterol and he hated baked chicken. I came up with this recipe," Alice said, beaming with pride.

"I can't wait to taste it. And I'm so glad it's Friday," she added.

"Sit down at the table, and I'll serve dinner at once."

But Bri noticed that Alice checked her watch.

"Alice, do you need to leave early? It's okay, I can serve myself."

"Aren't you a sweet thing. But, no, I don't have to leave. I just—"

The doorbell interrupted Alice and Bri realized that was what Alice had been waiting for. She was expecting someone.

Somehow it wasn't a surprise when she heard Hunter's voice. But there were some extra sounds she couldn't identify. Before she could decide to get up and do some investigating, Alice, followed by Hunter, entered the kitchen.

"Look who's here!" Alice said, pretending to be

surprised. "I asked him to join us since I had plenty of chicken made. You don't mind do you?"

"Of course not. How convenient that you made extra chicken."

Hunter sent her a rueful smile. "Alice, I don't think we fooled her. The truth is, Bri, Alice and I talked, and I told her I was going to do something for you in hopes that you'd help me. She asked me to dinner then."

Alice looked worried, and Bri couldn't upset her. "It's all right, Alice. We'd never turn down a hungry man."

"Kind of like helping Jenny Barrows," he said, raising one eyebrow.

Without looking at him, she said, "I'll file an expense account to cover that."

"Sure you will. You don't lie any better than Alice, Bri. The two of you are quite a pair."

Alice giggled, and even Bri couldn't hold back a smile.

"I'll practice," she said.

"Don't bother. You're perfect the way you are." After smiling at her, he turned to Alice. "Now, where's that special chicken, Alice? I'm starving."

Dinner was enjoyable. Hunter charmed both her and Alice, teasing them. Bri was glad Alice was there. It meant she wouldn't give in to the attraction that was the reason she was big as a house.

"This chicken is the best, Alice. You are a great cook."

"Wait until you try dessert. It's my special recipe for peach cobbler, still warm, with ice cream on top."

Hunter groaned. "I may have to deal with something else first. Then I'll have room for dessert."

"Something else?" Bri asked, frowning. "What something else?"

"Have you finished eating?"

"Yes."

"Then come with me. I have a surprise for you."

He took her hand and pulled her from her chair. Then he led her toward the living room.

By the time they reached the doorway, she already suspected what her surprise was. Standing in the corner was a full, fragrant Scotch pine tree, all ready for decorating.

Tears gathered in Bri's eyes.

He made it so hard to resist his care, his sweetness. He seemed to know her better than she knew herself. But that couldn't be true or he'd realize he only had to walk in the door to make her happy. Unless she remembered his abandonment.

Chapter Thirteen

Bri was back on the couch, among the pillows, her cup of hot tea in front of her. But she wasn't alone. Hunter and Alice were hanging ornaments on her Christmas tree.

She loved Christmas and all its trappings. This year, she'd thought she would have to give it all up. Just thinking about decorating a tree or doing anything other than the bare minimum made her tired.

But watching someone else do it was pure heaven.

Hunter turned and smiled at her. She smiled back. Perhaps she'd misjudged him. What if he had come back to her room, only to find her gone? It was possible. A sensitive, thoughtful man, as he was proving himself to be, wouldn't have simply walked away from her.

When he'd found out she was pregnant, the first thing he'd done was offer her marriage. Not a marriage of love, but at least he'd offered marriage.

She'd turned him down.

Did she wish now she still had that option?

Maybe, she admitted with a sigh.

"Tired, Bri? Do you want to go to bed? We can finish tomorrow or some other time."

Hunter again being thoughtful…and sensitive to her needs.

"No, I'm fine. I was just thinking how wonderful it is to have a Christmas tree. Thank you so much, Hunter."

"No problem. I'm having fun. I think Alice is doing all the work," he teased, winking at the housekeeper.

"No such thing. I wasn't going to decorate this year, since I'm all alone, but it does lift the spirits, doesn't it?"

"Yes, it does," Bri agreed.

But her mind remained on thoughts of Hunter. If she told him now she wanted to marry him, what would he say? She already knew. He'd agree at once, because he believed the girls were his babies. He'd agree, and she'd always fear she'd trapped him into marriage.

She couldn't do that to him.

"Uh, Bri, you haven't asked about the favor I'm hoping you'll do for me." Hunter said as he hung the last ornament on the tree.

Bri stared at him as he bent to plug in the lights. Suddenly the shadowy room was lit up with twinkling lights. She figured it didn't much matter what he asked. She'd agree to anything to thank him for his gift. "What?"

"Tomorrow afternoon, a real estate woman is showing me three houses. I'm going to need some advice. Would you come with me? I promise we won't be gone more than two or three hours. And I'll provide dinner."

"You want *my* advice? But I don't know what kind of lifestyle you have. I don't even know your favorite color," she pointed out.

He sat on the arm of the sofa beside her. "Hazel is my favorite color," he said, staring into her eyes.

"I would've thought blue to match your eyes."

"Blue was my favorite color until last spring."

She felt her cheeks flushing. "My dad might be a better choice. He knows the real estate market better than me."

"That's why I'm using a real estate agent. Please, Bri? I promise I won't let you get too tired."

"I suppose—I mean, I'll be glad to help you. Especially since you brought me my tree. I just thought there might be others who would be able to provide better advice."

He leaned down and kissed her cheek. "Nope. You'll have the best advice for me."

Bri hadn't even realized Alice had left the room until she reentered with a tray. On it were two desserts, hot tea for Bri and decaf coffee for Hunter.

"I'm not having dessert, so I think I'll go home now, if that's all right. Just put the dishes in the sink and I'll take care of them tomorrow," Alice commented.

"Thank you, Alice," Hunter said.

"Alice, I can't thank you enough for helping Hunter with the tree and for the wonderful dinner," Bri added.

"I enjoyed it. Do you want me to come in tomorrow?"

"On Saturday? Absolutely not. You enjoy your weekend."

Alice left and Hunter served Bri's dessert to her.

"Are these calories I need, too?" she asked.

"Yes. After looking at that teenager's babies, I definitely want you to eat well. You *are* taking your vitamins, aren't you?"

"Of course I am," she said before taking her first bite of cobbler. "Oh, my, Alice is a good cook."

"Yes, she is."

"Hunter, are Jenny's babies in bad shape?" They all knew the risks with multiple births, but it would be demoralizing to lose babies so early after the wing's opening. Or any time for that matter. She wanted the McCallum Wing to save every baby.

Hunter sighed. "Well, they're okay...right now. But they are small. And if she delivers right away, it will be touch and go. Zach is hoping for another couple of weeks."

"Christmas?"

"We'll be lucky if she makes it that long."

"Will I make it that long?"

He grinned. "I've told the girls they'll still get

presents if they wait until New Year's. Is that okay with you?''

''Oh, yes,'' she agreed with a sigh. ''New Year's would be perfect.''

HUNTER HAD BEEN in the hotel almost a week. The changes in his life had happened quickly. He'd decided to wait a few days before he committed to Austin by buying a house.

But once he'd discovered Bri's pregnancy, he'd known he'd be living in Austin for a long time. Unless she agreed to move away with him.

He'd called a Realtor a few days ago and given her very specific requirements for a house. He'd also begun applying for a loan. The Realtor had assured him that the three homes she wanted him to see today would meet his requirements.

Strangely, he felt nervous when he picked up Bri. Buying a house was a major move in life, and he wanted one that would hold his future with ease. His future was Bri.

''How are you feeling this morning?'' he asked as he led her to his SUV. After opening the door, he lifted her onto the high seat.

''Fine,'' she said, a little flustered by his assistance. It was becoming obvious to her that she loved Hunter's touch. ''I slept late.''

''Good. But you ate breakfast and lunch, didn't you?''

"Yes, mother hen, I ate everything in sight. And that's a lot since Alice started working for me."

"She's working out well, isn't she?"

"Yes, thanks to someone's good advice I'm having a much easier time of it now." Her smile warmed him as he circled the SUV and got behind the wheel.

Then she changed the subject. "Where are the houses we're going to look at?"

"All three are in the hills. Once of them looks down on Town Lake. And, surprisingly, they're not too far from the hospital."

"Sounds like Dad's and Adam's neighborhood."

"They live close together? Does that work out all right?"

"Oh, yes. They don't see each other all that often because both Dad and Adam are workaholics. Caleb, on the other hand, has a condo, like me. He's a loner, I guess. I worry about him."

Hunter grinned. "That's what being a family is. Worry. And joy."

He then told her stories about his family and their concern for each other. "Dad's the worst, since Mom's gone. But he'd do anything for either my brother or me. He's going to ship all my belongings down when I get a place."

"It must be hard living out of a suitcase," she murmured with sympathy.

"Not really. But I'm looking forward to having my own place again. Maybe when I do, I can hire Alice away from you."

''Oh, no, I can't let you do that!'' she exclaimed, laughing.

She thought he was teasing. But he intended them to share Alice…in one house…after the babies came.

''Here's the first one,'' he said as he pulled to a halt in front of a large home.

''Isn't this rather large for one person?'' she asked, frowning.

He shrugged his shoulders, not willing to explain what he had in mind. It would just throw her into a rise in blood pressure.

They met the Realtor and walked through the house with her. Then she gave them the address of the second house and they followed her to it. Again they walked through. While Bri admired both houses, Hunter didn't see any real enthusiasm in her face.

''Where is the third?'' he asked, getting discouraged.

''It's the one that looks down on Town Lake. I'll admit it's my favorite,'' the Realtor said.

Hunter mentally crossed his fingers. He wanted to get a house right away and have it ready for his family when he convinced Bri to move in with him.

The instant they drove up to the last house, he would've signed a contract.

Bri's eyes lit up and she softly sighed, ''Oh, my. How beautiful.''

''Yeah. I can't wait to see the inside.''

It was perfect. A large, welcoming home. It even had a downstairs bedroom off the kitchen which would be perfect for Alice. Four bedrooms upstairs, so each girl would eventually have her own room, and the parents would be nearby. Large closets, lots of baths and a huge family room downstairs.

"This house is perfect, but I'm afraid you'd rattle around in it by yourself," Bri warned.

"Maybe someday I'll have a family." He watched Bri's face as he said that, hoping to see a touch of jealousy.

"Yes, of course. I—you're right. This house will be perfect."

"You like the kitchen? I think that's one of the most important rooms in a house."

"No one could complain about this kitchen. It's huge with the breakfast room a part of it. It would be a great gathering place for a family. In fact, don't show it to Alice or you *might* be able to hire her away from me." She gave him a wobbly smile that made him want to hold her against him, to comfort her, to love her.

He hurriedly turned away. The Realtor had discreetly stepped into the hallway to give them time to confer. Hunter called her over. "I want this house. Can I make an offer today?"

"Of course. The couple had to move quickly and they're motivated to sell. I'll call them as soon as I get back to the office. What do you want to offer?"

Hunter didn't dicker too much. He figured the house would sell quickly, and he wanted to be the one who got it.

Bri joined him as they got ready to leave.

The Realtor smiled at her. "You're going to love this house. I hope you get it."

Bri flashed him a quick look, then said, "I hope Hunter gets it, too. It's lovely."

"But I thought—uh, yes. Me, too."

They got back in the SUV and she turned to him. "She thought—"

"I know. People assume things. After all, you don't look like a swinging single, Briana, you'll have to admit."

"No, I look like one who swung...and got caught," she said with a rueful laugh.

"Not by yourself." When she didn't respond to that, he added, "I love the house. Thanks for coming with me."

"Oh, I'm glad I did. The view from the family room of Town Lake is incredible."

"I'll let you know when I get word. How tired are you?"

"I'm fine."

"You always say that. Do you feel up to dinner out at a restaurant, or do you want me to get some take-out dinner and we can eat at your place?"

"I'm up for a restaurant. It won't be long before they ban me in case I break a chair, so I'd better enjoy eating out while I can. After the babies come, it will be impossible. In fact, mealtimes will become an Olympic sport."

"Three babies are a challenge," he agreed. "Did you ever think about having a multiple birth?"

"Yes, I did, but I really didn't believe it would happen." She rubbed her stomach.

"Are they jumping around?"

"Always. But that means they're healthy, right?"

"Yeah, or one of them is getting squeezed out by her sisters."

He pulled in at a barbecue place. "Barbecue doesn't bother you, does it?"

"No. I love it. Of course, I love Mexican food, too, but the girls don't." She chuckled.

"So we'll avoid Mexican for a few more weeks." He spoke without thinking, but the long silence that followed got his attention.

"What's wrong?"

Bri gave him a stubborn look. "You talk like we'll be eating together a lot. I appreciate your support, but you need to—to develop a social life. I can assure you the ladies of Austin will welcome you with open arms."

"You mean friendlier than the staff at the hospital? Wow, I'll be in hog heaven, as my dad says." He could've told her he didn't want any other Austin ladies. Just her. But not yet.

He parked the car and came around to help her down.

"I can manage," she protested, standoffish again.

"I thought maybe the girls were sleeping and you jumping down might upset them."

She glared at him.

After they were inside the restaurant and seated and the waitress had taken their order, he asked, ''Who are you naming Eleanor after?''

She appeared surprised by his question. ''Why do you think I'm naming her after anyone?''

''I don't know. I was worried that she'd be upset. Emily is named after your mother, and Elizabeth after mine. I didn't want Eleanor to feel slighted.''

''Elizabeth is not named after your mother. You must stop saying things like that. It's causing talk all over the hospital!''

''Stay calm. And tell me about Eleanor.''

Abruptly, she said, ''She's named after my grandmother.''

''Oh, good. Are you going to call her Ellie?''

''I don't know. I hate to make those decisions until after I meet her. All three girls will have different personalities.''

''Yeah, it's amazing how quickly they develop an attitude, isn't it?'' he said with a chuckle.

''Do you keep track of the babies you've delivered?'' She needed to believe he was thinking of babies in general and not her babies specifically. It was too easy to start to lean on him, as she had done in New York.

''Actually, I want to invite the mothers and babies that we deliver back once a year for a get-together. I've been meaning to talk to you about it. With

McCallum Wing's reputation growing, some of them may be too far away, but I'd like to try.''

Bri liked that idea. After they'd received their food and started eating, she asked, ''Will you use it for scientific study, or just as a social gathering?''

''I'd like to do both. Have them fill out some forms from which we can produce solid data. And just get a chance to see the results of our hard work.''

''Maybe you'd better get the doctors started on making a list of questions they want to ask their patients so you can all contribute to the questionnaire.''

''Right. Especially since we're beginning to fill up.''

''Do we have more patients?''

''Three more patients. Madeline Sheppard had success with one of her fertility patients. Looks like it will be another set of quadruplets, but the mother is only a few months pregnant.''

''Who?'' Bri asked hurriedly.

Hunter stared at her. ''I don't remember. A common name, something like Green or Gray, definitely a color.''

She released her pent-up breath. ''Oh.''

''Ah, I'd forgotten your sister-in-law is undergoing treatment with Dr. Sheppard.''

''Yes. Sometimes I feel so guilty, having three babies when Maggie can't have even one.''

''It's not your fault, honey. You didn't do it on purpose.''

''No, but—never mind.''

He tried to think of another topic of conversation, but she reminded him he hadn't mentioned a third patient.

"Who's the third patient?"

"Another set of twins. Our first set went home today."

"Oh, good. They were doing well. The mother was very happy with our performance."

"Are you going to personally interview every mother before they go home?"

"I like to give their stay a personal touch. And I think I'll get more information that way than I will with a form."

"Probably true. You're very dedicated to your work, aren't you?"

"Isn't that a good thing?"

"Yeah, but I was thinking about your condemning tones when you said Jackson and Adam were workaholics. Sounds like you set yourself some pretty big challenges, too."

"You're thinking I'm going to neglect my children, aren't you? I'm not going to do that!" She glared at him again.

"Whoa! I didn't say that. I know you'll be a good mother. But you're going to wear yourself out. Maybe you can hire another assistant. Train her the way you want and do more supervising than actually performing the tasks yourself."

His idea didn't impress her. "Maybe you'll stick to your side of the business and leave mine alone.

Unless you feel I'm not doing my job. Then, of course, you can complain. As I will if I don't think you're doing your job.''

"Bri, you're getting upset over nothing."

"Am I? I'm trying to support my family, and you keep suggesting I not work."

"I'm not suggesting that, but I'm glad you don't have to. You'll be surprised how much energy three babies take."

"And you know this because you've had triplets? You're like most male ob-gyns. You think you know everything, but you've never experienced any of it. I think that's why women ob-gyns are becoming more popular."

"I'm sure. However, a number of them have never been pregnant, and even if they have, they've seldom had multiple births."

"But at least they've experienced female problems!" she said, putting down her fork and continuing to glare at him.

"Why are you picking a fight with me?" he asked.

"I'm not. I'm simply disagreeing with you. And I'm ready to go home."

Well, so much for the brief thaw in the cold war, Hunter thought. Bri seemed determined to fight with him. Maybe the gossip at the hospital had gotten to her. It was easier for him to ignore it because he didn't know those people who were talking. And the man was never condemned for having babies out of wedlock.

Should he offer marriage again?

No, she wouldn't listen to him. Okay, so he'd keep his distance and encourage Abby to keep close tabs on her patient.

But soon he was going to make his move.

Chapter Fourteen

"Hunter, please tell me you're not calling to find out what Bri is having for lunch," Abby said in disgust. The man had driven her crazy for the past two days, wanting to know if she'd seen Bri, what she ate, whether or not she was getting enough sleep.

"No, I'm not!" he assured her. "I wanted to see if her checkup was at the same time as last week."

"I thought you were trying to avoid her?" He'd explained to Abby that he was going to keep contact with Bri to a minimum since he seemed to send her blood pressure rocketing.

"It's my job to monitor the patients," he said stiffly.

"You mean you're sitting in on every checkup?" Abby knew better. She was even pretty sure she knew why he was observing Bri so closely, which was why she couldn't complain.

"Uh, no, but—but Bri—I mean, she's the first triplet patient."

She heard the edginess in his voice. "It's okay, Hunter. I understand."

Dead silence.

Finally, he said, "You understand what?"

"I understand that these are your babies."

More silence. "Why do you say that?"

"I say that because Bri wasn't dating anyone when she went to New York for a medical conference last spring. And I noticed on your bio that you were at the same conference. Even more, there's an awareness between the two of you that wouldn't be there if you were strangers."

"Is that part of the rumor mill?"

"No, not yet. Everyone's talking about a romance between the two of you. The theory is that you felt an attraction before. Now that you've found her again, you're still interested in spite of her condition."

When he didn't answer this time, she added briskly, "Her appointment is at ten o'clock, my first appointment so she can get out quicker. Same routine? You'll wait until we do the ultrasound before you come in?"

"Yeah, if you think she can handle it."

"Of course she can. I'll see you then."

Abby hung up the phone and leaned back in her chair. Amazing how things got screwed up in life. Two perfectly lovely people, blessed with triplets, couldn't seem to straighten things out. She was going to do what she could to help them, but some things were beyond her.

BRI WAS growing more and more tired, but she didn't want to tell anyone. When she undressed for her checkup today, she determinedly tried to look cheerful.

The nurse made no comment, silently assisting her onto the table and then leaving to find the doctor.

Bri had decided that her feelings were the reason for the tiredness. Since Saturday, she'd only seen Hunter from a distance. She'd apparently upset him so much that he'd dismissed any concern for her condition. He hadn't inquired about her health even once in the past few days.

She hadn't realized how much she would miss his concern and support. Her father had called to check on her. Her brothers had checked in. And Grace. But she missed Hunter's concern.

Abby came into the room. "Good morning, Bri. How's it going?"

"Just fine," Bri responded, a bright smile on her face.

"Sleeping well?"

She wasn't that good a liar. "Well, the girls move a lot at night."

"Any discomfort?"

Bri chuckled. "You mean other than the normal discomfort?"

Abby grinned at her. "Yeah. Anything abnormal?"

"No. I think we're all fine."

Abby directed her for the physical exam. Then she ordered her nurse to prepare Bri for the ultrasound.

"Hunter is coming in, as he did last week. That won't upset you, will it?" Abby asked.

Bri nibbled on her bottom lip before saying, "I know he has a job to do." That would be the only reason he would be here. It couldn't be because he had any interest in her, she was sure of that.

"Good girl." Abby nodded to her nurse who went over and opened the door.

Bri could feel his presence, but she tried to keep her eyes on the monitor.

Abby took up the ultrasound roller and rolled it over Bri's stomach, pressing into her skin. "There are our little ladies," she said, a smile on her lips.

"You're about thirty-one weeks, Bri. The girls are doing well. We're past any critical problems. You can deliver any time now without endangering the girls, so I want you to remember that. If labor starts, don't panic."

Bri stared at Abby. "You're telling me it won't be long now?" she asked, unable to stop her lips from trembling.

She almost jumped off the table when a big warm hand squeezed hers.

In a cheerful voice, Hunter said, "You can't stay pregnant forever, Bri, even if you love it."

She groaned, then tried to smile. "Thanks, I'll remember that."

"Remember this, too. Everything's going to be all right." Hunter's authoritative tones would've convinced anyone.

"Yes," Bri said softly. She wanted to believe him. But her mother had died delivering her children. While intellectually, Bri could explain why she shouldn't be worried, she was forced to admit that emotionally, she was.

"What he's trying to say," Abby added, smiling, "is that everything is fine. Any additional time in the womb can't hurt, but we're fine."

Abby looked at her nurse. "Peggy, help Bri dress, please."

Then she and Hunter left the room. Bri released a pent-up breath, staring at the door longingly.

Peggy patted her shoulder. "There now, everything's fine. You heard the doctor."

Bri hadn't even realized she had tears on her cheeks. She hurriedly wiped her face and smiled at Peggy. "Of course it is. It's just these stupid hormones. They're out of control."

BRIANA DIDN'T SEE either Abby or Hunter when she returned to her office. As soon as she got there, she picked up the phone and called Caleb on his cell phone. "Caleb? I need—I need to talk with you privately. Can you come to my office?"

He told her he'd be over at once.

Then she pulled out a clean piece of paper and hand-wrote a long paragraph. Then, covering the paragraph, she drew a signature line. Then she wrote a brief paragraph and another signature line.

"Lisa? Could you come in here?" she called.

"Sure," Lisa called and entered her office. "What do you need?"

"I'm going to sign this paper. I want you to witness my signature and sign to that effect."

"Of course. What is it?"

"It's—it's private. All you're verifying is my signature."

"Okay."

After Lisa left her office, Bri put her head down, squeezing her eyes shut, hoping to hold back the tears.

"Sis?" Caleb called as he rushed into her office. "Are you all right?"

She sat up and wiped her cheeks. "I'm fine. You got here quickly."

"I was in the building. Are you in labor?" Caleb asked, a slight panic in his voice.

'No, I'm not. I'm fine. But I want to give you something in case—in case something goes wrong."

"Don't talk that way. Nothing's going to go wrong."

She smiled. Maybe it wasn't her best smile, but she tried. "Of course not. But—but I've been lying about something and I don't want that on my conscience." She handed him the folded paper.

Slowly he read the paper and then looked at her. "What do you want me to do with this?"

"I want you to put it in a safe place and give it to Dad if—if something happens to me."

"Did something happen to make you worry?"

"It—it won't be long now."

"Bri—" he began. Then he stopped and began again. "Everything's going to be fine. I'm going to call you every night before you go to sleep. And you keep my number written out beside your bed. You call me at once. I'll get you to the hospital in no time."

"I know you will, Caleb. You and Adam and Dad, and Maggie, too, have been wonderful. It's meant a lot to me."

"That's what family is for," he said and leaned over to kiss her cheek. "You okay, now?"

"I'm fine. I feel better now that I've—taken care of that."

"Okay. How about lunch? Want me to buy you lunch?"

Bri smiled at her younger brother. He wasn't comfortable with the emotional stuff, but he wouldn't back away when she needed him. Love swelled in her heart. Her family was terrific!

"Thank you, but I think I'll have Lisa bring me some lunch here. I can work and maybe knock off early for a late-afternoon nap."

"Good idea. Okay, I'm off then. But you call me if you need anything."

HUNTER WONDERED if his policy of avoiding Bri was a good idea. She seemed a little shaky today. And he agreed with Abby. He didn't think it would be long now. He was surprised at the nervousness that filled him. After all his experience he was facing this delivery as a first-time father—a new experience—and no one would know.

He tried bringing his concentration back to his work, but Bri's face filled his mind. He saw the fear in her gaze, the panic that something might go wrong. It was important that she remain calm. Maybe he should stop by her office every once in a while so that—

"Dr. Callaghan, Caleb McCallum is here to see you."

"Send him in." He stood and moved forward to greet Bri's brother.

"What happened today?" Caleb's hazel eyes were filled with concern.

"What are you talking about?"

"Bri! What happened at her checkup?"

"Abby told her it wouldn't be long now. That's all."

"So everything's all right?" Caleb demanded, his voice intense.

"Yeah, everything's fine. Why?"

"She just called me, insisted I come at once. I thought she was in labor."

"No. What did she want?"

Caleb stood there, his hands on his hips. "I'm not supposed to show anyone unless something goes wrong. But you already know."

"What are you talking about, Caleb?"

"You can't tell her. Promise me."

"Okay, I won't tell her."

Caleb pulled a folded piece of paper out of his back pocket.

Hunter took it from his extended hand, suddenly nervous about what he was going to read. "Are you sure?"

Caleb nodded.

Slowly, Hunter unfolded the piece of paper and noted the two signatures first. Then he began reading. His head snapped up. "She's acknowledging me as the father!"

"Yeah. That's why I was afraid something had gone wrong."

"No, but she's worried."

"Why?" Caleb demanded.

Hunter didn't want to be brutally frank, but he had no choice. "The same reason you, your brother and your father are worried. Your mother died giving birth to triplets. Even though there's no reason to worry, and you understand that in your mind, your heart tells you to worry."

"Yeah." Caleb slumped down in a nearby chair. "Tell me again everything's all right."

"Everything's fine. Do you think I'm going to let anything happen to my girls...or my woman?"

"I hope not. We're counting on you, doc."

Hunter folded the paper Caleb had shown him. But he was reluctant to hand it back to Caleb. "Can I keep this?"

Caleb hesitated. "I promised Bri that I'd keep it safe until—until after the delivery."

"I swear I'll do that. But it means a lot to me that she made sure that I would be acknowledged as the girls' father. Did you know one of them will be named after my mother?"

Caleb appeared startled. "No. How did that happen?"

"Just a lucky coincidence." Hunter grinned at Caleb. "But I'd like to keep this."

"Okay." He cleared his throat. "I guess you deserve that."

"Thanks, Caleb. And I'll be keeping a closer eye on Bri."

"Good. Me, too."

Hunter sat back in his chair as Caleb left. Bless Bri for her honesty and honor. He'd instinctively recognized her goodness in New York. Now he had proof that she would do the right thing. And bless Caleb for showing him.

He reached for the phone. "Hi, Lisa. It's Dr. Callaghan. Does Bri have plans for lunch?"

After hanging up the phone, he strode into Helen's office. "I'm going to be having lunch with Bri in her office if you need me."

BY FRIDAY, Bri was feeling better in one sense. Hunter seemed to be keeping tabs on her again. More unobtrusively, but he was around.

But she was also feeling worse. The girls seemed

to be gaining weight rapidly. Or she was imagining that they were. It was getting more and more tiring to make it through each day.

She was really looking forward to getting home, eating a good meal and going straight to bed. Several of her friends had asked her to go out tonight, but she'd refused them all. It was just too much effort.

A rap on her door startled her, but she smiled when she saw Hunter. ''Hi. What's up?''

After closing the door behind him, he strolled in and sat in front of her desk. ''I wondered if you'd take pity on a bachelor and ask me to dinner at your place. I checked with Alice, and she said she'd fixed plenty.''

Bri was surprised. While he'd checked on her often at work, he hadn't been back to her condo. ''Of course. If Alice says there's enough, I'm sure there will be.''

He studied her. ''About ready to switch to half days?''

She wanted to protest, to assure him she could make it just fine. But she couldn't, and she wasn't going to risk her girls' health for her pride. ''How did you know?''

''You've dragged a little lately. And I heard you turned down your friends for tonight.''

''And they told you?'' she asked, her voice full of surprise.

''Yeah. For some reason, they think I have some pull with you, Ms. McCallum.'' He shot her a teasing look that raised her blood pressure. For all the right reasons—feeling attractive because of the way a man looked at her—except that she was as big as a house with babies. No man would be interested in her now.

"Uh, well, I really am too tired for a night on the town."

"Too bad. It's going to be a lousy baby shower without you." He waited for her to realize what he meant. Then he said, "Do you think you can make it after a good dinner and half an hour's rest?"

"Of course. Oh, how awful of me. I didn't realize—they shouldn't have gone to so much trouble." She thought about April and Annabelle's proddings. Even Maggie had called and tried to get her to go out. "Why didn't they tell me?"

"It's supposed to be a surprise."

"But you told me," she pointed out.

"Yeah, but I know how stubborn you are. Here's how we're going to play it. Your father invited me over for the evening and I talked you into going with me because I don't know him so well."

"At my father's?"

"He offered April his house and his housekeeper when Maggie told him about it. Even though it's ladies only, he wanted to contribute to the shower."

"How sweet of him," Bri said, tears filling her eyes.

"Your hormones really are working overtime, aren't they?" Hunter asked, leaning forward. "Are you really too tired to go?"

"No. I wouldn't miss this for the world. But where will you and Dad go if it's ladies only?"

"Your brothers are meeting us down at the Lone Star for a beer."

"Okay. Thank you for making sure I get there."

"No problem. Now, pack up and go home. Stretch out on the couch until I get there."

"Good idea. And I think I will work half days until the babies come, starting Monday. You were right about it getting to be too much."

He stood, leaned over the desk and kissed her, a brief but potent kiss. "Good girl." Then he walked out.

She stood there, breathing deeply, hoping to regain control of herself before she faced Lisa. The man certainly knew how to send her blood pressure soaring.

Bri organized her desk and retrieved her purse. Then she went out to Lisa's desk. "I know it's early, but I'm leaving. I'm going to have to go to my father's this evening to accompany Hunter, so I'm going to take a nap first."

"Dr. Callaghan's going to your father's?" Lisa asked, her eyes rounded in innocence.

"Yes," she said with a disgusted air, hoping to conceal her knowledge of the shower from Lisa. "Hunter said he didn't want to go by himself. He's only met my father once." She shrugged. "Part of the job, helping him settle in."

Then she hurried away.

Two hours later, while Bri still lay on the couch as

ordered, drifting in and out of a light doze, her doorbell rang. Alice hurried to let Hunter in.

He immediately came to the couch as Bri managed to sit upright. "How you doing?"

"Fine. I've been resting the entire time. I'm sure after I eat I'll feel even better."

"Good girl," he said again.

She was disappointed that there was no kiss this time. She was getting greedy.

Alice thought Bri knew nothing about the shower, either. Fortunately, Bri had thought of that before she gave the secret away. Dinner was ready early. It was delicious, as usual, but Bri didn't have much of an appetite.

Hunter urged her to eat a little more as he was packing away his dinner, hungry as a bear.

"You must've worked very hard today, Hunter," Alice said, a pleased smile on her face.

"I did, Alice. And I ran five miles in the Wellness Center this morning."

Bri groaned. "That makes me tired just to hear it."

"You'll be back in shape soon, honey. Don't worry."

"No. I'm not." What a lie, but everyone was so busy encouraging her, she had to make the effort.

"We've got a few minutes before we need to leave. Why don't you go lie down again while I help Alice with the dishes?"

"I'm okay. I don't need to—"

"As your doctor, I say you do need to rest," he said, smiling, but he also winked at her.

"Oh, okay," she agreed, though her initial response was to inform him that Abby was her doctor. But it was clear he needed to tell Alice something.

When they got in the car and left, she asked him what he'd told Alice.

"I left all my numbers with her. I told her it wouldn't be long before you delivered and to call me if she was worried about anything." Then he reached in his coat pocket. "I'm telling you the same thing." He pulled out a business card and handed it to Bri.

Great way to keep her calm for the shower, she decided.

Chapter Fifteen

"Be sure and act surprised," Hunter reminded her as he helped her down from his vehicle.

"My memory hasn't disappeared along with my figure. I remember."

"Yeah, but you're not very good at lies."

"I told you I'd practice."

She marched up the driveway of her father's large home, wondering how they thought they'd surprise her with fifteen cars parked in the driveway and along the street. Cars she mostly recognized. They must've invited half the hospital!

The housekeeper who'd replaced Grace, Milly, told her her father was waiting in the family room. Bri nodded calmly and led the way to the back of the house. When she opened the door to the large, comfy room, it was filled with women.

They all stood and yelled Surprise! and Bri gave them a shocked expression. "What are you doing here?" she shrieked. Then she turned to Hunter. "But you said my father—"

Jackson McCallum stood. He'd been sitting among the ladies. "Isn't this great, Bri? Your friends are throwing you a baby shower!" He seemed as excited as her friends.

"But I thought you'd invited Hunter over."

"I did. We're going to meet your brothers at the Lone Star. You ladies have fun." Jackson gave Bri a hug and then shoved Hunter out the door ahead of him.

Bri was left to face her friends. They were all there, including her assistant, Lisa, and Hunter's assistant, Helen. She noticed her sister-in-law Maggie sitting beside Dr. Madeline Sheppard, the fertility expert who was helping her and Adam. Bri wanted to make her way to Maggie's side and find out how things were going. To her surprise, she even saw Alice, sitting beside Grace. Maybe that was why Hunter had driven slowly.

April took her arm and led her to a large chair. "We saved this one for you since you're the guest of honor. We're only going to play two games, though, because we know you need your rest. Abby warned us," April tacked on, waving to Abby. "But we found a couple of real cute games we couldn't resist."

Bri grinned, but she hoped April would keep to her word. The effect of dinner and a nap was already wearing off. "I'm ready," she assured her friend.

The first game was a word puzzle. They had to make words from the letters of each of the three girls' names. The three prizes, plastic baby bottles, were, of course, passed to Bri. Then they had a game that asked crazy questions of the expectant mother. Each guest asked a question that had been passed out. It was fun for a while. Until they got to Annabelle.

She'd taken the paper passed to her, but the game had already started. She didn't read her question herself until it was her turn. "What did the father say when you told him he was going— Uh, this isn't a good question. Let someone else go next!" she suggested, her cheeks red.

April hurriedly agreed. But the next question was about the daddy, too.

April said, "You know what? I'm tired of games. Let's eat. That's the best part." She indicated the big coffee table filled with covered trays. "Maggie, can you uncover the trays on your side? Let me fill a plate for Bri, then we can all dig in."

Abby patted Bri's arm. "You stay put."

"I will. I think I'm going to start doing half days next week, Abby. I've been getting really tired."

"Good girl."

That was the same response she'd gotten from Hunter. Without the kiss. She had to stop thinking about him. He was being nice to her. But that didn't mean he was interested in a future with her.

She fingered the card in her pocket. She shouldn't call him when she started labor. She'd call Abby, the way she was supposed to. Abby could call Hunter if she wanted.

"Bri?" April said anxiously.

Bri looked up. "Yes, April?"

"Here's your food. I'm sorry I didn't check out that second game better."

"Don't be silly, April. I'm not upset."

"Are you feeling tired?"

"A little. But sugar will pep me up. I'll probably be dancing on the coffee table before the night's over," she assured her friend with a grin.

April smiled back and went to fill her own plate.

While they ate, the discussion turned to hospital matters, since most of them were connected with the hospital.

"How's Jenny doing?" Bri asked. "I didn't visit her today."

Several people shrugged. Then April said, "I stopped by her room today. I've been checking on her since she has no family. She couldn't get comfortable. Seemed a little down."

"Dr. Beaumont checked her today," Annabelle added. "He didn't say much about it, but he frowned a lot."

"Some doctors just frown," Madeline Sheppard said. Since she was a doctor herself, everyone laughed. "You can't tell by that. Maybe he had a hot date the night before and didn't get much sleep."

"Dr. Beaumont?" Annabelle said with a gasp. "Oh, I hope not. What will I dream about if he gets hooked?" she asked with a laugh.

"Well, there's always Dr. Callaghan. He's definitely dream material. I heard he spent a lot of time with Barbara in physical therapy the other day.''

''Really? The only person I've noticed him hanging around is Bri!'' Joanna, manager of the cafeteria, said.

''Anything going on?'' Annabelle asked, looking at Bri.

''All I can say is if he picks me over any of you slim, beautiful women, then he's either blind or you all have bad breath!'' Bri grinned to make sure they all knew she was teasing.

The chatter continued even as they started Bri opening the gifts. She was touched by all of them. Grace had handknitted three little sweaters in pink, yellow and green. Apparently her friends had discussed the colors, because she got baby blankets and even tiny sleepers in those three colors.

''You coordinated everything so well. I'll admit I haven't prepared as well as I should. I have three baby beds sitting in boxes at home. My brothers promised they'd put them together before I brought the babies home.''

''They'll keep their promise,'' Maggie assured her.

''I know.''

Bri did get a minute alone with Maggie toward the end of the party. ''Is everything going all right?''

''Yes. Dr. Sheppard is wonderful. She thinks we have a chance. And she made Adam feel good about the process. That was a big step.''

''I'd heard she was good. I'm glad it's true. I

should be taking notes so I can be prepared when it's your time for a shower.''

Maggie's eyes filled with tears and she squeezed Bri's hand. ''I hope I get a turn.''

''Me, too.''

''Bri, is Dr. Callaghan going to pick you up?'' one of the nurses asked.

''I don't know. Needless to say, we didn't discuss that since I thought we'd both be here. Anyone want to drive me home?''

There were several offers, and Bri considered that point settled. But the nurse, a blonde who Bri and her close friends considered to be a little full of herself, said, ''I'm hoping he comes back. He was hitting on me the other day, and I want to give him some, ah, encouragement. I wore this dress just for him.''

Since she was showing a lot of cleavage, and the skirt had a split up the side of her thigh, the other women had been sure she hadn't worn it for them.

The sound of footsteps and the opening of the front door told them the men had returned.

Bri smiled firmly. ''Maybe you can get Hunter to give you a ride home, Rita. Who knows what will happen in the dark.'' Then she resumed talking to Maggie. She wasn't going to get upset just because Hunter was flirting with nurses at the hospital.

''The nerve of her,'' Maggie muttered.

''Just be glad she's not after Adam,'' Bri said. ''At least she's focusing on an unmarried man.''

"Yes, but I thought—I mean Hunter has been—everyone says—"

Bri squeezed Maggie's hand. "He takes his job seriously. It's nothing personal."

Then she pushed herself up from the chair. "Hi, guys. Hunter, April has promised me a ride home, but Rita needs a lift if you don't mind."

He frowned at her. "There's no need to draft April. My car's big enough for two of you."

Rita laughed. "I don't know. Have you looked at the size of her lately?" She fluttered her eyelashes at Hunter.

Caleb stepped forward and Bri cringed, worried about what he would say in her defense. However, Hunter stopped him and assured Rita there was plenty of room. Then he organized her brothers to help him load the gifts.

Almost before she knew it, Bri had thanked everyone and been loaded into the front seat of Hunter's SUV. Rita was sulking in the back seat.

When Hunter got behind the wheel, he asked Rita for directions to her house. She lived quite a way from the hospital. Hunter looked at Bri. "I'd better take you home first, so you can get to bed, Bri. Is that all right with you, Rita?"

"Very all right," she purred.

Bri gritted her teeth and said nothing. She should get used to seeing Hunter with beautiful women. But she wished he had better taste than Rita.

When they reached her condo, after a silent ride, Hunter got out to walk Bri to her door.

"I can make it, Hunter. There's no need to keep Rita waiting."

"I told you my mother raised me to have good manners." He grinned.

His words reminded her of their time in the deli, and she couldn't help smiling back.

"There aren't any rats around here, are there?" he asked, teasing her.

"No, just bats."

"Why didn't you tell me? I have a phobia about bats."

"Yeah, right." They reached her door, and she had turned to thank him when his beeper went off. He checked the number, then asked to come in and use the phone.

As soon as he dialed the number, he only spoke once, saying he'd be at the hospital at once.

"What about Rita?" Bri asked, afraid he'd ask if Rita could stay with her.

"I'll take her with me and put her in a cab. But Jenny Barrows has gone into labor and Zach can't stop it. I want to be there to help him. It's going to be a tricky delivery."

"I'm coming with you."

"You're not coming with me. You need your rest!" he said emphatically.

"I can sleep all day if I want. Tomorrow is Saturday. I want to be there for the first quadruple birth. Either you give me a ride, or I call a taxi.''

''Bri—you can't—''

She pulled back on the jacket she'd just taken off and headed for the door.

''Dammit! This is crazy.''

She ignored him.

He followed her downstairs and helped her into the back seat. Rita had already moved to the front seat.

''What's going on? Has she gone into labor?'' Rita asked.

''No, but Jenny has,'' Hunter said as he got behind the wheel and started to the hospital.

''Jenny? Who's that?''

''The teenager having quadruplets,'' he explained briefly.

''You're her doctor?''

''No, Zach Beaumont is.''

Bri was glad she knew Hunter was a good driver, since Rita seemed intent on distracting him.

''I'm sure Dr. Beaumont can manage without your help, Hunter, darling. And I had special plans for when we reached my place.''

Bri figured the woman couldn't spell out her intentions any clearer than that. She held her breath, waiting to see if Hunter put her in her place.

''Sorry, Rita, I'll have to take a rain check. I promised Zach I'd be there.''

Well, not exactly a rejection. Bri wanted to slap

him. Okay, she'd told herself—and him—there'd be other women. But not in front of her!

No one said anything the rest of the drive. When Hunter parked his vehicle in the hospital parking lot, he dug out his wallet and gave Rita a couple of twenties. "Take a cab home. Sorry I couldn't take you."

"Me, too," she said in the purry voice again and leaned toward him, her lips puckered.

He pretended not to see them, getting out of the car and coming around to open Bri's door and lift her down from the seat. Then he rounded the SUV, with Bri at his side, and locked the doors as soon as Rita got out.

Without another word, he hurried into the hospital, holding Bri's hand.

He tried to argue Bri out of coming into delivery one more time. "Look Bri, her babies are early. I can't promise they'll all survive. I don't want you upset."

"I understand," she murmured, her gaze focused on the door behind him.

"You'll have to wear a mask and gown," he pointed out, as if that would discourage her.

"I know." Then she circled him and pushed through the doors.

One of the nurses helped her don the mask and gown and showed her where to stand to be out of the way. She wasn't surprised to discover Annabelle already in the room, talking softly to Jenny. And she felt sure April would be prepping the nursery and would be in shortly to help with the babies when they were born.

Just as Hunter strode in, scrubbed and ready to assist, April slid into the room. She saw Bri and came over at once.

"You're easy to recognize, even with a mask on," she whispered.

"It's my disguise as a blimp. Gives me away everytime."

"What did you do with Rita?"

Bri smiled under her mask. "Hunter gave her some money and told her to take a cab home."

Jenny screamed, grabbing their attention.

"I'd better get over there. Are you sure you want to be here?"

"I'm sure," Bri whispered.

She watched Hunter lean over and say something to one of the male nurses. He left the room, then came back in pushing a chair the height of a bar stool over to Bri.

"Dr. Callaghan thought you might get tired."

"Thank you," she murmured and managed to climb into the chair. She appreciated Hunter's thoughtfulness. Without the chair, she probably wouldn't have made it longer than half an hour.

Four hours later, all four of Jenny's babies had been delivered. Though she hadn't been in labor long, the births weren't easy. One baby had been touch and go for a few minutes, but the staff had performed a miracle and resuscitated it. Bri breathed a sigh of relief.

Jenny had lost a lot of blood, but they had her receiving a transfusion before she left the delivery room.

Bri asked one of the nurses about her condition, and the nurse assured her that Jenny would be all right.

Then Bri slipped away to the nursery where they'd taken the babies. She watched the four nurses, April being one of them, wash the babies and prepare them for their first night on earth. They were so tiny.

"I've been looking for you," Hunter whispered, startling her.

"Don't worry about me. I'll take a taxi home," she said, staring at the babies.

"Yours are already bigger. She was only twenty-seven weeks. You're thirty-one weeks, Bri. Your babies are going to be fine."

"Yes," she agreed quietly as exhaustion slammed into her now that the tension was over.

Hunter wrapped an arm around her and led her away.

She dozed off in the car. He awakened her and guided to her door. "Where are your keys?" he asked.

She dug into her jacket pocket and pulled them out. Hunter unlocked the door and led her straight to her bedroom.

"Do you need a drink or anything? Want some milk?" Hunter asked.

"That would be nice."

"Here's your nightgown," he said, and left the room. Only after he'd gone did Bri realize he'd opened her dresser drawers until he'd found where she kept her nightgowns. She had the nightgown over her head, pulling it down as he came through the door.

"Here's your milk."

"Thanks." She drank part of it and put it on the bedside table. "Later," she mumbled and slid into bed.

Hunter covered her up.

"Lock the door," she managed to say and that was the last she remembered.

WHEN SHE FINALLY awoke the next day, it was almost noon. She stretched and rubbed her stomach as the girls started making demands.

"Easy, there, girls. Mama had a rough night," she whispered.

She wasn't eager to leave her bed. She shouldn't have gone to the hospital last night, but she wanted to see the team in action. They were impressive. As soon as she found something to eat, she'd call the hospital and find out how Jenny and her babies were doing.

She stretched again, resting just another minute, promising the girls she'd eat so they could get some food. "How about scrambled eggs? Or I could add cheese and ham and have an omelet. Mmm, that sounds good."

But she still didn't get up. Her bed was too wonderful.

"Okay, okay, I'm moving," she promised as the girls jumped about even more. With a sigh, she said, "You three are so demanding."

She slid from the bed and made a trip to the bathroom, as she always did first thing in the morning. There wasn't much room for her bladder, and it frequently felt like the girls did a tap dance on it.

A couple of minutes later, she emerged from the bathroom to find Hunter standing at the door of her bedroom, a tray in his hands.

"What are you doing here?" she shrieked, startled by his appearance.

"Serving you breakfast. Hop back in bed."

The smells filling the air made her stomach growl. "How did you get in? Didn't you lock up last night?"

"Sure, but I pocketed your keys, since I figured you wouldn't need them."

"What if people think you spent the night? You're going to completely ruin my reputation!" she snapped.

"Are you going to eat this breakfast or not?"

She crawled back into the bed, glad she was wearing a long gown. "Hunter, I'm serious. You shouldn't have taken my keys and come over this morning. Someone might think you'd spent the night."

He set the breakfast tray beside her, since it wouldn't fit over her stomach. "Eat your breakfast."

"You made a ham and cheese omelet?" She couldn't believe he'd read her mind.

"I hope you like it. It's one of my favorites."

"Mine, too."

"Guess that's something else we have in common."

She'd almost forgiven his appearance when the doorbell rang.

"Who could that be?" Bri wondered, an uneasy feeling filling her.

"I'll get it."

"No, Hunter—

He ignored her protest.

Bri heard voices. Then footsteps. The bedroom door opened, and Rita was glaring at her.

"Well, I see you'll go to any lengths to snare a man, Ms. McCallum!"

Chapter Sixteen

Bri took a deep breath. "Are you here for any particular purpose, Rita?"

"Yes. I'm here to collect my man," the woman spat out.

"Collect away," Bri suggested, but she did glare at Hunter.

Rita turned her back on Bri. "Hunter, darling, I've been looking for you all morning. I want to make up for not, uh, entertaining you last night."

Bri pretended disinterest, but she watched Hunter closely.

"Rita, I think there may be some misunderstanding. I didn't intend anything to happen between you and me. You're an attractive woman, but I'm focusing on my career."

"Oh, I see. You think Jackson McCallum's bucks are more important than sex appeal. Well, I'm glad to know what kind of man you are."

She turned around and stomped back out of Bri's bedroom, followed by Hunter.

Bri lay there, steaming. Hunter was parading his women in front of her? And telling everyone he was after her father's money? She never wanted to see him again!

He walked back into her bedroom.

"Get out! And take all *your women* with you!"

Hunter studied her with no apparent alarm. "What are you talking about now?"

"You come parading your women in my house? And you don't understand what I'm talking about?"

"*My women* consist of you and three baby girls, and you know it. I haven't had so much as a date since I made love to you, much less sex. I was trying to let Rita down easy so she wouldn't spread rumors all over the hospital. She is most definitely not connected to me in any way."

"She said you hit on her. And she said you were hanging around Barbara in physical therapy. Not that I care what you do. I want nothing to do with you."

"Bri, you're being ridiculous."

"Just go away!" she said again, afraid she'd start crying in front of him if he didn't go away.

"Bri—"

"Go!"

"Fine, I'll go. But call me if you need me."

So he left. And Bri cried a long time, hating that he'd left. He'd probably followed Rita, who had a small waist and a flat stomach. Unlike Bri. That thought brought on more tears.

She fell asleep, worn out by her out-of-control emotions, crying over things that even she didn't believe. When she finally woke up later that afternoon, it was because of wonderful scents coming from the kitchen.

"Hello? Is someone here?" She pretended she wasn't hoping Hunter would answer.

"Just me, dear," Grace called. "Hunter called and said you were having a difficult day." She came into the bedroom, took one look at Bri and hurried to the bed. "Whatever's the matter? You look like you've been crying!"

"I have, but it's just silliness. Hormones. How sweet of you to come over."

"Have you been in bed all day?"

"Yes. Except now I need to excuse myself." Bri hurried to the bathroom, leaving Grace standing there. When she came out, Grace had straightened her bed and had the covers turned down invitingly.

"Slip back into bed, darling, and I'll bring your dinner to you."

"I think I'd better eat at the table, Grace, and stay up a couple of hours at least, or I'll turn into a slug."

"Whatever you think, dear Bri."

They ate together, and Grace maintained a conversation that demanded very little from Bri. Afterward, Bri sent Grace home with a hug and a warm thanks.

"You're sure you'll be all right?" Grace asked. "I'll be over tomorrow to cook for you again."

"No, Grace, I'll manage. Alice has frozen some things for me. You take care of Douglas. I know he likes to go fishing on Sunday afternoons."

"He doesn't need me to bait his hook," Grace assured Bri.

"Still, I know you enjoy going with him. I'll be fine." Bri was feeling terribly guilty about her childish tantrum. And that's all it was. She'd been tired and easily irritated. And she'd taken it all out on Hunter.

Once Grace was gone, Bri cut herself a piece of cobbler left over from the other night, put it in the microwave and loaded it with ice cream. She was indulging herself.

Should she call Hunter and apologize? No, she'd e-mail him on Monday. And keep her distance until after the babies came. Being near him unbalanced her and made her act like a love-starved animal in mating season.

She only had a few more weeks. She would be all right. She'd just go back to bed as soon as she finished her dessert. She'd read that book she'd intended to read when Hunter had given her a foot massage.

When she did go to bed, all she could think about was Hunter. And she fell asleep with no more of the book read than before.

BRI DID e-mail Hunter on Monday morning with an apology and a suggestion that they avoid each other until the babies were born. He didn't respond. However, he didn't show up at her office, either.

Since she was going home at noon, there wasn't a lot of time anyway. On Monday, she ate at Austin Eats before she went home, since Alice wouldn't be there until one. By that time, Bri was in bed, taking a nap.

She followed the same pattern on Tuesday. She was a little worried that she didn't seem to feel any more energetic than she had before, when she was working all day. She wanted to call Abby and ask her about it on Wednesday morning, but everyone was in turmoil about what had happened during the night.

"Did you hear?" Lisa asked her as soon as she got in. "That teenager, Jenny? She ran away!"

"What?" Bri asked in shock. "Where did she go?"

"No one knows. But she left a note for April."

"A note? What did it say?"

"She left the babies in April's care."

Bri needed to talk to her friend, and find out what the hospital was doing about the situation. "I'll be back in a few minutes," she told Lisa as she hurried to the nursery where April worked.

"April!" Bri called when she saw her friend in the nursery with the four tiny babies. "What happened?"

April handed her a piece of paper. "She left this

note in my sweater pocket. I'd laid my sweater on my chair when I went to prep a delivery.''

Dear April Sullivan,
I know you'll love my babies and take good care of them so I want you to have them.

Bri read the note several times. ''Oh, my. What's being done?''

''They called the police. They've questioned me, but I don't know anything.''

''How are the babies doing?''

''They're fine. Still weak and on oxygen, but doing better every day. But it will still be a while before they can leave the hospital.''

Bri saw the tears in April's eyes. She gave her friend a hug. ''Let me know if there's anything I can do to help. Do we need more nurses on duty?''

''No, there's plenty, unless you decide to have your three right away. Then we'll need more. But everyone's prepared for that possibility. We just weren't prepared for a runaway mom.''

Bri left April, knowing how upset her friend was. Everyone had talked about how attached April was becoming to the babies. Bri was afraid her friend was facing heartbreak.

Back in her office, she received a phone call from her father.

''What's going on over there? They're reporting on

the radio that the mother of the quadruplets ran away!''

''I'm afraid so, Dad. We've called the police.''

''Are they going to find her? I don't like this kind of publicity for the hospital.''

''It's not the hospital's fault, Dad. We've taken very good care of her. And the babies are improving every day. But she's a teenager. It's pretty easy for an adult to be overwhelmed by having more than one baby. A teenager with no money and no family might decide she couldn't handle it.''

''Humph! I think I'll tell Caleb to investigate. He's still the best cop in town!''

''Dad, he's not a cop any longer. Are you sure—''

''A son should be willing to do his old man a favor. I'm calling him.''

Her father hung up the phone, and Bri replaced the receiver. But her concern was for Caleb. He avoided emotional situations. Would he want to investigate the disappearance of Jenny? She hoped her father didn't badger him into it.

''Abby called to remind you of your appointment,'' Lisa said from the door. ''It's in ten minutes.''

''Oh, right. Okay. I'll see you in a little while,'' Bri said as she left her office.

Soon she was on the examining table. But when it came time to do the ultrasound, there was no Hunter.

''Is Dr. Callaghan not coming?'' she asked quietly.

''He's trying to handle the disappearance of that

young woman, Jenny. I guess he doesn't have time today," Abby said with a smile.

But Bri knew the truth. She'd disgusted him with her outburst, her childish temper. She bit her lip to hold back the tears and watched as her babies came into view.

"Just four weeks until your due date," Abby pointed out. "You've done very well, Bri. And I really expect them to be born at any time. How are you feeling?"

"Still tired, even taking half days."

"I'm not surprised. They've grown this past week. You're carrying around more baby. Rest as much as you can, and call me as soon as you feel anything different."

"I will, of course. Do you think they'll find Jenny?"

"I don't know."

"Dad thinks it's bad publicity."

"It is, even though I don't think the hospital is the reason she left. But some people will think so."

One of the girls gave Bri a solid kick. "Ooh! That hurt."

"Where?" Abby asked at once.

"One of them is under my rib. It's nothing out of the ordinary."

Somehow, without Hunter present, the checkup wasn't much fun. And Bri, too, felt the babies were coming soon, which made her nervous. What she wouldn't give for a foot massage now. Or just Hunter smiling at her.

"It's your own fault!" She reminded herself in the elevator. Fortunately she was in it alone.

When she got back to the office, she checked with Lisa to see if there was any change in the situation, but there didn't appear to be any. Then she checked her messages and her desk. Nothing was urgent, what little there was.

Suddenly, Bri decided to go on home. She didn't want to be at work. Telling Lisa she had something she needed to do and that she wouldn't be back today, she slipped out of the hospital.

She crossed to Austin Eats to pick up lunch and take it back to her place. The café was alive with questions about what had happened at the hospital. Bri remained silent, got her food and hurried out.

She ate lunch and slid into bed afterward. She was getting to be very good about taking naps. Today, however, she couldn't seem to get comfortable. She ended up on the sofa, watching soap operas and re-runs, twisting and turning, trying to find a position that would let her relax.

Alice came in and cleaned, stopping to have conversation with Bri, which made her feel better. She didn't want to be alone today.

She guessed it was because she had hardly worked at all that she didn't have much appetite at dinnertime. Alice urged her to eat until Bri almost burst into tears.

After Alice left, Bri was so uneasy she began to pace the living room.

Finally she sat down on the sofa to watch more TV. When she got up to go to the kitchen, her gaze fell back on the sofa.

And she panicked.

HUNTER was tired.

It had been a long day, handling the police and the press, plus trying to be sure everything that should be done was.

Yet, with all of that, it was Bri who was on his mind. He'd had to miss her examination. He'd called Abby when he got a minute. She'd said everything was okay, but she'd sounded worried. He'd pressed her, but she'd said she couldn't put her finger on what was bothering her, but she'd stop by the office to see Bri in the morning.

He couldn't do anything else tonight. Bri didn't want him dropping by. That much she'd made clear. He sat on the bed in his hotel room and ate his take-out food, staring at the television, even though he couldn't have said what was on it.

When the phone rang, he almost didn't answer it. It was after nine o'clock. He'd told the press everything he knew. But it could be the police, saying they'd found Jenny. So he leaned over and picked up the receiver. "Hello?"

"Hunter, I'm bleeding!"

The panicked voice was Bri's. She was bleeding, like her mother. "I'll be right there!"

He grabbed his keys and raced to his car. As soon as he got on the road, he pulled out his cell phone and hit the quick-dial button that would ring the hospital. He explained that he was bringing Bri in. They should call Abby and prepare for their arrival.

When he reached Bri's place, he sprinted up the stairs and rang the doorbell. She opened the door at once. Her eyes were wide with fear, and tears had left tracks down her cheeks.

"It's okay, Bri. I'll take care of you," he said and swept her into his arms.

"My bag," she said, her voice weak.

"We'll get it later."

When he reached the SUV, she handed him a folded towel. "So I won't mess up your seat," she said, almost sobbing.

He did as she asked, putting the towel down before he set her upon it. Then he strapped her in and ran for the other side. He was trying to be calm before her, but he was finding himself playing the role of an expectant father, not an experienced doctor.

He drove as fast as he could, and they were at the hospital three minutes later. He stopped in front and two nurses rolled a gurney out the door. By the time he got around the vehicle, they were ready for him to put Bri on it.

"Hunter," she called, sounding even more panicky as the nurses began pushing her toward the door.

"I'm right here, honey. Everything's going to be fine. They've called Abby for us." He looked at one of the nurses for confirmation of that statement.

"She's scrubbing up, doctor."

"See, she's already here, honey. Everything's going to be fine."

It didn't take long to reach the delivery room. Abby had a calm smile on her face as she gave orders to the nurses for Bri's care.

Hunter drew several deep breaths before he conferred with Abby in a low voice, so Bri wouldn't hear. He and Abby worked well as a team as they staunched the bleeding and set up a transfusion. Bri began having contractions fast and furiously, as if Mother Nature knew it was time for the babies to be born now!

Abby and Hunter decided to let nature take its course, with a little help from them. Not half an hour after he'd gotten Bri to the delivery room, Emily made her appearance. Eleanor was next and she came fairly quickly after Emily, just three minutes apart. But Elizabeth wasn't in a hurry. It was almost ten minutes later before she was born.

Three beautiful baby girls.

"Bri, they're all perfect," Hunter told her. "Emily is already sleeping, Eleanor is complaining, and Elizabeth is simply staring at everything with big eyes.'' He bent down and kissed Bri. ''They're beautiful.''

''Did—did you get the bleeding to stop?''

''Yeah, it's stopped. You're going to be fine. We've improved a lot since your mother gave birth to you and your brothers.''

''Did you call Dad?''

''I'll do so as soon as they take you to recovery. There'll be a nurse there with you. I don't want to leave you alone.'' In fact, Hunter didn't want to leave her at all. He clasped her hand tightly, so relieved that his girls had made their appearance. And he and Abby had been able to make sure Bri was okay.

They wheeled Bri into recovery. A nurse was waiting for them.

''Keep an eye on her, and watch for signs of bleeding. If there's anything wrong at all, get a doctor,'' Hunter instructed.

''I've been a recovery nurse for thirty years, doctor. I think I can handle everything.''

''Be sure, nurse, because this is the mother of my babies. I don't want to take any chances.''

The woman gasped, but Hunter didn't care. Bri had called him when she was worried about the babies. And he intended to marry her as soon as possible.

He stepped into the hall and dialed Jackson's number. ''Jackson? It's Hunter. Bri just delivered the girls. Everyone's fine.''

"She's fine? She didn't die?" Jackson demanded, urgency in his voice.

"Nope. She's fine. Can you call Caleb and Adam? I want to get back to Bri."

"She's fine?" Jackson asked again.

"She's fine. The girls are fine. We're all fine. By the way, the babies are mine. I'll explain when I see you."

"O-o-okay," Jackson said slowly, as if he wasn't sure what he'd just heard.

Hunter hung up and reentered the recovery room, just as Abby came from the delivery room.

"Abby, are you going to check her again, be sure there isn't any additional bleeding?"

"Of course. But you can do it if you want."

"No. I'm discovering why they don't encourage doctors to work on relatives."

"She isn't one of the girls, Hunter. You're not kin to her."

"Not yet. But I'll be her husband as soon as it's possible," he assured Abby, beaming at her.

"Well, I'm relieved. Does Bri know that yet?"

"No. I was afraid to discuss it before the babies were born, because she kept getting upset."

"I wish you all the best. Did you call her father?"

"Yes, I did."

Abby checked Bri and assured Hunter she was doing fine. "I'm going to go look at the girls and make sure the nurses called a pediatrician."

"Good. Tell them hello from their dad."

"Will do," Abby said, grinning widely. The nurse was staring at Dr. Hunter Callaghan. Abby knew the news would be all over the hospital by morning.

BRI SLOWLY woke up, knowing something was different. When she finally opened her eyes, she realized she was in the hospital. Her girls had made their arrival. She tried to sit up, and Hunter opened his eyes.

He was sitting in a chair beside her bed. He stood and leaned over her, gently kissing her lips.

"Are the girls all right?" she asked hurriedly.

"The girls are perfect. We were waiting for you to wake up before I took you to your room. Want to drive by the nursery and see them?"

"Oh, yes, please. Hunter, thanks for coming for me so quickly. I'm afraid I was panicking a little."

"That's understandable. I'm glad you called me."

She blushed, knowing she'd promised herself she'd call Abby. But Abby wasn't who she'd wanted when she realized she might die. She'd wanted Hunter. She'd wanted to feel his touch, to see his smile, to feel his protection. As she always would.

He released the lock on her bed and pushed her into the hallway, turning a sharp right to go down the long corridor to the baby nursery.

"How big were they?"

"They were all over four pounds. Emily was the biggest. I think she weighed 4 lbs, 12 oz. Eleanor was the feistiest one with the strongest lungs. But she only weighed 4 lbs. 3 oz. Then Elizabeth, who wasn't in a hurry, weighed 4 lbs. 8 oz.''

They reached the windows that allowed the family to keep an eye on the newest arrivals. Hunter stopped the bed and helped Bri sit up a little so she could see the babies.

Tears filled her eyes.

Her father spun around. ''Bri! There you are. Those little girls are so beautiful! How do you feel?''

''Fine, Dad. I'm fine.''

Caleb and Adam and Maggie hurried up for a big family reunion. There were a lot of compliments for the three baby girls.

''So I understand there's going to be a wedding,'' Jackson finally said, looking first at Bri and then Hunter.

Bri stared at her father, then snapped her gaze to Hunter. ''What did you say?''

Jackson pointed to Hunter. ''While you were still in recovery, he said you two were getting married. He said he's the daddy.''

Hunter grinned and kissed Bri on her lips. ''Don't even think of denying it, honey. I've been telling everyone they're mine.''

Bri remained silent so long Hunter got worried. Finally, she said, ''I'm not denying you're the father, Hunter. But that doesn't mean you have to marry me. I won't ask that of you.''

Hunter cupped her cheek. "Honey, do you know why I took this job?"

"Because it's a good one."

"Nope. I took it so I could see you again. So I could find out if you were no good...or if you were my dream lover, as I'd thought until I found you gone."

"You really did come to look for me?" Her voice wobbled, but she kept her gaze fastened on Hunter.

"I really did. I wanted us to find a way to be together, because I knew what we'd found was special."

"But you didn't know where I was!" she exclaimed.

"Yes, I did. Once I learned your last name, I knew where to find you. I just wasn't sure I wanted to find you. But when I got a chance, I jumped at it. Then you walked in the door, pregnant. It took me a day or two to work everything out. But you already had me under your spell again."

"Oh, Hunter, I—I was so hurt."

"I don't understand any of this," Jackson protested. "Are you getting married or not?"

"Please, Bri?"

"Are you sure you love me?"

"With all my heart. But you'll have to share me with the girls. My four ladies." He kissed her again.

"Well?" Jackson insisted.

"Oh, yes, Dad, we're getting married," Bri said,

her gaze still fixed on Hunter. "Oh, I've missed you so much," she said, her arms going around his neck.

There was a cheer around them, and Hunter looked up, startled to discover about fifteen members of the staff listening to his proposal.

But he didn't care. He'd found his true love once more. He had no complaints.

"Will you move in with us? I don't want to live in a hotel," Bri said.

"I didn't get a chance to tell you. I got the house. By the time the girls can go home, we'll be moved in."

"Oh, Hunter, that's wonderful!"

He thought so, too, and swept her back into an embrace that he'd developed a need for in New York City, locked in a deli eight months ago.

Epilogue

Briana awoke the next morning when April shook her awake. "Hey, lazybones, breakfast will be here in a few minutes."

"Lazybones? I gave birth to three babies. I think I should get to sleep for days!" Bri exclaimed, but her smile told April she didn't mean it.

"True, but I've heard you're having company for breakfast. I thought you might want to comb your hair or something."

"Visitors this early?"

April grinned. "Well, when you're the doctor in charge of obstetrics—"

Bri was filled with excitement—and happiness. She hadn't admitted it to herself, but she'd feared Hunter might've changed his mind. "I need a shower!"

"I'm not sure—"

"Please, April," she pleaded.

"All right. A quick one. Stay in bed until I get everything ready."

Ten minutes later, Bri was back in bed, her hair

still wet, but the rest of her ready for a special visitor. The door opened, after a brief knock, and a nurse came in carrying her breakfast tray, followed by Hunter, carrying a second tray.

"Do you mind having company for breakfast?" he asked with a smile.

"I'd love it," Bri assured him.

April followed the other nurse out the door. "Ring us when you want the trays collected."

Hunter didn't move until the door had closed. Then he set the tray on a nearby table and reached for Bri, his arms sliding around her. "How are you?"

With his arms around her, she felt better than she'd ever felt. "Wonderful." Then he kissed her and she felt even better.

"You haven't changed your mind?" she asked afterward, her voice a little wobbly.

"I'll never change your mind. And I'll never leave you or our girls. We're going to be married as soon as you feel up to it."

"Today?" she suggested.

"I think you'd better recover for a couple of days at least." He kissed her again.

"Will it always be this wonderful?" she asked as she relaxed in his arms.

"Yeah. The seven months we were apart, I missed you every day. I was mad at you, but I still wanted to be with you."

A knock on the door brought a frown to Hunter's

face. "Come in," he called. The frown went away when he realized who had arrived.

A deliveryman came in carrying two large vases of roses, one with white roses that had deep pink streaks in them, the other with pale yellow roses with pink streaks. He announced, "Flowers for Miss Emily Callaghan and Miss Eleanor Callaghan."

Bri stared at the flowers while Hunter showed him where to place the vases.

"I'll be right back," the man said. When he entered again, he carried another vase like the others, this one filled with peach roses with pale yellow streaks for Elizabeth Callaghan. But in his other hand he had a vase with two dozen scarlet roses for Briana.

When he'd gone, Briana asked Hunter to bring her the cards. Each of the cards for the girls said, "Welcome to our family, love Daddy." Her card said, "Thank God I found you again. All my love, Hunter."

Tears filled her eyes and she slid her arms around his neck for another magical kiss. "You're wonderful."

"There's just one thing we need to negotiate," he murmured, and Briana's heart clutched.

"What?"

"In a year or two, we might do this again, and have boys this time so I won't be outvoted all the time."

"How about I just promise to vote with you?"

"I don't know. I'm thinking one of these girls will have to be a really good shortstop, then."

''We'll see.''

Another knock on the door interrupted them. Hunter frowned again. ''I thought they were going to leave us alone!''

But these guests were welcome. Two nurses brought in three little girls, identically perfect. The first nurse announced, ''Here are your babies, Mommy and—'' She stopped abruptly, staring at Hunter.

He stood and crossed to take one of the girls. ''And Daddy,'' he said with pride.

''And Daddy,'' the nurse repeated.

Briana reached out for one of the babies and Hunter took the third baby, too.

Bri smiled at Hunter, his arms full of babies, and her own precious bundle, and believed in the future. Together, with Hunter, they were going to have a wonderful life, starting right now.

* * * * *

QUADRUPLETS ON THE DOORSTEP

BY
TINA LEONARD

Tina Leonard loves to laugh, which is one of the many reasons she loves writing books. In another lifetime, Tina thought she would be single and an East Coast fashion buyer forever. The unexpected happened when Tina met Tim again after many years – she hadn't seen him since they'd attended school together. They married and now Tina keeps a close eye on her school-age children's friends! Lisa and Dean keep their mother busy with soccer, gymnastics and horseback riding. They are proud of their mum's "kissy books" and eagerly help her any way they can. Tina hopes that readers will enjoy the love of family she writes about in her books. Recently a reviewer wrote, "Leonard had a wonderful sense of the ridiculous," which Tina loved so much she wants it for her epitaph. Right now, however, she's focusing on her wonderful life and writing a lot more romance!

To Kasey Michaels, for being an inspiration and a
friend, and to my Mimi, because she's cool.
Lisa and Dean, you guys make me smile.
Tim, I guess we've done OK so far – thanks for
doing my classwork in the first grade.
See what it got you!

Chapter One

Caleb McCallum peered through the glass window of the McCallum Multiple-Birth Wing Neonatal Intensive Care Unit. Four plastic isolettes were marked Baby Barrow number one, Baby Barrow number two, three and four—the four abandoned children whose case he'd been sent to monitor. A nurse moved from isolette to isolette, touching each baby gently, tucking a blanket here, replacing a baby cap there. He was caught by her loving touch as she lingered over each small form.

Caleb's mind automatically went over a previous conversation with his father. Jackson McCallum, founder of the Emily McCallum Multiple-Birth at Maitland Maternity Hospital in Austin, had commanded him to ''look'' in on the situation and ''find out what you can. Use some of your police contacts in Missing Persons, Caleb.''

''Dad, the police will handle the problem fine.'' He was an ex–police officer. Ex. Using his old contacts was something he'd prefer not to do, and he'd definitely not wanted any part of this latest request.

"It's my wing, son," Jackson had replied. "I feel responsible. I want to know that this young mother is found, and quickly. There are four young lives missing the most important part of their world's new beginning."

Caleb hadn't reminded his father that he knew damn well what it meant to be raised without a mother. Jackson knew it, and was trying to pull Caleb into the situation, fully aware that Caleb wouldn't want to relive any part of his former life as a cop.

"Not to mention that a young girl who's just been through a difficult birth shouldn't be out of bed, much less running around town. She needs to be in the hospital where she can be cared for. I'm worried like hell about that."

It wasn't so much that Jackson was worried about the wing's reputation. His father would be reliving the moment his beloved wife had died in childbirth—the result of giving birth to Caleb.

"All right, Dad," he'd finally said. "I'll go to the wing and do some asking around."

"Only right that you do," Jackson said. "To him whom much is given, much is demanded. It's your duty. You were the finest officer on the force."

"Were, Dad. Were." And he'd hung up the phone, but the conversation lingered, refusing to be switched off replay.

Dad did a good thing by building this wing, Caleb admitted reluctantly. Even if it did exist as a monument to the mother he'd lost, Caleb knew he should be proud of his father's generosity. But to him it signified loss, not gain.

The nurse hovering over the isolettes no doubt would disagree. He didn't think the missing real mother could spend more time nurturing those babies.

She glanced up, catching him staring at her. *She's cute,* he realized at once—*real cute.* Big green eyes assessed him in a face surrounded by long, curly auburn hair. Creamy skin dotted with light freckles across a tiny nose was accented by full, rosy lips.

Before he realized what she was doing, she'd left the nursery and come to stand beside him. She'd just reach his midchest, if she took a deep breath and stood poker-straight.

"Aren't they sweet?" she asked him.

Caleb stared at her, lost for just a moment, his gaze locked on her beautiful smile.

"They smell like…like new spring," she said dreamily. "Sometimes soapy-clean, and sometimes formula-burpy, but precious beyond words. I think of spring when I hold them, even when they smell like formula."

"It's only late December."

She gazed through the window. "You'd have to hold them to understand, I guess."

He cleared his throat, uncomfortable with the

emotions the petite nurse was setting off inside him. "Has anyone heard from the mother?"

Slowly, she turned to face him. "I'm afraid not."

Her eyes were so sad he wanted to comfort her—and yet, he was here in a more or less official capacity. The cop in him went into command. "I'm Caleb McCallum," he said, putting out a hand for her to shake.

"The son of Jackson McCallum who dedicated this wing?" she asked, sliding her hand into his. "Bri's brother?"

He nodded, registering with all his old sensory training that her skin was soft, her touch gentle, her fingers small-boned, like the fragile bones in a mourning dove's wing.

"I'm April Sullivan. It's nice to meet you."

Her hand withdrew from his, and he shoved his own into his jeans pocket. "How well did you know the mother?"

"Jenny Barrows?" Auburn eyebrows lifted quizzically. "She was here for about two weeks before she gave birth. I suppose that she preferred me to the other nurses. But I certainly didn't know her well enough for her to leave her children to me, not that I would have suspected that she was even considering such a thing."

"How did she let you know she wanted you to have them?"

"I'd laid my sweater on my chair when I went to prep a patient. Jenny left a note in my sweater pocket asking me to take care of her children. I was…shocked. I still can't believe it.''

''How many hours after the birth did you find the note and realize Ms. Barrows was missing?''

She stared at him, her eyebrows drawing into delicate crescents. ''The questions you're asking are so official. You sound like the officers who've been interviewing me.''

''I used to be on the police force.''

''I see. And now?''

''I work as a security consultant and trouble-shooter at McCallum Enterprises. Dad asked me to see how the situation is progressing.''

''That's nice of you. And him.''

''Why?''

''Well, to be so concerned.''

''He has a strong affinity for this wing, and if he thinks there's anything he can do to help the mother once she's found, believe me, Dad will do it.''

''That's kind.''

If living in the past was something to be proud of, maybe. But Caleb didn't say that to April.

''I have to get back to the babies. If you'll excuse me—''

He really didn't want her to go just yet. ''You didn't answer my question.''

It seemed to him that she set her jaw with a tiny bit of defiance. ''I found the note in my pocket at eight a.m., which would have made it four days past the delivery on Friday. She left four days before

Christmas, the babies' first Christmas,'' she said softly. It seemed she straightened suddenly to stare at him. ''Anything else you'd like to know concerning the particulars of this case?''

Spunky, and cool when riled. Red hair definitely a warning of some warmth in the temper zone. ''You don't like me asking you questions?''

''I don't mind you asking questions,'' she said, passing him. ''I mind you questioning me in that detached-cop voice, like you're recording data. These babies aren't data, Ex-Officer McCallum. They were left in my care, and like your father, I have a vested interest in seeing that they are treated with the utmost devotion.''

A fierce guardian she apparently planned to be. ''I would guess Ms. Barrows chose pretty well when she picked you for surrogate mother.''

''I didn't ask to be the stand-in mother to these children. But until *Jenny* is found, I plan on doing as she asked.''

She returned to the nursery, keeping her back to him as she ministered to the infants. He shifted uncomfortably. White pants trimmed a tiny little tush– the woman was made like a doll. Even her shoulder blade-length curls seemed like doll dross.

Well, he couldn't stand here and stare at her posterior all day. She'd clearly noted the lack of warmth in his soul when it came to children, so it was best to move along.

But then the devil seized him, and he tapped on

the window. She turned, clearly aware that it was him by the raised eyebrow she shot him as she neared the glass.

"Coffee at 2 p.m.?" he asked.

"Help yourself. The cafeteria's open then."

But he saw the challenge in her gaze, and he knew she'd be there.

Because she wanted Jenny Barrows found. And she'd made her point clear about the human element being the key to finding a scared young girl.

He really admired April Sullivan's grit.

APRIL LEFT CALEB sitting in the cafeteria for ten minutes past two o'clock before she slid a doughnut over his shoulder onto the table in front of him. "I heard police officers love doughnuts. This one might be a bit stale."

He fake-frowned at her as she took the plastic chair across from him. "You didn't see the sign that says, 'Don't feed the cops'?"

"But you're ex, right? So I'm free to ignore the sign."

"I couldn't help noticing the sign you're wearing says, 'Questions can be directed to the appropriate department, but not necessarily answered. And all in my own good time.'"

"Glad you can read." She popped open a soda can. "I'll do anything I can to help find Jenny, but I don't want to be questioned by RoboCop."

"I got it, I got it. There *is* a heart behind my bulletproof vest."

She gave him a stern eyeing, noting that his chest was broad, but not thick enough that he was wearing a vest. "Do you wear one as a security consultant?"

"Not usually. If I'm on the golf course with Dad, maybe."

That earned him a smile. "Now you're sounding more human."

"So, do you have any idea why Ms. Barrows—sorry, *Jenny*—might have disappeared like she did? And left those adorable bundles of joy to a virtual stranger?"

April drank some of her cola before answering. "Believe me, in the last several days, I've tried to put myself in Jenny's shoes. She was too young to be a mother, really, and certainly to quadruplets. Seventeen, widowed, her husband killed in a construction accident, no family support..." She shrugged. "It was a lot for her to handle, without even mentioning the stress of finding out what all had to happen to care for quads."

"If she doesn't return or isn't found, the children will go into foster care."

April froze. "Not if I have anything to do with it, they won't. Not for one damn minute."

"Hey, it's okay—"

"Not to me, it isn't. I don't even want to think about Jenny not returning. For goodness' sakes, she needs medical care herself! Surely one weak girl can be found. And these children deserve a true home.''

''What's your beef with foster care?''

She bristled. ''I simply…would not want that, considering that Jenny entrusted her children to me. A home isn't a home unless it's built on love, and a family isn't a family unless it's based on love. The babies should be ready to go home in a month. In that time, a lot can happen, like the mother being found by you, if Austin's finest can't do it. Isn't that why your father sent you? He wouldn't want them to go into foster care, either.''

''Hey,'' he said, gently putting his hand over hers. ''Chill, lady. I didn't mean to get you all upset. I'm beginning to think maybe you don't like me too much, kind of like oil and vinegar naturally repel each other.''

She snatched her hand from under his. ''It's good on some things.''

''But it has to be shook real hard to stay together, and even that's not for long. Let's me and you work together on this without a lot of shaking, okay?''

''I don't want to talk about the babies going into foster care,'' she said stubbornly. ''I want you to say you'll do your best to assist the officers and everyone else who's looking to find Jenny, since that's why you're here.''

''You've got a lot in common with my dad.''

His grim tone caught her ear, but she didn't heed it. ''The man dedicated a wing to helping children and mothers who need extra attention. If you're putting me in the same category with him, I call that a good thing.''

He sighed, looking at her with some admiration. ''Beneath that delicate appearance, you're wearing steel determination, lady.''

''What would you do in my place? If you'd been left a heartbreaking note asking you to take care of someone's children?''

''I'd be scared as hell, if you want to know the truth.''

''Well, I am, Mr. Troubleshooter. I'm scared. I want to see the happy ending to this fairy tale right this minute.''

She stared at him to see how he was taking her brave words. But she wasn't exaggerating. She was frightened out of her wits, for Jenny's sake. The babies were fine, loved and stroked by everyone who was admitted to the neonatal nursery. But Jenny might be in pain, and she was most certainly frightened to have left the way she had. She had no money, nothing of value. She could be putting herself in danger, and the thought of it was more than April could bear.

Caleb looked at her, his hazel eyes dark with compassion and empathy. Okay, maybe he wasn't all data-seeking ex-cop. He was tall and well filled out, no doubt in shape from his days on the force. She suspected his story would be a tale of heartache, because he didn't strike her as an easy quitter. Witness how he'd overridden her cold shoulder and enticed her into a coffee break. "Are you going to eat that doughnut or not?"

He shoved it toward her. "You want it?"

"Never touch them. I watch my fat grams carefully."

That brought a laugh from him. "Why? Afraid to weigh more than ninety pounds?"

"I'm afraid to coagulate my bloodstream and arteries with sludge when I work twelve-hour shifts. And I weigh a very healthy one hundred five, thank you."

She stood, and he did, too.

"Then I'll pass on it as well." He tossed the doughnut into a nearby trash can. "Since I'll be working around the clock to find the missing mother of those babies."

"Thank you," she said quietly. "I would appreciate anything you could do. Not that I don't think the police won't find her eventually. But they have lots of cases and I'm afraid, Caleb. It's been nearly a week since anyone has heard anything."

She looked up at him, unwilling to think that maybe Jenny wouldn't be found, especially if she didn't want to be. The girl wouldn't have credit cards which would leave a paper trail. No family she might run to.

"Do you know anything at all about the husband?" Caleb asked. "Did either of them have family?"

"No. They were both orphans. She was living with a grandmotherly type named Mrs. Fox whom she mentioned from time to time. But the police have already checked with her, and Mrs. Fox had no more information than I do."

"There's got to be a school she attended."

"She'd dropped out," April said sadly. "Her husband as well, since he had to work to support them both. Jenny couldn't work because of the difficulty of a multiple-birth pregnancy."

"Okay. I'll check the buses and the airlines, though I don't guess she would have had money to get anywhere. And I'll check the teenage hot spots, in case anyone has seen her."

"You don't think she might have left town, do you?" April was horrified by the thought.

"Anything's possible."

Upset, April turned to go, then slowly returned her gaze to his. "I was in foster care," she said softly.

"Tell me something I couldn't figure out on my own," he replied gently. "Can you give me a description of Jenny which includes weight and height?"

She blinked back sudden tears. *Jenny, come back!* she thought. *These little lives need their mother. They need more than being broken up and shuttled through the cracks in the system.* "I'll have that description waiting at the nurses' desk when you're through eating,'' she said, hurrying away from the cafeteria.

It would be so unfair, so cruel if that's what happened. April just had to put her faith in the police force.

And if not them, then Caleb McCallum, troubleshooter and ex-cop, would have to be her knight in shining armor. He was a bit scarred. He didn't hang out with his family much—until Briana's surprise pregnancy, his sister didn't hear all that often from him. She knew that from her close relationship with Bri; she was aware of the family tree.

She also knew that since Briana's babies had arrived, Caleb had thought up one excuse or another to visit her house.

Now that April had finally met the big bad ex-cop, she decided he was a man who didn't want his bluff called. He wanted to act as if he didn't care about these quadruplets—but he did.

She wouldn't call his bluff on that matter. But she wouldn't allow him to underestimate her, either.

IT WASN'T THAT he minded his job as a security consultant, Caleb thought as he waited at the nurse's desk for April to give him the weight/height description of Jenny. What bugged him was being called in on family matters, with his dad's constant reminders of his past. Maybe his dad wanted to live in his grief by building a monument to it—the birth wing—but Caleb preferred to let time heal his wounds. If time, in fact, could do that.

Since the death of his close friend and cop partner a few years ago, Caleb was pretty certain time had slowed to a crawl.

It was either his dad's disbelief that his son would never return to the force, or perhaps Jackson's desire to remind Caleb that time *was* passing him that made him keep asking him to "use his contacts" about matters that concerned babies.

Okay, when his unmarried sister, Bri, had become pregnant with triplets, Caleb hadn't needed too damn much convincing to want to find the father. He'd very much felt that he would use all his contacts, and every bit of cop determination he'd ever possessed to find the guy and explain to him how much he *really* wanted to be married to his sister.

Bri, ever independent, had stayed his search. That situation had resolved itself fine.

Maybe this one would, too. On the other hand, he had to admit a strong desire to see the case closed with a happy ending. It sure would upset April Sullivan if those babies were taken by the state. Goose pimples ran over his hands at the thought. What a feminine little woman! When his father had asked him to look in on this case, he could have had no idea about the compact bundle of steely determination he would meet up with.

Caleb frowned. And then again, Jackson had been dropping hints for some time about Caleb needing a woman to help him through the rough time in his life. Romance. A wife.

That was the last thing he wanted. A wife should be a partner, and he didn't want any more partners. He didn't want to get close to anyone; he didn't want to feel responsibility for a single soul. Take April, for example. Now, she'd suck up a lot of attention. For one thing, he'd sensed she had emotional baggage a lot like his. Clearly, she was a woman with a lot of weather, and while he liked a storm or two, he also wanted calm more than anything these days. And she was so *fragile*. Those tiny bones in her hand had instantly made him relax his handshake to the point that he'd almost been holding her hand rather than sharing a greeting. It had been like palming warm satin.

He bet those hands felt good to those tiny infants. From pictures, he'd seen that his mother was a fragile flower compared to his father's hearty stature and—

Oh, no. No, no, no. He was the youngest triplet, the one his mother had brought last into the world. The scrawny one. Yet, might she have lived had there been one less child? What made one woman bear four infants and be strong enough to run away, and another woman unable to withstand the arduous process of birthing three? He wasn't certain, but it might have something to do with constitution and frame, and April, while she had tugged on his male instincts, was a big red stop sign. Well, a petite red stop sign, but a woman he wasn't going to allow to get under his skin. He definitely didn't need a dainty flower that couldn't withstand the rigors of his roughhouse cop personality.

"Here's a description of Jenny," April said, handing him a slip of paper. "All the pertinent details."

Starting, he found himself looking into her deep green eyes. Eyes that looked at him no-nonsense, as if she fully expected him to walk out into the street and come back inside the hospital, producing Jenny Barrows in all of ten minutes.

"Social Services called a moment ago," she told him. "They plan to come by today to begin overseeing their role with the children. For now, these babies are too frail to leave the hospital, but in a month, maybe sooner, that won't be the situation. If Jenny isn't found, I fully intend to do everything I can to make certain I comply with her wish that I raise the babies."

He cocked an eyebrow at the determined diminutive redhead. "How are you going to do that? Raise four babies by yourself? You'll have to quit your job."

"I am prepared to do whatever it takes, Mr. McCallum."

Waving a hand in surrender, he said, "Caleb. Don't go all formal on me again. I'm on your side, all right? I'm just asking you how you're going to do it."

"How could I *not* do it?"

"Okay, okay. Do you have a boyfriend, or someone who can help you?"

She put a hand on her hip. "If you want to know my status, why don't you just ask me rather than phony-baloneying about it?"

Whoa, she was a Tartar. What she lacked in size, she definitely had in spirit. He tucked the information she'd given him into his pocket. "I'm just trying to determine if you have any resources that might make Social Services look favorably upon you as a temporary mother."

"I'm a nurse trained in neonatal intensive care. I was the one Jenny Barrows turned to. And I want to do it. I'm not afraid of a challenge. Other temporary-care situations will split the babies up."

"All right, April. You let me know if you hear anything. This is my cell number," he said, scribbling on a piece of paper and handing it to her. "It's always on. I'll let you know if I find out anything the police haven't been able to turn up themselves."

"I hope you're better at asking questions with other people than you've shown yourself to be with me." She raised an eyebrow at him.

Oh, brother. She just wasn't going to leave it alone, because she'd squarely caught him trying to figure out if she was unattached, and she knew it. Denial wasn't going to work here; she was too smart for that. But a man had his pride. He frowned at her and said, "You're entitled to your opinion, Miss Sullivan."

She laughed at him, not fooled for a second, then turned around and walked to the other side of the nurse's desk, giving him a view of that sweetheart-shaped tush in action.

And then she glanced over her shoulder, dead-on catching him staring at her fanny.

Oh, brother.

Chapter Two

"You didn't answer my question," he said.

"It didn't merit an answer. Social Services will consider my skills and other matters as a single mother, I hope, if it comes to that. You find Jenny, and I'll focus on spiffing up my foster parent qualifications in case you don't locate her in time. But I fully intend to do what I can for the children," she replied, disappearing into a hospital room.

It was an empty room, which was good, because she needed to collect her thoughts. Her words were almost all bravado. Even she knew that she might be an unlikely candidate because of her marital status. Possibly even a married couple might not be allowed to take in all four children.

The best thing for these children would be for Jenny to come back today. But if Jenny didn't return, and Social Services didn't look favorably upon her request to take them, they would be split up and put into varying foster care situations.

The thought was enough to tear April's heart in

two. It wasn't that her adoptive family hadn't loved her—they had. Yet all the years of being moved from one home to another had taken its toll. Friends, schools, addresses—nothing ever stayed the same. No relationship ever cemented for her, and she'd grown wary of trying to build any relationship in her life.

In fact, she'd learned to simply rely upon herself. By the time she was adopted, she was a teenager. While appreciative of her new mother and father, she'd almost felt as if she were adopted to take care of them. That wasn't fair, because they loved her to this day. They'd seen she was put through college and then nursing school, and that she had everything she needed.

But the foundation of love she'd lacked all her childhood couldn't be filled in. Independence became her sole weapon against pain; any friends she maintained knew that although she was kind and loving, she could be bullheaded about staying whatever course she chose without allowing anyone to help her.

That's why Caleb McCallum sent prickles of panic running all through her. While she'd recognized that this unexpected source of assistance might be beneficial if Jenny could be located for her children, she'd also perceived a strength and determination in Caleb congruent to her own.

Strong men always seemed to want to take care

of her—and then they were disappointed when she wouldn't allow that to happen.

While knowing that Caleb's personality was equal to hers, she also had to admit to feeling a thrill that he found her attractive. Sometimes, she spent so much time in a nurse's uniform that she forgot that she was a woman with a feminine wish to be attractive.

Caleb's gaze had told her she was—and so, for the moment, she could almost forgive him for trying to figure out her relationship status, a point she didn't want to dwell on because he'd been right about Social Services favoring married couples. She smiled to herself. He'd fished so badly that she almost found it cute—almost.

Poking her head into the hallway, she saw that it was devoid of the big, strong ex-officer and hospital personnel, so she slipped into the nursery for a last stroke for the babies before she went home. Each lay sleeping, with either a fist or a finger in their mouths. "I'll be so glad when these tubes come off," she told them softly. "And I'll be even happier when you have healthy birth weights."

They'd been alive so short a time. Four flannel wrapped responsibilities in cocoons of warm softness, blissfully unaware of the turmoil their mother's disappearance was causing. Caleb hadn't wanted to see them as anything more than an impersonal case his father had tossed at him. "It's going to be okay," she murmured, reaching in through the rubber-glove opening to touch the smallest baby's foot. "What you children need, I think, is to be called something other than babies one, two, three and four. Since you're supposed to be mine, why don't we think up some names, temporarily at least? Then maybe everyone will see that you're real little people, not numbers."

They didn't move, too content for the moment, but this would change soon enough. As soon as one awakened, usually all of them would begin flailing tiny fists and feet. "You're the big sister," she said to the baby in the first isolette. "You can be Melissa. When I was a little girl, I was in a home with a girl whom I desperately wanted to become my big sister. Her name was Melissa, and I remember her telling me that her name meant bee in Greek."

Picking up a pen, she wrote Melissa on the card attached to the front of the isolette. Then she reached for a baby names book. "Let's call you Chloe," she told the second pink-wrapped girl, "because it's pretty. And according to this book, it means blooming. I guess every bee needs a bloom, huh?"

She chuckled to herself. "Number three, lucky number three. A man should have a strong name, right?" Caleb was a strong name, as was Jackson. "But I don't want you to be so strong that you're tough and unreachable," she told the tiny boy. "Yet I believe that comes from nurture not nature." Frowning, she thought about what she knew about Caleb. Bri had said once that Caleb was the sibling who didn't really fit in somehow. They loved him, but many times he wanted to be alone, choosing a harder path for himself than any his two siblings took. If they went hiking at summer camp, he had to go over the rocks to get where they were going, while they took the marked trails.

"Craig," she whispered to the baby. "It means crag. And we'll take care of the nurture thing so that you don't grow up too tough and unreachable. A little is good, too much is...well, it means a lonely path for you. And now you," she said to the last, smallest baby. "You need a special name. I'll call you...Matthew. Did you know that means gift of God? Well, it does, according to this handy-dandy book."

Closing the names book, she finished writing all the names on the cards. Satisfied for the moment that she'd given the babies a reason to become real people and not just numbers to even the most stalwart of tough hearts, she went to sign off her shift.

Slipping her hand into her pocket, she felt the note that had changed her life. Pulling it out, she read the note for the hundredth time:

Dear April Sullivan,
I know you'll love my babies and take good care of them, so I want you to have them.

Jenny Barrows

The words, written in immature lettering on a piece of school notebook paper, cried out the young teenager's despair. *She had to have been so desperate to appoint a near stranger as the guardian to her precious babies!* April was twenty-seven, and she knew she'd feel overwhelmed by the thought of raising four tiny infants alone, as precious as they might be. But she would do it.

Replacing the note in her pocket, she headed to the nurses' station. To her dismay, a Social Services worker was at the desk, speaking to the head neonatal nurse, Cherilyn Connors.

"April, this is Mandy Cole from Social Services. April Sullivan is the nurse to whom Jenny left the note concerning her children."

"How do you do?" Mandy said.

April looked the tall brunette over without trying to seem obvious. "I'm fine, thank you," she said carefully, wondering if the woman would be sympathetic to her plea for temporary custody.

"I'm going to examine the infants," Mandy said. "Is there anything you feel I should know about them?"

The question was directed to either Cherilyn or April, she noted. But it was April who wanted answers. "We can go over their files together, if you'd like. What will you do after you examine them?"

"We'll continue to monitor them. If Ms. Barrows doesn't return, or if the children become healthy enough to leave, they'll be placed in temporary care

until the situation can be resolved more satisfacto-
rily.''

Misgiving rose inside April. ''Jenny's wish is that
I take care of her children. I am willing to do so.''

Mandy looked at her with some surprise. ''The
paper Ms. Barrows left itself is not a legal document. I'm certain you realize the difference, Ms.
Sullivan, between a legal document and an emotionally distraught young girl's note?''

''I recognize this, Ms. Cole, but I also am willing
to take the emotionally distraught young girl's
wishes into consideration.''

''May I ask how old you are?'' Mandy asked. ''I
see that this particular wing is new. How long have
you been employed as a nurse, here or anywhere
else? And are you married, Ms. Sullivan? This is
information germane to any application you might
wish to put forward.''

With those words, April realized Caleb had been
right. Regardless of what Jenny had wanted, or what
she, April, might be willing to do for those sweet
babies, she would not be considered as a temporary
foster mother.

And that meant the babies would go into the system.

CALEB HAD RETURNED to the hospital, after going
down to the nearby Austin police station to talk to
some guys he knew who would give up the information on the missing mom, when a small dynamo

swept past him, walking fast toward the parking lot. "Hey," he said, reaching out to grab April's arm gently. "Going somewhere? Remember me?"

She kept her head down, and he realized she was upset. "Hello, what's going on?" he asked, encircling her with one arm. "Are you okay, April? Did something happen?"

She shook her head, a sniffle escaping her as she blew her nose into a tissue. Despite the parking-lot lights, it was too dark outside for him to see her face, but clearly, the calm tigress of a lady had some unexpected troubles.

"Ah," he said soothingly, tugging her up against his chest. "Didn't you know it's okay to talk to police officers? Police officers are our friends," he said in a singsong teacher's voice.

Though she didn't laugh at his attempt to cheer her, she didn't pull away from his chest. He decided to shut up and go with the physical comfort, because one, it was working, and two, she felt good. Underneath the nurse's smock, delicate shoulder blades quivered. And man alive, was her waist ever tiny.

"You were right. Social Services isn't even going to remotely consider me as a temporary mother for the babies. You've just got to find Jenny somehow!" she finally cried on a wail.

He felt a little better now that he knew the issue they were confronting. "No single moms, huh?"

"No single, young, barely-out-of-nursing-school

moms allowed. Scraps of paper are not legal documents, and don't you forget it.''

''Whew. You didn't enjoy that conversation, and I think I understand why.''

''Well,'' April said, finally moving away from the shelter he'd tried to give her. ''I understand her point. Social Services has a job to do, and they do it under sometimes impossible situations, and always highly emotional ones. I was just hoping so much that, in this case, they'd allow me some leeway.''

''Not a chance?''

''Not a chance.''

He moved his fingers down to her elbow. ''Let me walk you to your car.''

Nodding, she began walking the way she'd been going when he'd stopped her. He let his hand fall away from her, just keeping up easily with her quick pace. ''Did you know that Jenny was actually a good student?''

She stopped abruptly, swiveling to stare up at him. ''No, I didn't. How do you know?''

''Because I've been doing my job. She was a better-than-good student. According to some of my buddies who did the initial interviews of the hospital staff and the landlady when Jenny first went missing, the teenager was a remarkable student, as was her husband. They felt a need to prove themselves. Apparently, their relationship was for real, and they expected to get married and go on to college, where they could live in married-student housing, work, and rely on each other for emotional support. Finding themselves pregnant moved the timetable up, and they had to marry and drop out of high school. But these were not troublemaker kids.''

"No. Jenny didn't strike me as that type. But I would never have guessed that she had planned to go to college."

"Mrs. Fox told the police that both David—the deceased husband—and Jenny planned to get their GED, and they had both applied to the same colleges, also with applications for student aid. They were sincere in their efforts, and they meant to make it happen. After David died a few months ago and Jenny moved in with Mrs. Fox, Jenny began to become uncertain as to whether she would even try to attend a local college. The babies, of course, would need every minute of her time for the first several years. But without income, Jenny knew she'd have to work at a minimum-wage job. All this stress began weighing on her. She mentioned several times that she wished she could give the babies the home they deserved."

April stood still, looking at him.

"She must have seen an awful lot of good in you," he said softly, "to decide that you were just the answer to her prayers."

April shook her head. "She was desperate. I don't think Jenny knew what she was doing. After giving birth, many women suffer postpartum blues. With

Jenny, this would have been doubly manifest, I believe, because of the grief she was already suffering from losing her husband.''

''Maybe. But I now have to look at it from a different angle, based on this information,'' he told her. ''You're saying she was grief-stricken, and once she comes to her senses, will return. I'm saying, yes, she was grief-stricken, but moreover, she desperately wanted her children to have everything she couldn't give them. She met you, saw a kindred spirit who had made it where she had once dreamed to go, and she knew you'd love her children. Like a dying mother who fights to the last instant to create the best world she can for her offspring, Jenny gave you to her babies.''

''Rather than giving her babies to me.''

''Right. You were the gift, the way of a better life. I believe Jenny has no plans whatsoever to return. None.''

Chapter Three

April could hardly take Caleb's words in—and yet,
there was a core of logic she couldn't ignore. "I
would never, ever have thought what you just said."

"Because you're going from the perspective of
empathy," he said. "In an optimum world—
yours—the mother is tired and frightened and will
return once her medical condition, the blues exaggerated by grief, is overridden by the love for her
children. But Jenny's world was far from optimum.
Though I don't believe she thought her actions
through with any sense of clarity or comprehension,
I believe she was acting on the survival-of-the-fittest
theory. Because she was desperate, and she was
fighting for her children's survival."

"You know, you're very good at this," April said
slowly. "You were an awesome cop, weren't you?"

He raised an eyebrow at her. "Now who's asking
bad questions? Let's get you to your car and get you
home. You look like you could fall asleep on your
feet."

April ignored his guiding hand as she thought through the picture he'd drawn. "So what you're saying is that you feel Jenny didn't know that her children would be split up and put into foster care."

"I am positive that, while she was book smart, she was quite innocent about how the system works," Caleb said. "She'd gotten pregnant, which, in hers and David's history of being orphans themselves, they would have most likely been eager to avoid. While many teens get pregnant because they're bored, or they're subconsciously wanting someone to love them, David and Jenny were not bored. They were working toward a common goal. And they didn't need anyone to feel loved by, per se, because they had each other. I'd bet the pregnancy was a total accident. You see that it changed their plans, and therefore, their lives, forever."

"Being unsophisticated about birth control doesn't mean Jenny was unsophisticated about what might happen to her babies if she abandoned them. She watches TV like any other teenager."

"But," Caleb said, tugging April forward so he could take her to her car, "she chose her replacement. Would she have known that Social Services wouldn't heed her request? *You* seemed to think her wishes might make a difference. You told me you're willing to take those babies. Jenny probably felt that your bond with the babies and your training might make a difference." He paused for a moment, then said, "You are determined, and you are capable, and

Jenny no doubt sensed you'd do your best to stand up for her children's rights. What she didn't know is that she has to sign a legal document giving up all rights to her children before you could ever adopt them legally. They can't be adopted by anyone until the living mother authorizes adoption.''

April's heart stilled inside her. ''So although Jenny meant to provide for her newborns, she's actually put them in the very situation she grew up in herself. Orphaned. Oh my God.'' April couldn't help the tears that swept down her face all over again.

''Here, here,'' Caleb said, pulling her into his embrace again. ''Crying's not going to help, April.''

But she was shaking and she couldn't stop, so for once she allowed herself to take comfort from someone else. *Just for this moment, I need Caleb. I'll cry it all out, and then I'll be strong again.*

''You're too upset to drive. Let me take you home. Come on,'' he said, trying to move her.

She shook her head against his chest, but he was adamant. ''I'm at least going to follow you home to make certain you get there safely, so you might as well give in gracefully.''

''I don't think I know how to give in gracefully,'' she mumbled, wiping her nose on a tissue she jerked from her purse.

''Now, why does that not surprise me? Miss Chock-Full-of-Spit-and-Fire doesn't give in gracefully. Surprise, surprise.''

She laughed reluctantly through her tears. "I don't think I like you when you're being sarcastic."

He snorted. "That doesn't bode well for our working relationship. I like to be sarcastic sometimes. It keeps me from getting bowled over emotionally by little red-haired women who wail all over my big strong chest."

"Oh, please!" But that brought the smile to her face he'd been trying to find, so she decided just this once she would give in gracefully and let Caleb follow her home.

"I guess you're going to want coffee or a nightcap when we get to my house."

"After that nasty doughnut you tried to give me earlier, I may be too frightened to take anything else from you. But I deserve a nightcap after all the thinking I've done today. It's not easy running lithely through the trails of the teenage feminine brain."

She suspected it was very easy for him, and was even more convinced that seeing different angles in every situation had made him a damn fine cop. Never would she have seen Jenny's dilemma the way he had.

"I warn you that the trails of the feminine brain are tricky at any age," she teased. "Do you still want to join me for a nightcap?"

"I'm on duty until the case is solved, aren't I? If you've got orange juice, I'll take you up on it."

"That I have." She dug in her purse for her keys.

"Bri did tell me once that women fell for you like mad, and that you rarely noticed it happening. She said you were an accidental seducer." She raised an eyebrow at him. "I'm inviting you in for orange juice, but please, do not think I can be accidentally seduced or otherwise."

He laughed, not offended. "My big sister has a head full of romantic rocks. Ignore her."

"One should never ignore their best friend."

"Well, if anyone is safe with me, it's you, babe. Come on. Let's get you home."

What the heck did he mean by that? She turned quickly before he could see that his casual statement had unsettled her.

Much more than she wanted to admit.

"WE NEED a plan B," April told him once they'd stepped inside her house. Caleb hadn't been too shocked by the white compact car she drove—very clean and spare—and the house was what he would have expected as well, although something niggled at him, though he couldn't put his finger on it. Everything was in its tidy place, with delicate hues on the walls and in the carpet. The word he would have used to describe it was *dollhouse*.

"Plan B for what?" he asked, distracted by the lace drapes. In his apartment, he never bothered to open the plastic shutters. April's drapes hung like fairy-tale wisps, tied with soft blue bows. He scratched at the back of his neck, wondering if he was beginning to break out in a rash. Or hives.

"For making certain the babies aren't put in four separate homes. There has to be something we can do. We know for sure that Jenny didn't mean for that to happen."

"Did you sew your own drapes?" he asked, absently taking the glass of orange juice she handed him as he stood awkwardly in the living room.

"Of course." She laughed at him. "Why do you ask?"

His gaze roamed the kitchen she'd stepped from. Tiny vases sat in a collection atop a counter; china dishes were placed along the wall for ornamentation.

He swallowed uncomfortably. "If your toilet broke, what would you do about it?"

She looked at him as if he'd lost his mind. "I'd fix it, of course. What's hard about that? There's a ball and a chain and some plumbing. I laid the tile myself in the kitchen. One reads the directions, takes a do-it-yourself class at the local repair store and then goes home and puts the tile in. What are you really asking me?"

"When Jenny was in the hospital for those two weeks before she gave birth, did you talk about your house at all? Or sewing? Cooking? Woman things of that nature?"

Her forehead wrinkled up delightfully as she thought about his question. "Yes, I'm sure I did. What else was there to talk about? Before I'd go off duty for the days I wasn't scheduled, she'd ask me what I planned to do with my time. And so I told her. At the time, I believe I was working on a cross-stitch for your sister's nursery."

He drained the juice and reached around her to put the glass on the counter. "Okay. Well, thanks for the libation. Guess I'd better let you get some rest."

"Not until you tell me what you're thinking. You're working on something, and I want to hear what you've come up with, since I now realize you've been running through the trails of my brain."

"Okay." He drew a deep breath. "But don't go all ballistic on me."

She shrugged. "I can't make any promises. Hope you've got your flak jacket on."

"I think you'd like a baby someday."

She blew a raspberry. "You can do better than that! You didn't have to stand here asking silly questions about toilet repair to say, 'Okay, she's a female, and females approaching their thirties want children ninety-five percent of the time.'"

He held up his hands. "But did you *know* you wanted a baby?"

There was no way she was going to share her dreams with him—not now. "You're safe, Caleb, I promise you. Even if I did install my own tile floor."

Brushing that aside, he said, "And did you also

know you might have subconsciously projected your dreams very clearly to Jenny?''

APRIL HAD THOUGHT any number of things might happen if she allowed Caleb inside her house. Bri had mentioned that the opposite sex seemed terminally tempted by his loner appeal. Maybe she'd thought he'd make some attempt to hold her again. Quite possibly, that's why she had allowed him inside her home on the pretext of serving him a drink. She'd answered his questions about her home with a sense of pride.

Never had she thought he might be analyzing her. When he'd said she was safe with him—she hadn't known how safe.

''Caleb, if you're trying to say that I subconsciously told Jenny I wanted children—her children—I've got to tell you that you've gone way off the deep end.''

He sank into the sofa, uninvited. She could tell he was so deep in thought he didn't realize she was becoming angry. ''Could she have chosen you out of a sense of gratitude? Maybe even as a way to make your dreams come true? That would definitely lead me to conclude that she's not coming back, which would also mean that it would be good to start checking bus stations—''

''Caleb,'' April interrupted. ''Stop. I did not push my dreams onto Jenny. I did not position myself as the answer to her prayers. You're supposed to drink your orange juice, possibly murmur something nice about seeing me soon and then leave. Definitely you're not supposed to be conducting a case file on me.''

Surprise touched his face. ''April, I'm working all angles. You wanted me to find Jenny, didn't you? Well, when am I supposed to turn off the sensors?''

Feminine annoyance made her voice sharp. ''When you start checking me over as a suspect.''

''Not a suspect. An unsuspecting, maybe even un-willing, player in Jenny's desperation.''

She wasn't sure she was mollified, so she went into the kitchen for a few moments, examining whether she was upset because he just might have a point, or if she was miffed because she'd hoped he might try for a kiss before he left—and clearly had no intentions of that. She'd noticed he was tired, anyway. ''I'd better let you go. You probably need some sleep before your inner-cop clock runs past a twenty-four-hour shift.''

There was no answer, so she turned to see the expression on his face.

But the big, rough-and-tough man had fallen asleep, his head cradled on one of the soft ribbon pillows she'd made.

''Yo, dream man,'' she said, nearing him.

He gave a tiny snore of exhaustion.

Rolling her eyes, she got an afghan out of the closet. ''Your sister was wrong about you being ter-minally tempting to the opposite sex. And by the way, I crocheted this myself, you lummox.'' None too delicately, she tossed his booted feet up onto the sofa and dumped the afghan on him. "And I upholstered the sofa you're snoozing on, and I painted these walls myself, and I'll have you know, none of it was done with any thought of trying to snare you, so you can rest easy.''

CALEB AWAKENED, bolting upright as he wondered if he'd heard a sound. It was dark; he was sitting on April's sofa. Touching a button on his watch, green numbers glowed the hour. It was 5:00 a.m.

It was the first time he'd spent the night in a woman's house in quite a while. But there had been no up-close-and-personal time before he'd snoozed. He wished he hadn't fallen asleep on her. *Scintillating conversationalist*—that's me. *Real impressive.* Reaching to a table beside the sofa, he flipped on the lamp. Two blankets covered him, put on him by April. He'd brought her home to comfort her and make certain she was all right. Their roles had reversed, and he found it an embarrassment to the macho bravado he'd been wearing around April.

Time to make himself scarce. But first, he decided to check on Nurse Sullivan. Just a glance, to make certain she was securely tucked into her bed.

Folding the blankets, he tossed them onto the sofa, then headed down a narrow hallway. He switched on a light, seeing that there were two empty bedrooms on the left, a sewing room on the right and a hall bathroom. At the end of the hall, there was a closed door—the only place she could be. Quietly, he reached out a hand and edged the door open, every sense sharp as he waited for his eyes to adjust.

A double bed centered the room, with white sheets, white bedspread, white pillows—too much, if you asked him. But in the center of the ethereal white, April lay sprawled, a tousled yet relaxed flame at rest. Her hair was flung over her pillow; one slender leg poked from covers that had twisted around her waist.

He felt heat rising inside him, and decided waking up with April could take the chill off of late-December mornings real fast. She looked like pure temptation to him.

Yet, the clear reminder of who April was lay clustered in every window, in every edge of free space on dressers and the window seat. Dolls of every nationality, type and material kept a gentle vigil of forever childhood, satisfied to watch over April's most vulnerable moments.

That vulnerability frightened him—and yet drew him inexorably to her bedside. He couldn't stop looking at her delicate skin, her lips as they curved in her sleep. The leg so frankly exposed made him nervous even as he couldn't take his gaze from her. So, to return the favor she'd provided him, he took hold of the white blanket she'd kicked to the foot of the bed and slowly pulled it up over her until he reached her neck.

He glanced at her face, instantly finding her eyes wide open and watching him.

''There for a minute I thought you were going to frisk me,'' she said, her voice husky with sleep.

''Well, if you want me to—''

''Mr. Troubleshooter, I think you missed your chance last night.''

Her smile robbed him of the ability to decide if she was lodging a complaint or not. ''I apologize for falling asleep. I'm usually better company than that.''

She sat up against the pillows, keeping the blanket tight to her. ''I wouldn't know.''

''Oh, come on. You do know. You like me, in some way.''

''Maybe. Not when you're yelling in your sleep, though. That gave me the heebie-jeebies.'' Auburn eyebrows rose over concerned eyes. ''Do you do that often? Because if you do, I'm going to send some dolls home with you to chase away the monsters in your mind.''

He sent a glance around her room. ''Does it work?''

''In lieu of pets, they're less bother, cost, and my work schedule suits them. Sure. They're great company. Take a few with you. Or ten. If you have those doozy nightmares often.''

Swallowing, he tried to forget about the dainty

body beneath the sheets. He'd noticed she wore only
a short, pink T-shirt and some pajama shorts. Not
enough to tame his libido, and in fact, keeping his
brain busy with electrified hormones. "Believe it or
not, I slept better than I have in a long time."

"Really? On a sofa, in your jeans and boots."
Her eyes twinkled at him.

"Well, no doubt I could have slept better in
here—"

"And that's my cue to say grab a glass of orange
juice from the fridge and show yourself out," April
said with a smile. "I'm sure you need to get back
on the case."

"Do you have to work today?"

"No. But I will go in to see the babies." At that
thought, her shy smile disappeared.

"Don't think about it," he said quickly. "Either
Jenny will be found, or…or—"

"Or not. And as I mentioned last night, I need a
plan B."

"Are you losing faith in me?"

She shook her head at him, her gaze solemn.
"Just the system."

He grunted. "You only have your marital status
and age mainly working against you, right? Not in-
surmountable odds. Unless it's Social Services
you're pitted against. But they do have a job to do,
under thankless circumstances."

"I know. But there isn't a doubt in my mind that,
unless Jenny returns, I can provide those babies with

much of what they need for a balanced and happy life.''

Glancing around the dolls keeping silent watch, he nodded. ''You don't have to convince me that you, better than anyone, maybe understand the odds those children are up against.''

''And I love them.''

''And you love them.'' There wasn't a doubt in his mind about that. He'd seen how she lingered over each baby's bassinet, tenderly touching them. *It's all wrong. Too many children get left behind in a system that means well. They should have a mother. It's not that April is the only woman who would love these babies, but she already does.*

April is already their mother.

The phone rang, startling both of them in the cold morning light illuminating her room. April picked up the phone by her bed. ''Hello?''

She listened for a few moments, and as he watched panic stretch its shadow over April's face, Caleb felt his gut tighten with apprehension.

Chapter Four

"Baby Matthew's missing," April told Caleb, jumping out of bed and trying to keep the view of white, freckle-spattered skin to a minimum as she snatched on a green terry-cloth robe. Caleb may have appointed himself her one-night guardian, but she didn't know him well enough to forgo modesty. "I'm going to have to get down to the hospital. I hate to toss you out, but—"

"Wait. Who is Baby Matthew?" Caleb demanded.

Frantically, she pulled her hair up into a knot as she hurried into her closet. "Baby Barrows number four, the littlest of the babies," she called. "I named him Matthew."

"How can he be missing?"

"I don't know! I didn't stop to ask the particulars. If Cherilyn calls me at five in the a.m. to tell me he's missing, I can assure you it's not bad hospital humor."

"How can that happen? The baby had tubes in him."

"I don't know." Her heart was beating almost too hard for her to think clearly. "I can't think about that right now. I just want to get there."

"I'll drive you to the hospital."

"I'm okay." She didn't know if she wanted to continue allowing this man to look out for her. He was definitely trying to be caring, but independence was a hard habit to break. "No, thanks. I'll probably stay at the hospital all day with the babies, anyway."

Having fully dressed in the walk-in closet, April grabbed a coat, stuffing her arms into it as she looked at Caleb. His stance was stiff, as if he didn't quite know what to do with himself. "I don't want to start leaning on you. You're a nice man, but I've gotten used to taking care of myself."

"I know." He nodded his understanding. "We'll skip over the fact that you're upset and it would be better if you weren't driving. I'll follow you, and if you do anything vehicularly heinous—like drive eighty in a fifty-five—I'll honk the horn. Just in case you miss the speed limit signs or something."

"How can one tiny baby be lost?" she fretted, pulling on walking boots, not even registering his effort to keep the situation light. "He was too fragile to go anywhere. And surely no one would remove his tubes to slip him out."

"Let's just get down there and find out what's

happening. It doesn't do any good to envision scenarios. The police will have been called, and probably soon the media will be, too.''

They left the house, April locking the door and hurrying to her car. Caleb followed in his—and the sight of his car behind her gave her some measure of reassurance.

CALEB COULD HARDLY believe that someone would take a tiny baby, especially under the watchful eyes of so much hospital personnel, but the grim expression on the head nurse's face told the story.

''The quads are never alone,'' she told him. ''There is always supposed to be at least one nurse inside the neonatal care room. They are special needs babies, requiring constant care, especially as not all problems show up immediately after birth. Early this morning, we were short on personnel, and the nurse stepped out to retrieve something—which took only moments—and when she returned, the isolette with Baby Barrows number four was gone.''

''Matthew,'' he murmured. ''Someone rolling an isolette couldn't have gotten far without being seen.''

Annabelle Reardon, a delivery nurse, spoke up. ''We immediately had security posted at every exit we could cover. Unfortunately, at the hour that this occurred there are not many patients awake, and the hospital crews are a bit more understaffed. Particularly in this new wing, there are many empty rooms where someone could have hidden until they saw the hall was clear.''

''Someone knows something.'' Caleb thought about April, down in the nursery with the remaining three babies. She'd told him she'd watch over the infants, and he could investigate this latest turn of events. He admired that she came in focused and ready to do her part, and leave the searching to him and the officers on duty. She could have been frantic—which he knew she was, but trying to keep her panic at bay—and his attention would have been divided between Matthew's disappearance and her fear. ''My first thought is that a patient took the baby,'' he told Annabelle and Cherilyn.

''We have no one we're caring for at this time. Just those four Barrows babies,'' Cherilyn told him.

''In the main hospital, where the regular deliveries take place, there are many patients, though,'' Annabelle said.

''How do we find out if anyone recently had a pregnancy that might have ended unsatisfactorily?'' Caleb asked.

''As in a stillbirth?'' Annabelle asked.

''Possibly.''

''Well, the records of births are in the computer. To my knowledge, only one stillbirth occurred, and that was a week ago. A Mrs. Cannady, first child.''

''Okay,'' Caleb said. ''Let's start by having every single room of the main hospital searched. I'll check these rooms, although I don't think the kidnapper is here.''

"You don't think someone would harm baby Matthew?'' Cherilyn asked.

"No. I believe that someone heard about these quads on the news, and knows that the mother is missing. My guess is that someone desperately wants a child, and is figuring that here are four no one wants. She may even feel like she is doing Matthew a favor by keeping him from a life of foster care.'' He knew how apprehensive April was about foster care.

"I heard one of the officers say they needed to question April about this,'' Cherilyn said worriedly.

"Not a chance,'' Caleb said. "I might have thought the same thing, knowing April's fear of the system. However, I went home with her last night, and know for a fact she slept all night.''

"Oh-h-h,'' Annabelle and Cherilyn said together. He shook his head. "Not the way it sounds.''

"I suppose we should have known that,'' Annabelle said with a sigh. "Knowing April the way we do. Oh, well.''

They looked upon him so pityingly that Caleb realized they felt sorry for him, as if April had chewed him up and spat him out as date material.

"It's not quite that way, either. I was concerned about her and told her I was going to follow her home. She invited me in for a glass of orange juice, and I fell asleep on her sofa, where she tossed a couple of blankets over me and—'' He suddenly remembered the sensation of warmth covering him. For all the nights he couldn't sleep through the night, that gentle warmth had lulled him right back. April had covered him, not once, but twice.

"You were saying, Caleb?" Cherilyn prodded. "You fell asleep?"

He realized they were having some fun at his expense, but that was all right. "The details aren't important. Let's just leave it at the fact that Matthew isn't hidden in April's house, as much as she might like to have him. All of them."

Cherilyn shook her head. "I'd like to see that happen as well. But Social Services let her know fairly plainly that a one-parent family wouldn't be considered."

"I know." He nodded to both women. "I'm going to go check on her."

"Good idea," Annabelle said. "She doesn't know it, but she needs someone to think of her, at least until this is all over."

April hadn't let him do anything for her. In fact, *she'd* cared for him. There wasn't any way he could think of to get her to lean on him. Yet, everyone needed someone they could shift some emotional weight to from time to time.

He shifted his emotional weight to…no. No one, anymore. Once upon a time, Terry Jakes had been his partner. But now…he kept his emotions solely under wraps.

Walking to the nursery, he'd found April exactly where he knew she'd be. "April," he said softly, tapping against the glass to get her attention.

She looked up, put down the towel she was folding and came into the hall. "Hi."

"I shouldn't have said that you might have projected your dreams onto Jenny so that she began to see you as someone she could gift with her children. I'm sorry. When I'm thinking through angles, I let my mind go pretty much."

"Your mind was definitely gone at that point," April said wryly. "I didn't pay any attention to that nonsense you were spouting. Any man who falls asleep on my sofa after exercising his brain to that extent deserves a stiff back and a sore neck." Her eyes suddenly darkened. "Do you think Jenny came back?"

"And what? Stole her own son? For what purpose?"

"Well, I don't know. If I ascribe any reality to your nonsense, maybe she would take one and leave me three."

"Nah." He shook his head. "She wouldn't take the littlest one. Jenny had strong survival instincts in her for her children, or she wouldn't have left them to you. She's not back, much as I wish she was."

"Then where is Matthew?" April demanded, her voice high and shrill, almost a wail as she started weeping. "He needs to be in there with his brother and sisters, where I can make certain he's getting everything he needs!''

''Shh,'' he said, pulling her close to him so that she was enveloped against his chest. ''I have the main hospital being searched. That's where he'll be found.''

''How do you know?'' she asked, her voice watery.

''Because for every harebrained angle I come up with, I come up with one that's dead-on. Every time.''

She stared up at him, her shamrock-green eyes hopeful. ''You really think he's that close? I'll go search every room myself.''

He had to smile at her earnestness. There was nothing this lady wouldn't do for the children in her care. ''You stay here with the babies, and I'll do the searching. Okay?'' he asked, gently stroking her hair back from her face. ''Isn't that the way it's always been between the sexes? Woman nurtures, man hunts and protects.''

Her shoulders went stiff as she jerked out of his arms, just as he'd known she would. A devilish smile leaped onto his face. ''That's the lady I know, the one with the iron spine and the spirit of the Tartars.''

''The what?'' she demanded.

''Never mind. I've got a baby to locate. Although I'm expecting Matthew to return in his runaway isolette any moment now. Remember that in cases of newborns kidnapped from hospitals, they are almost always found quickly. Someone will notice when a new baby turns up unexpectedly somewhere.'' And then, because she looked so put out with him, he reached out and touched the side of her lips, gently turning one corner of her mouth up. ''Later on, I want you to smile for me, April.''

''Why?''

He laughed at her pugnacious question. ''Because you make me feel warm when you smile that big smile of yours.''

The wheels were turning in her head; he could nearly hear them whirring at full speed. She was trying to figure out exactly what he wanted from her, besides the smile.

But there was nothing he wanted.

Except, maybe, quite possibly, her.

He shut the voice out of his mind, told himself it would never work, and left to do a little detective work, something that never failed to put his mind on a single track.

This time it didn't work.

When this child is found, he vowed, *I'm going to offer April the only thing I have to give her: my protection. All these children can be under one roof, safe. In April's arms, safe. And together, safe.*

IT WASN'T THAT HARD to locate the baby. Caleb merely had to put himself in the shoes of a desperate person, likely female, likely recently disappointed in a birth process, and he headed to the main birth wing at Maitland Maternity.

A quick count at the nursery window showed ten newborns engaged in healthy squalling or being fed by attentive nurses. "I'm Caleb McCallum from the McCallum wing. Are these all the viable deliveries within the last twenty-four hours?" he asked a nurse.

"These are all of them. We only had one unsuccessful delivery—the placenta separated and caused problems."

"Where is the mother?"

"In her room, resting."

"Are you certain?"

The nurse's eyebrow shot up. "Come with me, Mr. McCallum."

Indeed, the mother was resting. Sitting up, she slept, at peace with the world, no doubt dreaming of happy moments she had waited for nine months to experience. One of her hands was in the plastic bassinet pulled up next to her bed, resting gently upon a sleeping baby's back.

Matthew.

"That baby shouldn't be in here," the nurse gasped.

Caleb put his hand on the nurse's arm. "It's all right," he said softly. "She hasn't done any real harm. If I were you, I'd talk to the head nurse about getting a grief counselor to this woman immediately."

"But the baby—"

"I'll take him back. He belongs in the McCallum wing."

"If you're certain—"

She clearly was not, as the whole situation was terribly out of order. But Caleb was more concerned about the grieving birth mother. "Let's put our focus on the mother. This baby has a lot of people cheering for him, but she…" His voice faltered as he looked back at the mother. All she'd wanted was to feel the precious skin of a child. Sometimes a simple touch could mean everything in a moment of despondency. "I'll get the baby."

As soon as he touched Matthew's bassinet, the mother's eyes snapped open. "It's okay," he said, putting his hand over hers. "I'm just going to take Matthew back to the nursery now. He needs special care." He massaged her fingers gently in his before moving her hand from the baby's back. "Thank you for watching over him."

"I just wanted to—"

"Shh. I know. Go back to sleep," he told her, his tone soothing. "You need special care and rest now, too."

"I didn't mean any harm, I just—"

"It's okay," he repeated reassuringly. "You're not in any trouble, but we do have to take Matthew back where he belongs. Right now, you need to rest." He smiled at her, focusing calm on her so that she would relax.

"Thank you," she whispered as she closed her eyes, exhausted.

"Go to sleep," he softly commanded, stealthily wheeling Matthew from the room.

The nurse followed in astonishment. "You handled that like a police officer talking a jumper off a bridge."

"Thanks," Caleb said grimly. "I'm taking Matthew back to McCallum." He rolled the isolette in front of him, his heart thundering as he stared at the tiny bundle of life, innocently unaware that his disappearance had caused an uproar. "Little man, back you go in your flying isolette. I know several people who are going to be delighted to see you, and one spicy little nurse in particular."

CALEB WASN'T CERTAIN where the idea came from. It hit in the split second after he wheeled Matthew beside the nursery window. The squeal of pure joy that left April's throat as she flew into the hall seared his brain with the fear she'd suffered, and he'd instantly thought, *I can do something about that.*

"April," he said as she prepared to wheel the bassinet into the nursery, "I think we ought to get married."

Chapter Five

In her overwhelming relief at having Matthew back, April wasn't certain she'd heard Caleb right when he spoke. Or maybe he was teasing. Concern was flying through her mind as her eager fingers touched Matthew's skin, checking him over as the nurse and the mother in her warred to know he was safe and sound; perhaps she'd missed the resonance in Caleb's flat comment. Men didn't deliver proposals the way he had, did they? And why would he want to marry her?

"I'm sorry, Caleb, I wasn't listening. Could you repeat that?"

A muscle twitched in his jaw; his Adam's apple jumped in his throat. "Maybe we ought to get married."

She searched his face for signs of teasing, reluctance, medication, *anything*. But his expression was genuine, his posture stiff.

He was *serious*.

"Let me put Matthew back into the nursery. I

want to change him, and get him where he can hear his brother and sisters. And then we'll talk. Okay?''

He nodded, and April wheeled the bassinet into the nursery, her heart thundering. *My first proposal. And I don't think it's because he's in love with me, either.*

Her hands shook as she fixed Matthew's diaper, and then checked the other babies. Making a notation on the charts, she counted to ten, tried to gather her courage and went out into the hall to meet Caleb.

''Where was he?'' she asked, unable to help herself.

''At Maitland. A mother had an unsuccessful pregnancy and was distraught. I'm guessing she crept down here during the early shift, when the desk wasn't fully staffed. She just wanted to touch a living, breathing baby, I believe, in order to save herself from—'' he blew out a breath ''—I don't know. Probably going around the bend.''

''Oh, poor thing,'' April said, her heart struck. ''I wouldn't want to be in her shoes. I mean, she shouldn't have done it, and technically, the hospital should—''

''Let's not go into technicalities right now. I asked you a question, April,'' he said.

She swallowed uncertainly, perceiving that he might have blurted out the question, surprising even himself, but she knew there was some strong reasoning behind it.

''Not that this is the first thing I thought I'd say

when I received my first proposal, but why?'' she asked him.

"You're not going to get temporary custody without a two-parent home. I'm willing to provide that."

"Why?" she asked again, unable to see where he was heading.

"Because I can. And I don't want them shuffled off, either. And it scared the hell out of me when Matthew was missing. If I have all five of you under one roof, I can...you know."

April cocked her head. "Protect us better?" she asked softly.

"Of course."

She sensed behind his brisk tone that he was hiding his feelings as much as she was. "I don't know what to say."

"It makes sense."

"Yes, in a strange sort of way. We'd have to file for emergency temporary custody. It's possible. But...that's an awful lot of adjustment for you, Caleb. Four babies, a wife, a very small house, diapers, crying, feeding—"

"I hope you don't cry too much," Caleb said. "As for feeding, there's always fast food. Cops are used to eating on the run."

"I meant the babies."

Caleb gave her an abashed grin. "I knew what you meant. I'm trying to inject some levity into a moment where my heart's about to leap out of my chest. I don't do much of anything without a lot of methodical thought, so I've just about used up my allotment of proposal courage.''

"Oh, that's sweet of you, Caleb," April said quietly. "Here comes your father."

To her astonishment, Caleb turned pale before her very eyes. *He really hasn't thought this through,* she realized.

And in a way, she liked the fact that he hadn't calculated what his proposal would mean in terms of turning his life upside down and inside out.

"Mr. McCallum, my best friend, your daughter, Bri, is not the only McCallum to marry, it seems. Your son has just asked me to marry him," April said to Jackson as he joined them in the viewing area.

"He has?" Jackson seemed stunned as his gaze riveted to their faces.

"Yes. I'd like to know what you think about that."

The elderly man eyed his son with some amazement. "That you're getting the short end of the stick, April, but if you think you can put up with him…" His attempt at teasing fell flat as his hope caught up inside him. He stared at Caleb. "I didn't know you were contemplating such a serious move."

Caleb shrugged. "I didn't, either. But the time feels right."

Jackson scratched his head, glancing at April.

"Um, how can I put this delicately? Is there—or will there be—a grandchild in the mix?"

Apparently, Jackson thought that there had been some nights of passion between April and Caleb, a quick fling even, and there were results for which to be accounted. April smiled at him, and then glanced toward the four babies in their isolettes. "We hope so. That's the main idea."

Jackson followed her gaze, then snapped his own to his son's face. Caleb stared back at him, unperturbed. Slowly, Jackson glanced at the babies, then brought his focus to the hint of a smile on April's face. "Oh, I see," he said softly. "I do see. Well, thank you for letting me in on the scheme. I'll do everything I can to help you."

He kissed April on both cheeks, his style old world, and April sensed he was being chivalrous in a moment that had totally knocked him off his feet. Clearing his throat, he said gruffly, "April, what I said about you getting the short end of the stick—" he glanced toward Caleb "—I'm very proud of my son. I don't always show it."

Her smile was understanding. "I know, Mr. McCallum."

"Jackson. You're going to be part of the family." He shook his son's hand, took April's hand in his, and as he stood in between them, keeping a tight hold on both, he looked through the nursery window. "Quadruplets," he said under his breath. "I'd better get busy!"

"Well, we don't have our hopes up too high," April said. "And rest assured that we will have a prenuptial agreement drawn up."

"Prenuptial agreement?" Caleb and Jackson echoed.

"Of course. In the event that…our situation doesn't come to fruition, I wouldn't want you to think that you have any lingering responsibilities for me. Or to me."

"A prenup is not necessary, April." Caleb looked stoney.

"I feel it is," she said, her tone quiet yet firm. "It's very important to me that all the expectations are known by everyone up front. I'm doing this for the children, not for me, or for you. You're giving me your name, and a marriage contract for a clear-cut reason, and I feel that I should treat it as such."

"Well, I don't think—" Caleb began.

"I think April has hit upon a very sensible arrangement, myself. After all, there are all my millions at stake, and a prenup would make me rest easier at night."

April smiled. "Precisely what I was thinking."

"Now, wait just a minute—" Caleb tried again.

"Caleb, can I see you in private?" Jackson asked. "Congratulations, April, I think this is a very satisfactory arrangement for everyone. I am delighted to welcome such a forward-thinking and intelligent woman into our family, for however long."

"Thank you, Jackson."

"If you'll excuse us…" Caleb said reluctantly.

"Of course." April smiled at him, and walked back into the nursery, touching each child with fingers that gently, firmly pressed their skin. So that they would know she was there. And that she loved them.

JACKSON FAIRLY DRAGGED his son into the Austin Eats diner next to the hospital. "I don't have to tell you how happy I am about this, son."

Caleb sank into a booth. "I'm not certain what I am."

"Look. Let the prenup thing go. The girl is obviously independent, and wants us to know she doesn't expect anything from us."

"From me, Dad, she's marrying *me*."

"Not exactly. When you marry someone, you marry the in-laws too, Caleb. And that means *me*— and my money, about which she's trying to reassure me. I say give April her breathing room. Who cares about the prenup?"

"I do. I don't think a marriage starts well with a road map. You and Mom didn't have one."

"Well, your mother was a delicate little flower who did everything I wanted and lived to please me. I haven't married again because I'll never find that kind of devotion."

"April's a delicate flower—"

"Not really, son. She got that spine of independence from somewhere. I say, tell her our lawyer will draw up the prenup, and then, I suspect you two will be so busy that she'll forget that the lawyer doesn't get around to it.''

Caleb frowned. ''Are you saying we'll trick her?''

''No, I'm saying that I don't think we really need to go to the trouble with this gal. If you don't get the children, and you decide not to stay together, you'll just annul the marriage. Right?''

He didn't want to think about that scenario—it meant admitting that April might not get temporary custody of the children, and it meant she might not want to stay with him if she didn't. He really didn't like that thought.

''I don't think I like it, Dad.''

''Look.'' Jackson blew out a breath and scratched his white-maned head. ''Ever since your mom was gone, you've wanted reassurance from everyone that they weren't going to leave you. You didn't realize it, but that's what you were doing. When your partner died, you took it hard, which is natural, especially since you blamed yourself. But you never got over it because it was a piece of yourself you couldn't hang on to. That's left over from your mom's death. I've stayed a little aloof from you over the years because I was worried about how you'd take it if I up and croaked. You took your mother's death harder than the other kids, Caleb.''

''There was a reason for that,'' Caleb said on a growl.

''I know. I know. Self-induced guilt,'' Jackson

said. "But it's time you let go, son, and realize that you can't hold on to people so tight. You're gonna scare this little girl, because all she wants is to think she's always gonna have her independence. You see how this is a recipe for sure disaster?"

A glimmer of recognition was starting to intrude in his brain, and Caleb didn't want to let it in. "Not really."

"Okay." Jackson put the saltshaker in the middle of the table. "This is April. She's salty and independent because she's had to be that way. This is you," he said, placing the pepper shaker next to April the saltshaker. "You want to share the same space with her, but you can't. You can't go on watermelon, you can't go in ice cream, you can't go in cookies."

"You are making no sense at all."

"You can't make the pepper go where the salt wants to every time, or you'll ruin the recipe," Jackson said, out of patience. "Isn't there a rock song that has to do with if you love something, you gotta let it go? She wants her independence; you can't hold on to her so tightly. Pretend the prenup is okay with you, and she'll appreciate you for it, Caleb. It's the first thing you can do that shows April you're not going to try to squash her with overbearing solicitousness."

Caleb shook his head at his father. "I want to take care of her. That's my end of the bargain."

"And she doesn't want you to," Jackson said

stubbornly. "You can't hold on to everything with both fists, son. Life is fleeting, like water in your hands."

"All right," Caleb finally said on a sigh. "I'll try not to squish her."

"Squash."

"Whatever. Oh, jeez, I can't believe this."

"Well, I never got around to the birds-and-the-bees talk with you when you were a teen, so now I figure having a chat that keeps you from putting your big foot on top of your newly budding engagement makes up for it."

The waitress came to their table. Jackson ordered chicken and mushroom chowder, and Caleb ordered a cheeseburger—not that he really had any appetite.

"You know, Caleb, it's probably time for you to let that bag of guilt go, especially before you get married."

"What bag of guilt?" Caleb demanded, certain he didn't want to have this conversation.

"About your mom." Jackson looked out the window at the hospital for a moment, then brought his gaze back to his son. "There isn't a week that goes by that I don't think maybe it was my fault. I knew she was a fragile little thing. But, Caleb, babies were what your mom wanted. It's what made her happy. Her health never entered her mind, not by the doctor's caution or my worrying."

He stared at his son. "Think about that. I had the chance to say, 'Have a selective elimination procedure.' But I didn't, because three was what God had given her, and that's what she wanted. Yet, also a single day never went by in our children's childhoods where I didn't think why her? Why not me? She was the one who wanted these babies, she carried them, she worked for them, she endured the pain to carry and deliver them. And then she never got to enjoy the blessings she so dreamed of.''

Caleb thought about the suffering woman in the hospital who had felt the same way. It was almost as if, for one split second he'd seen his mother in her. Tears pricked the corners of his eyes. Impatiently, he rubbed at them, demanding that they retreat.

''Great gravy, son, if anyone should have been feeling guilty, it was me. But no little innocent baby had anything to do with her death.''

Caleb sighed as the waitress put their food in front of them. ''April is very delicate, too.''

''Yes, and you can't do a damn thing about that. If you love her, then accept that she has to make some choices for herself, and you gotta let her.''

He stared into his father's compassionate gaze. ''All right,'' he said finally. ''I'll bow to your wisdom and experience on this one.''

Jackson nodded slowly, his gaze appreciative and empathetic, too, and for the first time in his life, Caleb felt a bond growing between them.

''So, how long is this supposed to last?'' Jackson asked.

"We discussed filing for emergency temporary custody until the birth mother returns. April really believes that since Jenny left them to her, it's up to her to keep the babies from being parceled out among strangers."

"I couldn't agree more." He was thoughtful for a moment. "You know, son, if you go slowly, bit by bit, this marriage agreement might stick longer than April plans for it to."

"I don't think I should expect more from it than I know it to be, Dad."

Jackson waved that away. "I didn't say anything about expecting. I said, if you go slowly and gently, treading lightly, she just might learn to trust you. And then to love you."

"You make it sound so easy."

His father shrugged. "If anyone can put themselves in April's place, I'd put my money on you. Bit by bit, son. No leaping tall buildings in a single bound. Just a nice, slow walk holding each other's hand can conquer a path of great resistance."

Jackson took a spoonful of soup, and then as an afterthought, stared at his son. "She *did* say yes, didn't she? Or did she just give us a bunch of qualifications?"

APRIL'S HEART was still fluttering over Caleb's surprise proposal when she left work. She hadn't even mentioned it to Cherilyn or Bri, she was that rattled.

When she saw Caleb walking toward her in the

parking lot, bearing florist-wrapped long-stemmed roses, her heart went into full-speed motion sickness. "You really mean it," she said when he came abreast of her.

"Of course. No man fools around with the M-word unless he means it."

"Oh…" Shyly, she buried her nose among the red, satiny blooms of the roses. "They're lovely. Thank you."

"I was afraid maybe I didn't hear you accept me," Caleb said, his face serious. "If you hadn't yet, I thought I'd better do a little better in the convincing department." And he pulled out a jeweler's box, handing it to her opened, so she could see the lovely emerald-shaped diamond inside. "Four sides to this stone, four babies in our lives. I hope you'll say yes, April."

She nearly dropped the roses. Heck, she thought she was going to faint. "Caleb! You don't have to give me a ring! It's just something I have to give back once Jenny returns."

"No." He shook his head, staring into her eyes. "It's for you, April. You gave me a gift I've wanted all my life, the beginning of a relationship with my father. We're actually relating to each other rather than not relating at all. This is yours, no strings attached. No prenup needed for this." And taking the ring from the box, he slipped it onto her finger. "Besides, we want everyone to believe that we're in love, and ready to be a happy family of six."

"Oh, Caleb." Surprised tears jumped into her eyes. "I have said yes, haven't I? Because if I haven't, *yes*. And thank you so much for taking up my cause. You're the knight I hadn't expected, and you can't possibly know how much it means to me."

They looked at each other for a few moments, awkwardly. April wondered if he was going to kiss her, or if she should just reach up and kiss him.

In the end, that's what she did.

And when he wrapped his arms around her, heedless of the roses, April realized this big, strong man had given her a gift she'd wanted all her life, too.

Babies of her very own.

Even if it was only temporary.

Chapter Six

"I suppose I shouldn't have done that," April said, pulling away, immediately aware of strange longings rushing through her, longings that had nothing to do with wanting to stop at a friendly kiss. The moment their lips touched and he wrapped his arms around her to enclose her against his chest, her brain had instantly responded *Oh, yes, oh my stars, yes.*

What her mind and body were saying yes to was so much different than what she'd expected to want from Caleb. It was best if she remembered that this was pretend. Their relationship had a goal: the well-being of four children.

"It was fine by me," Caleb said, his hands in his jeans pockets, looking incredibly handsome for a man she didn't want to recognize in this sexy manner. His gaze was level, open and intense. Very aware of her as a woman.

Shivers claimed her skin; her nipples tightened, and the most feminine area of her body went warm with desire.

I'm in way over my head with this man.

She calmed herself with rationale. There really wasn't any rhyme or reason for her to get sidetracked by Caleb's enormous capacity for making her feel like a treasured doll. She knew all about collecting and caretaking of wonderful things. Yet she also knew from painful experience that her heartstrings snapped long before any man managed to get her down the aisle in a real wedding. The only way she'd manage to get through this wedding was because it was fake. A faux fiancé. She couldn't bend enough to allow a man to take care of her, as if she were a collectible doll. Being forced to learn to rely solely upon herself was a blessing in many ways; yet it had also left her with the inability to structure a lasting relationship.

This one wouldn't be any different—unless it remained a masquerade for Social Services.

So why had her heart jumped like a heartbeat on a monitor when he'd kissed her? She'd nearly melted into a feminine puddle of desire—and she had a funny feeling he was completely aware that he'd had her guard down for a split second.

Like the time she'd caught him staring at her posterior. It was a crack in his armor, and she'd kind of liked seeing him check her out.

By the fiery burn in his gaze, she was pretty certain he was enjoying this crack in *her* armor.

"I have to go," she murmured swiftly, holding

the roses in front of her like a shield. ''Thank you, Caleb. For everything.''

She made her escape as quickly as she could, totally aware that she was running like a scared rabbit that flees, uncertain as to what it's fleeing from, but the scent of danger hurrying it ever faster.

April couldn't get to the shelter of her home fast enough.

THERE WERE A FEW THINGS Caleb knew for certain after April's impulsive kiss. She'd been touched by the ring, if only for the sake of the ruse they were perpetrating. She wasn't immune to him. Her lips felt like a dream under his, soft and supple and clinging, the way he liked a woman's lips to be.

And she was scared to death of liking him. This marriage was all about the babies, and there was no subtle trap waiting to spring its jaws on him. She wasn't marrying him with the notion that she needed a husband, or that the situation was a good way to rope him blindly into something long-term.

Oh, no. She'd innocently kissed him, and been very startled by the blaze that had very nearly erupted. He'd felt her tremble in his arms.

That tremble had told him everything a man needed to know about a woman. She was attracted to him—and she was going to fight her feelings every step of the way.

He'd just have to help her make up her mind to

allow him to kiss her again and this time not cut it so dramatically short. *The next time I kiss her, she won't go running from my arms. She'll stay—because she wants to.*

Chapter Seven

There wasn't a moment to waste. As soon as the mandatory blood tests had been reviewed and the marriage license waiting period ended, Caleb McCallum married April Sullivan in a quiet court-house ceremony performed in a justice of the peace's chambers.

All the while, April's heart was in her throat. Caleb held her hand despite the delicate bouquet of white roses she clutched. She could feel a tiny pulse in his thumb.

The moment felt all too real to her for something that was supposed to be simulated. She was certain her skin could not have felt more moist, her pulse more erratic, if this was a wedding for keeps.

Jackson looked so proud of his son. Though it was a daytime ceremony during courthouse hours—noon, before the courthouse closed for New Year's—he wore an elegantly formal charcoal-gray suit, with a black-and-white striped tie so satiny it could have complemented a tux. Caleb wore a suit strikingly similar, which made his short dark hair and hazel eyes stand out richly.

He's so incredibly handsome, April thought. *And so giving.*

Between Caleb and Jackson, she felt as if she would be well protected. It was clear they were determined to take care of her, a thought that both comforted and worried her.

Bri looked fetching in a short pink dress, suitable for tonight's New Year's Eve dinner at the Mc-Callum mansion. Jackson had insisted the whole family get together for dinner to celebrate both the wedding and the new year. *A wedding and a new year—we'll ring them in together,* he'd said.

April felt a tiny chip of reluctance drop from her heart as Adam gave Caleb a brotherly pound of congratulations on the shoulder when the ceremony ended.

And then Bri kissed her cheek, murmuring, "I never thought I'd see this day, and I couldn't be any happier, even if that was the shortest dating period in history. One night. Wow."

April embraced her new sister-in-law, remembering all the times she had thought Bri was the closest thing to a sister she'd ever have. And now she was—for a while.

Caleb, Jackson and April had agreed not to tell anyone that the marriage was short-term, a means to an end, in case Social Services might get wind of the posthaste wedding and decide to question the circumstances.

"Thank you, Bri," April said, hugging her tightly as she told the tears at the corners of her eyes to stay in place.

"You've made my father so happy," Bri said. "He thought Caleb would turn to stone before he allowed anyone to get close to him."

April separated herself from her best friend and now sister. Caleb put his arm around her. "Mrs. McCallum," he said, his voice unsteady, "you look wonderful."

She felt a blush tint her cheeks as she looked up at him. Not for anything would she admit that when she'd tried on this short wedding dress in a vintage clothing store, she'd been struck by its simplicity and charm. It had a short fingertip veil as well, but she'd left that at home, content to make do with the fifties-style wedding gown. The style wasn't incongruous in a courthouse, yet she felt very fairy-tale princess. The dress had been a bit pricey for her budget, but she'd bought it anyway, something in her heart wanting very much for Caleb not to be disappointed in his bride.

"I'm glad you think so," she said nervously, wondering if she could be any more unsettled if this moment were the real thing. "You're very handsome, too."

Caleb winked at her. "Did you expect anything else?"

Bri popped him lightly on the shoulder. "Behave, or April might change her mind."

"She can't. She's mine, fair and square."

Ringing began in April's ears, running through her brain. Her hands began to tremble, and her stomach pitched. "I think I'll get a drink of water," she said breathlessly, heading toward the courtroom exit.

The rows of the courthouse were full of strangers, but April paid them no attention as she hurried past. She had to get out of there fast, before she began to get lost somewhere between the reason and the reality of her new situation.

"Slow down, April," Caleb said, catching up to her and taking her hand in his.

They were outside the main courtroom now, and she could take in more than a stifled breath of air.

"Was it getting to you?" Caleb asked.

"A little," April admitted. "I didn't expect it to feel so real! All your family, I mean, I didn't even think to ask my mom and dad because this is just pretend. I wasn't even planning to tell them, and now I feel horrible, like I've left them out of something really important."

"Focus, April," he whispered against her hair. "Day after tomorrow, we file an emergency application with Social Services. That starts the interviewing process, I'm certain. Meanwhile, I'll be hunting Jenny for all I'm worth. You'll be back at work keeping an eye on the little muffins, and all will be good."

An unbridelike sniffle escaped her. "You're right, of course."

"Of course I am." Patting her back as he held her close to him, he said, "Pull yourself together and act like a happy bride or Bri is going to yell at me. All right?" he asked gently, wiping the tears from the sides of her eyes.

"You're an annoyingly confident male, do you know that?" she asked, pushing his hands away so she could wipe her own face, but smiling at him just the same.

"I expect to hear you say that many times in the course of our short marriage. And if you're worried about your folks, why don't you and I go by and get them and have them to Dad's house for dinner?"

"Would he mind?" April asked.

"He'd be delighted. He asked me if your parents were coming today, and I told him we hadn't discussed it. I didn't know how you'd want to handle it."

"Well, I just can't all of a sudden be up and living with you, I guess," April said. "They'd wonder when I'd met you."

"They're going to wonder anyway, since we're married. We'll have to tell them we eloped to save on money."

April laughed. "You think of everything, don't you?"

"Every angle, lady, and any angle can be promising. Now come back with me before Jackson thinks I've got a runaway bride on my hands.''

She smiled, feeling better now that her head had cleared. ''I'm better now.''

''I hope so,'' Caleb said, taking her hand in his. ''Because if you freaked out thinking the wedding was real, us living under the same roof may be shaky.''

''As little shaking as possible,'' she reminded him.

''That's right. I just wanted to see if you remembered.''

She remembered, all right. It almost dimmed the beauty of the marital vows they'd just spoken.

THE ENORMITY OF WHAT he and April had done came rolling in on Caleb as they drove up in the driveway of the Sullivans' small home. He'd married her—and never given a thought to asking her father for her hand.

Of course, that's because their marriage agreement had been fast, and tied to four young babies. But if he'd been marrying her for real, he would have asked her father's permission first.

Walking in to a stranger's house and announcing he was now family was going to be fairly wild for a man who didn't like change.

''Why am I suddenly feeling apprehensive?'' he asked out loud.

''Same reason I felt apprehensive after your family began congratulating me?'' April guessed. "It feels like we're lying.''

"We *are* posturing, but in the most honorable sense.''

"I guess there's such a thing. I'm telling myself this is okay. But I think my parents are going to be so...well, so surprised.''

"Unpleasantly so.''

"Maybe. They couldn't have children, and so they adopted me, and they've kind of lived vicariously through me. And they're older, quite a bit older than your father.''

"Well,'' he said, sighing, "we'll sound cracked if we tell them we did this in the hopes that we can foster four children until I can find the birth mother.''

April bit her lip. He wanted to lay a finger against her soft skin to stop her, but if he did, he'd probably start kissing her, and then they'd never get inside the house. "I didn't kiss you after we got married,'' he said suddenly.

"No, you didn't. I assumed it was because we were in the justice's chambers.''

Caleb shook his head. "No, I think I was worried about you because I could feel you trembling.''

"I could feel the pulse in your thumb,'' she said, giving him a cautious look. "I think you were nervous.''

"If you felt my thumb right now, you'd *know* I'm nervous.'' An elderly gentleman came out onto the porch to stare at their car. Caleb took a deep breath as the man waved to them, and without further hesitation, he got out of the Acura.

"You coming in or not?" April's adoptive father shouted.

Hard-of-hearing, Caleb guessed. "Yes, sir," he called back loudly. "Let me get April."

Opening April's car door, he helped her out. "Did I tell you you're stunningly beautiful?" he whispered urgently.

"No, you didn't, but thanks." She hurried up the slate steps to kiss her father. "Hi, Daddy."

"April, love. You should have let us know you were bringing a gentleman by. We would have had some supper for him."

Her mother came out on the porch as well, looking with pride at April's beautiful dress. "My, don't you look lovely, April. And your gentleman friend is so handsome."

"Thanks, Mom, Dad." April glanced at Caleb, and he shrugged at her. The twitch in his thumb had moved to his eye, and he was pretty certain that, if they didn't get on with the big announcement and whatever reaction was due him, he was going to have a tic for life.

"Well, bring him in," her mother told her. "Please do come in, Mr.—"

"Mom, this is Caleb McCallum," April said quickly. "Caleb, this is my mother, Donna, and my father, Webb."

"Well, bring him in, April. We don't want him to think we're rude the first time your friend meets us."

Caleb held the door open for the two fragile people. April lingered to whisper, "This is not going to be easy."

"I wasn't signed on for easy, remember. I'm okay with it," he said, not one hundred percent truthful but telling himself a brave front could make up for the percentage he was fibbing. "When this is all over, I'll let you kiss me."

April ignored that.

Donna perched on a green velvet antique sofa, and Webb gestured to a rocking chair for Caleb. That left no place for April and him to sit together, which might have been her father's intention. He wasn't certain. April went to sit by her mother, who clasped her hand.

"You see, Mom, Dad," she said, swallowing. Caleb could tell she was nervous. "Caleb and I got married today."

Both the Sullivans stared at Caleb.

The room went deathly quiet.

"Why?" Donna asked.

Caleb stared at their hopeful faces, realizing that they wanted a reassuring explanation. Hopes and dreams lay in their curious eyes as both parents waited patiently. April was the child they'd adopted late in her childhood, late in their life. They wanted to know that he loved their only child.

He thought about the way he'd wanted to find Bri's boyfriend and make him marry his sister when he'd learned she was pregnant.

Caleb wanted to know that Bri would be loved. Bri wouldn't tell anyone the name of the father of her babies. Hunter Callaghan had come to the wing to become its administrator and reunited with Bri. He thought about the immature writing of Jenny's note, as she left her children to the one person she knew would love them.

What the Sullivans wanted badly to hear was so understandable, so normal, that it had him sweating in his suit. His shirt collar felt stiff as he swallowed.

"Because I love her," he said.

APRIL GASPED at Caleb's unexpected pronouncement. Her mother clasped her hands together with delight. "Oh, I couldn't be happier," she said with sparkly tears in her eyes. "I can't tell you how we've waited, hoping that a young gentleman would see all the gifts April has to offer a man. Webb and I were so afraid we'd pass on before the right man discovered our special girl." Donna got up to cross to the rocker, taking Caleb's hands in hers. "Welcome to the family," she said to Caleb, kissing his cheek.

Webb gruffly cleared his throat. "Yes. Welcome to the family."

"Wait. I've got something for you, April." Donna rushed from the room, returning a second later with a cameo. "It was my mother's on her wedding day, and mine when I married Webb, and now it's yours." Gently, she clasped the antique necklace around April's neck. "And doesn't that go just beautifully with her hair?" she proudly asked Caleb.

April flushed, still overcome by his declaration. He didn't mean it, did he? Love was not in their agreement. Of course he didn't love her. He was merely trying to make her elderly parents happy.

"Just think, Webb," Donna said happily. "We could even be grandparents before we pass on. Wouldn't that be a miracle?"

April leaned back against the high-backed sofa as she caught Caleb's eye. She was expecting a wink of job-well-done or something of the sort, but his expression was so solemn that it made her uncomfortable.

"And you love him, too, April?" Webb asked. "This marriage is what you wanted?"

How could she lie to her parents? They both stared at her so hopefully, waiting for her to say that this was the man she had waited for all her life, this was the man who made her dreams come true. After all their love and care in raising her, she'd found the man who could give her what they wanted her to have.

Caleb watched her, and if she didn't know better, she'd think he was holding his breath. His tie looked tight on his neck.

"Yes," she said, her whole being miserable.

Chapter Eight

"You said it first," April told Caleb in the car after they'd left her parents' house. Donna and Webb weren't used to getting out much, and the cold weather seemed an invitation to light rain and slick streets, so they'd declined to come to the party at Jackson's house. "You said it, which made *me* have to say it."

Caleb snorted. "I haven't had much practice with in-laws. I couldn't let them down."

"I couldn't, either," April said. She stared out the window at the streets that seemed hard with the freeze.

"I thought they took our marriage well." He glanced at her, noting that her face was strained. "And we get to fake it for my family tonight, and the hospital staff tomorrow, and after that, Social Services. Piece of cake."

"My parents will be so disappointed when we divorce."

He scratched the back of his neck as he braked at

a stop sign. April's low voice told him she was wondering if she'd made a mistake. And maybe they had. "Are you regretting our marriage?"

"I don't think so." She sighed, stretching her arms around her knees. "I'm not regretting it at all for the babies, if we can keep them together. I do feel a little sorry for my folks. They had their own dreams for me."

The intersection was clear of cars, so he moved the Acura forward. He didn't suffer April's worries, because his father was in on the "scheme," as Jackson had called it. Clear as anything, Caleb had read the Sullivans' hopes, too. They wanted the prince to come riding up for their daughter, and reassure them that in their old age, they had nothing to worry about where she was concerned. She'd be loved, and taken care of, and swept off to his castle.

He didn't have a castle. And he wasn't much of a prince.

"Do you want to talk about living arrangements?" he asked, trying to get her mind off her parents. "Now that we're getting the big stuff out of the way, maybe we ought to talk about the incidentals, such as keeping up a good front."

"You could…move into my house."

The dollhouse? "Do you think that's a good idea?" he asked carefully.

"Well, we can't raise four babies in an apartment. I mean, we can, but there's no reason, since I have a house. And a yard for them to play in."

He frowned. "I don't know if I can live in your house."

"I don't know if you can, either," April said. "You're going to have to get a futon or a rollaway."

"A futon?" he yelped.

"You won't fit into my bed, unless you're lying right on top of me."

"Well, now, there's an idea."

"No. There is not an idea." April shook her head to discourage such notions, even though she knew he'd been teasing her—to a point. But it was a point she didn't even want to bring into the conversation. "We said nothing about marital relations when we discussed the prenup."

"Wait a minute. The prenup was about money, wasn't it?"

"That, among other things. The prenup is about independence, you see."

Caleb pulled up in front of the McCallum mansion, parked the car, turned off the engine and turned to look at her. "I do not see."

"I keep my house, you keep your apartment. You keep your car, I keep mine. You get a futon, I sleep alone. Independence."

He blinked. "Forever?"

"Caleb, you're not really my husband."

She looked confused but beautiful in her innocence—white gown and pretty, upswept hair. Caleb wasn't sure how long he could live with her without being driven mad. "Maybe I should stay in my own apartment."

"You could," April said brightly. "At least until we find out if we get the babies."

"You don't want me with you at your house, do you?"

Her eyes softened as she looked at him. "I'm not sure I do."

"I promise to put the lid down on the toilet and the cap back on the toothpaste."

"Why do you *want* to stay in my house?"

He couldn't say for sure; he was only teasing her right now because he could tell she was resisting him so badly. "You're worried that I'm going to try to claim my husbandly rights."

"Oh, for heaven's sakes!" She crossed her arms and stared forward through the windshield. "I kissed *you,* if you recall, not the other way around."

"So you did." He wound the slight tendril that had escaped her hairdo around his finger. "And I liked it."

Her lips twitched with reluctance. "I didn't."

Gently, he tugged the tendril. "That is the second fib you've told today."

"It's the third. I said I'd love you and cherish you and keep you, or something to that effect. And we know that's not going to happen."

"Well, you're turning into a real dishonest young bride." He tsk-tsked her. "Maybe you're being dishonest about the reason you don't want me to stay in your house.''

''There really isn't any reason for it, is there? You probably watch wrestling. I'd go mad.''

''You'd probably want me to mow the yard and learn how to make string pot holders. *I'd* go mad.''

That made her laugh, and he moved his finger from her hair to the back of her bare neck, stroking lightly. ''It's happened fast, but it doesn't have to be fast between us, April.''

She turned to look at him. ''Do you mean it?''

''Of course. I know what my role in this charade is.''

''It's not a charade. You're kind to try to help me.''

''I like it when you're grateful,'' he teased. ''It makes me want to kiss you.''

''Caleb!'' She flicked his hand from her neck, but her tone wasn't angry.

''I think I know what you're worried about,'' he said quietly. ''And I'm not going to expect you to become 'my woman,''' he said, the final words in a gruff, manly tone.

''Your woman?''

''Yeah. Kind of like the caveman days. I promise not to drag you off by the hair and—that's why you won't come to my apartment, isn't it? You're afraid to leave your safe little nest to come to my cave.''

A charming moment of hesitation gave her away. ''*No,*'' she denied vehemently.

"Yes you are! April Sullivan-McCallum," he said, sticking a hand under her ribs to tickle her, "your nose is growing a foot. You're afraid I'm going to sweep you off your feet, carry you off to my cave and ravish you."

Her pert nose went into the air as she caught his hand in hers, stilling him. "I cannot be swept, carried or ravished."

His eyebrow lifted. "Why not?"

"I won't allow it." And she opened the car door, hurrying to the mansion door, her white puffy skirt billowing in the cold New Year's Eve breeze.

"Is this a battle-of-the-sexes kind of thing?" he called after her, slamming the door as he followed. "Mrs. McCallum, I promise never to encroach upon your emotional territory. That's a vow I can keep."

She waited for him on the long porch. "You told my parents you loved me. That made *me* have to say it."

"Yes, but it made them so happy." Taking her face between his palms, he captured her lips in a surprise kiss.

"Oh," Bri exclaimed as she suddenly opened the door. "You *do* love her, don't you, Caleb? I did wonder, but then I could tell you did in the courthouse. It was written all over your face!"

Now he was trapped, fair and square. Bri's expression was so delighted. He couldn't bear to disappoint her. April stared up at him, her emerald eyes huge, and he could feel her holding her breath.

Well, this whole conversation was about independence. Little Miss Freedom was determined to keep him at bay, with a prenup and any other thing she could think of.

But he was holding her now and that's what made this New Year's Eve moment so special. He had her face in his hands, and his sister waiting for an answer. "Yes," he said softly, his voice warm and meaningful. "Yes, I believe I do." And he lowered his lips to hers, kissing her much longer than he knew she would want, and reveling in that knowledge. "I forgot to do that at the courthouse," he said, explaining the kiss in a way April couldn't refute in front of Bri.

Her eyes snapped sparks at him, but he'd felt a slight response in her supple lips.

"Well, don't stand out there all night kissing her, Caleb," Bri said, laughing. "She's going to become the ice princess. Even though April looks like there's no place she'd rather be than on that porch with you. But come on, you two. There's time enough for that later."

April followed Bri inside, and he could almost feel the indignation in his bride as she stiffly walked, her knee-length, bell-shaped skirt snapping from side to side.

He was starting to think that warming up an ice princess might be challenging. He loved a challenge.

In the drawing room the whole clan waited until Caleb and April entered to erupt into approving applause. Astonished, April halted, so he took her hand in his to steady her. "Smile," he said. "We're in love."

"When you say it, I end up having to say it, so I wish you'd quit!" she complained under her breath.

"Were you a flop in high-school theater?" he asked, also under his breath as he nodded his thanks for his family's compliment to his bride.

Glasses of champagne were lifted high to them as a butler passed by offering April and Caleb a flute. Adam called out, "Here's to Mr. and Mrs. Caleb McCallum. May they be happy all their lives, and enjoy the fullest fruits of marriage!"

If April turned any redder, Caleb thought, she would match the berries in the Christmas holly. "You're cute when you're caught," he told her.

"You're annoying when you're full of yourself."

He lifted his flute, clinking hers. They drank at the same time. "Don't throw the glass," he said with a wink.

"At you?" she asked sweetly.

"Into the fireplace. If you want to throw something, we'll have a pillow fight later. In your house, where I'm going to walk in every night and call, 'Honey, I'm home!'"

"You're going to learn to love that futon," she said as he swung her into a dance when soft waltz music started.

But he didn't answer. Her waist was tiny in his

hand, and she was beautiful, and not afraid of his admittedly somewhat overbearing cop personality, and...despite all their squaring off of territory, he couldn't remember the last time he'd felt so happy.

That was the way he always wanted to remember this New Year's.

Happy.

JUST BEFORE the stroke of midnight, Bri pushed Caleb and April under the mistletoe, which had been hanging in the big den since before Christmas.

He playfully shooed Bri away. Then, knowing April was uncomfortable standing under the green-leafed token to encourage kissing while his family watched them, he said for April's ears alone, "Make a wish. A wish for the new year."

"I wish with all my heart that you find Jenny," she said quietly as he took her into his arms to the satisfied, happy laughter of his family. "Yours?"

"The same," he said, lowering his face to hers as his family counted, "Three, two, one! Happy New Year, everyone!"

The family began singing auld lang syne, crackers were pulled, kisses enthusiastically exchanged—and none of it registered to Caleb as he finally kissed April, his bride.

Bride for a while.

APRIL WAS EXHAUSTED, as Caleb had to be as well. It had been a fast week, and no doubt they were both still suffering the aftereffects of the tension of Matthew being missing, and then jumping into tonight's wedding.

The electricity that snapped between them constantly was wearing, too. Possibly she'd had too much champagne to drink as she tried to act the joyful new bride.

Caleb's kiss at the stroke of midnight had taken the last of her reserve of energy to protest. It felt so good when he kissed her. She didn't mind when he slipped his hand through hers and tugged her to the front door. His family tossed birdseed on them as she and Caleb ran to the car. Caleb helped April into the seat, then got in the driver's side and switched the car on to warm it.

"How about a honeymoon suite tonight?" he asked.

She looked at him, surprised.

Shrugging, he said, "Maybe it's a good compromise for us until we figure out what we're doing. I don't really look forward to a futon on my wedding night, even if tonight is 'just for looks.' Your sofa is fine, but..."

"A honeymoon suite just to sleep in?"

"Dad said he knew my brother and sister would ask where we intended to spend our honeymoon. Since we're not really having one, Dad fobbed them off with an excuse about our busy work schedules. Bri moaned that it wasn't very romantic, and that she couldn't bear the thought of us just going back to your house or my apartment after the wedding. Dad decided to try to put her mind at rest, and made reservations at a hotel just minutes outside of Austin as his wedding gift. I told you my sister has romantic rocks in her head,'' he said with a grin. ''But I think staying in a hotel tonight is probably a good idea, anyway.''

''Why?''

''I think it might be a good way to keep things from being awkward.''

April considered that, admitting to herself that she was feeling anxious about their partnership. Maybe she might be less so if she weren't so aware of Caleb as an attractive male—her senses tightened her body like wire every time he touched her. ''Well, it *would* save us from having to debate sleeping arrangements. We could even get separate rooms at the hotel. Bri would never know.'' She waited for his reaction to her offer, wondering if he was as apprehensive about tonight as she was. There were definite undercurrents of attraction between them—and it was probably best to try to ignore them.

''Okay,'' Caleb said. ''We'll take Dad up on his offer. And Bri said she and Adam loaded some wedding gifts in the trunk for us. We can open those later.''

''Definitely later.'' April turned her head to stare out the window, hiding her feelings of swift and startling disappointment. ''In fact, we should just save them so that your brother and sister can return them to the store after we get a divorce,'' she said, telling herself that was a rational plan.

''That's an idea.''

But April wasn't watching, so she missed the sudden worried look on Caleb's face.

TWENTY MINUTES LATER, April was awakened by Caleb saying her name. ''Nurse Sullivan-McCallum,'' he said in an official-sounding voice.

''Not funny,'' April replied, sitting up to tuck some wisps back into her upswept hair. ''For just a minute, I thought I'd fallen asleep at the hospital and you were a doctor who'd caught me dozing.''

''We're here. Let's go check in and I'll carry you to your room. But not over the threshold.''

''I can walk, but thank you for trying to be such a gentleman.'' She got out of the car, waiting for him to meet her. They hurried inside the lobby, going straight to the desk.

''We're Mr. and Mrs. Caleb McCallum,'' he told the desk clerk. ''We have a reservation.''

The clerk checked the computer. ''Ah. The honeymoon suite. Right away, sir.''

''We'd prefer two single rooms, if that's possible,'' April told the man, standing up on her toes so that she could see over the high, elaborate desk better.

The clerk eyed her wedding attire with a carefully studied glance. ''I'm sorry, ma'am. The conference that's here has taken all the rooms except the honeymoon suite. You were lucky to get that.''

April sank back onto her heels. "Oh, I see."

"It's quite large," the desk clerk said suddenly, his face noncommittal. "I'm certain you'll find that the spacious accommodations will suit your needs."

She blushed, and Caleb took the key from the helpful man. "Thanks." He tucked it into his pocket, took April by the hand to drag her across the marble floor to the elevator, punched the button, and when the doors opened, swept her up into his arms and carried her into the elevator.

April could see the clerk staring over the counter, his studied expression gone, his mouth wide open.

"Why did you do that?" April demanded, staring up at Caleb as her heart began a nervously thrilled hammering.

"You said you couldn't be swept, carried or ravished. I have now swept you off your feet." The doors brushed open, and he purposefully carried her down the hall with long strides. "I have now carried you."

"Caleb—" April said, becoming slightly worried, and even worse, somehow warm with desire. All her tiredness and the calming lull of the champagne were gone.

"But no ravishing," he said as he opened the door to their suite. "I'm trying to set your mind at ease, because I can tell you're just about to jump out of your skin with mistrust of me. That is, unless your unease is because *you* prefer to do the ravishing?''

His hopeful tone broke the alarm she was feeling and made her laugh—as well as notice the twinge of regret she felt as he put out a hand, signaling for him to precede her into their suite. ''I'm not much for ravishing, myself. Sorry.'' But had the idea sounded kind of enticing to her love-starved ears?

''Wait a minute,'' he said, reaching out to snatch her back outside the door.

''What are you doing?'' she gasped, taken totally aback by his reversal.

''I've had a change of heart. Every bride, even a short-term, impostor bride, should be carried over the threshold. I'm sorry, but I have to stand by my convictions.'' He lifted her into his arms again, cradled her against his chest, held the door open with his foot and backed into the suite.

She gazed up at him silently.

He stared down at her, his eyebrow cocked. ''No protests?''

''I don't think so,'' she said, her voice tiny and somehow wondering. ''What would you say if I told you I liked it? Very much?''

Without another word, he laid her on the honeymoon bed. ''I'd say nothing at all. I might even take it as encouragement.''

They watched each other for a few seconds, April hesitating as she lay back, Caleb at her side, his arm crossed over her hip as he leaned on his hand for support. There was nothing in his eyes to be afraid of, she told herself. If she didn't know it was all a cover-up, she'd say that their wedding night couldn't have gone better. And she'd want it to last forever, if it was real.

Swallowing nervously, she said, "I did like it very much."

"I am taking that as encouragement," he told her, the warning there if she cared to heed it.

"I think that…I hope you do," she said, her heart in her throat, her whole body trembling with wonder.

Chapter Nine

Caleb's heart began a wild pounding in his chest. "I know that you don't love me, April, and that we're not long-term. I know I make you nervous, I could tell that at the desk downstairs. I don't want to frighten you in any way."

"I know," she said, her gaze on his, trusting.

"I would never hurt you."

Her eyelashes lowered for a split second before she said, "Tonight was the most beautiful night of my life. I wish it would never end, Caleb. But there's one thing I can't stop thinking about."

Caleb stroked her hair and then down along her neck. "Did you know white is sexy on you, whether it's part of a nurse's uniform or a wedding gown?"

"Caleb." She pecked lightly at his chest to hold his focus, and he realized his mind was in a far different place than hers. But what could he do? Everything about this petite woman made him want to hold her in his arms and shelter her from life.

"What is it, babe?" he asked huskily. "Tell me what you can't stop thinking about."

"I know nothing about you, really." She took a deep breath. "I know your family. I know that you're the son of the McCallum Wing's founder."

He couldn't stop the withdrawal from her, as much as he tried. It was in the cooling of his hands, and the stiffening of his spine. What she wanted was to get inside him, know him better than just a surface presentation to the world.

One thing he would never allow himself to do was pair himself so tightly to a human being that there was a bond, a sealing of spirits.

He looked into her earnest green eyes. Her need for emotional satisfaction was reasonable. Here they were, man and woman, husband and wife, without anything more between them than the reason they'd married. "I'm not trying to be mysterious. I just don't make it a habit to get close to people. Or to spill my guts."

"I know. It's just that..."

What she was thinking was in her eyes. Her body wanted his, the same way he wanted her, and yet, her mind asked for a connection to his soul. Nothing wrong with that. A different thing than he wanted from her, but the same, in the end, since he needed to protect her, keep her safe, and that was an emotional level she wasn't comfortable with him seeking. "Neither of us is right for the other," he said huskily. "We both want something the other can't give."

"I know that. I'm not completely innocent."

Touching her face, he enjoyed stroking the delicate skin. "I wonder if either of us could compromise."

"Probably not." She caught his hand and held it against her cheek. "Not enough, anyway."

"And yet I want you, April. More than anything I've ever wanted in my life." He turned the hand she pressed to her cheek, so that he carried her hand to his lips to kiss her palm.

"Nurses help people get well. You wouldn't have asked me to marry you if you weren't suffering, Caleb. It wasn't all about the children. Your actions told me it was also about making your father happy. Laying some demons to rest. You'll have to let me get to know you at some level, or I'll never know which shadows of yours you don't want disturbed."

If she wasn't a vision in angel-white lying on the hotel bed, he'd have been long gone by now. If they hadn't said vows—vows that meant nothing and yet reverberated inside him somehow—he'd have pulled a major disappearing act. Staring at April's sweet heart-shaped lips, meant for giving and receiving pleasure, stayed him. In a split second, a window in his mind opened. April had hit a salient point, whether she realized it or not: He wanted from her exactly what he did not know he wanted to be given.

Healing.

From screaming dreams in the night. From loneliness. From darkness.

The realization frightened him. This petite redhaired woman was too delicate to heal him. He'd take her under with him, just as a drowning victim might accidentally drown his rescuer. As a former cop, he knew better than to recklessly undercut his position.

He started to pull away. April swiftly put her arms around his neck, pulling him down to her, and before he could heed the warning, she'd touched her lips to his in a way that invited more intimacy.

Groaning, he gave himself up to her because he was tired of running away.

And because she was right. He did need to be healed.

APRIL HAD NEVER been kissed like this in her life. She melted into Caleb's arms, unwilling to give up the moment they were sharing. His tongue swept into her mouth, possessing her the way she'd once dreamed would happen for her; long strokes of need had her whimpering for more connection, more depth, more Caleb.

His hand stroked up her thigh, rasping on the white stockings. At the garter, he hesitated, and it seemed he took a shuddering breath as he investigated the skin encircled by the garter. Then he went to her lacy thong, pushing the full white skirt up as he sought the top of her thigh. She gasped, feeling as if she was going to fly apart if he didn't release her from the anguish her need was demanding.

"Caleb," she pleaded.

"No," he whispered, kissing her deeply again. "I can't rush this."

She arched underneath him as he kissed her neck, her earlobe, her collarbone. With unsteady fingers, she undid his tie, pulling it from his neck and dropping it to the floor. It was harder to undo his shirt buttons, and she sat up to push his jacket off of him.

He undid her zipper while he gnawed lightly on her neck. Shivers shot over her skin.

"Are you okay?" he asked against her earlobe.

"Yes," she said, her voice unsteady, her heart going crazy inside her. To show him she was, she pushed his shirt from his shoulders, helped him unbutton the cuffs and dropped that to the floor as well.

Bare-chested, he was breathtaking. The dark trousers emphasized a toned waist and an ebony trail of hair that led to the place she wanted to be.

She popped the fastener on his trousers, and he tugged her bridal gown off. His swift intake of breath told her he hadn't expected her to be braless. "The straps were so thin—"

His lips closed over her breast, cutting off her explanation and any chance she might have had to form a reason for refusal. Moaning, she clasped his head to her, sighing as he licked, nipped, suckled her. "Oh, Caleb. That feels *so* good. So *very* good."

She wanted him to feel pleasure, too, so bravely

she slipped a hand inside his trousers, inside his briefs, to massage him. For just a moment, her hand stilled as she considered his girth. He felt large, almost overwhelmingly so, and for just an instant she wondered how they would fit together.

"It's all right," he said, lying her back against the pillows. "Don't worry. I'll take care of you."

Standing, he removed his pants, and his socks and shoes. Last, his briefs. April's eyes grew wide as she stared at him. He was big all over, and more handsome than she could ever have dreamed.

She wanted to be beautiful for him. As attractive as she found him to be. Shyly, she found herself freezing into uncertainty. He seemed to sense her sudden hesitation, because he gently drew the bell-shaped gown over her hips and down her legs, tossing it onto a nearby wingback chair. His gaze drank in her bare breasts; his finger caressed a path from her waist to her hip where the white garter belt began.

"I knew you'd be beautiful, April, but I never dreamed you'd be this beautiful."

The words calmed her like a balm to her undernourished spirit. Gently, he removed her high-heel jewel-patterned shoes; he reached around her to unsnap the garter and take that and the stockings down, over her knees and down her ankles, so slowly she thought she might scream from the way he was staring at her.

There was nothing left but the thong. Caleb

seemed content to let his gaze rove from her pink-painted toenails to the cameo at her throat. To her lips, then back to her pink-tipped breasts. She wondered why he hesitated. "Caleb?" she asked, reaching out to touch his face.

"You're so much sweeter than I could have imagined," he said, his voice raw with emotion. "You're like a doll. I'd like to sit you up in my bed and look at you all night long."

His approval warmed her. "This doll would rather be held," she said. "I won't break."

It seemed a sigh of indecision left him. Whatever was battling inside him lay defeated, because ever so slowly, he reached for her white thong, and as carefully as if he were peeling petals from a rose, he took it down her legs.

Stroking lightly up her thighs, he seemed to admire her femininity, then suddenly his fingers teased inside her. She closed her eyes, swept by growing desire. When his tongue parted her, sliding inside her in a way she'd never expected, moving deeper to possess her, she grabbed his shoulders to hold on to him.

"Oh," she murmured. "Oh, Caleb!"

He sought her secrets with his tongue. "Caleb!" she cried out, feeling herself ride up on a giant wave that suddenly exploded. She felt a scream rising inside her, begging for something she couldn't understand, and then Caleb moved over her, parting her with his fingers as he eased inside her.

Tears of release began to spill from her eyes. "Yes," she told him, urging him with her hands. "Yes, yes, yes!"

"Come to me, baby, come to me," he patiently encouraged.

The building scream she'd been holding back erupted, pushed out of her by the uncontrollable pleasure driven by the shattering fire sweeping her, even more thrilling because his hoarse cries signaled his release was as passionate as hers.

"Don't leave me," she begged softly as he slumped against her, his lips against her shoulder in supine gratitude. "Stay inside me."

"Be careful," he said against her ear. "I could be easily tempted to stay inside you all night."

"Could you?" she whispered, thinking that would be nothing short of heaven.

"Oh, my, you are so sweet." He groaned and she thought it was a sound of pleasure. He turned, cradling her so that he stayed in her as she'd asked, and yet allowing him to lie more underneath her so that his weight was not on her.

She felt him kiss the top of her head, and for some reason, all the worry and tenseness left her body.

For the first time in her life, she felt sheltered. And whole.

MORNING CAME FASTER than April wanted. She was a morning person, always eager to greet the day.

Today, she just wanted to lie in Caleb's arms. Yet

that was not possible. Without disturbing him, she rose from the bed, showered, and changed back into her wedding dress. This time she didn't add the silk garter or stockings. Those she tucked into her purse. Her hair she pulled up into a knot, and then slipped her shoes on. It just didn't feel right to walk around wearing the same wedding finery she'd worn the night before. She wasn't truly a bride in the forever sense, and somehow, she felt a sham. The gorgeous wedding ring sparkled on her finger, a reminder that Caleb was a considerate gentleman, a man who would stand up and protect what he believed in.

The lovemaking had been so shattering and wonderful because she knew she could trust him, knew that his credo of "your cause is now my cause" had given her the security she'd needed. But she had so little to offer him in return.

When she came out of the bathroom, Caleb was dressed as well, but without his tie and jacket. His hair was rumpled, as if he'd run a hand through it. She couldn't believe she was married to such a devastatingly handsome, altogether-too-sexy man. Had he really held her in his arms last night, murmuring sweet words of passion she had never thought to hear said to her in her life?

"We look just a little different than we did last night," she said, her smile regretful for the night of passion that would never be theirs again.

His expression was rueful as well. "It was quite a night."

She didn't know how to take that, exactly. But she knew she'd reached out to him last night for shelter; he'd provided it. Now was the time to walk away gracefully, without putting more entanglements into the relationship than they had both agreed upon. Hadn't she been the one who'd been eager to set boundaries with which they'd both be comfortable?

"I'm anxious to get home and change and do some things so I can get to the hospital," she said softly.

"With it being New Year's Day," he said, "I'm curious to see if there are any teens hanging around the local hot spots, blowing off boredom."

So it was back to work, back to the normal routine for both of them. She nodded, knowing it was best if they both went on about their separate lives.

"Monday morning, we go put in the application for the quads," he told her. "Agreed?"

"Agreed. Definitely." She gave him an appreciative smile. "Thank you, Caleb."

He shrugged. "Nothing to thank me for. Yet."

There was, in so many ways she couldn't tell him. So she picked up her purse and waited for him to lead the way downstairs. He had his car brought around, and while they waited, April tried to ignore the cold wind whipping against her bare legs. Last night she'd been so warm.

Last night had been the most wonderful night of

her life. She wondered if Caleb had any idea just how much she'd needed him.

That was not the basis on which to start this partnership, she reminded herself. The need in the marriage was the quads', not her own personal yearnings. So she remained silent as they got in the car. She didn't say a word when he pulled the car in front of her house. No protest left her lips as he walked her to the porch, clearly having no intent to enter her house with her.

But after she opened the door and hesitated, not looking at him, and lost for words, he took the hand dangling at her side and raised it to his mouth. He pressed a kiss against her palm without lingering, a kiss that didn't seek more but was a gesture of chivalry.

Anything more would have spoiled what they'd shared, and what they both knew would not happen again. She offered him a tiny smile of understanding, and then murmured goodbye as she went inside and closed the door behind her.

A moment later, she heard Caleb's car pull away. A deep sigh of relief left her as she closed her eyes, remembering one more time what he'd given her. Then resolutely, she walked down the hall to her bedroom.

It was time to give up the past. There was not a doubt in her mind that she and Caleb had qualifications not even Social Services could ignore. He was the son of the wing's founder; he and his family were well known for their generosity. He had been a respected police officer. She was a neonatal nurse. There really was nothing now that Social Services could nitpick. Today, she felt certain that the quads would be awarded to them as soon as they could leave the hospital. Marrying Caleb had given her that reassurance.

So now she needed to make some changes. The babies could sleep in one of the guest rooms, or two in each guest room. The cribs and other paraphernalia would certainly fit very nicely.

Caleb couldn't always sleep on the sofa. She could easily move a bed for herself into one of the rooms where the children would be, thereby being able to keep close to them in the night. Caleb could use her room.

She went out to the garage and gathered up some boxes left over from when she'd moved into the house. Carrying them to her bedroom, she retrieved some packing tape and taped the boxes back into shape from their collapsed state. With one last glance around her room, she eyed the doll collection she had built over so many years. A beautiful ensemble, certainly, but nothing a man would want in his space. She wanted Caleb comfortable.

Without hesitating, she took the dolls, one by one wrapping them in tissue paper and storing them in the boxes. "Goodbye," she said as she carried the boxes to the garage. "Someday you'll mean a lot to someone. But I don't think Caleb will want to sleep every night with you watching over him.''

That vision made her laugh. It hadn't been so bad packing up her cherished memories. In a way, she felt as if she'd closed a door in her life. Where the dolls once had comforted her, now she had someone who comforted her in a much more tangible way. It was only for a short while, only until they found Jenny and got her resettled with her family—but for April, who had never known the depth of that support before, it was something she knew she'd never forget.

Chapter Ten

Monday morning, Caleb picked April up at her house. It was still her house, of course. That would never change. For a moment, the irony struck him. She was his wife, and yet, she wasn't.

A woman like her would be a real right angle chunked squarely into his neatly ordered life. He didn't want the emotions, the deep commitment, the abiding connection they would have to forge. The magic they'd allowed to sweep over them on their wedding night would never happen again. Neither of them would want it, for so many reasons.

So he put on his cop face, and gave her doorbell a serious stab with his finger. No way was he going to let his bride-for-a-while make him go all soft.

She came to the door wearing a lavender skirt and wool top, and sensible heels by no means old-fashioned, but by no means stiletto, either. Her hair was up, and she took his breath away faster than the cold breeze.

"Hello," she said, her voice quiet and unsure.

He knew exactly where her head was at. Despite their agreement, there was so much tugging between them that it was tempting to give in to the pull and go with it. See where it took him. "Hi," was all he said instead. "Got all the pertinent papers you'll need to satisfy the first round Social Services throws at us?"

Her smile was tremulous and apprehensive. "I hope so."

"Good." Taking her hand, he helped her down the porch. "Now remember, you and I have known each other for some time. That's not exactly a fib, because we knew of each other because of Bri."

"I feel like I've known you forever."

"Right. So we decided to get married. I don't think they'll be interested in the whys or wherefores of our relationship past that."

April was breathless as he helped her to his car. Nerves, he thought. "Don't be nervous," he said automatically. "We've got a great chance."

"Do you really think so?"

They got in the car, and he started it without looking at her. The less he maintained eye contact with those dazzling eyes of hers, the less likely he was to drown in her feelings. "You see anybody else lining up to take in four newborns?"

"No, but that doesn't mean there aren't. We don't know who might want them."

"I'm prepared to make the case that the mother's wishes should be considered, whether the document was legal or not. I'm willing to say that I'm working on the case, I believe I can find the mother, and it would greatly help if this grieving person who was little more than a child herself found that her family was taken care of in the manner she'd hoped. Even Social Services won't want to scare Jenny half to death by discovering that her babies were separated. Clearly, what she had in mind was giving them a family she felt she couldn't give them herself.''

''I hope you're right. And thank you for saying that you're willing to go to bat for me.''

''I believe in my heart it's best for all concerned, or I wouldn't do it. I wouldn't have offered to...to—'' He couldn't finish, uncertain as to how to put his opinion without insulting her. She was his wife, after all.

''You wouldn't have offered your protection to us if you didn't believe it was the right thing to do. It makes me feel good that you trust me that much, Caleb.''

''Trust you?'' He turned to stare at her, forgetting all about his vow to keep himself from drowning in her gaze. ''Anybody can see that you love those children, April. They need that right now.''

Her smile lit on him like a bright star. He felt a groan go through him. So he turned back to face the road, and reminded himself that April was a place he had vowed never to go again in his life. Partnership and caring. Being there for someone.

He told himself he was way too scarred to get lost in his heart again.

"Have you been able to find any leads on Jenny? Or have the police?"

That question centered him again, in a place where he was comfortable. The cop in him came strong to the fore. "I talked to some of her friends. Acquaintances, actually, but in the teen years, friendships are fairly liquid. They haven't seen her since she gave birth. That's a bad sign."

"Why? You don't think something's happened to her?"

"No," he reassured her. "I think she's not in the city any longer. Possibly not in the state. There had to have been someplace she had family."

"She never mentioned it to me."

"Someone somewhere knows what I need to know. It's simply a matter of patience until I knock on the right door and talk to the person with the golden key."

April rubbed her hands over her arms. "It's so hard to have that patience."

"I know. But I believe this case is by no means hopeless. I almost feel like we're holding all the cards. I can totally sympathize with what Jenny did."

"You can?" April's tone was astonished.

"Sure. She had a lot on her plate all at once. It was too much. Given time, she might even work through what happened, and want her children back without us having to encourage her to feel that way.''

''You really believe you're going to find her, don't you?''

''Yeah. Sure.'' He sent her a fast glance. ''I'll keep playing the angles over in my mind until something sticks out funny, and then it'll come to me.''

She was silent for a moment. ''One day, when you feel like it, I'd like you to tell me about your time on the force.''

That surprised him. It didn't surprise him that she'd want to know; women usually didn't have the caution not to try to push into his feelings. Like they could bind him up and cauterize the wound if they could only get him to talk about it. Well, his was a wound which couldn't be cauterized, so he never talked to anyone about it.

But the tone of April's voice wasn't intrusive. She seemed to really want to hear about his life. He caught no false sympathy, no egged-on encouragement in her voice.

Yet, he really didn't need to talk about it. His story was safely bottled up and stored where it couldn't come out and ooze into his life.

''I enjoyed being a police officer,'' he said, surprising himself. ''Being able to help people is something I find rewarding.''

''Me, too,'' April said, seemingly pleased that they shared this in common. ''I feel worthy, like I've found my reason to take up space on earth, when I'm helping other people. Especially people who really need to be helped.''

That was what it was all about for him. ''Exactly.''

He intended to be no more forthcoming than that. Waiting for her to draw more out of him now that she'd hooked into an empathy scenario between them, he was surprised by her silence. He sensed her waiting, and also her patience. If he wanted to talk now, he could. If he didn't, he perceived she'd just return to looking out the window, understanding that he could only give to her when he had something to give.

Somehow, that noncondemning, nonwaiting silence encouraged him. ''You know, I don't think I realized that we had something in common. I mean, something other than wanting the babies to have one home, one safe situation.''

''What do you mean?'' She turned inquisitive eyes upon him.

''I just think it must take a special woman to take care of babies who are so helpless that all they can do is trust. And the parents, who have to trust that you can make their children healthy. Not everyone can do it.''

''Serving the public has its wrenching moments, as you know,'' she said carefully. ''It also has its extremely rewarding moments.''

Man, did this woman ever know how to say exactly what he'd always felt.

"And when something goes wrong, it's like…a sweeping loss you can't help feeling is your fault. I mean, you're the one everybody trusted, right? It was your job to be the best, to be the trustworthy savior."

Too close to home, he thought raggedly. This woman was reading his emotions. And yet, somehow, he wasn't as resentful as he'd expected he might be. "My partner was killed in a drug bust that went wrong."

She didn't reach to touch his hand. She merely said, "I'm so sorry, Caleb." Softly, with the right touch of shared commiseration. "And you believe you should have been the trustworthy savior."

"Right."

"Tell me something I couldn't guess on my own," she said, softly mimicking words he'd once spoken to her. "If not the details, then pretty much the story. But you know what fascinates me, Caleb? In spite of all that, here you are, willing to be the trustworthy savior once again. Just in a different capacity. And I really, truly admire that."

Nothing to admire about letting somebody down. But he had to smile at her refusal to coddle him. It annoyed him when people tried to understand his pain in their well-meaning manner. He hated it worse when they tried to give him advice.

April, perhaps true to form, did neither. She just offered him some sass and a little salute, and it added up to just what he needed.

"One day, maybe I'll be able to sleep at night. In the meantime, I'm not making any plans to move into your house until we have the babies. There's really no reason to do so."

"I couldn't agree more."

Well, it couldn't be said that she was after his body. He wondered if he should be irritated that she wasn't more enthusiastic about an encore performance of last night. "You're not the kind of girl to go all gooey on a guy about anything, are you?"

"I hope not. That sounds very unattractive."

Her teasing response took the last edge off his reserve with her. "I took it pretty hard when my partner died. I keep replaying that night, thinking of everything I did wrong. I just think I could have saved him if I'd been a better cop."

"Jenny might not have left if I'd been a better nurse. If I'd been paying closer attention to the signs. To her emotional condition."

He gaped at that logic, as much as he could clearly see the parallel she was drawing. "Do you really think that?"

"Yes." She shot him an impatient glance. "Is it not my job to be the one to pick up on the signals and make certain nothing goes wrong?"

"Yeah, but—"

"There's no buts for me, just like there aren't for you. And the worst part is, I don't know if Jenny's dead or alive."

"She's alive."

"She was not a healthy patient when she left the hospital. Anything could have happened to her."

An infection just by itself could zap a woman off the earth quicker than anyone could figure out the cure... A shudder shook him. They'd reached the offices of Social Services, so he parked and switched off the engine. "I think you're good to talk to. For the first time, I feel like someone knows what it's really like to be on the front line."

Her gaze was even. "It doesn't solve anything for either of us. We still have all the baggage."

"Yeah, but the compartments just shifted. Maybe, eventually, we'll just lose the baggage, kind of like the airports lose it."

Rolling her eyes at him, she said, "Come on. We've got babies to safeguard."

So they got out of the car, and he grabbed her hand, her soft, delicate hand that hid a gentle touch and a strong heart. The weird thing was, he didn't mind rushing to April's side to try to shore her up. He believed in her, the way she believed in him.

And that felt strangely nice.

In a nonpermanent sort of way, he reminded himself as they walked through the doors into the Social Services offices.

TWO HOURS LATER, April and Caleb were finished with the initial paperwork, and the questions she was so afraid she'd answer wrong. It had been draining. Wrenching. And somehow, painful.

"Are you okay?" Caleb asked when they left the building to get into his car.

"I'll feel better when we know if they're taking us seriously as candidates."

"It's going to be okay. I just know it. Do you want to get a bite to eat at Austin Eats? You could go right in to the hospital after that."

"You know, I don't think I feel like seeing a whole bunch of people right now, and there'll probably be a lot of staff hanging around, catching up after the holiday. I think I'd like to go get my car, Caleb, so you won't have to pick me up when I'm ready to leave the hospital."

"All right. I need to go by and see Dad anyway. He's going to want to hear about how our meeting with Social Services went."

"Tell him I said thank you for the honeymoon suite."

Caleb gave her leg a quick pat as he drove. "I have to say I enjoyed it a lot myself."

She stared out the window, wondering if there was a double meaning in his words.

"By the way, I went by and saw Mrs. Fox yesterday."

"You did?"

"Yeah. She was actually pretty happy to have company on New Year's Day."

"Oh," April murmured. "I guess she might have enjoyed not being alone. It's got to be quiet without Jenny around."

"She's a pretty nice lady. I can see why Jenny leaned on her after David died. But she didn't have a whole lot of details on Jenny's history, besides the fact that she was really grieving for her husband. Mrs. Fox said she didn't think Jenny might ever get over losing him, and that she was frightened to death of having four children on her own."

"Oh, dear." April could imagine the level of deep grief herself. It had to have been so overwhelming for a teenager without family.

Just walking into Social Services and doing paperwork to temporarily foster the quads had nearly panicked her. Knowing that someone had filled out paperwork on her when she was a child—actually, many people—had given her a nearly physical pain in her stomach. The process seemed so cold, and yet it had to be straightforward and nonemotional. Yet there were people's lives involved, and children.

As an orphan herself, Jenny would have understood what she was doing if she abandoned the children to the system. And yet, her own situation was intolerable. April might have been the only person she felt might understand.

"I think I mentioned to Jenny once that I had been in foster care," she said suddenly. "And that I'd been adopted."

He nodded. "It's really not too hard to figure out. I believe that she realized you were the only person who might understand her panic over her children not going into the foster care system. You and Jenny shared a similar belief system, a common background. Just like you and I have discovered something common between us.''

She stared at him, stunned by his admission. It was almost as if he was saying that they had achieved some level of closeness. Why did that shock her? ''I don't think I ever expected you to…I mean, that sounded so—''

He grinned at her loss of words. ''So hurray-for-the-home-team? Maybe I have to think of our relationship in terms of sports.''

''Oh.''

''That's the spirit. Now I'm going to do a few things today, but you call me if you hear anything, or need anything.''

''Okay.''

He parked the car at her house and April started to get out, halting when he caught her hand.

''I mean it, April. Call me if you need *anything.*''

The look in his eyes was deep and purposeful. He really meant that he would take care of her, in any way she needed, while they were married.

It was so wonderful to know that he wanted to be there for her—and it was so scary to find herself wanting to rely on him. Every other time a boyfriend in her life had wanted to let her rely on him, she'd taken off like a shot. Bonds had not been easy for her to form.

She felt one forming with Caleb, whether she wanted it to or not, and yet, she found herself drawn to it like a sunflower to the sun. *I could fall in love with him,* she realized faster than a blinking eye. *I like being married to him.*

That shocked her more than anything. Managing a quick smile for goodbye, she got out of the car and hurried up the sidewalk, letting herself into the house without another look back at him. Her heart thundered.

"What was I thinking?" she asked herself. "This will be over one day. And it's going to hurt so much more than being passed over at the orphanage when I have to face that Caleb doesn't want to stay married to me."

The dawning of her feelings for him were outside their agreement. She couldn't have foreseen that she'd begin to feel this way. There was so much good wrapped up in Caleb. Him. His family. His beliefs. Their mutual understanding. His lovemaking, and the way he treated her so gently.

It was balm to her spirit; it was a magnet pulling her heart inexorably toward his.

Nothing about this was going to feel good when it was gone from her.

Chapter Eleven

"So how's the newlywed?" Bri asked when April came in to check on the babies.

"I'm fine. Better than fine."

They hugged each other, reveling in the knowledge that they were sisters now.

"I'm only here for a quick visit, but my brother treats you good?" Bri asked.

A blush stole over April's cheeks. "Your brother treats me better than good."

"Oh my gosh," Bri said in wonder, her eyes not missing a detail of the glow in April's eyes. "You didn't say anything about how you and Caleb had decided to make the big leap. But you really like my crazy brother, don't you?"

April laughed. "He's not crazy."

"No, but he can be tough as old rawhide. Yet, the way you're smiling tells me you really like him. It all happened so fast I thought...well, I don't know what I thought. But there's something special between you two, I can see it in your eyes.'' She hugged April again, close.

''He hasn't been tough as rawhide with me. I couldn't ask for better.'' That was the truth, considering the circumstances, and it was painful to admit it, and to keep up the pretense even though she knew her marriage to Bri's brother wasn't forever.

''Did you enjoy the honeymoon suite?'' Bri's eyes sparkled with some teasing, and some womanly interest as well.

April shifted, mildly embarrassed. ''Thank you for suggesting it to Jackson. It was very sweet of you,'' she said, trying to sidestep the question.

Bri laughed. ''Okay, it's none of my business. But you look happy, and glowing, and I take that to mean you enjoyed more about the suite than the accommodations.''

Even with her best friend, this was almost more than she could share about Caleb and herself. ''It was a lovely suite,'' she said primly. ''I'm going to go check on the babies now.''

''They've been in good hands, April. And they're getting stronger every minute. Though they will require constant care for a long time.'' Bri smiled at her, content to let wedding matters and honeymoon suites go for the moment. ''Before you go, I do want to tell you how happy you made my father. He's thrilled that you're part of the family, April. I think Dad was always afraid Caleb would bring home a woman Dad wouldn't be able to relate to.''

"Why?"

Bri shrugged. "It's the radical element in Caleb. He's different from the rest of us. His feelings are in a deep dark place. But Dad thinks you're wonderful, and that you're going to be great for Caleb. All that sweetness is bound to rub off on him somehow. Anyway, it's wonderful to have someone in the family who's blissful. My brother, Adam, and his wife, Maggie, are at the other end of the marriage spectrum. Not that they don't love each other, but they've been praying for a child of their own for so long. Fertility treatments have been unsuccessful so far, and it's all beginning to take a toll on them. I'd like to see them happy together again. Like you and Caleb. I'm telling you the truth, Dad was the happiest man at the wedding yesterday."

April didn't answer, not certain how to reply. Clearly, Jackson had spun their relationship to the family as a love match. She offered Bri a shy smile and a nod before making an excuse and hurrying down to the nursery.

"Oh, you little sweethearts," April murmured as she went to stand beside their isolettes. "You'll never guess where I've just been. Soon, I hope you'll be coming home with me. We'll find your mother, and we'll help her get started with you. And just you wait until you meet your temporary father. You're going to like him, because he's a special man."

As she touched the delicate toes and baby skin

she had come to love, April allowed herself to become lost in a hazy daydream. *If only these were my babies, and yet, my heart so wishes for their real mother to return.*

But still, I do love them as if they are my very own.

"Hi, April."

Her head snapped up as the daydream was snatched away. "Hi, Madeline," she said.

Madeline Sheppard smiled at her. "I wanted to come by and give my good friend my best wishes. Congratulations on your marriage."

"Oh. Thank you." April's face warmed as she realized her "happy" news would have spread throughout the hospital, fairly shouted by her exuberant sister-in-law.

"Bri is ecstatic that you're part of her family now."

"I am, too."

Madeline touched a few baby toes as she smiled wistfully. "My biological clock is ticking so loud it sounds like it might detonate any minute."

Madeline was a fertility specialist, and maybe for that reason, April had never thought of her as lacking anything where babies were concerned. And yet, Madeline had to think about babies all day long as part of her job—it was only natural to want the same for herself that she tried to help other couples achieve.

"I'm approaching a ripe old thirty-five in a few

weeks. If I had my way about it, I'd be married and expecting my own child by my next birthday. That's what I'm going to wish for when I blow out the candles on this cake, anyway.''

April smiled at her. ''I'll cross my fingers for you, too. Your prince could always be closer than you think, maybe just a wish away.''

''Yours certainly appeared from out of the mists. I thought all you ever did was work. Of course, now we all know you found a little time for romance,'' she teased.

April blushed. ''Caleb kind of...swept me off my feet.''

''Well, you seem so happy. Congratulations. Oh, I wish I could stay and hear all about it, but I've got to get back to work.''

''Thanks for stopping by, Madeline.''

Madeline left the room, and once again April turned to consider the infants. It would be so wonderful to have children of her own. She wasn't that different from Madeline. Actually similar, because she had no man with whom to become a partner in pregnancy. Caleb was temporary. No other man had suited her as either husband or father-to-her-children material.

It seemed almost too ironic to accept congratulations from Madeline when there was nothing to celebrate. ''Oh, well,'' she told the babies, ''for now, I've got you to hold, and who knows, that prince might be just a wish away for me as well.''

JUST AS A MATTER OF COURSE, Caleb decided to leave no stone unturned when it came to idle conversation. Someone had talked to Jenny and had heard something they didn't realize. The trick was finding out who had the information he needed.

He'd already tried the teen scene. Speaking with Mrs. Fox had been illuminating, but not necessarily the gold mine of clues he wanted. "Next stop, hospital staff," he said under his breath.

He caught Madeline Sheppard in the hall as she was leaving the neonatal nursery. "I'm Caleb McCallum," he said.

"Oh, the handsome groom who nabbed our sweet nurse. Bri can't stop doing cartwheels over your marriage."

"Bri's a romantic, but thanks." Caleb grinned, then got down to business. "Madeline, did you ever talk to Jenny, the mother of those quads in the nursery?"

"Once, maybe." Madeline's forehead creased. "I'm a fertility specialist, so I didn't have much reason to talk to her. She'd already hit more of the jackpot than most people ever do in their lives. But I did stop in once to say congratulations."

"So she never mentioned anything to you of a personal nature?"

Madeline smiled. "All she did was lie there. She could barely smile. When I saw Jenny, she was pretty exhausted from the delivery. I don't think she said a word, as a matter of fact."

Caleb nodded. "I can understand that."

"You might try her obstetrician," Madeline offered. "Zachary Beaumont delivered the quads."

"Thanks. I will."

"Congrats." Madeline gave him a friendly smile and walked away.

April came out in the hall, her eyebrows raised. "I thought I heard your voice. Are you flirting with the single women on the staff?"

"No. I'm kissing married ones." And he reached out and swiped her close to him, laying a big kiss on her lips.

She jumped out of his arms as if she'd been snapped. "Caleb!"

He laughed at her. "I can do that. We're married."

She visibly relaxed. "I forgot. I'm sorry."

His expression turned serious, though it was clear he was teasing. "We have to keep up appearances, you know."

"Of course. Well, goodbye."

She scurried back into the nursery as fast as her little white shoes could take her. Caleb laughed under his breath. She was so cute when she was unsettled. It served her right for teasing him about flirting. He wasn't a flirting kind of guy, and she knew it. That would be the last time she asked a question like that, because she knew what his answer would be.

A big smooch, where anybody could see.

He had really enjoyed that.

TEN MINUTES LATER, Zachary Beaumont gave Caleb a benign glance. ''I really didn't know Jenny Barrows very long. She was here at the hospital for a couple of weeks because having quadruplets requires special care, of course. But two weeks isn't long enough to know much about a patient.''

Caleb hated turning up big fat zeroes.

''She was a stellar patient, though. I'm surprised she left the way she did. The way she acted about those children, oohing and aahing over each of them as they were born, I thought she was more smitten than scared.''

''It was a lot of personal stuff, I think. Thanks, Doctor.''

''You're welcome. If anything else comes to mind, I'll let you know.''

''Thanks.'' Caleb headed off, deciding he'd go by his father's offices and talk with him. By now, he wondered why his father hadn't called him for a full report.

Of course, he might be less anxious for a report on the case now that he and April were married and applying for temporary custody. Caleb snorted to himself. No doubt Jackson hoped Jenny would stay gone long enough for he and April to figure out that they actually liked sharing residential square footage. Liked being married.

Wouldn't Jackson be surprised when he learned that Caleb and April maintained separate quarters and would continue to do so, at least until the babies went home with April?

JACKSON LOOKED at him from under beetled brows. "So the first round of paperwork at Social Services went fine?"

Caleb shrugged. "As far as we can tell. They keep their cards pretty close to the vest. Still, the babies may be able to go home soon. They'll have to go somewhere, and April and I are a ready-made family who can give them the constant care they require."

Jackson nodded. "How does it feel to be married?"

"Better than I thought it would." Caleb sent his father a sheepish glance. "Maybe I feel okay about it because I know that there's a timed release in it."

His father shook his head. "Well, you seem to like that little gal. Don't be in too big a hurry to push the destruct button. Great women are real tough to find."

"Don't I know it." Caleb rubbed a palm over his chin, ready to be off the subject. "I'm having no luck finding Jenny Barrows."

"That's unusual for you. Bloodhounds don't do any better at tracking scent than you do at putting missing pieces together."

Caleb frowned. "I know. I'm missing a huge piece, and it's bugging me. Teenagers don't disappear without a trace, especially when they have no money, no family and no resources. There had to have been someone she talked to.''

''I bet you stumble on it soon enough. You ate your black-eyed peas on New Year's, didn't you?''

''Don't tell me that superstitious tale of eating peas for luck is going to help me find Jenny.''

''No. I'm just asking you in a roundabout way if you and April cooked, or if you went out after your honeymoon.''

''We actually went our separate ways. She went to the hospital and I went to chat with local teenagers.''

Jackson grunted. ''I take it the honeymoon wasn't a sufficient lure to keep you two together then.''

''Dad,'' Caleb said, his tone no-nonsense. ''Don't try to make a romance where there isn't going to be one.''

''All right.'' Jackson sighed. ''But damn, I like that little girl.''

''I know you do.'' Caleb sighed. ''But I gotta like being married. And she's got to like it. Believe it or not, I'm not the only reluctant mule in the marriage.''

''Oh, I believe it, all right. That young lady's full of sass. Say, did she ever ask you about the prenup?''

''No. It was just as you said. She'd made her point, knows we accepted it, and beyond that, I don't guess the details interest her.''

"I sure do appreciate honesty and a good, hard-working stubborn streak in a woman," Jackson said wistfully. "April reminds me so much of—"

"Dad. I'm not going there." He stood, clapping a strong hand on his father's shoulder. "Thanks for everything you did to help us and to make things nice for the wedding. I've got to get back to work."

"You do that. Thanks for stopping by."

Caleb nodded, seeing the lines around his father's eyes and the concerned fold to his lips. "It's going to be fine, Dad," he said soothingly. "Don't worry."

"I'm not so old that you need to start parenting me," Jackson said, uncharacteristically petulant. "I've been around the track enough to know that everything eventually works itself out."

Caleb laughed at his dad's who-is-in-control-here tone. "That's my dad. Bye."

"Bye." Jackson waved him away, watching as his son walked out the office doors. Great gravy, was that any way to start a marriage, staying apart from one another? What would it take to get these two stubborn kids in one place long enough that they had to begin to work within the boundaries of the marriage agreement they'd made? Life was way too short to be so damn mule-headed.

And yet, as much as he wanted to wave his hand like an all-powerful genie to cast the proper spell that would make April and Caleb want to be husband and wife, he knew that wasn't the way marriage worked.

It took mutual craving.

There was no way to kickstart a craving.

He'd done his best, and he'd have to be satisfied with that. The rest was up to Caleb and April. Maggie and Adam. Bri and Hunter.

"You'd think, Emily," he said to his deceased wife, "you'd think that any man who dedicated a wing of a hospital to multiple births would get tons of grandkids. Adam and Maggie, I just don't know what to say about that except that I wish you were here to talk to your son and comfort his wife. Caleb's so ornery you might as well forget about any bundles of joy coming from that son of yours. Bri's coming along fine with her three, but it sure would be nice if her brothers would join in the fun and have a few kids of their own." He sighed deeply, his soul lonely. "You'd know what to say to these kids of yours. I miss you, woman, I truly do."

Chapter Twelve

After four weeks of interviews, visits to April's home and countless questions of their family members and work associates, a miracle happened. April and Caleb were allowed to take the four babies home for temporary foster care.

The moment April learned the news, she shrieked with joy she never really thought she'd get to feel. After that, everything happened fast. All the things that had been bought for the babies by Bri were taken to April's house. A minishower was given by Cherilyn, much like a shower for a woman expecting her very own child. Since this foster situation was temporary, there was a twist to the gifts. There was something small for use with the babies, like a set of washcloths with little ducks from each nurse—but then there was something for April from each friend as well. Lovely, breathtakingly sheer webs of lacy lingerie.

"You got married so quickly we didn't get you wedding gifts," Cherilyn explained. "And you won't have the babies forever, so we didn't buy any clothes for them past the six-month size. But your marriage to Caleb calls for something to keep that hunk right by your side,'' she teased.

So April ended up opening up beautifully wrapped gift after gift of lingerie, tasteful and exquisite. Meant to make a man look. And touch.

Of course, her friends had no way of knowing that the marriage was meant to be more short-term than the foster care.

The party was given for her on the last day of her employment, as she was taking an unspecified leave of absence until the babies were no longer in her care. The nurses and some of the doctors threw confetti at her and Caleb as they left with the babies, followed in a car by Jackson and Bri, who were coming to help move them in.

It almost felt like a real homecoming day. It was more than April had begun to believe could happen.

She carried Matthew's carrier inside her house, nearly trembling with excitement. Caleb carried in Craig, Bri brought in Melissa, and Jackson, who couldn't bear to be left out, carried Chloe in as if she were a fragile piece of china.

''An instant family, that's for certain,'' Bri said as they all took a baby to diaper and get changed for bed. ''You've decorated their rooms beautifully, April.''

Too distracted by all the excitement, April barely heard Bri's compliment. But she was glad that her

sister-in-law thought the nurseries were suitable for
the babies. On the days when she'd been off, she
had decided to paint bright yellow colors on the
walls in both bedrooms. She'd found huge cutouts
of the moon, the stars, and even a castle, decorations
that she realized the infants couldn't focus on yet,
but during the waiting days, as she'd called them,
the busywork kept her mind relaxed.

She'd even sewn tiny bumper rails. That had been
a challenge, and after that project, decided she'd
done enough and was just going to drive herself
crazy.

She and Caleb hadn't seen each other much. He
came by every once in a while with a pizza or other
food item, making sure she ate. He'd help her paint,
or hang the big cutouts, change some lightbulbs or
help her with drapery rods, but beyond that, they
didn't share affection. It was as if their wedding-
night lovemaking had never occurred.

He seemed as content with that as she did. She
couldn't have asked for more in a partner, because
he seemed to understand that she needed to throw
every ounce of her energy into what she called nest-
ing. In a way, she felt almost expectant herself, as
if she was simply waiting for her own day of giving
birth.

Of course it was a silly fancy, but he didn't seem
to think so. And once she'd shared that idea with
him, he'd gone out and bought two sliding rockers,
one for each room.

April had been delighted with the gifts. "You didn't have to do that, Caleb. But thank you!"

"We're going to need them for those all-night feedings. I figure the chances of four babies sleeping through the night is about nil."

He'd grinned at her, his hair rumpled from carrying the rockers in with a cold breeze blowing outside. The chill had touched his cheeks with a healthy ruddiness, and his eyes glowed even brighter. She liked him in jeans—too well—and the blue-and-black flannel shirt gave him a rugged appeal she couldn't help admiring.

Their lovemaking flashed into her mind, and April felt need warm her body. Attraction like she'd never known sped into her.

But that was outside what they'd agreed upon, and a sure way to destroy a good friendship. Because after this time in their lives was over, and Jenny was found and reunited with her children, what would she and Caleb have together?

Nothing but an agreement to wed for the sake of four tiny babies who would no longer be in their care.

But for now, the babies were here, and she had to focus on the short time they might have them. "Thank you," she said quietly to Caleb after he'd secured one baby in its crib. "You've been a wonderful partner."

"It's okay." He tugged at a long curl of her hair.

"I haven't done anything I haven't wanted to, babe."

"This little baby wants something, and I can't figure out what," Jackson said gruffly, coming in from the other nursery room, carrying a squalling Chloe in his arms. "You'd think after three of my own, I'd know what I was doing."

Bri laughed, coming to take the fitful baby from her father. "Not necessarily, Dad. Babies are puzzles sometimes. And crying is not always a bad thing. She may know she's been moved from her secure environment and feeling out of sorts. Or she could just be tired."

April smiled as Bri expertly checked Chloe over, trying a bottle and a fresh diaper. Then Bri placed the infant in a crib, and covered her with a warm blanket. Bri rubbed the baby's arms and legs and back soothingly, and Chloe finally allowed herself to relax.

They turned the Peter Rabbit lamp on, switched off the overhead light, and April picked up the baby monitor as they left the room.

"Good job, everyone," Jackson said, sinking into the sofa as they filed into the den. "I'd call that a successful transition. And I'm exhausted."

"Caleb, get your father a glass of tea from the kitchen, please," April said, smiling at her father-in-law fondly. No one could have tried harder to be a real part of the newly growing family than Jackson. In fact, she'd heard from Bri that Jackson might have placed a few calls to Social Services, offering them badly-needed diapers and formula donations and anything else he could do to help.

"It wasn't bribery," Bri had explained to April with a shrug. "Dad had the McCallum Wing finished, operating and out of his hands. Your struggle to win emergency custody of the quads gave him a new mission. He'd made a call to see if there was anything he could do, got to talking to Mandy Cole, realized there were needs as with any agency, and that gave him a new goal. He said Emily told him it was the right thing to do." Bri smiled at her sister-in-law with some sympathetic exasperation. "Emily was our mom."

"Yes, I know," April murmured. "Bless Jackson's heart."

"Oh, he talks a pitiful game. But behind that I'm-dying-until-I-have-my-own-grandchildren exterior is a man who's pretty content with life. He's got us all married, three grandchildren, four temporary babies to love and daily communiqués with Mother. He just likes to keep us all feeling like we could do a little more to make his golden years extra-shiny golden."

April had laughed, but now as she looked at Jackson on the sofa, she saw a man who simply loved his family. Adam, Bri and Caleb had been so fortunate to have Jackson for a father. Whatever bonds he hadn't been able to form with them as children, he seemed eager to tie now.

She wondered if Caleb had the same latent seed

of bonding in him. He'd said he didn't want to get close to anyone, but did he have the same capacity for allowing himself to heal and move on that Jackson possessed?

"Thank you for all your help," she said to Jackson, leaning over the sofa back to hug his neck. "It's meant an awful lot to me."

He caught one of her hands in his. "Not as much as it's meant to me, my girl," he said, his voice tight with emotion.

She couldn't help herself. After all the years of wanting a family of her own as much as she had, she felt so blessed to have the McCallums embrace her with open arms. Pressing a kiss to Jackson's cheek, he held her head against him for just a split second. "Thank you," she murmured.

"You're welcome," he whispered back.

Straightening, she caught Caleb staring at her, watching the exchange. To her surprise, he had a baffled expression on his face.

Almost as if he was perplexed by the affection that they shared.

CALEB WATCHED APRIL with his father, and with some surprise—and a lot of consternation—he realized that she loved his old man. Not just loved him, but wanted him to be happy. Appreciated him.

Why he should find this disturbing, he wasn't certain. He laid the glass of tea she'd requested for Jackson on the coffee table in front of him, glancing up to see his father watching him with some approval and gratitude.

"Thanks, son," Jackson said.

Caleb nodded, never very comfortable in anything but the role of renegade son. But that need seemed to be falling away from him more and more these days, and it was a direct result of April being in his life, he realized. With April, he found approval in his father's eyes. Because of her, he'd found a way to give his father exactly what he wanted—family, most especially a second chance to enjoy a large family—and yet Caleb hadn't had to do a damn thing. Put forth little effort and almost no emotion. April required no true love, no lasting commitment. Zippo. All he had to do was treat her the way he'd treat any woman, with respect and caring, and marry her for the length of time she needed, and he'd won the jackpot of instant "good" rapport with the old man.

The lovemaking had been a helluva bonus, of course.

But other than that, he could skip the emotional connecting he so wanted to avoid, paste a temporary wife and four babies onto the cardboard cutout of his life, and faster than he could say, "Look, Dad, no hands!" he'd won his father's respect and love.

Damn. Life didn't really work out that easy, did it?

April smiled at him, a soft glow of happiness and joy on her face, and his stomach sank. He wasn't supposed to feel pride when he looked at her. He wasn't supposed to feel attraction when she carried the babies, nor when she bent over to change diapers. He wasn't supposed to go into a soft, droopy daydream when she fed them a bottle, rocking them to sleep with a contented hum under her breath. He wasn't supposed to want to hold her in his arms at night and kiss her neck until she turned to him with the same want he felt burning him.

Life wasn't easy at all.

He had a feeling it was going to get more difficult.

AFTER HIS SISTER and his father left, the closest emotion he could remember since his partner's death swept over him.

Panic. Sheer raw panic.

He was alone with four babies and a woman, and they needed to become a family.

For the first time in his life, he truly realized how his father must have felt after his mother had died. He had no idea how to proceed. The flight instinct pushed at him surprisingly hard.

"You get Melissa," April said, "and I'll get Matthew. The others will lie quietly for a moment, but these two are a little more rambunctious when they wake up from their nap."

He did as she asked, mainly because courage was required at this moment, and if there was anything he could call up instantly when needed, it was courage. Cop training. He approached Melissa as if she were a time bomb. Gently, precisely, carefully. "Now, you and I are going to do this successfully," he told the tiny baby. "Because there's no one here anymore to hold our hand and bail us out. It's just me and you, babe, so let's make it good."

Melissa, unimpressed with his offer, let out a squall that seemed as loud to him as detonation. "Now, don't take that attitude," he told her. "I know you don't recognize my hands on your little body, but I assure you, I'm very gentle," he said soothingly. It didn't really matter what he said to her, did it, as long as he said it with baby-pleasing tones?

Unconvinced, she tore loose a greater shout, her little tongue curling into a tiny disk in her mouth. "My goodness," he said in the same quiet voice as he carried her over to the rocker. "You *are* a noisy young lady. If your daddy was here right now, he'd be so proud to know he had given life to either a cheerleader or a carnival barker."

She was unappeased, and disinterested in the bottle he offered her. "All right, young lady. If you have something else on your mind, why don't you let me know."

Melissa cried louder.

"Okay, I think I got the general consensus of the complaint you're lodging."

He heard a scraping sound in the hall and poked his head into the hallway. April was dragging the rocker across to the girls' nursery. "What are you doing?" he demanded.

"I think it was a mistake to separate the children while they're still so young," she said, breathless from trying to tug and push the heavy rocker while she held Matthew. "They're used to sleeping side by side in clear isolettes where they can see each other."

Baloney. Those babies couldn't see each other worth flip, he'd be willing to bet. April wanted to see him—and make certain he was doing his job right. Obviously, Melissa's forlorn attempts at a college-size yell were causing her new mom some angst, rather like a mother bear who hears her newborn cub yelping and rushes to the rescue.

"Hang on," he said to Melissa over her din. "Your mom is showing some anxiety. You crying is making her think she has to come in here to monitor me."

But he went out, picked up the rocker and carried it into the girls' nursery, the one with the castle on the wall, so that he and April could sit across from each other. He decided it might be best to show April that he knew exactly what he was doing.

"I think she wants her diaper changed," he said over Melissa's cries. "I am particularly adept at this."

"I'll just bet you are," April said, her eyebrows raised. "Don't you want me to do it?"

"I said I am an expert at this," he explained

loudly. "In crisis situations, particularly where a perpetrator is resisting, I like to perform what I call the sneak attack. Watch closely."

Gently, he turned the baby on her back and laid her in the crib. "Now, most women don't complain about this part, but I sense you're going to show me you're different, so it's going to be over before you know what happened, sweetie." Deftly, he undid the tapes, tossed the diaper aside, scooted a new one underneath the baby, gave her a couple of quick swipes with a diaper wipe and taped the new one in place, before picking her up to snuggle her against his chest—all in under fifteen seconds.

"And that, little one, is a sneak attack. It's best if you know about such maneuvers on the part of the male species so you can fend them off later." Sitting down in the rocker across from April, he said, "Don't you have anything you want to say? Questions? Comments? Praise?"

"I do have a question. Is the sneak-attack part of the cop manual, or just yours?"

He grinned at her, calming the now-almost-still Melissa with the warmth of his arms. "Are you asking out of professional curiosity, a need to learn my diapering skills or a desire to experience my sneak attack?"

Chapter Thirteen

Well, Bri had once mentioned that Caleb was fairly confident with his appeal to the opposite sex. Not interested, just confident. And he'd already shown her that he could back up his confidence, April thought with a warming of her female anatomy.

He was suggesting none too bashfully that he could have her panties off before she knew it—and that she wouldn't even protest.

He was right.

How she'd *love* to wipe that smug grin off his face.

Melissa did it for her, burping up a giant bubble of formula all over his shirt. "Oops, I think I hear Craig waking," she said, scooting swiftly from the rocker. "You've already proved you're equipped to deal with all female emergencies and otherwise, so I'll leave you to it."

And she hurried from the room, cherishing the surprised and somehow appalled expression on Caleb's face. "Well, he deserved it," she said, snuggling her face against Matthew's warm neck. "I'll leave him with Chloe and Melissa, since he thinks he's got all the know-how when it comes to sugar-and-spice-and-everything-nice. I'll settle for snips-and-snails-and-puppy-dog-tails, not that I can claim to have his experience with the opposite sex, but just because it's good for him to recognize that sneak attacks on a female might give him unexpected results, like Melissa's sneak attack on *him*."

Matthew didn't seem to care about the battle of the sexes, though, as he allowed her to slip him into his crib. Slowly, she drew a blanket over him, then went to check on Craig. Though she'd pretended she heard him crying, the baby slept peacefully.

She might not have this much quiet again for a while. With Caleb here to take care of Melissa and Chloe—and keep an ear out for the other two—she decided to shower and change. Creeping from the room, she peered into the girls' nursery.

Caleb had his back turned to her. The babies were safe in their cribs, and he had just finished pulling off the offensive shirt. She held back an instant gasp. Broad and strong, his muscular back tapered into a trim waist. A thick leather belt corded through the blue-jeans loops. His feet were bare, as if he was planning to…he reached to his front, and she realized he was undoing his belt buckle. Those jeans were about to come off, and it didn't matter that she'd lain in his arms one night enjoying more bliss than she ever thought possible. She hadn't seen him up close and personal in fairly good light, and as much as she secretly might want to see him in the raw, she simply couldn't. She fled, heading into the bathroom and quietly closing the door so that he wouldn't know she'd passed down the hall.

"Okay," she said, her heart beating hard in her chest. "Rule number one of communal living. We don't take off clothes unless the door is closed. Maybe we need a bell. Something to alert the other person that clothes are about to be shed." No, not after Caleb's sneak-attack theory. She had a funny feeling ringing a bell when she was about to undress could cause a Pavlov's-bell type of reaction.

The door to the bathroom suddenly opened, and April gasped, startling Caleb as much as he'd startled her.

He was wearing nothing but a baby blanket around his waist, tied in a knot, Roman-style.

Swiftly, she turned her back on him and covered her eyes.

"Sorry!" they both said at once.

"No, I'm sorry. I thought you were in the boys' nursery," Caleb said.

"It's okay," April said on a rush. "Of course, you need to take a shower to wash that stuff off you. I wasn't thinking. I'll just squeeze past you, and—" She backed up, determined to get past him without seeing more than she had. Instead, she bumped into him, and he put a hand out to steady her.

"I'm okay!" She darted around him, reaching out

to grab the doorknob and pull the door shut behind her. Pulse racing, she leaned against the wall, relaxing only when she heard the shower turn on. "Oh, boy," she said under her breath. "Now I know why women throw themselves at him like grenades set to explode on impact."

Great-looking in clothes, he was even better nude. With a baby blanket around his waist, he was awesome.

She'd made love with him. And though she hadn't been able to see much on their wedding night since neither of them had stopped what they were doing to flip on a light, she knew what that pink-and-blue-giraffes-print blanket was hiding.

A groan escaped her, and this time it wasn't because his confidence annoyed her. It was because she remembered—and because he was right about sneak attacks.

She wanted to be in his arms again, making love—and she shouldn't have in the first place. There was no reason to make love with a man with whom she wasn't in love. Wasn't going to marry.

"Not marry for real," she qualified to herself.

"Got any towels?" Caleb asked, jerking the door open and peering through the crack.

She barely stopped the scream that nearly tore from her throat. His hair was wet, his chest glistening from the shower. She didn't dare let her gaze wander any lower, instead remaining steadfast on his face. "Under the sink," she said quickly.

"Thanks." He gave her a devilish smile, and slowly closed the door.

Darn it! He knows exactly what he's doing to me—and he's loving it.

BY NIGHTFALL, they were both exhausted.

"I knew it was going to be a lot of work. I just didn't know how much," Caleb said. "It's a good thing you've got me here."

She had moved an extra chair into the den area so that they wouldn't both have to sit on the sofa. Her chair was plush and comfy, and she'd curled her feet up under her, relaxing into the softness. "Having all these children will probably make me very ready to see you whenever you're going to be around," she said, her voice already sleepy.

Did he ever have a surprise for her, little-miss-I've-got-to-do-everything-myself. "I've taken indefinite leave from my job as well. I plan to be here until things get a bit more manageable."

Her eyes snapped open, and he couldn't tell if she was pleasantly or unpleasantly shocked. "Why?"

He shrugged, trying to act casual. It was her house, after all. He was the interloper, even though they'd planned for him to stay here once the babies arrived. But he was pretty certain April had been thinking more of a nighttime schedule for him rather than around-the-clock. His feeling was that the tiny lady might need more help than she thought, and he didn't even want to envision a scenario where she might get herself in a jam with no one here to help her. "I want to put all my efforts into finding Jenny, for one thing. It's tough to do that, and work a full-time job. I had a lot of leave built up, since I don't like to take vacations."

Hell, he'd never had any reason to. Where would he have gone? Staying busy kept him from remembering and thinking about things he didn't want to. He hadn't even really had to ask for an indefinite leave because he had so much paid time coming to him. "I plan to do nothing but help you take care of the babies, and find Jenny." *And make certain you don't overwork yourself and make yourself ill. That wouldn't do anyone any good, and it would worry me real bad.*

But he didn't make the pronouncement out loud because it would bring Independence Day with all the stars and stripes and marching-band protesting forth from April.

"Are you sure? I hate for you to have to give up your life because of me, Caleb. What about your dad? Doesn't that make an awful lot of work—"

Caleb held up a hand. "It's fine, April. You ought to know by now that Dad would rather have me here so he can get hour-by-hour reports. In fact, it's probably either me or Dad."

She smiled a little, her eyes sparkling. "You're probably right about your dad."

He intended to be right about a lot of things.

Mainly, that he thought it was best if he was here with her.

"But I'm not used to living with a man around the clock," she said worriedly. "There's only one bathroom. The hall is narrow. The kitchen is small. I never did buy a futon."

"April, I'm pretty adaptable. You're not announcing a headline by telling me this is a dollhouse. It's just right for you, and I like it because of that. I would have been fairly weirded out to find out that you lived in a house with massive leather furniture and an animal's skull and horns on the wall."

She giggled. "You'll have to settle for needlepoint flowers."

"I find it rather peaceful," he fibbed. He hadn't looked closely at the walls of her house. Mainly he looked at her.

"Maybe we'd better set some ground rules," she suggested.

"Okay. I'll take the babies at night. That will leave me free during the day to talk to people about Jenny. And I'll never, ever, walk out of the bathroom nude. What do you think about that set of ground rules? You don't have to make the same agreement, of course," he said smoothly.

April considered his suggestion. She felt her skin blush, and by the raising of Caleb's eyebrow, she knew he was fully aware that she'd been mulling over the last part of his idea rather than the baby arrangements.

"I never walk around nude, which may disappoint you," she said, making her voice stern. "Did you walk around in the buff in your apartment?"

"Not much," he admitted. "I only put blinds up in my bedroom. Didn't spend much time in my apartment, actually. Too quiet."

"Well, it won't be quiet here." April got up, hearing a baby squawk come over the monitor. She crept down the hall to check on the babies, but the squeak she'd heard was only Matthew letting out a tiny wail before going back to sleep.

"You'll like me being gone during the day," he said softly when she returned. "It's the best way, April, because you'll be asleep when I'm doing duty with the babies. I know you're not going to be one hundred percent comfortable with me in your space."

She shook her head. "I guess I won't. I wouldn't with anyone, most likely."

"It's hard when you've been on your own to suddenly share living quarters. I'm going to try to keep my intrusiveness to a minimum."

I'm not certain that's exactly what I want, she thought. "I'd rather have you here than anyone else, though."

"You would?"

He seemed so astonished that she felt sorry for him. "I'm sorry, Caleb. I haven't meant to make you feel unwelcome. I'm simply so focused on learning to be a mom that I haven't taken the time to say thank you. But I do appreciate everything you've done. None of this would have been possible without you.'' *That* she meant from the bottom of her heart.

He was so quiet. His stillness told her that her words had touched him. She'd have to file that away for the future: *Caleb really likes to know his heroic efforts are truly appreciated.* She wasn't used to that sort of give-and-take since she hadn't had many relationships. She didn't like to count on anyone, or for a man to try to take care of her. Somehow, Caleb was doing it without setting off the old alarms she normally felt.

Maybe it's because I know it's not forever. And yet, she liked knowing she'd made him happy with her sincere gratitude.

And then it hit her. Caleb liked to know his heroic efforts were appreciated—because he felt as if he'd failed the only other person he'd let really close to him.

So that was the cementing ingredient in this arrangement. She had never wanted anyone to take care of her. He needed to take care of her because he'd let his partner down, in his mind.

Caleb was trying very hard, with teasing and sensual innuendo, not to let her become aware that he was trying to take care of her and the children. But it had turned into a mission for him, much as it had for Jackson. She and the babies filled a gap for them, healed something Caleb needed healed.

She was a nurse. There was no way she couldn't respond to his desire to heal.

He had given up a lot to help her with what she most wanted.

She could make a supreme effort not to mind his care and protection. He wasn't trying to take her independence; he wasn't wanting her to become dependent upon him, as some men did. She didn't have to be afraid that he'd desert her, because they both knew this marriage was nonpermanent.

It was a small thing to do for a man who needed something she could provide so easily. What it would do to her heart, she wasn't certain, but then, her heart wasn't the only one on the line.

AFTER ONE LAST RUSH of feeding, diapering and comforting with the babies, April finally decided she'd easily take Caleb up on his offer of nighttime assistance. "Good night," she told him. "Please make yourself at home in any way, Caleb. I mean that."

"Thanks," he said sincerely. "You get some rest."

Her eyes communicated uncertain tension. Beneath all the teasing he peppered her with was a desire to ignore how much he wanted her. Caleb had never wanted anything so bad in his life. Making love to her, feeling her underneath him, being inside her—all of that felt as if he'd been welcomed home.

But he knew their lovemaking was a one-night

happening. April wasn't cut out for a short-term affair, and he didn't regard her in that light. But it was enough to be here with her now, the closest thing to a family of his own he might ever know. Husband, wife, children.

But the tension he saw in her eyes, *that* he could erase. "Go to bed," he said softly. "I've got it all under control."

"Okay. Thank you." She backed away, still hesitant, before turning down the short hall and disappearing into her room.

"And that's that," he said to himself. "Newlywed night number one. No problem. Under control, tight lid, cool temps." He flipped a few channels on the television, keeping a tight ear on the monitor for the babies over the next hour. The late-night comedians weren't that funny, the classic sports channel had lost its appeal and a romantic movie wasn't what he needed tonight, of all nights. Not when he couldn't be diverted from thinking about April, tucked in her white bed.

Kicking his feet up on the sofa, he let the cushy softness surround him, forced everything from his mind and fell asleep.

A WARY SENSATION hit him early in the a.m. He'd only dozed, he was pretty certain, listening with one ear to the monitor, and his consciousness unscrambling what he'd learned about Jenny in his mind.

Something he couldn't put his finger on had

awakened him. His eyes snapped open in the darkness, adjusting to the flickering light of the television. Warm fingers rested lightly against his neck; a bare arm trailed over his shoulder.

April sat on the floor, her forehead against the sofa seat cushion. She slept in a sideways kneeling position that had to be uncomfortable. He registered that she was touching him in a manner which was clearly nonsexual. Comforting.

He sighed, realizing he must have shouted in his sleep again. She'd mentioned it before, and the only reason he didn't realize he did it so often was because there was no one around his apartment to complain about it.

Or comfort him.

Hopefully he hadn't awakened the babies when he'd yelled. Slowly, he pulled to a sitting position, then gathered April into his arms as if she were a child. *Well, definitely not a child,* he thought as her curves melted against him, accepting his action. More like a very delicate, very delicious woman.

It appeared he was going to keep her up every night with his nightmares; she was going to keep him up every night with a serious case of unquenchable desire.

Eventually, they'd have to find a way to sleep, or they'd be no good for the babies. Slipping her into her bed, Caleb stared down at April.

What the hell. He pulled off his shoes, kept everything else on and got in the bed, scooting up against her back. She sighed in her sleep and reached to pull his arm over her waist.

Promising, Caleb decided as he closed his eyes. *A little scary, but promising.*

Chapter Fourteen

Sneak attack. Caleb had clearly pulled one on her. He was in her bed, lying spoon-style up against her back, snoring quietly in her ear.

Far different from what he'd been doing in the early a.m. The shrieks of agony had pulled her from her bed in a fright as she rushed to the sofa. A hand on his forehead and quiet murmurs had chased away whatever was torturing his mind's eye, yet still she'd been unable to leave him for fear the nightmare would recur. It ripped her soul to hear such a strong man cry out, calling for back-up.

Shuddering, she knew that whatever he'd seen was locked in his mind forever, lying in wait to feed on his unguarded moments. She could not allow the man she'd married—for however long—to suffer in such a way. Not when he'd done so much good for her, easing her suffering. For better, for worse, in sickness, and in health.

She'd kneeled beside the sofa and stroked his head. He'd never wakened again—until he'd carried her to bed. Obviously, he'd decided that sleeping with her in the bed was preferable to both of them being uncomfortable on the sofa, and a mature reflection of their situation made her agree.

Of course, it was the simple symbol of the bed which alarmed her. A bed was intimate with two people in it, inviting closeness and a feeling of bonding that worried her.

Jenny would come back, as she should. And Caleb would leave.

Was it wrong for her to guard against feeling more for him, when she already realized she felt far too much as it was?

A weak cry came over the monitor Caleb had parked beside the bed. She snapped it off before he could wake, slid from the bed and changed into sweatpants and a top. Closing the bedroom door, she left her husband sleeping in her bed.

The truth was, she really liked seeing his broad form in her pristine, delicate room. The dolls had kept her from being lonely and scared before, but nothing had ever felt as good to her as waking to find Caleb's strong warmth against her, a strange shelter from everything she'd wanted to chase away, and never could.

"WHY DIDN'T YOU wake me up?" Caleb asked.

"You needed your sleep." April shot him a look, taking in his hair, sexily awry, his jeans rumpled and somewhat loose.

"So did you. Apparently, you didn't get much."

Turning away so she wouldn't think too much about how handsome he was, April fussed with a baby diaper. "I feel very refreshed, actually."

Silence met that. Apparently, he didn't want to bring up them sleeping in the same bed, or the nightmares, any more than she did.

"I did some thinking last night," he said suddenly.

"Oh?"

"Despite the missing person's report, and the police looking for Jenny, no one has come forward to say that they've seen her in a little over a month. If she were in the area, she would have seen the news reports on television, read in the newspaper about her babies going home. She's not in the area."

A sick shiver slid along April's spine. She laid Craig in his crib and went to tend Matthew. "What's next then, if that's what you've come to believe?"

"It occurred to me last night that anyone I talked to hasn't had the knowledge of Jenny's past that you do."

She glanced up at him, her mouth open. "No, Caleb, I am not holding back anything I know about Jenny just so that I can keep her children."

"I didn't say you were," he said, his tone soft.

April drew up sharp. "Please don't play mind games with me. I didn't like it when you theorized that I might have projected my needs onto Jenny, filling in the realization of the mother she needed for her children. And I don't like you overtly suggesting that I might be harboring information about her."

"April. Relax, babe."

His soothing tone did take some of the steel out of her spine. She went back to fixing Matthew's diaper. "I want Jenny to come back."

Silence met her statement, and that unnerved her. "I do, Caleb," she insisted. "I believe that children belong with their parents whenever possible, whenever it's best for that to happen."

"I know you do."

"I won't tell you that having these babies in my care and in my home hasn't opened up a longing for children of my own. A true family of my very own. It's intense, and it's a deeper wish than it's ever been before. But I can have my own children, Caleb. In fact, I dream of it. I've always wanted children, and so, one day. One day."

He was silent, so she peered his way again. The look on his face startled her. "What's wrong? What did I say?"

"I don't want children," he said slowly.

She frowned at him. "What are these?" she asked, pointing to the children.

"Mine for the time being. Little people who need a good start in the world, that I am capable of providing. But I don't want any of my own."

His stark reaction puzzled her. "I don't know what you're getting at."

''I don't know, either.'' He swept her with a gaze that seemed longing, and yet, somehow, unhappy. ''I'm sorry. I don't know why I said that. It was just a...gut reaction.''

He *had* surprised her, and somehow she was disappointed that he wouldn't want children of his own, but the topic was too personal to discuss with him. ''Were we talking about something else before we got sidetracked?'' Picking up Matthew, she held him close. ''Something about Jenny?''

His hand went up in surrender. ''Without you thinking that I'm accusing you of anything—''

''Well, you did before, and it was an unpleasant leap you made.''

''Okay. I apologize. It's in my nature to—''

''Run through the trails of someone's mind. I know. Jenny talked to me a lot, but I've told you everything I know, and I'm not hiding anything.''

''Okay. Slow down a minute. Listen to me. I want you to think about your childhood.''

She creased her lips together. ''I won't think about it for long, so hurry up with what you want to know.''

''Hold Matthew, close your eyes and listen to my voice. Jenny's childhood was somewhat similar to yours. You had that in common. You grew up in what state?''

''Texas.''

''Did you have that in common?''

Her eyes opened. ''Ohio. Jenny was from a small

town in Ohio, David had once lived on a farm in Texas. They had some kind of tree in common. Um, pecan. I think.''

He nodded at her, and April's stomach seemed to reverse inside her. ''I didn't withhold that from you. And it could mean nothing.''

''It could mean nothing, and no, you did not keep that information from me. Idle conversations of no seeming importance take place all the time. But hopefully, with any luck, that may be a salient piece of something I can go on.''

''How could Jenny have gotten to Ohio?'' Panic began to rise inside her. ''She was sick, she had no money. It was Christmastime.''

He nodded. ''And those may be many of the reasons why she could have gone back to a place where she had something in common with the man she loved—and lost.''

CALEB DIDN'T KNOW why he hadn't thought of it before, but somehow sitting in front of the television watching everything and anything had brought the question to the fore of his mind: Why would Jenny not come to her children after seeing them on the news at night? He knew she'd had no intention of coming back, but there was only one reason she wouldn't have sent some kind of message to April once she knew that the children had gone home healthy from the hospital: She wasn't anywhere where she could see the local news.

"I'll be back tonight. Count on a good night's sleep," he told April, shrugging on a black cloth jacket with a warm lining. First, the truck stop on the highway out of town. He'd already checked the bus stops once in the beginning of his investigation; no names had matched Jenny's or any variation thereof.

But the truck stop—until April had said Ohio, Caleb hadn't had an idea of how far the quads' mother might have intended to go. There was lots of goodwill at Christmastime, and truckers were a notoriously helpful lot. It wouldn't have been all that hard for Jenny to have found a softie to give her a ride "home for the holidays."

And a desperate young girl wouldn't think twice about telling such a tale if she meant to return to the last place that might hold happy memories for her. Anyplace but where she'd lost her husband.

He was the champion at trying to outrun memories. It wasn't all that hard to understand Jenny's motivation.

Milling around the truck stop for thirty minutes asking questions, he came upon an older lady named Rosemarie who worked there. Yes, she'd seen a young girl about a month or so ago, and the only reason that stuck out in her mind was because the girl seemed weak and somehow disoriented. At Christmas, she was concerned that the teenager was a runaway. The girl, whose name was April, said she'd just delivered a stillbirth and her husband had left her.

Her tale had elicited sympathy and a hot meal from her, as well as a ride from her sister, who was a trucker.

To Cleveland, Ohio. But from there, the girl meant to go to some small town in Ohio, where her family had once lived.

Sharp instinct twisted Caleb's gut. Jenny didn't want to be found, but he had to find her, for everyone's sake. She needed help, and grief counseling. The babies needed their mother, and she needed them. April needed Jenny to return, not the least of the reasons was that she could never truly adopt the children without Jenny's legal approval. As April's was a temporary foster home, the babies could be removed at any time and assigned to different homes. Caleb needed Jenny to return before he fell any farther into the pretend marriage he'd suggested. Because he was seriously in danger of that—and when April had mentioned wanting her own children this morning, he'd known that there was no future in their marriage at all.

He would do anything on this planet, anything at all: run into gunfire to try to save a buddy, protect the innocent, serve the public, be a father to four abandoned children.

But he would not get a woman pregnant with his child. And most definitely not April. Delicate, gentle, sweetly caring April.

Never.

JACKSON CALLED that morning before he stopped by, ostensibly bringing baby blankets in case she didn't have enough.

"It's going to be cold outside," he said gruffly.

But April could tell by the hungry look in his eyes that he was starved to hold the babies. And she was glad of the company. It gave her a fast break and a chance to eat some lunch. "I'm glad you stopped by, Jackson. These babies have kept me busy. They may be having trouble getting used to the new environment. Although it's quieter here, they may have gotten used to the constant lights and voices and sounds in the hospital. They just can't seem to settle today."

She knew them well enough from taking care of them in the hospital to know that they were out of sorts. Of course, the second that Jackson picked up Melissa and balanced her in his arms, she quieted.

"I think she feels the resonance of your voice."

"Anything this tiny thinks my deep voice sounds like a bass drum. But I'll talk quietly," he said to Melissa.

The baby's eyelids drooped. Jackson seemed delighted that he had comforted the baby as he settled onto the sofa. "The night was uneventful?"

April felt a blush sweep her. She knew he was asking about the babies, but the night had been uneventful for *her*. As every night would be. "Yes.

They slept most of the night, then only required one feeding.''

"How are you and Caleb working the schedule?"

"He's nights, I'm days. But I'm not expecting the babies to sleep all of another night. I think it had to have been a result of all the excitement of moving locations, and they were extra tired. I'm paying for it today."

"I could come over every day for a feeding time so that you can nap," he said eagerly. "I don't do much for lunch at the office, and until they're more settled, I'd be happy to do it. Bri offered to do the same, one or two days a week. We could switch out."

April smiled to herself as she made a sandwich in the kitchen. The McCallum generosity was more than she'd ever expected. It was what being a family was all about—and as much as she loved her adoptive mother and father, the McCallums were a bonus. As were the babies.

I almost wish it would never end. I wish it wasn't a watercolor dream-come-true that might wash away any minute.

It wasn't just her dream; it was Jackson's, too. "Don't you and Bri have enough to do where babies are concerned?"

"I figure this crew's not permanently ours. And they may need us more. Bri's got a real husband for her, and a real father for her children. She also has a housekeeper. You're mostly on your own, and I admire that greatly, but I don't think it should mean you have to do it all on your own.''

"Thank you, Jackson.'' She came to sit in the den, watching him drink up the babies in their four rolling bassinets crowded throughout the small room.

"Well, you're a daughter to me. You're married to my son, and that makes you family.''

Jackson didn't look up, and April paused in the act of putting the sandwich in her mouth. He knew that the marriage was bogus, contingent upon the situation with the infants. But he'd sounded so serious. As if he wanted to believe her marriage to Caleb would become forever.

"Where is Caleb?''

April shrugged. "Trying to follow leads for Jenny.''

"You know he'll find her. Eventually.''

She waited, wondering what Jackson was trying to tell her.

"There's no one like Caleb,'' he said heavily, "when it comes to thinking through a case. He's got a special talent, and he was a damn fine officer.''

"He says he'll never go back,'' April said. "He says that part of his life is over.''

"That's true. I don't always agree with it, but now that I see these children, I think it's best if he didn't.''

"It's not forever, Jackson,'' she said gently.

"I know.'' He laid Melissa in her bassinet, stroking her back before covering her with a blanket. "I just want you to be prepared for the fact that Caleb will find Jenny. It's his job, and he won't quit until he does. And I think you should be prepared for whatever happens when Jenny returns."

"I think it's best that she does. As soon as possible. Children need their mother, if at all possible and appropriate."

"I agree. But take it from me, April," he said, his voice distant and emotional, "what's best isn't always what happens."

Chapter Fifteen

Caleb drove his car, not really certain how to tell April that he had a strong lead now on where to find Jenny. Technically, he should probably tell the appropriate law enforcement agency. The thing was, the fact that Jenny had gone out of state pretty much left local authorities without much jurisdiction, even if they felt like pursuing his flimsy information.

But what really nagged at him was the truck-stop lady's words about Jenny. He'd gotten the feeling that Jenny had been so tired and so desperate that folks had taken pity on her. He really didn't think unfamiliar police officers tracking her would do anything to alleviate the upset the girl was already under.

Though she didn't know Caleb, either, the fact that she'd used April's name while traveling gave him hope that she might see in him a comforting presence. He was helping to care for her children—surely those two combined facts would tame Jenny's fears.

Taming April's would be another. Envisioning going home with his news that someone had, in fact, seen Jenny and helped her leave the state, he felt April's first reaction would be relief. And then concern for Jenny.

Whether she would admit it or not, some trepidation would be mixed in there as well. In her mind, April knew these children weren't hers forever. She had already decided to have a child of her own when the inevitable day of reuniting Jenny with her family arrived. He'd seen her decision and the desire in her eyes.

But she hadn't looked at him as if he'd had the answer to the other side of the parenting dilemma— and he'd let her know in no uncertain terms that he was not a father candidate.

That left him with an uncomfortable, gnawing feeling in his stomach. His mother had died in childbirth after delivering him. April wanted children of her own; he would not jeopardize her health. That meant that no matter how much he knew himself to be falling for her, she would never be his. Not his wife, and not the mother of his children.

It meant he had to find Jenny fast, and get the hell out of April's house. This convenient marriage needed to come to a swift, merciful conclusion.

He was in serious danger of losing his heart. Maybe he'd already lost it—a terrified voice inside him was warning that he was ever more deeply involved in a matter outside his control.

Going inside the small dollhouse of a home, he saw the wreckage of the day by the dim lamp April had left on. Blankets and burp cloths lay over bassinets; empty bottles littered the coffee table. He smiled, seeing at once that April's day had been busy.

He felt pretty certain that she'd loved every minute of it.

Laying his keys on the kitchen counter, he began putting away the bottles in the sink, washing them out for the next day. The scattered burp cloths he tossed in a washer filled with hot water; he checked the nighttime supply of premade bottles in the fridge. Everything looked good to go, and since he was the nightshift, he decided to go down the hall and swipe the monitor out of April's room. He should have called her; should have checked on her; should have told her when he'd be home.

But that would have smacked of a real marriage. He wasn't ready for *Honey, I'm on my way home.* Not now. Not when he knew what he had to do.

Before he could open April's bedroom door, his cell phone rang. Swiftly, he pulled it from his pocket. "Hello?" he asked quietly, moving back toward the den.

"Caleb?"

He frowned. "Yes?"

"This is the lady you spoke with at the truck stop. Rosemarie."

"Yeah. Right. I remember." He'd given her his

number in case she thought of any further details after he left. Many times people did, once they had a chance to think things through without him standing around. And sometimes they just needed enough time to think through airing their conscience—and to give him a call.

"I just needed some time to think about what you wanted to know about. The girl," she said uncertainly.

"That's all right, Rosemarie."

"I didn't tell you everything. I needed to think about what the right thing to do was. I mean, that gal was so frightened. And I didn't know her, but I sure did feel sorry for her."

"I know. She needs help and understanding right now."

"Well, it was Christmas and…anyway, she's at my mother's in Pecan Grove," Rosemarie said on a rush. "My sister took her there so she'd be safe until we could find her family, or until she got well enough to do whatever she needed to do. I can give you the address," Rosemarie told him, her voice soft, "but my mom's grown real fond of her. She's good company. All I ask is that…is that you be gentle with her. She's too young to be as sad as she is."

"It's okay, Rosemarie," Caleb said, his voice soothing. "I appreciate all you've done for her. I'll go and get her, and I promise you, I'll keep in touch with you and let you know that she's getting along fine. She's been through a lot, but she's got people here who are going to help her.''

"You looked like a kind man. You looked like you honestly cared about what happened to her. I wouldn't have called you if I hadn't thought so.''

Conscience attack. He admired Rosemarie for choosing to call him. She clearly wanted to protect Jenny. "You've done the right thing, Rosemarie. I'll be in touch.''

Shutting off the cell phone, he scribbled the address she'd given him on a piece of paper in the kitchen. He called the airport and scheduled a flight into the nearest big city around Pecan Grove for tomorrow, early a.m.

Then he went down the hall, slowly opening April's door to grab the monitor. She was clearly exhausted, one leg thrown out of the sheets, her arm over her eyes. The light from the hallway showed him that she was wearing a cozy flannel gown. Nothing sexy about that—and yet, there was. He just thought everything about April was delicate and feminine.

He so wanted to take care of her. He so wanted to shield her from all the bad hurts in the world.

The cop instinct to protect had to be turned back. She had warned him that men wanted to take care of her, and that she did not welcome that.

But he was going to get the biological mother of the children whom she loved. With one simple plane flight, he would irreversibly change the course of their marriage. Once Jenny realized how much support she had in helping to raise these children, she would want her family back together.

April and he would have no reason to continue their marriage. Social Services would no longer impact their lives.

Tonight would be the last chance to touch April, to hold her, and to feel her shallow breathing in the deepest part of his body. It was wrong, maybe it was taking from her something she wasn't willing to give, it might even be unchivalrous as hell, but just for tonight he wanted to sleep up against her again.

He could sincerely apologize in the morning. Or tomorrow night, when he came home with Jenny. It really wouldn't make any difference, because everything between them would be finished.

He'd return April's key, and pretty much walk out of her life to sleep in his own bed. His barely furnished apartment with the blinds only in the bedroom because he wasn't there enough to bother with them anywhere else.

Something that felt unnaturally like dread filled him. He didn't hesitate any longer, but pulled off his boots. Same as he had last night, he slid into the bed fully clothed.

Same as she had last night, April reached for his arm, pulling his cold, windswept body up against her back, so that his knees securely pulled up under her flannel-covered body and his arm over her waist to hold her.

At that precise moment, Caleb knew he was forever lost to the petite nurse. The wife he couldn't keep.

WHEN APRIL AWAKENED the next morning to the cries of babies going full tilt, she knew she'd slept hard. At some point in the night, she'd relaxed into the deepest sleep she'd experienced in some time. The babies hadn't cried, or if they had, she'd slept right through it, knowing that Caleb was on duty. She'd heard no yells from him, either, so he'd slept soundly as well.

The only evidence he'd been in the house were the clean bottles and dried, folded blankets and burp cloths. And yet, she remembered being held in the night.

Think I've found Jenny. Gone to check, was the note he'd left written on the table. Holding Matthew against her, April felt her stomach pitch at the words, just a little. Hope that Jenny would be found and reunited with her children. Fear for Jenny's condition. Some regret that the babies might not be in her care much longer.

All of these emotions smote her at once. It was almost too much. With tears stinging her eyes, she brought all the babies into the den, changing their diapers and then beginning the juggling act of feeding them.

The doorbell rang and her heart jumped in her chest. "Who is it?"

"Bri."

"Oh, good. Help is on the way, you guys." Still holding the baby she was feeding, April got up and opened the door. "Please excuse my nightgown. I have never been so glad to see you."

Bri laughed. "Did Dad tell you I was planning to stop by?"

"He made some vague reference about the two of you plotting a schedule to assist me. Grab a bottle and help yourself."

Bri did just that, shrugging out of her coat and scooping up Chloe, whose racket seemed the most intense at that moment. "So, how's it going?" She swept a glance around the room. "It looks very successful, I must say. If I didn't know better, I'd think you were handling everything with your customary aplomb. Are you?"

"I don't know. Some things, yes. Other things, no."

"Well, let's start with the things you're not handling as well." Bri gave her a mischievous grin. "Those are the most fun, usually."

"I don't know how to tell you this," April said carefully, "but I think I'm crazy about your brother."

"Oh. Bad thing to be crazy about your husband," she teased.

With a stab of conscience, April remembered that

Bri thought the marriage was a love-at-first-sight match. "Well, I mean that I...I don't know." She sighed, wishing she could tell Bri more. They hadn't had much reserve with each other in the past—and yet, there was no one else she could confide in. "Caleb left a note this morning that said he thought he knew where Jenny was."

"Really? That's awesome! Dad said Caleb would find her, and Daddy really does know best in this instance."

"Yes." April lowered her gaze for just a moment. "Bri, Caleb and I got married so that we could get temporary custody of the babies."

Bri stared at her. "The pieces are beginning to fit. I'm sure I suspected, but decided I would over-look it in the hopes that you two might decide mar-riage was too good to pass up. Not many women would want to throw my brother back into the dating pond. I mean, he can be annoying—he is my brother after all—but I'm not blind to how women feel about him. I just wouldn't want you to leave our family, so I was hoping his charm would affect you the same way."

It did. His charm and so much more than surface effects had caught at April's heart. Unfortunately, she was keeping a secret, one that she knew wasn't going to be pleasant for Caleb.

"So, basically what you're trying to tell me is that since Caleb's gone to get Jenny, most likely any reason you two had to stay married is about to be null and void.''

''In a nutshell, that's it.''

''I see. Well, that stinks,'' Bri said, shifting the baby to her other arm and adjusting the bottle. ''But you said you think you're crazy about him.''

''Yes. I fear I am.''

Her smile was teasing, and yet sympathetic. ''Dad has the notion that Caleb really likes you, April.''

''I think we...have a mutual attraction. Still, some things are off-limits for both of us.''

''Oh, I see,'' Bri said, her tone changing to one of awareness.

''No, no. It doesn't have to do with what you're thinking.'' April frowned for a second, realizing that her problem did have to do with sex, though Bri obviously thought she'd meant their problem had something to do with the bedroom, which it most definitely didn't—or that they hadn't made love, which they most definitely had.

''I'm late,'' she said suddenly, needing to get it out of her system, no matter what happened once her worry was voiced.

''Where are you going?'' Bri asked, sitting up to glance at the clock.

''My period is late,'' April said, slowly enunciating the words so Bri would understand.

Bri sank back into the sofa, cradling the baby in her arms. ''You are?''

''Yes. I was approximately three-quarters through

my cycle when we married. Since I've always been regular as clockwork, I thought it was a safe time. But with all the stress about the babies, and Jenny, and Matthew being…rolled into another part of the hospital for a while, my schedule might have been off.''

Bri's eyes were wide. ''And you think you might be expecting.''

''I don't know. I've never been late before. Never.''

Bri stared at her, her expression stricken. ''Well, there's no point in jumping the gun before you know for certain. You should get a home pregnancy test next week, or make an appointment at Maitland. I can arrange to be here with the children if you decide to go see an OB-GYN.''

''I might have you do that,'' April said miserably. ''You know, I've always wanted to have a child of my own, but this is not going to be good news.''

''You know, then? That Caleb isn't going to take it very well if you are?''

She nodded, hearing the sympathy in Bri's voice. ''I know. He's always been clear about the fact that he doesn't want children of his own. And that's what worries me so much.''

''So let me think this through for a minute.'' Bri got up to put the baby in the bassinet, reaching for the last infant who was quite ready for breakfast. ''My brother has gone to get Jenny. You're both expecting Jenny to want to come home to her children, once she sees them again, and once she realizes she has a larger support system than she knew."

"I think so. That's the way it seemed."

"And so then, you and Caleb can quietly divorce because you were only together for the sake of the children. Only now you think you might be pregnant, which, while it won't make Caleb happy, he would never dream of going through with a divorce then."

April nodded.

"And you didn't want him that way."

April shook her head.

"You got married because of someone else's babies, but you worry he won't want you if you're expecting his baby." Bri bobbed her head. "It's convoluted, but it's Caleb. But you could be borrowing trouble. In a few days, you might start."

"It's true." She hoped so.

"Wait a little longer before you worry too much. Work through the Jenny aspect of your marriage, and once the babies are reunited with their mother, I'll be curious to see if my brother is as easy to get rid of as you seem to think he will be. By then, a home pregnancy test will show something, and you'll know whether you have anything to tell him or not. But since there's really not a good sure way to know until then, just wait a couple more days. At least, that's my take on it."

"All right." But she couldn't help worrying somewhat.

"From a medical point of view, I can't help wondering if you're late because you're tired. The month has been stressful. You don't really want to give up these children, though you know it's for the best if Jenny is in any way able emotionally to handle parenting them. It's a lot, April. And you've shouldered a lot of it alone."

"Actually, Caleb is very supportive. I couldn't have asked for more."

"Well, then," Bri said softly, "don't give up on him so soon. He's a bit of a chicken when it comes to certain things he doesn't want to face, but so are we all. You happen to be accidentally picking at his biggest bogey of all, but…"

"But what?" April demanded, not comforted at all.

"I don't know. Will it help if I tell you I'll pound my brother if he doesn't take it like a man if the two of you are expecting?"

April laughed shakily. "It helps that you say it, but the actual action wouldn't do me much good. I'm a healer by nature, and couldn't bear to see you hurt him."

"Well, then don't you hurt him, either," Bri told her in a gentle voice. "If Dad says Caleb really cares for you, April, then I suggest we give Caleb a chance to find that out for himself."

Chapter Sixteen

"I actually like the idea that I could be an aunt in nine months," Bri said, her face turning impish with delight.

"Don't even say that out loud!" April cautioned. "Let's not put it in the air where it might hang and somehow become fact."

"Like a speech balloon in a comic strip."

"I suppose, except that there is nothing funny about this." April carried some diapers into the laundry room and came back. "I know that I have what it takes to be a good mother. What concerns me, though, is do I have what it takes to be a good wife?"

"Why would you think you don't?"

April shook her head. "Inability to willingly form attachments, maybe?"

"You said you think you're falling for my brother," Bri pointed out. "He might be falling for you. Without an unexpected fly in the ointment, matters might proceed in a surprisingly romantic fashion.''

''You don't think that me being pregnant wouldn't be a fly?''

''Well, is he kind to you?''

''Caleb's kind to everyone.''

''Yes, but does he hold you at all? Kiss you?''

The question brought a sudden blush to April's face. ''He kissed me the night we got married.''

''Obviously,'' Bri said, her tone dry. ''But other than that?''

''No,'' April admitted. ''We probably both tacitly agreed that the one night was somehow a reaction to all the champagne and good wishes flowing our way.''

''Or a reaction to secret wishes in your souls. Caleb's a pussycat, April, though he rarely allows anyone to know it.''

''He sleeps against me in the night,'' April said softly, ''when he thinks I don't realize he's doing it.''

''I don't get it. Details.''

She took a deep breath. ''When I'm in bed, for the past two nights I've awakened to either find him in my bed, or some clue that he was there. And then I remember that I felt him against my back, kind of snuggling me.''

''Oh, that's sweet,'' Bri breathed. ''Almost like he wants to give you affection and to receive it but is too worried about making things uncomfortable between you to ask for it.''

"Maybe," April said doubtfully. "I would never ask him why he does it. The truth is, I like it, hard as it is to admit. So I don't mention it, because I don't want him to stop."

"Oh, April. You guys have got so much airing out to do in so little time. The biggest part of all of this is that you've had to compress so much into so little time. I know you'll miss them, but if Jenny's coming home, and the babies and her start a family, it may be the very best thing for your marriage. I always have faith that illusion is some parts real. Isn't that the basis of fairy tales?''

April didn't answer. Fairy tales were a matter reserved for children who didn't grow up in orphanages—or at least not for her. Reality had always been her companion, and the main reason she depended upon herself.

Caleb sleeping with her was comforting, but the reality was, their marriage was an illusion.

AFTER THE BABIES were settled into their bassinets for their naps, and Bri left, April picked up the mess left from the morning round of feeding and diapering. Then she decided that a homecoming—if Caleb did bring Jenny home—called for a celebration.

She decided to bake a cake. The fragrance of warm chocolate cake alone would be soothing. Mixing the ingredients was a comforting process, giving her something to concentrate on other than whether her marriage would essentially end tonight or not.

But when she got to the canned frosting, it seemed that there was nothing left to focus on. Jenny belonged with her children, and Caleb and April had done the right thing. Not a forever thing, but a right thing.

Bri was right: So much had been compressed into such a short time that April almost felt as if *she'd* been the one to give birth to the quads. And the quads had birthed her marriage. She was going to miss them, and she was going to miss Caleb.

Tears filled her eyes. Sinking onto the wooden stool, she popped the top on the canned chocolate frosting and ate a big spoonful right out of the can. And then she let the tears fall because the frosting splurge wasn't going to make her feel any better.

It tasted good, but it wasn't sugar-and-spice-and-everything-nice like the babies were. And it wasn't snips-and-snails-and-puppy-dog-tails like her big strong husband.

IN THE END, April managed to get more frosting on the cake than in her mouth.

She was actually fairly pleased with her efforts. Little yellow frosting flowers adorned the top edge of the cake. Squeezing those out of the frosting gun had only taken a little while longer, and it made the cake look pretty.

She took a shower, checked on the babies and fell asleep on the sofa for a nap.

Fifteen minutes later, by her watch, all four babies wanted attention again. "You didn't sleep very long," she cooed, wondering if they sensed her unsettled state. "I wonder if your formula is the wrong kind."

Checking in diapers, she decided that the babies had simply returned to their routine in the hospital where there'd been a lot of noise and action. Or at least more than there was in her tiny home. "Maybe it got too quiet and startled you," she said. "When it gets warmer in the spring, I'm going to put all of you in a stroller and walk you every chance I get."

She could do that even if the babies weren't living in her house. Brightening, she realized that Jenny would still need help. *Her* help. She wouldn't be separated from them the way her mind was envisioning.

The front door opened, and to April's astonishment, Jenny walked in, followed by Caleb.

"JENNY!" Leaping to her feet, April rushed to hug the girl. Over Jenny's shoulder, she could see Caleb looking at her, his face concerned. "I'm so glad to see you!"

"I'm glad to see you, too." Jenny pulled from her arms, slowly going to look at her babies sleeping in their bassinets in the den. "I knew you'd take good care of my children. They look wonderful."

But she didn't reach to touch the squirming bundles that were now starting to wail to be picked up and comforted.

"They don't like me," Jenny said, whirling to face Caleb and April.

"They don't know you. They just want to be held." April rushed to scoop up Matthew, whom she knew could be calmed the quickest, and thereby hopefully alleviate Jenny's worries. "See? Just as easy as can be."

"Not for me." Jenny shook her head. "I'd be afraid to pick them up. They're bigger than they were in the hospital, but they still look so fragile."

Caleb put two babies in his arms, sitting on the sofa with them. "They don't break, Jenny. But don't think about that right now. Let us just take care of you first. The babies are fine."

Refusing to sit down, Jenny finally met April's gaze. "I have to tell you something, April."

"Tell me. It's okay, whatever it is."

"The day I left, you'd put your sweater on your chair. You had some money in the pocket, I saw you put it there after someone paid you for picking up something. I took twenty dollars."

"Oh, Jenny," April said, relieved. "Thank you for telling me, but I didn't think a thing about it. I'm glad you had money. I was so worried you left without a dime. Please don't go anywhere without telling us. We were so worried about you!"

"Caleb said you were. That's why I agreed to

come back. I wanted you to know that I'm fine. In fact, I'm better than I thought I'd be.''

''And you'll be much better in the future. How about a piece of chocolate cake and a glass of milk?''

''I'm not hungry, thanks.''

Jenny went to stand by the window, looking out at the street. April had a chance to run a quick glance over the girl. She was dressed in jeans and a loose shirt. Her hair hung lankly, but it was clean. Other than seeming thin—and somewhat depressed—Jenny looked much better than she'd expected.

''February is such a gray month,'' Jenny murmured. ''I'd forgotten how ugly Texas is in the winter. It's all concrete in the city.''

Caleb and April glanced at each other. He shook his head. Clearly, Jenny's reaction puzzled him as much as it did April. But she was a nurse—and a female. She should have some insight into Jenny, and unfortunately the girl just seemed so sad that it concerned April terribly. ''Jenny, why don't you come sit down next to me.''

To her surprise, Jenny did, suddenly leaning her head on April's shoulder. ''I miss David so much,'' she said. ''I miss my husband, and I can't bear the thought that I'll never see him again. I'd give anything just to hear his voice one more time. And I can't stop thinking that if he hadn't taken that job to support me and the children, he wouldn't have gotten hurt. We'd have gone off to college, and he'd still be alive.''

Caleb's and April's eyes met in a sudden flash of realization. The problem went much deeper than postpartum depression, April realized. So much farther than deep grief.

''You can't understand what it's like to lose your best friend, the only one you ever had,'' Jenny said, talking out loud now to no one in particular.

FROM APRIL'S ROOM so he wouldn't wake Jenny who'd fallen asleep on the sofa, Caleb alerted the authorities, Social Services and the hospital that Jenny had been found, and that her health appeared reasonably good. He called Jackson to let him know as well.

''Fine work, son. I knew you'd find her.''

His father's praise was of no particular comfort to him. Whether Jackson meant to or not, Caleb always felt his dad was bringing up his past, trying to show him that he was a damn fine cop. Had been, and could be again.

Caleb wouldn't, and that was the way he wanted it. The second that Jenny had said that they couldn't possibly understand what it felt like to lose a best friend, the only one in the world, he'd known exactly how deep her suffering went.

''Does this mean your marriage is over? Since a mom and children reunion was the goal of the mission?'' his father asked him.

He rubbed his eyes, tired from the flights, and the emotional seesaw of picking Jenny up and bringing her home. The sadness in April's eyes was there, too, pulling on him, though she'd never admit she was going to be devastated to give up the babies.

"I don't think it's going to be that easy, Dad."

"No? Is there a problem?"

"I think we underestimated Jenny's degree of depression. I'm no doctor, but I don't see a quick resolution on this matter."

He wondered if the sound he heard on the other end of the phone was Jackson rubbing his hands with glee. Closing his eyes wearily, he said, "You like April, don't you, Dad."

It was a statement of fact, not a question.

"I do, Caleb. She reminds me an awful lot of your mother. Gentle souls draw me, I suppose."

The last thing Caleb wanted was a woman as delicate and frail as his mother. "I'll talk to you later, Dad."

"Call me if I can help out in any way."

"I will. Bye."

Clicking his phone shut, he sat on April's bed, thinking for a moment. He was in this for the short term, and he had a bad feeling it had just turned into the long haul.

April walked into the room, softly closing the door behind her. "Jenny fell asleep on the sofa. I think it's best if she rests all she can."

"Definitely." He saw so many questions in

April's eyes that he didn't know where to start. "She was staying in the home of an elderly lady who had taken her in. She was fine, and she wasn't that hard to convince to come home. It was almost as if she was grateful to be brought back. I think she couldn't make herself do it on her own, and yet she knew she had to."

"We may have underestimated her situation," April said. "I feel foolish saying that, because as a nurse, I always think I can assess a patient's health fairly well, but this time I didn't."

"You're used to working with babies. They don't have issues. They poop, they sleep, they eat, they want to be held. Fairly simple in comparison to what Jenny's going through. There's no way you could have assessed that."

She sat on the bed next to him, staring into his eyes. "It occurs to me that you might be kicking yourself right now."

"For what?" he demanded.

"You made an offer to secure the babies for me. We'd bring the mother home, give her some time to adjust, make certain the children weren't separated or shuffled into undesirable situations, and then we'd...wrap up the case."

He nodded. "That's what we thought. Or at least, as close as it can be described."

She reached to touch his hand. "Has this turned into more than you bargained for?"

How could he tell her that he was falling for her—

had fallen for her—and yet, he had no right to?
"This situation has forced me to evaluate my life.
And myself. Who I am, and who I want to be."

Silently, she nodded. "What do you think happens now?"

"Are you asking me what I want to happen, or
what I think will happen?"

"Does it matter? Can't it be one and the same?"
He shook his head slowly. "I don't think so."

Chapter Seventeen

With those words ringing in her ears, April knew her marriage was over. Caleb had never wanted something long term, and now that Jenny had returned, it was clear that nothing about her situation could be short term. He regretted the marriage bargain they'd made.

There was nothing she could say about that. The sound of her heart shattering was louder than any words she could speak anyway.

"Let's give her a night to sleep on everything," he suggested. "We're all tired. In the morning, we can figure out how we're all going to fit together."

She raised her gaze to his.

"There's not enough sleeping space here, for one thing," he reminded her. "We'll have to buy a cot or something. And since Jenny seems unable to care for her children, that presents a whole new problem."

"I'll make an appointment for her with a doctor

at Maitland. No doubt they will refer her to a clinical psychologist after assessing her general health.''

He nodded. ''Social Services is going to want to talk to her as well. That's something we need to think about.''

''What do you think will happen when they realize she is unable, at the moment, to care for her babies?'' April couldn't help being concerned. She and Caleb were only approved as a temporary foster care arrangement.

''I hope that by the time Jenny talks to them, she's made some kind of recovery in her emotions. But if not, maybe we persuade Social Services that the best thing for the children is to be here, with us, where their mother can spend some time adjusting to them.''

April looked down at her hands. ''Caleb, thank you for thinking all this through. And for helping her.''

He sighed. ''I want to, April.''

''You do?''

''Yeah.'' He gave her the most serious look she'd ever seen him wear. ''It's my chance to make up for a lot of things. And that's the way I see it. You have nothing to thank me for.''

They stared at each for a few moments, their eyes searching each other's. Then he said, ''I'm going to run by my dad's and pick up a cot I just remembered he's got over there.''

"Okay." Silently, she wondered if the cot was for him or for Jenny, but she was too afraid to ask.

"YOU DIDN'T HAVE a boyfriend before I left," Jenny said when April came out of her bedroom. She'd waited to leave her room until she heard the closing of the front door. She hadn't wanted to watch Caleb leave. One day she'd have to watch him go out the front door, and know he'd never come in it again. "Much less a fiancé. As I recall, you didn't even mention a significant other."

"No, I suppose I didn't," April said.

"That was sure fast."

April looked at Jenny, who was perching on the sofa at an odd angle, as if she was trying to avoid looking at the bassinets that contained sleeping babies. Jenny had a soap opera running on television, a soft hum of voices punctuated every once in a while by a dramatic shriek. A tissue box lay propped against a pillow. "Some things happen quickly sometimes."

"You said once that you wanted children of your own someday, but that you hadn't met the right man. You met him in the space of a couple of months."

"Guess I was lucky. He's actually the brother of my best friend, so it wasn't all that far-fetched."

"Still."

April held her breath, hoping Jenny wouldn't ask any more questions.

"Did you marry him because I asked you to take care of my babies?"

How much truth and details could Jenny handle? Was any of it important?

"I'm not certain what the relevance of your question pertains to," April said honestly. "If you're asking me if I married Caleb because I needed help with your children, then the answer is no."

"Are you in love with him?"

"Why do you ask that?"

"Because people fall in love and get married. I don't know why, but I don't feel like that's what happened. Maybe you got married and are hoping to fall in love."

April tried to give a nonchalant shrug. "Maybe."

"Then if that's what happened, you did it after I left, because you didn't mention it beforehand. That means you did it because of me, because of the children."

"It's more complicated than that," April said, uncomfortable.

"I know you're trying to spare me, April. I know I haven't handled some things as well as I could, but this is something I can handle. I need to know because it affects everything."

"Everything?"

"Yes. If you're married to someone you don't love because of me, that's not fair."

April shook her head. "I can't answer your question."

"Can't, or won't?"

"Sincerely cannot."

Jenny drew in a deep breath. "Caleb says Social Services is going to ask me a lot of questions. He says that they're going to want me to be with my...with them. My babies."

"I think that's what we all want, Jenny. After you've had time to grieve, and some time to come to grips with everything, it might be what you want, too."

Caleb came back inside the house, startling both of them. He was windblown, and his ears were red, as were his cheeks.

"I thought you'd gone to get a cot," April said.

"I was leaving, when your neighbor's dog escaped," he said before going into the kitchen to warm up his hands with tepid water. "Little-bitty poodle thing, running for all it was worth across the street, and enjoying its freedom to the max. Unfortunately, the little boy who went running after it was extremely unhappy, and he knew better than to go into the street to get it." Caleb shrugged. "So I chased the damn dog to the next block before I finally tackled it."

"You tackled his puppy?" Jenny asked.

"I had to catch him. If he'd gotten run over, and I had to go tell that kid what had happened, I don't think I could have taken it. Damn it, but it's cold outside!"

He wasn't wearing a coat. April said, "What happened to your coat?"

"That's what I tackled the dog with. I threw my coat over it like a net, then sort of leaped to make certain the pooch didn't wiggle out and take off. Unfortunately, when I picked it up using the coat as a blanket—and a shield, I'm not too embarrassed to say—the damn dog peed on it."

April shook her head, trying very hard not to laugh. "I have never heard you say damn so many times in one conversation."

"I wish I'd seen it," Jenny said, the first smile she'd shown touching her lips. "I'll bet you were mad when it peed on your coat."

"It was a reflex action to wrap the dog in the coat after all the bundling I've been doing lately with these babies," he said sternly. "And I was no more mad at that dog than I am when the babies wet as soon as I get them diapered. Sometimes, the boys do it *before* I get the diaper on. I just vow to be a little quicker next time with them, but I told the little boy he'd have to find someone who was in better shape to chase his dog next time." He sank into a chair. "Forget the cot. I'll get it later. After I've recovered."

April laughed, but Jenny's face turned serious again. "Actually, Caleb," she said, "you don't have to get the cot. I called Mrs. Fox, and she said I was welcome to stay with her until I get back on my feet. For as long as I need to."

CALEB TOOK JENNY to Mrs. Fox's, promising to pick her up again the next day. He found himself driving to April's as fast as the speed limit would allow, knowing that they had to talk, and they had to talk a lot. There were some decisions that had to be made, and he wasn't certain either of them had the answers.

The aroma of something cooking greeted him at the door. April popped her head around the kitchen frame. "Your coat's clean now. It wasn't all that bad."

She'd washed his coat and cooked a meal. He liked it; he liked it very much. "Why aren't they yelling or squirming or crying?" he asked.

April came out of the kitchen. "All I can think of is that they're comforted by the sound of the TV. Jenny had it on this afternoon, and I left it on after she left. I guess it soothes them somewhat to hear quiet noise."

"Quiet noise. Now that's something to ponder." His stomach growled, and he decided to be very male about it. "Is that dinner I smell cooking? And am I invited?"

"It's dinner, and it's for the man who chases neighborhood puppies." April went back into the kitchen and Caleb followed, intrigued by her attempt to please him.

"I have no offering of my own. No bottle of wine, no box of candy."

"Baked chicken and rice isn't romantic, Caleb. It's just an easy dinner."

"I could run up to the store and get a bottle of wine."

"Sit down and watch TV. I'm going to tear some lettuce for a salad."

"I can do that." He further encroached upon her kitchen. "Mmm. And a cake."

"That was for Jenny. Yet, it didn't seem that a homecoming cake was warranted, considering how she feels about everything."

"Time is supposed to be the great healer." He stuck a fork into the chocolate cake, sighing with happiness. "My favorite. I could sit here and eat just this."

"Dinner's not for an hour. You want to?" April got herself a fork out of the drawer and sat across the dinette.

"Maybe it'll make the conversation we need to have a little sweeter."

"I don't think so. No matter what, we have to admit that our plan didn't work out the way we hoped."

"No. It didn't." He stabbed a forkful of cake and enjoyed it, his eyelids closing for a moment. "Have any suggestions?"

"Don't fill up on cake? Don't use your coat as a net?"

"That's about all I can come up with, too."

He put his fork down and looked at her. "Remember when I told you that running through the trails of the teenage mind was challenging?''

April raised an eyebrow. ''Yes.''

''Jenny told me in the car that there's no way she'll ever be able to see these newborns without feeling pain. She loves them, and she wants them to have what she cannot give them, but to her they represent a painful loss she wants to forget. She said those aren't the feelings a mother should have for her children.''

''She told you that?''

He nodded. ''She left because she was frightened, she was out of her mind, but she was also too desperate to face the future alone, and she feels that she'll never be a good mother. She and David were too young to get pregnant, but with him, she could have done it. All those babies do is remind her of him. And it's not something she can face. Ever.''

''Oh my God. Poor Jenny. Poor babies.''

''Exactly. She wants to sign them over to you and me for adoption. On two conditions. One, that we want them, and two, that we plan on staying married.''

April felt her heart drop straight into her stomach. She wondered what Caleb thought when he'd heard *that* pronouncement. ''What did you tell her?''

''I told her I thought she needed to take some time to make such a drastic decision. She said it was only drastic to me, that she's been thinking about it ever since she left. She didn't want to come home with me, but she knew she had to face what she'd left behind, and do whatever legal work needed to be done for her children. When she found out you and I were married—that you actually had a spouse—it seemed like a gift from God.'' He spread his hands on the table. ''That's what she called our marriage, our family. A gift from God. An answer to her prayers.''

''Well.'' April sighed. ''We are certainly perpetuating a successful fraud then.''

''Her conditions beg an interesting question we certainly hadn't foreseen.'' He reached across the table, gently taking her fingers between his. ''First, April, you have to decide if raising these children is what you really want to do, for a long time. We had planned on a somewhat less extended situation.''

''True,'' she murmured, her heart hammering.

''We talked a lot about our own personal baggage a long time ago. Can you make a commitment to her children?''

''I can,'' April whispered, wondering if he meant a commitment without him.

''Then if you know that's what you can do and want to do, we have to move on to the second condition. Part of Jenny's motivation is that she wants the children to have what she never did, and what she cannot give them now—a stable, loving home with two married parents.''

April stared at him. He rubbed her fingers between his before touching the lovely engagement ring he'd given her.

"Do we want to be married to each other, all or nothing? Do or die? The real deal, the whole enchilada, close-the-escape-hatch type of married?"

The half smile on his face belied the seriousness of what was in his question. "I can't answer for both of us. But..." The secret she was keeping floated inside her consciousness, pressing her guilt buttons. "I don't know, Caleb. I know I'm not unhappy with what we have."

It seemed his features shifted in an expression she didn't have time to analyze, almost as if he was disguising his own feelings. "I'm not unhappy, either."

"But it's a lot for two people who don't know each other very well to decide on overnight."

"Exactly."

She thought he looked relieved. April wasn't sure what she was. "You know what, I think I'll go lie down for a while. If you don't mind eating alone, that is."

He wouldn't let her pull her fingers from his. "April."

"Yes?"

"Are you upset with me, or upset about the situation?"

"Both, I think," she said quietly. "But mostly with myself."

"Commitment-phobia?"

"I think so. I've never liked depending upon any-one, and I find myself needing you more and more."

"Because of the babies."

"Yes." Her head drooped. "I do like you, though, Caleb. Like Jenny, maybe all we need is time."

"What if time isn't the healer in this instance?"

She shook her head. "I don't know. I've just about run out of answers, while the questions just keep piling up."

Does he want to stay with me? Does he feel the same way about me I feel about him? Should I tell him how I feel? Should I tell him there's a chance we might be expecting more than quadruplets on our doorstep?

The questions piled up; the answers ran faster than puppies and a young mother and little baby fists and feet flailing the air.

In the morning, April awoke to two realizations: One, her brief lie-down had turned into seven hours of fitful sleep.

Two, she'd slept alone.

Chapter Eighteen

"You're here," she said with some surprise—and a lot of gladness—as she walked into the den. An adorably whiskered and jeans-and-T-shirt-clad Caleb sat with two babies in his arms, rocking them in one of the rockers he'd dragged from the nursery.

"These little darlings decided they'd party all night. They invited me, and I figured you needed the sleep."

She went to sit beside him on the sofa. "My turn. You go get some rest now."

"Now that Jenny's been located, I have no place pressing to be. No reason to snooze. It's probably best if you and I take a day to see how we feel about making a real marriage out of this."

"No ideas came to me in the night. You?"

"Nah. I think we have to give ourselves an A for effort now, and not worry about flunking the course."

April smiled. "Your approach to school was relaxed."

"Confident."

"Ah. You're confident about a lot of things."

"It's either face a crisis situation with confidence, or fold because you don't believe in yourself. If we stay married and look into adopting these children, April, I'm going to approach our marriage and our family with confidence."

He was so darn appealing when he looked stubborn about something. She wished Caleb wasn't quite as appealing as he was—it made it hard to think about a time when he might not be her husband.

On the other hand, if anyone was worth unpacking her baggage for, it was him. "How can you be so certain we're not taking advantage of Jenny's distress?"

"Because she's thought her dilemma through. She knows what she's capable of right now. I'd worry if we'd have the children in another town, but we won't. We'll be right close by whenever she wants to see the babies. In a way, I think this would be better because she could adjust to them without being so frightened and so overwhelmed."

"Remember what you said about me projecting my needs onto her?"

"Forget about it. I told you, I work through every angle of a case. What I know now about this case is that I think I understand Jenny very well."

"You do?"

"Now that I've talked to her a couple of times,

yes. It's not wrong for Jenny not to want to be a mother if she knows she can't do it without David, if she'd dread it horribly. We can't judge or predict her grief cycle. Only she knows best.''

"How do you know this so confidently?"

"Because it took me nearly all my life to give up a chunk of what was bothering me." He held up a hand to make a point. "And still, it remains a part of me I can't forget. I don't know when I will, either."

She thought about her elderly adoptive parents, and how much they had done for her. Without them, she might have never had a chance. "I guess we do get over some things in time." Glancing at him shyly, she said, "Caleb, I never saw myself as the type of woman to be a good wife."

He shrugged, not waking the babies he held. "I sure never saw myself as dad material. Believe me, me and the old man have gone a round or two that would lead you to believe that I'm lacking some parental training. If we learn by example, anyway."

Her secret burned inside her. He was trying so hard to acclimate himself to the situation he'd had no part in making; only that he tried to make her happy. She couldn't bear to upset him, especially if it was for no reason.

"Let's take a few more days to think about it," she said.

"Worried that Jenny will change her mind?"

Worried that you will.

But she only smiled and began making breakfast. "I know what's wrong," she said suddenly, coming back into the room. "I know what I'm afraid of."

He looked at her.

"We're making it work, not celebrating it," she said. "Caleb, there's nothing wrong with realizing that this isn't what we started out thinking we were doing, and it's not what we'll celebrate. It should be the biggest moment of our lives."

"April," he said kindly, "you need a day off. Away from the babies. A day of pampering should be on your to-do list."

She gave him an impatient glare. "You're not listening to me."

"I am. I'll watch the babies if you want to go get your nails done. Maybe a massage, but not by one of those guys who makes a woman want him to remove her towel."

"You've lost *your* mind," she told him.

"I can't help it. I'd be a little jealous to think of another man near your nude body."

That stopped her. She'd been talking about his assertion that she needed a break. Jealous? Caleb? "Would you really?" she asked, fascinated by this emerging side of his personality.

"How did we get from you having cabin fever to me having a slight distrust of men who run their hands over women for a living?"

"You're sidestepping an issue you raised," she

pointed out, "as well as not being very politically correct, I might add."

"Since when is it politically incorrect to be slightly jealous? Very, very minutely, I might emphasize."

"Never mind," she said with a sigh. "Can we get back to celebrating? My point is that we've sewn this little piecemeal family together with our love and our heartstrings. We've done something pretty good, Caleb."

"Do you want me to take you out to dinner? We could pop a bottle of bubbly?"

She smiled at his tentative offer. "It's more an emotional celebration I mean. But thank you. I'll definitely take you up on some bubbly another time. I had a phone call from Bri yesterday, by the way."

"And what did my sister have to say?"

"She filled me in on the latest gossip. It's probably what's got me thinking maybe we've pressed so much into our situation that we haven't taken the time to examine if we're happy about it."

"Bri is a troublemaker," he grumbled, his tone loving in spite of the words.

"She told me that Adam and Maggie are finally going to have the baby they've longed for. It's a wonderful blessing, because you know that Adam and Maggie have undergone so many trials with the fertility treatments that their marriage had begun to show some stress. But now they'll be a family. Sometimes people don't know how they're going to get to be the family they want so much, but it should be celebrated when it happens. You're going to be an uncle again, Caleb.''

''Well, isn't that something,'' he said, enormously pleased. ''Another baby in the family.''

She smiled, her lips stretched to simulate pleasure for the news, but all she could do was hope that he'd be as pleased when she told him *her* news.

Their news. She had a feeling he wouldn't want to celebrate, then.

THEY SPENT a fast morning with the babies keeping them on the go. Caleb was starting to think he could handle this project pretty well: four babies and a wife. Maybe he could do this permanent-marriage thing as good as he'd ever done anything he'd tried.

The instant he thought about the marriage as a project, he knew April had a point. One of them was assuming a life he'd never seen for himself out of a sense of duty.

''You're right,'' he said suddenly. ''Maybe I've been on autopilot.''

She paused in the act of bending over a bassinet to check on Craig. Her head turned to stare at him, and he couldn't help thinking that it would kill him not to see that spunky face every day. That tousled auburn hair alone felt like silk to his hungry fingertips.

''Autopilot for you is to serve, protect and defend,'' she said. ''I think that's just what you've been doing, for us. And as long as that's the case, I don't think I have anything to offer you that you'll let me give you, Caleb.''

He hadn't expected her to read his feelings. Chewing on the inside of his jaw, he said, ''I suppose the healer in you has a suggestion?''

''Maybe.''

When she bent over like that, making her hair hang forward a little, and then shot him that teasing smile that said oh so clearly that his smart-aleck question hadn't rattled her, he had a suggestion of his own. He desperately wanted to put that woman back in her white bed and christen it for their own. ''I'm listening. Let me hear your best shot.''

''I think you miss the police force like crazy. And I think you've put us in the place of what you're missing.''

He stared at her.

She gave him an innocent look as she stood up. ''You're not the only one who runs through every angle, Caleb. I was a pretty good nurse, and I'm a very astute woman.''

The wink she gave him was unsettling. He wasn't certain if he liked realizing he'd met his match. She'd hit the bull's-eye, dead center. ''I guess you'll have a diagnosis, Nurse Sullivan?''

Her shrug was way too unassuming. ''Talk to someone at the force about how you feel. I've never heard you mention that you talk with anyone, Caleb.

And I know you don't talk to me. You're too busy trying to take care of me, the babies, Jenny.''

"Are we back to that independence thing?"

"No." She gave him a smile that was somehow sad, somehow knowing. "But I do think you need to give some thought to how much your partner's death impacts how close you'll want to be to this family. And to me."

He sighed, the tone unwilling even to his ears.

"You can't receive love if you're not willing to, Caleb."

"Do you want to give it to me?"

"Maybe," she retorted. "But I'm not going to force it on a man who slips into my bed at night and then skitters away before dawn."

"I was trying to be considerate."

"And I liked having you in my bed. I just think you've got to want to stay in it, all the way."

"Are you suggesting you wouldn't mind if I went back to my old life?"

"I want whatever you want. But I want you to do what you want, instead of living with fear and regret. You won't be any better off than Jenny if you do."

"Technically frozen."

"Right. Her grief is fresh, though. You and I owe it to these kids to move on."

"I'll think about it," he said, wanting it to be way down on his to-do list.

She gave him that foxy smile as she bent over

Matthew's bassinet, and he decided maybe he'd think about it sooner than later.

"SO, YOU'RE NOT THINKING about returning to cop work," Andrew Mulligan, Caleb's former captain and close friend, said offhandedly.

"I don't think so. But it is a big part of me that will always be there."

"Sure. We can use you if you think the time is right."

Caleb wasn't certain of anything. His old life, his new wife and the in-between-the-two knife that had once seemed to separate the two so clearly. "I've got these four children now," he said with some wonder.

"I heard. I also heard that you're the one who brought the missing mom back."

"Yeah." He nodded, feeling satisfaction with his part in bringing Jenny successfully to her children. Initially, he'd been afraid that she'd resist returning, but somehow a bond had forged between them. She trusted him. It was a matter of time before she began to trust her love for her children. She'd never be equipped to handle the emotional needs of the quads—were there any single teenage parents who could?—but one day she'd find her footing with them. And sometimes that was enough.

"You're a great cop, Caleb."

Present tense. The past was still a part of him. "My dad always says it just that way, Andrew."

"The old man's right. You are. I just sense your heart's not in it anymore."

"No. I don't think it really is." Yet there was still something there, a question unsolved.

"Your new family will begin to replace your relationship with Terry," Andrew said softly. "In case you're wondering if there's light at the end of the tunnel after losing a partner."

"How do you know?"

Andrew shrugged. "I know."

"Okay." Caleb accepted that, hearing the deeper edge in Andrew's voice and knowing that personal experience was speaking.

"By the way, Terry's wife is dating again. Did you know that?"

His skin prickled with electricity. "Dana is dating?"

"Yeah. A real good cop, too. Something wrong with that?" Andrew asked with a patient smile.

"No. I guess not. I mean, I guess I just…"

"It's been a few years," Andrew said gently. "She'll always grieve for Terry, but she has a family to think about. She knew it was best to move on."

Caleb didn't know what to think about that. Had it been that long since that fateful night? So long, and yet it seemed like yesterday.

"Let go of the guilt, Caleb," Andrew said softly. "We've replayed that night a hundred times. All the officers in the area said the same thing. You did exactly what a good cop should have been doing. No one could have saved him.''

''I keep seeing it, thinking I could have moved faster, should have covered better,'' Caleb said, his voice uncertain.

''Anytime an officer is lost, we go over the details, debriefings, and every other angle to learn what went wrong, and what can be done better in the future. From what I read and heard, you saved a few other lives that night. Just not his. And sometimes, no matter how much we want it to be different, it's just out of our hands.''

''Maybe.''

''Some things *are* in our hands, though,'' Andrew said. ''This marriage of yours, for one thing. Terry would want you to be happy, Caleb. And it sounds like you've got a helluva good thing going.''

''April's pretty sweet,'' Caleb admitted. ''And those babies are something else.''

''Like 'em, do you?''

''They've turned me inside out pretty good.''

''Think of them as making up for your partner, if you need to, then,'' the captain told him. ''Think of everything they're going to need emotionally that you're in a prime position to provide. Consider it a gift to Terry. He'd want that, you know.''

Terry had felt damn strongly about kids, that was for certain. He'd felt damn strongly about drugs on the streets that got into kids' hands, which was one of the reasons he'd been such a fierce warrior.

"You're right," Caleb said, feeling the past recede from focus. It was as if the present became crystal clear to him in that moment, and everything he wanted and needed and hoped to have in the future.

April. And the quads. And helping Jenny walk through the burning wall of grief until she could make it to the other side. Not as a parent, maybe, but as a whole person.

"Thanks, Andrew."

"You're welcome. Anytime. By the way, this conversation hasn't been totally unselfish on my part."

Caleb settled a gaze on him. "April doesn't have any unmarried sisters, Captain."

Andrew laughed, not offended in the least. "No. I'm not cut out for the job you're undertaking, Caleb. I was thinking of something more force-specific."

"As in?"

"I know you're working for your dad, but we could use a crack detective on the odd case," the captain said. "There's simply no one that works the angles and brings in the goods the way you do. It would be occasional, and I'd make certain only the real knuckle-crackers came your way. You'd be off the street and safe from harm, because I think we both agree that with four children, you'd better keep your head down. But you'd still have the opportunity to do something that's close to your heart, and that you're damn good at.''

A chance to do what he really loved again. Police work. It would mean spending less time working for his father, but no one would be happier than Jackson if he returned to what he was best at. Relief spread through him that he'd never expected to feel again, and a well of need opened up inside him.

For April.

She'd understood exactly what he needed to do. Suddenly, he felt healed.

Chapter Nineteen

Caleb hurried home to see April, to tell her that he understood it all now. She'd been right. Until he'd put the past away, he'd been simply giving, and not allowing her to give to him. It was as if he'd shoveled in all the dismay and guilt he'd carried into her life, like a giant piece of earthmoving equipment.

He was ready to be a partner rather than a martyr.

To his surprise, April was gone. So were the quads.

Maybe she'd gone to see Jenny. Quickly, he rang Mrs. Fox's house, asking to speak to Jenny.

"Hey, Caleb."

"Hey. Is April over there?" Maybe she'd taken the babies to Jenny, to try to get them together in small, easy-to-manage doses.

"No. I haven't heard from her, either."

"Oh."

"Caleb, I've been thinking about something."

"Go."

"I do want to be a part of my babies' lives."

His eyebrows raised. "That's great."

"But I still want you and April to adopt them. It's just that...I'm still at the age where I wish I could be adopted," she said quietly. "I wish I had a family who wanted *me*. Y'know? It's not that I can never love them, it's just that...I think you guys are what I would have wanted if I'd been able to have parents of my own."

"I'm so glad you explained your feelings to me," he said. "It helps a lot, Jenny. I don't think I'd ever quite seen it that way before, but don't worry about that anymore. April and I will be there for you. Consider yourself part of our family."

"Thanks, Caleb," she said softly, her voice teary with gratitude. "You've taken on an awful lot for me."

"I've gotten a lot, too. I'll come by and get you later so you can see the babies."

"I want to."

"Good. And then we'll talk about your future, and what we can do to help you."

"Thanks."

He hung up, strolling into the kitchen to look for a note from April. But there was nothing there, either. She could have gone to see Jackson, or Bri.

But packing up four newborns by herself required a mission, he was pretty certain. If there'd been an emergency with one of the children, she would have called his cell phone. Whatever it was, it didn't seem that she wanted him to know about it—just yet.

"MOM, DAD," she said to her adoptive parents as they stared at the newborns in their carriers. "I haven't told you the one-hundred-percent truth. This is Craig, Melissa, Chloe and Matthew, and it looks as though I will be officially applying for them to be my children."

It was clear that Donna and Webb were thunderstruck, as they sat on the high-backed green antique sofa, with a fan of babies in front of them. April felt terrible for not telling them the truth about her marriage sooner. As a short-term solution to Jenny's problem, she hadn't seen a need to bring it up. Now she realized that her decision had been pretty narrow-minded and selfish. They were her parents.

She'd been dutiful, but not loving. She'd shut them out of her life to the extent that she could. Adopting her as a teenager had been a leap of faith for them. Too afraid of a bond being ripped from her again, she'd protected her heart instead of allowing herself to be close to them.

She was a fine one to tell Caleb he needed to resolve his past unless she resolved hers as well.

"I wasn't totally honest with you. Caleb and I didn't get married as a love match." She swallowed, touching the cameo at her neck that her mother had given her on her wedding day. "We did it so we could apply for these children for temporary foster care."

"So these children are not Caleb's?" Donna asked.

"No. He married me so that we would have a two-parent home in order to secure temporary care, if possible. A girl who had come to the hospital bonded with me, and after she gave birth to these children, she sneaked out of the hospital. She left a note that asked me to take care of her children."

"And so you have, it appears," Webb said. "You have a kind heart, April, which other people see. But temporary and permanent are two different things, and Caleb isn't here with you, so it leads one to worry."

"Well, we weren't expecting the situation to need to become permanent. We thought that once Caleb found Jenny—he used to be a police officer and his father asked him to make use of some of his skills— Jenny would see her babies and fall in love with them."

"As you had," Donna commented.

"Yes," April admitted. "I couldn't imagine not falling for these children. They're all so special, they all have their unique moments. Craig impatiently waves his fist when he wants something. Matthew wrinkles his nose when he cries, Melissa can kick her feet like a Rockette and Chloe stretches her fingers as if one day she'll get whatever she wants on her own, without asking for help. Yes. I loved these children from the start."

"What about Caleb?" Webb asked.

"My feeling is that he's still in shock. He's offered to stay with me, but I'll know when the time is right to take him up on his offer.''

"Do you love him?'' Donna asked.

April bowed her head a little. "I do. I have for so long. But it's so easy to fall in love with a man like Caleb, Mom. He takes care of me and the babies so sweetly. And it's not just us. He went running off after my neighbor's puppy the other day. And he worries about Jenny. There's not a woman on earth who wouldn't appreciate what he has to offer.''

"You don't want to be a burden,'' Webb stated.

"No,'' she said, shaking her head sadly. "I don't.''

Her parents glanced at each other before Donna spoke. "That was always your number-one worry once we adopted you, April.''

"It was?''

"Yes.'' She nodded. "Other girls your age thought about boys and dances and cheerleading. You thought about how you could help around the house, and worried about what scholarships you could get to colleges, so you wouldn't be a burden to us.'' Donna smiled at her a bit wistfully. "We wanted you to be a child, but it was as if you came into our home already an adult, feeling that you had to care for us.''

"I did feel that way,'' April said uncertainly.

"We were patient with you, realizing that your situation had made you feel uneasy in our home,''

Webb said. "And we've always been proud of you. Very proud."

"Maybe you should be willing and comfortable with your answer if you ever feel that Caleb is asking you to stay with him because he wants you, honey, not because you're a responsibility he's shouldering. We certainly didn't feel that way," Donna told her gently.

"I feel like I'm starting all over today," April said, surprised. "I don't know why I didn't see any of this clearly, but I'm starting to feel like I didn't know you very well. That I didn't give you a chance. Is it possible to be born again? Because that's the way I feel."

Donna and Webb smiled at her.

"Hello, baby girl," Webb said. And then he held out his arms to her.

Without hesitating, April rose up on her knees and clasped her father's neck. Then she moved to kiss her mother on both cheeks. "I love you," she told her mother. "Thank you so much for being my mother, and knowing just what I needed to hear."

"It's what I always wanted to say," Donna said, "but I just knew it wasn't the right time. You needed to make your own way. And now, you have. Congratulations on your beautiful children, April. You'll make a fine mother. And a wife."

"It means so much to hear it," she whispered. "You can't know how much I've worried that I'd be unable to be a good wife."

Donna slowly got onto her knees beside April so that she could take a better look at the babies. "You'll be a wonderful mother now that you've let go of the past, too." She touched her daughter's hair with a trembling hand. "A word of caution, my sweet. The adoption process will be arduous."

"Was it?" she asked Webb, who rustily got down on his knees to peer into Matthew's carrier.

"It was," he confirmed. "But it was worth every minute. Look what we got, after all."

He took her hands in his, squeezing them for just a minute.

"Well, Webb," Donna said to her husband as he sat on the opposite side of April. "We always prayed for grandchildren."

The three of them looked at the carriers. Donna clasped her hands in delight. "I don't know how, and I don't know why, but the day I saw you standing in the orphanage, April, I knew you'd be the best daughter a mother could ever have. Four grandbabies! I can't wait to tell my church prayer group!"

CALEB FLEW OUT the door when he heard April's car pull into the driveway. He pulled open her door, unable to wait for her to get out of the car. "I was so worried!"

"Why?" April smiled at him, a new emotion for him residing in her heart. "We just went for an outing."

"That was some outing! It seemed you were gone for hours."

And there was a different air about her, a seeming peacefulness he'd never seen before. He liked it; she wore contentment well. "You didn't go see a masseur, did you?" he asked gruffly, unstrapping two of the baby carriers in the back seat.

"No." April laughed, the sound carefree and joyful to his ears.

"Well, whatever you did you look like it did you a whole lot of good. Stand there for a second with the other two while I take these little guys inside. I don't want you doing any more lifting than you've already done today."

He carried Matthew and Craig inside out of the chilly breeze. Returning to the car, he lifted out Melissa and Chloe, whom April had already unstrapped. Silently, they both went inside the little house, and each began unbundling babies and putting them on a puffy quilt on the floor.

Awkwardly, he wondered if she'd go ahead and mention where she'd been. It was about to kill him! For a man as good at figuring things out as he liked to boast that he was, he had no idea where she had taken the quads. After an hour had passed after his return—and he'd talked to the captain a while—he'd called his sister to ask surreptitiously nosy questions.

Bri had had the nerve to laugh at him. "Are you going to make a habit of calling me every time April gives you the slip? I'm going to install caller ID if you are.''

He'd hung up, disgruntled, but only because Bri was the only one who would dare to call him on what he was doing—and then tease him about it. Deciding that he'd just have to wait, he had thrown himself onto the sofa, making certain his cell phone was on and nearby. Just in case.

''I went to see my old captain,'' he said, deciding the onus was on him to put April's concerns about him at rest. Where she'd been might forever be a mystery to him, but if she always returned looking that renewed, he'd let her go without question.

''You did?''

He sat up a little straighter, realizing he had her complete attention. ''Yeah. I'm going to start doing an occasional case.''

''What does that mean, exactly?'' She wrinkled her nose at him, and he thought she looked just like Matthew when she did it.

''Detective work. Nothing big.''

''It sounds big. It sounds like something you'd be very good at.''

Her praise felt great. ''The captain seems to think so.''

''I think so, too. What did your dad say?''

''Congratulations. But he was very quiet, and when he's like that, I know he's trying to disguise his emotions. Dad had wanted me to go back to what he thought I was naturally good at for a long time. I'd resisted his encouragement.''

''Well, you and I have something in common, then.'' She folded a baby blanket and looked up at him. ''I've been known to resist a little encouragement myself.''

''Did the babies enjoy the outing?''

''They slept mostly. But when they were awake, they were darlings. Totally.''

She smiled at the babies on the blanket beside her, and Caleb's heart warmed like a sea in warm summer. He pulled her up into his lap, but she surprised him, straddling him instead of reclining against him.

''I missed you,'' he said.

''I missed you more,'' she told him.

''I want you.''

It had to be him who said it, April knew. She would have waited forever to hear those words from this man, because it was so important that he want her, because of everything that came with her. ''I want you more.''

''I have condoms,'' he told her, ''if you're of a mind to tell the children we're going to take a nap.''

''Condoms?'' April looked down into his eyes from her perch in his lap.

''And champagne. I went by the store today because I agree with you, April. We should be celebrating.''

''Oh, Caleb,'' she murmured, sinking into his outstretched arms. "I feel like it's the Fourth of July in February."

"Not New Year's all over again?" he asked, pulling her down on top of him on the sofa so that he could touch her hair, her face, her breasts.

"No," she said against his lips. "We've both moved forward, and that calls for a hotter, more intense holiday."

"Firecrackers work for me." With great speed, he pulled her sweater over her head and undid her jeans.

"I'm thinking Roman candles in February is perfect." Stripping off his jeans and pushing them down over his hips, she worked them off him until he was as nude as she was.

"You're beautiful," he said, taking hold of the blanket over the back of the sofa. "Too bad I have to cover you, but I don't want you cold, and I don't want to shock the children."

"The children appear too ready to sleep to care about watching us," April said, sighing as Caleb's mouth closed over her breast. She reached between his legs, massaging him, already wanting him.

"I've got to get the condoms," he said, splashing cold water on the shooting emotions inside her. "I don't want to take any chances on getting you pregnant."

It was so hard to stop the magic she was feeling, but she had to be honest with Caleb. He'd gone to the captain as she had suggested. He was making an honest attempt to put the past behind him.

Only she held the key to knowing if it ever truly would be. Sitting up, she wrapped the blanket around her as she stared down at him. "There's something I have to tell you."

She had to. No easy way to put it, either.

"Can it wait? It'll only take me a second to jog down the hall, babe. I promise it's going to be worth the wait."

She smiled and shook her head. "You've been so good to me, and to Jenny, and to the children." Her breath came deep from inside her as she pulled up courage. "It involves our marriage. The question of whether we want it to be a permanent marriage. There's only one thing I think we have to work out between us." She hesitated, but only for a second. "I know how you feel about having a child with me, Caleb."

The look on his face was not forthcoming. Instinctively, he had an idea where she was going with this.

"April, I would give you anything. I would do anything for you. It's not you. I don't want to have a child of my own with *anyone*."

Her secret forced her to probe the conversation more deeply. "Caleb, could you at least consider it?"

He shook his head.

''I think it's probably no secret to anyone that I've always wanted—''

His back went straight as he jumped up from the sofa and began putting on his clothes with unyielding haste. ''What you want I cannot give you. I cannot give anyone. I will not *do* to anyone.''

She frowned. ''Caleb, please. You're not leaving any room for—''

But she'd pushed him too far, far past his breaking point. ''No. The answer is no today, it will be no tomorrow, it will always be no. I thought you accepted me the way I was, the way I accepted you, April, past hurt and all. I can't really explain the depth of why I feel the way I do, but it's me, it's etched in my soul, dug in like damaged cells, and I'm never going to be any man but the one I said I was in the beginning. Like Jenny, there are some things a person only marginally heals from, and this is something I cannot do. I'm sorry. I'm really, really sorry.'' He took a deep breath, his face hard, his body nearly rigid from the assault of her plea. ''And now, I'm leaving.''

Chapter Twenty

"Please don't leave like this," April told Caleb as he tossed his things into a duffel bag.

It wasn't that he wanted to, but there was too much fear in him. He'd fallen in love with her—and it scared the hell out of him. She had needs he could not fulfill, needs she had a right to have fulfilled by someone. Not him. "I'm sorry."

She started to sob, wrenching his heart in two. "You care about me. I know you do."

True. That was, precisely, the problem. He'd meant to alleviate her needs, take care of her and the children. He'd never meant to start needing her the way he knew he did. And he'd meant to only give to her—but this, what he knew she really wanted, he could not give. He saw it in her face every time she held the adorable quads; he knew the depth of love in her soul. "I do. But I just can't get you pregnant, April. I could be responsible for you and the babies, because we thought it was short-term. And then it was a question of long-term, and that seemed possible, and maybe even right. But you're safe now," he said, his voice pleading for her to understand what even he could not explain. "I'll always be around to help you with all of this, just not in a husband capacity."

"I think I'm pregnant," she said hoarsely, her face torn with the agony of finally revealing her secret.

His whole being stilled in the act of jumping off the emotional cliff he'd been heading for. *"What?"*

"I think I'm pregnant. I'm not certain, but there's a possibility. I've got an appointment at Maitland tomorrow for accurate testing." This time the words were a hushed confession. She wiped her eyes, staring at him.

So helpless. And so sweet.

And so deeply embedded in him.

Coward if he jumped now; thief if he ran with her heart; bastard if he deserted her.

April would be such an awesome mother to his child. She'd already proved herself as a mother, so Madonna-like.

And yet so fragile.

"We need you," she said.

His mind blew into darkness, the impact tearing a crater in his soul.

Of course he'd been drawn to the gentle mother in her. She was, in so many ways, a frame for the delicate mother he'd never known.

There was too much pain swimming in his head.

So he sat down, tugged her into his lap, and, burying his face in her hair, burst into tears he'd never before allowed himself to cry.

"I know what I've been doing," he said finally as she silently wiped his tears away from his eyes with her fingertips. Her loving action was the final push to break down his wall of reserve. "I haven't been honest. I've been in love with you since the day I met you."

"Oh, Caleb," she said, her panic beginning to recede. His gaze was so clear, so honest, that she knew for the first time she was seeing the real him. All of him.

"I do love you," he told her.

"I love you, too," she whispered.

"I think I was taking the easy way out. We'd get married on a pretense. I knew in my heart Jenny couldn't handle the children, it was too much for her after losing her husband. She wanted you to have them, and then, so did I." He drew a deep, shuddering breath. "But I have to admit that I must have been trying to create a family without..."

April touched his face with her hand. "Endangering me?"

He stared into her eyes. "I'm so sorry. I admit my mom dying when I was born is a fact that has haunted me. Badly. It's not very brave, is it?"

"I think you're a hero," she said softly. "I love you more, as of this moment." Then she tapped her finger against his lips in a gentle rebuke. "But,

Caleb, if I am pregnant, can I just remind you of one thing?''

He nodded slowly.

"I am a nurse. I can take care of myself. *Good* care of myself. That's something you can't do for me.''

She felt a ripple go through him. "I know. And I know it will be all right. But I'll still be scared.''

Then he smiled at her, and she knew he had made peace with his past. "You can pace in the waiting room.''

"I'll be right there in the delivery room with you. You should know that by now!''

It was true. He had been with her through some of the hardest, darkest moments. "I know. And I love you for it.''

"And I love you, Nurse Sullivan-McCallum. But if you don't mind, I'm going to have to insist upon moving you and all these children into a bigger castle. With many bedrooms, and many bathrooms, and many phone outlets for the teen years. It won't be quite a dollhouse, but I give you my word that you can decorate it any way you please. Pink flowers, teacup wallpaper in the kitchen, I don't care. Five children! And I was the guy who said I wouldn't have any. Bri is going to tease me *unmercifully.*'' He groaned, but his face was happy. "Let's start looking for the perfect house, just the right thing for us—and our growing family.''

"That's fine,'' she said with a smile, drawing his

head to hers for a kiss. "I was scared, too. I'm not anymore, Mr. Troubleshooter. And I'm ready to make that move with you."

"FALSE ALARM," April told Caleb as she snuggled up against him later that evening.

With the reading lamp on, Caleb was lying in her bed, bare-chested above a white sheet, as if he'd always done this before. He'd been circling real-estate ads in the newspaper, but he dropped the paper at her announcement, and sat up straight. "Really?"

"Really." And then she laughed.

"What's so funny?"

"I used a cop term, and you didn't even notice."

"Because it elicited the same kind of relief I'd always felt whenever I heard *false alarm*."

"But you seemed so surprised. If I didn't know better, I'd think you were disappointed, Caleb."

He thought about that a moment, realizing he'd been ready for whatever had come to them. That was the difference between then, and now.

He was ready.

Taking April in his arms, he said, "Nah. Hearing you talk cop to me turned me on, babe. I suggest we practice babymaking often and see where that takes us. *Stat.*"

She moaned underneath him, her need for him thrilling him. "Very funny, Caleb. A medical term. I got it."

"I'm so glad," he whispered, taking her with him, "I'm so glad that I've got you, to have and to hold. *Forever.*"

THE McCALLUM QUINTUPLETS

BY
KASEY MICHAELS
MINDY NEFF
MARY ANNE WILSON

Kasey Michaels is the *New York Times* and *USA TODAY* bestselling author of more than sixty books. She has won the Romance Writers of America RITA® Award and the *Romantic Times* Career Achievement Award for her historical romances set in the Regency era and also writes contemporary romances.

Mindy Neff published her first book in 1995. Since then, she has appeared regularly on bestseller lists and won numerous awards, including the *Romantic Times Magazine* Career Achievement Award.

Mary Anne Wilson is a Canadian transplanted to Southern California, where she lives with her husband, three children and an assortment of animals. She knew she wanted to write romances when she found herself "rewriting" the great stories in literature, such as *A Tale of Two Cities*, to give them "happy endings." Over a ten-year career, she's published thirty romances, had her books on the bestseller lists and received a Career Achievement Award in Romantic Suspense.

GREAT
EXPECTATIONS

BY
KASEY MICHAELS

Chapter One

The room was dark, the only light filtering through the slats in the vertical blinds on the single window overlooking Austin's Mayfair Avenue. The Texas sun wasn't all that strong at five on this March afternoon, but Dr. Madeline Sheppard still squinted slightly as she watched the illuminated screen in front of her.

The room was silent, the only sound the purring motor on the ultrasound machine pulled up next to the examination table where Maggie McCallum lay, also watching the screen on the ultrasound machine.

Madeline leaned a little closer to the screen, her lips moving silently.

"Dr. Sheppard?" Adam McCallum asked as he stood on the other side of the examining table holding his wife's hand, giving it a reassuring squeeze. "Is anything wrong?"

Madeline looked at Adam from overtop the tortoiseshell-framed half glasses she'd worn for close work since her thirty-fourth birthday, hoping she wouldn't be in bifocals for her thirty-fifth. She'd taken to attaching the glasses to a strap hung around her neck, although most times the glasses perched low on her nose because that was even easier than having them hang from the strap.

"Hmm?" she murmured, her mind still concentrate on the screen, what she was seeing on that screen. "Oh I'm sorry, Mr. McCallum. No, no. Nothing's wrong. Quit the contrary. You just lie still a little longer, Maggie. want to recheck something, that's all."

"Hey," Maggie said, laughing nervously, "take all th time you need. And I still don't know how you can se anything on that little screen."

"Oh," Madeline said, tongue in cheek, "I'm seein, something. Trust me, I'm seeing something."

She squirted a little more warmed gel on Maggie' belly and continued moving the sensor, watching th screen as, under her breath, she did a little arithmetic.

"Doctor, you're beginning to worry me, even if yo keep saying everything's all right," Adam complained walking around the bottom of the examination table t come peer over Madeline's shoulder as she used the smal dials on the machine to box section after section of th screen, then repeatedly hit the Print button.

"Okay, all done," Madeline said, sighing as she lifte the sensor from Maggie's already faintly rounding belly then wiped her patient's skin free of the lubricating ge "How about you just zip up your slacks, and we'll g into my office, where we can all be more comfortable."

Before Adam, still hovering at her shoulder, could as another question, Madeline grabbed the printouts an walked into the adjoining room. She shrugged out of he white examination coat, smoothed her loose-fitting, ankle length dress and seated herself behind her desk. Sh folded her hands together on the small stack of printouts took a deep breath and collected her thoughts.

The conversation she was about to have would be won derful, at first. But then the questions would come, th fears would surface—all of them understandable, all of them possibilities that had to be addressed.

They came into her office holding hands, two good people. Good-looking, good hearts, good friends. Maggie, a schoolteacher and wife as well as an anxious, expectant mother. Adam, the son of Jackson McCallum who, providentially it would seem now, had financed this very building, the latest addition to the Maitland Maternity Clinic.

Officially, the new unit was called the Emily McCallum Multiple Birth Wing, in honor of the woman who had died thirty-one years ago giving birth to the McCallum triplets, Adam, Briana and Caleb.

Emily McCallum's delivery-room death would be very much on Adam's mind in a few moments, and Madeline mentally rehearsed how she would address those concerns.

How ironic that Adam and his wife had come to seek Madeline's advice as a fertility specialist several months ago. How wonderful that she had been able to help them. Now they would learn that the three of them were going to be a close-working team for the next seven months, along with Zachary Beaumont, the wing's highly qualified perinatologist, who specialized in high-risk pregnancies and multiple births.

Madeline watched them closely as the couple sat down in the leather chairs, still holding hands, both of them looking at her expectantly. Good word, expectantly. Because, boy, were these two ever *expecting!*

"Dr. Sheppard?" Maggie asked, her voice overly bright with nerves. "Are we right about the timing? I'm just two months along? Because I'm really having trouble with my waistbands, and I thought it would be too soon for that."

Adam laughed. "Maggie sees no relation between the chocolate-covered marshmallow Easter eggs she's discovered and her weight gain, Doctor. Me, I'm considering buying stock in the company, if their candies are really that good."

"Ha, ha," Maggie said, glaring at her husband for a moment, then smiling.

These two smiled at each other a lot lately. Madeline liked that; it made a nice change. Infertility strained many a marriage to the breaking point, and as both doctor and friend, she hadn't been unaware of the tension Maggie and Adam had been under through the months of fertility testing, the "come home, my temperature has gone up" pressure that took a lot of the romance out of any marriage.

But all that was over now. Maggie and Adam were pregnant. Now it was Madeline's job, and Zachary's job, to get Maggie to a healthy delivery.

"Okay," Madeline said, putting a smile on her face. "First, yes, Maggie, I'd say we're right on the money with your due date, especially since we've been routinely running pregnancy tests and monitoring your cycles. You're two months pregnant. Your uterus, however, is nearly twice the size of a two-months' gestation."

"It's twice as large *because*…?" Adam asked, leaning forward in his chair.

"Maybe because," Madeline suggested, "there could be more than one baby in there, Adam. We did discuss this possibility, remember?"

Maggie nodded. "Yes, we did. Adam was one of triplets, so that made us more likely to have a multiple pregnancy, even without the fertility drugs I took. You told us, Doctor. We knew the risks."

"And we told you it didn't matter. One baby, three

babies—we'd love them all,'' Adam added, his eyes going to the small stack of printouts Madeline had just picked up. ''We're having more than one? Is that what you're saying? Can you see them on there? I mean, really see them?'' He stood up, held out one hand. ''Let me see.''

Madeline deliberately put down the printout she'd been holding, folded her hands over the stack once more. ''In a moment. And, yes, Mr. McCallum, I can see them. I counted, counted several times, and there's no question. You and Maggie are going to become the parents of what we in the medical profession so ridiculously call multiples.''

Maggie gave a little cry and reached out to Adam, who held her close, kissed her hair, her cheek.

And Madeline watched, smiling with them...and waited for the other shoe to drop.

Adam was the first to sober, to look at Madeline, his eyes dark. ''How...how safe is this, Doctor? I mean it, be honest. My...my mother—''

''Your mother, Mr. McCallum,'' Madeline interrupted quickly, ''gave birth over thirty years ago, in a small-town hospital unequipped to handle her special circumstances. You know I've seen her medical records, and her complications, although still dangerous today, are much more manageable now. And, as we've also already discussed, the McCallum Wing is the most well-equipped, up-to-date facility in this entire region. We're going to take very good care of Maggie and your babies.''

''Babies,'' Maggie said, lightly pressing both hands against her belly. ''How many, Doctor? Two? Three?''

''They're still incredibly small, but I tried to capture them each separately.'' Madeline picked up the grainy printouts and began dealing them out in front of the expectant parents like playing cards, watching Maggie's and

Adam's eyes widening, their cheeks going pale. "One... two...three...four...and *five*."

Then she grabbed the ammonia packet from her top drawer and broke it under Adam's nose. Funny, it was usually the mother who fainted....

"WE'RE GOING to have to pile pillows on the floor of the delivery room," Madeline joked as she ended her story about her newest expectant father. She sat low on her spine on the soft leather couch, her bare legs and feet propped on the glass-topped coffee table. "Otherwise, mother and babies will be fine, and Daddy will be admitted for a concussion. I mean it, Ian," she said, looking at her friend, who was looking at her bare feet, "the poor guy went out like a *light*."

Ian Russell picked up Madeline's crossed legs and slipped a section of the morning newspaper under them. "I'd do more than that," he said, heading to the small wet bar in the main living area of his spacious apartment to snag a bottle of soda from the refrigerator. "I think I'd be on the next fast jet to anywhere but here. Five babies at one time? Damn, Maddie, that's a litter." He held up a green plastic bottle, wiggled it. "Want one?"

"It is *not* a litter, Ian," Madeline replied testily. "And no, not that stuff. That stuff has no caffeine. I have about five medical journals to read tonight. I need caffeine. Lots of caffeine."

"Really? Sorry, all out," Ian said, grinning at her. "How about I spoon-feed you some of the coffee grounds left over from this morning? That ought to give you a kick start on staying up all night."

Madeline rolled her eyes, indicated with a wave of her hand that, yes, reluctantly, she'd take the soda he'd offered. "You don't really think multiples are litters, do you, Ian?'' she asked as he sat down next to her on the couch, rested his head against the back cushion.

"No, Maddie, I don't. But I get a real kick out of the way your nostrils sort of *flare* whenever anyone dares to say the word *litter* in your presence. Hell, I think you're doing a great job. Bringing happiness to previously infertile couples, bringing children into the world who will be loved, cherished—really wanted.'' He turned his head to look at her. ''Okay? Am I forgiven?''

''I'll think about it, while you think about groveling. Because I absolutely love it when you grovel,'' Madeline said, raising the bottle to her lips, drinking deeply. Then she closed her eyes, tipped her head back and gave every indication of going to sleep.

Ian looked at her, shook his head. What a woman. She worked harder than any two men he knew, practically *lived* her job. No, her profession. What Maddie did, what she achieved, was a whole hell of a lot more than just a job. She had been this way, this dedicated, ever since he'd met her.

How long had he and Maddie known each other? Fifteen years? No, more like seventeen, ever since their freshman orientation class that first day at the university. Almost half a lifetime, considering they'd both turn thirty-five this year, Ian just two weeks after Maddie's birthday.

The Gruesome Twosome, that's what they'd called each other, a fairly uninventive name, but they'd liked it. He'd given her a little whirl, because that's what he liked—giving the ladies a little whirl—but it hadn't worked. She'd been too caught up in her studies to have much time for romance, and the one time he'd tried to kiss her, she'd laughed at him. Laughed!

But she'd been right. They were compatible. As friends, they were compatible. They'd even shared an off-campus apartment the last two semesters of school, Maddie doing the cooking, Ian the cleaning. And cleaning up after Maddie in the kitchen had been a full-time job.

Still, they were friends, great friends. Best friends. Nobody applauded louder when Maddie received yet another academic honor. No one laughed harder when Ian had to take to wearing dark sunglasses and a big hat to avoid the latest lady in his varied love life.

They'd gotten drunk together the night he learned that his father, from whom he'd been estranged for years, had died. They'd spent a month backpacking through Europe together before their last year of school. Maddie had cried on his shoulder when her first big love affair went belly-up, and he'd written her application for her internship.

And here they still were, not roommates anymore—Maddie lived in the apartment across the hall—but still best friends. She could tell him anything, and he'd listen, he'd understand. He could show up on her doorstep, feverish, hacking and sneezing, with a morning beard and bed hair, and she'd take him in, cluck over him, make him all better.

In fact, if they weren't such good friends, he'd marry her, except that marriage would probably just break up their friendship.

"Maddie?" he said, pushing a dark curl that had slipped onto her forehead, tucking it behind her ear.

"Hmm?" she said, her eyes still closed. "If you've got a hot date and you're asking me to move, you can just forget it. I'm staying right here."

"Long day, huh?"

"No more than most," she said, seemingly trying to open her eyes by raising her eyebrows—a fruitless exercise, to say the least. "But I had to tell one of my patients that the in-vitro didn't work. That was hard."

"Are you going to try again?"

"Uh-huh, thanks to the fund Jackson McCallum set up to help pay for the procedure for those who can't really afford the high fees." She finally succeeded in getting her eyes open, her deeply brown, wonderfully compassionate eyes. "I hate it that sometimes a couple's checkbook comes between them and the chance for a baby. It just doesn't seem fair."

"And she's off," Ian said, smiling. "I would have thought you'd be too tired to climb up on any of your many soapboxes tonight."

She wrinkled her nose at him. "When you're right, you're right. Topic closed. Now, do you want me out of here or not, because if you don't have a date I think ordering out for pizza sounds like a real plan. We rent a movie, pop some popcorn later? What do you say? Those darn journal articles can just wait for another day."

Ian winced. "Sorry, babe. Definitely a hot date." He pushed back his sleeve, looked at his wristwatch. "As a matter of fact, she'll be here any moment now, so if you wouldn't mind?" he ended, picking up her bare legs once more, pushing them off the coffee table so that Madeline had no choice but to get up. It was either that or slide onto the floor in a heap.

She gave her thick black mane a toss, then pulled at her extra-extra-large gray sweatshirt that all but hid the fact that she was also wearing a pair of cutoff jean shorts. Maddie had great legs, Ian knew, but that body of hers pretty much remained a mystery, even after all these years. He'd never met a woman so careful to conceal her body, mostly with goofy granny gowns or oversize sweats.

He stood up with her, flicked a finger against her shiny, makeup-free nose. Her naturally curly hair—and there

was a lot of it—was still damp after her shower, and he
liked the way it waved around her face. Such a change
from the tight braid or the bun she usually squeezed it all
into because she thought the scraped-back styles made her
look professional. Professional, hell. Just as he'd told her
about ten million times, in those granny gowns, with that
hair, she looked like a gunnysack with bangs.

"Tomorrow night?" he asked her as he took her by the
shoulders, turned her, aimed her toward the door. "Pizza,
popcorn, the whole nine yards. My treat."

"You're on," Madeline told him, accepting the sneakers he picked up, held out to her. "Oh, no—wait. I can't.
Dammit, Ian, I can't."

"Hot date?" he asked, a little surprised to feel a slight
twinge somewhere inside him. A twinge? Of what? Certainly not jealousy. That would be ridiculous. Besides, if
it was jealousy, it would only be because he enjoyed their
movie nights so much. Maddie never missed a joke in the
comedies, always guessed the murderer in mysteries and
just about crawled inside him when they watched horror
movies. And she made great popcorn. With cheese on it.

"No, silly. No hot date. Not even a lukewarm one,
more's the pity. The girls are taking me out for my birthday."

"Your birthday? That's not for another two days. And
besides, you're spending it with me, remember? Saturday
night, you and me, reservations at Lone Star, two very
thick, very rare steaks. You couldn't have forgotten?"

She reached up, kissed his cheek. "Relax, I haven't
forgotten. How can I forget? You're paying the check.
No, this is just a girls' night out, that's all. Just April,
Annabelle and yours truly. We'll go to the mall straight
from work, grab something to eat and do a little shopping."

"Really?" Ian said, looking at her, one eyebrow raised. "You're going shopping? At the mall? For *clothes?* And that would be voluntarily? I don't believe it."

"Very funny," Madeline said, heading for the door once more. "I'll have you know that I've agreed to let April and Annabelle pick out a new outfit for me. It's their birthday present to me, and I think it's a very nice gesture. Really." She wrinkled her nose. "Kind of. Sorta. Oh, how I'm going to *hate* this."

"Hold it right there, pal," Ian said, walking after her, grabbing her elbow as she reached for the doorknob. "There's got to be a story attached to this. Let's hear it."

Madeline pulled a face. "Man, you're a pain. Okay, okay, so there is a story. Sort of. I was speaking with a patient the other afternoon, out in the hallway of the unit, and the patient's little girl pointed at my stomach and asked when *my* baby would come out."

Ian's smile faded for two reasons. One, he knew Madeline's absolutely atrocious taste in clothes had caused the child's mistake—Omar the tent maker used less cloth—and two, he knew how badly Madeline wanted to be pregnant. Married and pregnant. Just pregnant, if she didn't marry soon.

He hated to hear her talk about becoming a single parent. She deserved so much more. She deserved a man who loved her, a family, even the requisite white picket fence around the family home.

He shook away his thoughts, tried to keep the conversation light. "When is the baby coming out? Ouch, babe, that had to hurt. What were you wearing? That green granny dress your mom sent you? I told you—"

"I know, I know. You've definitely told me. And, yes, the green granny dress my mom made for me, which is now residing in a charity bin outside the hospital. Anyway, Annabelle overheard the little girl, and the next thing I knew she and April had a conspiracy cooked up between them. Tomorrow night they're buying me a new outfit for my birthday. And they've told me I'd better come prepared with my plastic, because they fully intend to talk me into an entire new wardrobe. I'm going to hate every moment of this. Just *hate* it.''

''But you'll play nice?'' Ian prodded. ''You won't do what you did to me the last time I suggested you wear clothes at least *close* to your own size?''

''I didn't do anything to you, Ian, and you know it.''

''Sure. Right,'' he agreed. ''Now, what did you say again? I'm afraid my ears are still ringing. Wait—if I listen, listen closely, I can still hear it. 'Ian Russell, you can take that pitiful excuse for a dress and shove it straight—'''

He broke off as Madeline put down her head, as her shoulders sort of slumped. ''Ah, hell, Maddie, I'm sorry. I didn't know that was such a sore spot with you.''

Her head flew up, her chin jutting out. ''It is *not* a sore spot with me, Ian. I just don't see the point. Do you know how many times a day I can be getting in and out of scrubs, my street clothes? It's just easier to dress as I do. Loose clothing, no buttons, no restrictions.''

''No style, no glamour, no hairstyle, no makeup—okay, okay,'' he ended, putting up his hands as she growled at him. ''I'm backing off, right now. But, man to woman, Mad, if you plan to go fishing, it's smart to put out a couple of lures.''

Madeline opened her mouth, probably to tell him to close his, when there was a knock on the door. She grinned at him rather evilly. ''Oh, gosh, your dress-up doll's here. Guess I'd better hit the road.''

''Very funny,'' Ian said, heading toward the door

"And Rosemary's not a toy. She's a software whiz. Very creative."

"I'll just bet she is," Madeline said as he opened the door. She breezed past Rosemary, who frowned at her, then smiled at Ian.

"Who was that?" Rosemary asked as she waited for Ian to close the door.

"Nobody. Just a friend from across the hall," he told her, wondering why he suddenly felt lower than a snake's belly. He looked at Rosemary, his hot date. Blond hair, legs that went on forever, some pretty impressive cleavage showing above the neckline of her little black dress.

He wondered how soon he could get rid of her.

FRIDAY NIGHT, Madeline met April McCallum and Annabelle Reardon at the Austin Eats diner next door to Maitland Maternity, racing in about twenty minutes late.

She slid into the booth alongside Annabelle, smiled at April, who sat across the narrow table. "Thanks for agreeing to meet here instead of at the mall. I'm so sorry for the last-minute change of plans. Mrs. Halstead kept saying, 'Just one more question, please.' But I think she's okay now. Poor thing, she spends all her free time on the Internet, looking up ways to scare herself."

April sipped soda through a straw, then sighed. "I know how she feels. I mean, I didn't have to worry about all the problems of a multiple pregnancy, but the problems that can arise *afterward* certainly aren't minimal. I can scare myself silly about the babies, and I'm a trained neonatal nurse."

"It's *because* you're a trained neonatal nurse that you can scare yourself so badly," Madeline said reasonably. "You just know too much, have seen too much. Besides, those babies are fine."

April smiled weakly. "I don't know, guys. I should be doing handsprings, but I just...well, I just worry, that's all. I love those little scraps so much. So much," she repeated, blinking back tears.

"Yes, you do love them, April," Annabelle, the baby of this trio of women, said with a wink at Madeline. "Along with a certain new husband you're pretty gaga over, right?"

"Oh, and look who's talking," April countered, nudging Madeline in the ribs. "Have you seen the way our little girl here looks at Zachary Beaumont, our esteemed obstetrician? Some of those looks could melt rock at fifty paces."

"That's not true!" the young delivery room nurse protested, blushing. "I have nothing but the greatest respect for Dr. Beaumont."

"Oh, yeah, here we go. She *respects* him. Let me count the ways. She respects his yummy chocolate brown eyes. She respects that sexy smile. And, oh boy, does she *respect* the way that man looks in scrubs. Did I miss anything?" April asked, leaning her elbows on the table, which only goaded Annabelle into more protests.

As April and Annabelle went back and forth, Madeline pretended to read the menu she already knew by heart, as Austin Eats wasn't just convenient; the food was good, so good that the place had become almost a home away from home for the Maitland Maternity staff.

Madeline felt comfortable here, comfortable with these two women she both liked and admired.

She'd watched April closely these last months, ever since the birth of the quadruplets last December. What a conglomeration of complications that had caused! The birth mother, hardly more than a child herself, had disappeared shortly after the birth of the quads, leaving beind a note that she wanted April to care for her babies. April, who had been assigned to the quads at birth, had allen completely in love with them.

The desperate teenage mother had seen that, even the ocal child welfare agency had seen that, but April's ap-lication to become foster mother to the babies once they vere able to leave the hospital had been tabled, and all ecause she would be a single mother.

April had been devastated, and everyone at Maitland Maternity rallied around her, did everything they could to elp change the agency's mind.

Madeline had written a long letter to the child welfare oard, detailing April's exemplary work ethic as a neo-atal nurse and assuring them that medically, as well as motionally, April would be a perfect foster mother for hose abandoned children with their special needs.

And they were special needs babies; premature, needing onstant care, requiring close monitoring until at least heir fifth year of life, as not all problems showed up mmediately after birth. She sometimes felt that she had o educate the whole world about multiple births, and she ever backed down from a fight.

Madeline ran a finger down the list of specials as she emembered the day Adam's brother, Caleb McCallum, ad entered the picture. A whirlwind courtship and mar-iage followed, but those first weeks of marriage had been retty rocky for her friend. And yet, as Annabelle said, April was definitely gaga over Caleb now, and the man ouldn't be more obvious about being in love with his vife.

It had become a ritual for Madeline to stop by the nurs-ry every night before she went home, to watch April and Caleb with their babies, the babies they'd both come to ove. And now they were a family, at least a foster family, and if the courts had any brains at all, they'd be a real permanent family.

Because Jenny, the quads' mother, had at last been located and seemed to still want April to care for her children. If she would give her final legal approval to the adoption, all of April's and Caleb's worries would be over.

"Okay. Let's order, eat and get this girl to the mall. It's makeover time," April said.

Madeline immediately felt her stomach clench. "Oh, do we have to?"

April's expression as she looked at Madeline said *You're kidding, right?*

"Oh, no, Madeline, we have to do this," Annabelle, younger and less tactful, blurted. "You *have* to do this. I mean—look at you."

Madeline looked at her comfortable cotton granny dress. Slightly scooped neck, cap sleeves, button front, a little bit of smocking over the bosom, high waistline. Pretty little blue flowers on a gray background. Short gray cotton vest sweater hanging over the dress. Okay, so maybe the sweater was a *little* baggy. "What? What's wrong with this?"

"Annabelle?" April said, covering her smile with one hand. "You want to take this one?"

Annabelle's cheeks turned rosy, and she stammered slightly as she said, "Oh! Oh, Madeline, I...I didn't mean. I mean...I don't want to *criticize....*"

"Oh, sure you do," April said cheerfully. "Start with her sandals, why don't you?"

"My sandals? What's wrong with them? I thought you were talking about my clothes, not my sandals." Madeline sat back, sighed. "Oh, all right, all right. It's not like this is the first time I'm hearing this. Ian keeps telling me must shop in the dark. But the thing is, I *like* my clothes. They're comfortable.''

"So's going around naked, Madeline," April countered, "but I don't think it'll ever catch on."

Their food arrived, double cheeseburgers all around, but Madeline had lost her appetite. "How do I explain this?" she asked, addressing the French fry in her hand. "Okay, here goes. I was an only child. Neither Mom or Dad had the faintest idea how to raise this daughter they'd ended up with due to one of those fabled menopausal pregnancies. They never really adjusted to me, so I had to adjust to them. Which meant I spent most of my time with my nose in a book and not thinking about the latest fashion fads.''

"That still doesn't explain why, at nearly thirty-five, you're dressing like a throwback to the sixties. Or did you grow up in a commune?"

Madeline lowered her head. "Just until I was twelve," she admitted, then looked at her friends, who were goggling at her. "No, seriously, I did grow up in a commune. It was wonderful. Really. Stop laughing.''

"I can't help it, Madeline," April said, wiping her eyes. "I'm trying to be serious, but I keep seeing you tripping through a meadow, a daisy chain in your hair, a loaf of homemade bread under your arm.''

Annabelle clapped her hands for attention. "Another discussion for another time, ladies. Okay, so now we know where the granny gowns and sandals and that braid came from—and may they all leave quickly, please. But we're here together tonight to turn Madeline Sheppard from—and I mean this in the nicest way, Madeline—dull and dreary and into *ka-wow!*''

"Oh, sure." Madeline groused, wiping her hands on her paper napkin. "I can see it now. I open a couple of

buttons on this dress, take off my reading glasses—which
means I won't be able to see my French fries—take down
my braid, shake my hair free and—bam!—suddenly I'm
Catherine Zeta-Jones.'' She rolled her eyes. ''Cut me a
break.''

''Hey, it could happen.'' April ignored the sarcasm.
''And another thing. Are you saying that there's something under that dress that would be improved by opening
a couple of those buttons? I'll bet you are. Well, then,
we're on our way, aren't we, Annabelle? Hot dog!''

''Oh, no,'' Madeline moaned, and buried her head in
her hands.

Chapter Two

Madeline walked to the tall T-stand and lifted off a hanger, holding up the soft cotton flowered ankle-length dress to her friends. "See? It's not just my mother sending me her efforts, sewn with her two arthritic hands, bless her. There have to be dozens of these dresses here. How can you say I'm out of date?"

Annabelle and April exchanged pained meaningful glances. "I'll take this one," April volunteered after a moment. She relieved Madeline of the dress, which she then shoved onto the rack. "Madeline. Sweetheart. Honey. Yes, they still make these dresses. Yes, they still sell these dresses. *To teenagers.* You're thirty-five years old."

"Thirty-four," Madeline grumbled under her breath. "Maybe for only one more day, but I'm hanging on with both hands, thank you anyway."

"Thirty-four, thirty-five, whatever," April continued, taking Madeline by the elbow and steering her toward another section of the largest department store in the mall. "The point I'm trying to make is that, if you're not either eighteen or pregnant, the time has come to say goodbye to the cutesy, little-girl look, okay?"

Madeline cast one last look over her shoulder at the

rack of dresses, sighed. "Okay, but what do I tell my mother? She sends me at least ten new dresses a year."

"Tell her you still want them to donate to the thrift shop run by the hospital auxiliary. Those high waistlines, those gathered skirts? Your mom puts enough material in those dresses to take a woman carrying sextuplets into her third trimester. In fact, maybe you ought to think about donating your entire wardrobe to the hospital thrift shop."

Madeline blinked back sudden tears. "You sound just like Ian. I swear, if that man had his way, all women would wear nothing but bikinis."

"Really? He's a sexist?" Annabelle asked.

"No, not really. I was exaggerating," Madeline said. "He just thinks it's time I paid more attention to myself, that's all, instead of taking the easy way out, which is what he calls my clothes. Which are *comfortable,* not to belabor the point. I don't even have to waste time like this—shopping. You have both figured out that I *hate* shopping, right?"

"Ian said you should pay more attention to yourself?" April nodded, pulling out a soft pink silk blouse, holding up the hanger. "Sounds like a smart man. Life in a commune, working your way through college and med school, working twelve-hour days at the new unit? I know you're busy, Madeline, but you're not just a doctor. You're a fun, lovely, intelligent woman. It's about time you stopped hiding behind those yards of material."

There was no getting around, over or under these two women. She'd have to tell the awful truth. "I've got a gut," Madeline said quietly, so quietly that Annabelle leaned closer, made her repeat what she'd said.

"A gut," Madeline said, more loudly than she'd intended. "A belly, Annabelle. I always have. There are the medical terms for it, but in layman's terms, I'm an apple. You know—apples and pears. Pears have small waists, flat bellies, bigger hips, heavier thighs. We apples have skinny arms and legs, narrow hips, but tend to gain all our weight in our bellies, waistlines. And our busts,'' she added, knowing that every drawback had at least one bonus, and her generous bust was hers.

"She says she's an apple," Annabelle said to April, shrugging.

April shrugged in return. "So? I'm a pear. I've been waging war on my upper thighs since I was twelve. No problem. We camouflage."

Madeline rolled her eyes. "Isn't that what I've *been* doing?"

"Madeline," April said reasonably, "you could hide *Oklahoma* under that dress. We don't need that much camouflage. We just go for short skirts—to show off your legs—and longer, more swingy tops, to hide this massive waistline you say you have. Now, what size are you?"

Madeline tried to make her one-hundred-and-forty-pound, five-foot-six-inch frame smaller—knowing she couldn't make it disappear. "I don't know. I have to go larger to be able to comfortably button my waistbands, which is just another reason Mom's dresses are easier and definitely more comfortable. And slacks? Forget it! By the time the waist fits, the crotch is at my knees, the seat sags, and my legs disappear. Which—" she ended on a sigh "—is why I don't wear slacks or jeans."

"Oh, have *you* ever been shopping in the wrong stores. Except you don't shop, right?" Annabelle shook her head. "Come on, Madeline, it's just us girls here. The size?"

Madeline sighed. "A fourteen? A sixteen?"

"Sixteen? No way!" Annabelle exclaimed, eyeing Mad-

eline with what looked to be a practiced eye. "You probably just chose the wrong designers. Some seem to design
for those of us with smaller waists and bigger butts—
pardon my French—and others design for, what did you
call yourself? Oh, yeah, an apple. We just have to find a
designer who caters to apples."

"And elastic waistbands," April added, dragging Madeline across the carpeted floor to yet another section of
the women's department. "According to my mother, a
definite apple, elastic waistbands are the greatest invention
since sliced bread, or something like that. A sixteen?
Never! I'll bet you're a twelve, once we find those elastic
waistbands."

April was wrong. Twenty minutes later, with Annabelle
running back and forth between dressing room and selling
floor to exchange sizes, Madeline stood staring at herself—and wearing a size ten.

The collarless Wedgwood blue silk suit jacket she wore
had long sleeves, a lovely row of covered buttons, a hem
that hit just at the top of her thighs and a softly nipped
in waist that actually gave her a shape. A real shape. And
the skirt? Lined with slinky taffeta, the straight skirt—
with elastic waist—barely skimmed the top of her knees,
exposing her slim, well-shaped, very long lower legs.

"Now I ask you, ladies and gentlemen, who *is* this
gorgeous creature?" April asked, obviously quite pleased
with herself. "So, Madeline? What do you think?"

"I think I don't believe it," she answered, pulling up
the tag hanging from the sleeve. "A *ten?*"

"Welcome to the wonderful world of camouflage,"
Annabelle said as she hung up rejects, then sat on the
small chair in the dressing room. "You look great, Madeline. Professional, yet sexy. We'll take it, right, April?"

"Definitely. Happy birthday, Madeline," April answered with a grin. "Thank heaven the mall is open late for the pre-Easter sales. Now that we know the style and the size—and the great elastic secret—Madeline, it's time to pull out the plastic, because we aren't leaving here until you've got a whole new wardrobe. Suits for work, slacks and tops for casual wear, you name it."

"And then we do the shoes, the purses—because you're *not* going to ruin that suit by carrying around that knitted feed bag anymore, Madeline."

"And makeup," April added, unwrapping the elastic tie around Madeline's braid, unwinding the braid itself. "Oh, would you look at those curls! Madeline, you've been hiding naturally black, naturally curly hair? How could you? That's positively criminal. And you've got fabulous skin, Madeline, white and creamy. That's probably because you've never worn makeup. Snow White skin, Snow White hair—all we need now is a prince."

"Yes, definitely a prince," Annabelle said, jumping up from her chair to kiss Madeline's cheek. "You look *wonderful,* Madeline."

"True, Annabelle, but there does come a time when we all need a little...embellishment. Even princesses. With those brown eyes, I'd say some two-tone beige and brown shadow, some peachy-colored blusher and lipstick. And, of course, mascara and eyeliner. Madeline? Madeline, are we pushing too hard? Are you okay with this?"

Madeline, who had been staring at her reflection, half frightened, half pleased, knowing she still wouldn't give Catherine Zeta-Jones a run for her money—but, then, who could?—just nodded. "Okay. Sure. I mean—" she gave her head a small shake, watched her curls settle onto her shoulders "—sure. Let's do it."

IAN LOOKED at his watch, calculating how much time it would take to get across town to the Lone Star in time for their six o'clock reservations.

He'd had it all planned so carefully. Up early, go for a run. Golf with the guys, a nap, some power shopping to locate a reasonably good birthday gift, dinner at six.

Except he'd come home to a note Madeline had slipped under his door, telling him that she might be a little late because she had to go back to the mall with April and Annabelle for "some last-minute idiocy."

Ian pondered that line for a while, then tossed the note aside, found the channel changer and surfed for whatever sports might be on the tube the week before the NCAA March Madness started next week. He lucked out with a great game for one of the last divisional tournaments and settled in to watch, one ear listening for Madeline's footsteps in the hallway.

Not that he wasn't interested in the game on the screen, because he was. But he and Maddie usually watched the games together. Baseball, basketball, football, ice hockey—anything that wasn't soccer, because she always fell asleep during soccer games.

Maybe, after dinner, they'd come back and watch the video he'd rented last night. He'd started to watch it by himself, but only five minutes into it he knew Maddie would love it, so he'd ejected the tape. Then he'd read two chapters of a book. Then he'd walked around his apartment, straightening up, and found one of Maddie's hair clips under the kitchen table. He put it in the dish on the counter, the Maddie Collection Plate that she raided every time she ran out of hair clips or needed postage stamps, emery boards, even her extra pair of reading glasses. Her sandals he kept in the hall closet, along with a tweed vest he hoped she never remembered she owned.

nd the crutches she'd used that summer she broke her
oot.

Not that he minded that Maddie, left to her own de-
ices, could quickly have his entire apartment littered with
er stuff, because he didn't. He liked that they were so
omfortable with each other that they just about lived in
ach other's pockets. Sharing, caring. All that good stuff.

Except now Maddie was going to turn thirty-five. If
e'd thought she'd panicked at thirty, it had been nothing
o compare with the teary monologue he'd listened to one
ight a few weeks ago, wherein Maddie lamented her sin-
le state, her ticking biological clock and her conviction
hat she was speeding headlong into old maidhood.

He was also going to be thirty-five. Did that mean he
vas racing down the road to old bachelorhood?

Not according to Maddie, Ian remembered, as he
ooked into the mirror above his dresser, twisting his tie
nto a neat Windsor knot.

"You're just entering your prime," she'd told him—
ccused him, actually. "Men have it so much easier.
You'll be able to take your pick of women—especially
ounger women—well into your fifties. But not women.
And especially not if we want babies. Do you know how
nuch more difficult it is to even *become* pregnant for the
irst time after the age of thirty-five? And the complica-
ions of having your first child after forty? Not good, Ian,
ot good. Trust me. So I'm thinking about getting preg-
ant. I mean, why not? Women like me are doing it every
lay. Of course, I'd have to find a donor."

"Yeah?" he'd said, trying to keep the conversation
ight. "Well, don't go to strangers."

Ian checked the collar of his shirt, still looking at his
eflection as he thought over Maddie's words, his flip re-

ply, the rather shattered look that had passed over her features before she'd smiled, laughed rather hollowly.

Was that when everything had changed?

Probably.

Maddie was his best pal, his good buddy—his other half, when he got right down to it. There was nothing they didn't know about each other, nothing they couldn't share—not their pains, their joys, their highs, their lows. Theirs was the friendship of a lifetime, the sort only a few were blessed to have and one he knew had to be fed, nurtured, in order to endure.

Except he'd been taking advantage of Maddie. Oh, not intentionally, but he'd been monopolizing her time all these years while keeping his social life in full swing.

Was that his fault? If Maddie didn't date very often, didn't actively look for dates—was that his fault?

Did he keep her that busy? Sure, they saw each other every day, sometimes sharing breakfast in her apartment, sometimes meeting near the hospital for lunch. Madeline cooked dinner for them at least four nights a week.

And on Friday and Saturday nights Ian went out on dates…and Maddie stayed home to read medical journals.

"You've been getting all the perks here, bucko," Ian told himself as he ran a comb through his dark hair. "You don't just count on Maddie hanging around, waiting for you to show up in her life—you *expect* her to be there. And that's not fair."

Maddie should be married. Ian knew that. She should have a gang of kids, definitely. But if she stayed with him, let him be the platonic man in her life, she'd never find a romantic man for her life. Maybe Maddie didn't see that, but he did. Now. The damn dirty shame was that he hadn't seen it for fifteen long years.

"Yeah, but don't tell her that tonight," he warned himelf as he went to the closet and pulled out his sport jacket, lid his arms into it as he headed out of the bedroom. 'Happy birthday, Maddie. Go away, find a life.'' He hook his head. "Oh, yeah, that would do it. That one vould nail down that Prince of the Year award for sure.''

But what else was he to do? What Maddie wanted, what Maddie needed, he couldn't give her. They were friends, not lovers. Hadn't they tried that back in college? It hadn't vorked then and it wouldn't work now. They knew each other too well to change their comfortable friendship into omething so much more complicated.

Besides, if he tried to kiss her, tried to do anything at ll, she'd probably laugh at him, just the way she'd done he one time he had tried to kiss her in something other han a brotherly way.

What was it she'd said to him at the time? Oh, yeah. Something really nice. "What, are you nuts, Russell? I'm not even blond.''

"See?'' Ian said to the ceramic dalmatian Maddie had bought him for Christmas, the one that stood sentinel in front of his gas fireplace in the living room. "That's how he sees me, Spot. Playboy of the western world. Not that haven't done my best to live up to that reputation. But man, Spot, I'm getting tired. Dancing all night, ruining my new sneakers with romantic walks in the rain, fielding veiled questions about how many kids I'd like to have. Who needs the hassle? I'm just getting too old for this. Right, Spot?''

Spot just sat there, that sort of sickly half smile on his ace that had gotten him marked down to half price and won the heart of Maddie, who believed the underdog hould be able to catch a break from time to time. So he'd brought Spot home, given him to Ian, saying he houldn't worry, she'd feed the mutt if he'd walk him.

Ian smiled, shook his head again. What an idiotic pres
ent. He wouldn't take Spot's weight in diamonds for tha
stupid, crooked-mouth dog.

Okay. He checked his watch one more time, decide
he'd killed enough time on introspection, or whatever i
hell it was he'd been doing—and he certainly wasn't go
ing to examine his rambling thoughts too closely, becaus
then he might find out. Maddie should have been knock
ing on his door fifteen minutes ago, maybe twenty.

"Yeah, well, if the mountain won't come to Muham
mad," he grumbled, scooping his car keys from the tabl
beside the couch. "Don't wait up," he called over hi
shoulder to Spot, and headed across the hall to Maddie'
apartment.

"GO AWAY!"

Ian knocked again, harder this time.

Madeline should have known. The man never had taker
direction well.

There was that time she'd told him not to make a
U-turn at that intersection with the No U-Turn sign. Yes
she'd been called to the hospital for an emergency, and
yes, she'd wanted to get there as fast as possible. But did
he listen? No. That one had cost him a hefty fine.

And then there was the time—okay, about six hundred
times—she'd told him not to take the wooden spoon from
a pot, take a taste and put the spoon back in the pot. And
then he'd wink at her, the rat.

Or the day he swore he wasn't too sick to go camping
with some old college friends and ended up with pneu
monia. That had been a big "I told you so" betweer
them, considering she had been the lucky one who'
ended up playing nurse for a very uncooperative patient.

She could go on. And on. The man was a menace

There were times she threatened him with divorce—and they weren't even married.

"Ian, go away!" she called, definitely in the grip of panic. "I'm…I'm not ready yet."

"Well, I am, Maddie. Come on, I'm starving," he called through the door, then turned the knob—just as Maddie realized she hadn't locked the door. Damn him for knowing she rarely remembered to lock the door during the day. He'd give her another lecture. Just what she didn't need, someone else telling her what was best for her.

Madeline turned on her heels, ready to make a break for it all the way to her bedroom, to her bathroom, to the door that would lock behind her once she was in the bathroom.

"Whoa!"

Too late. Madeline remained where she was, her back to Ian, her eyes closed as she waited for whatever would follow that whoa.

It wasn't long in coming.

"Maddie? Is that you? In *slacks?*"

She looked at herself. At the tangerine-colored silk top that flowed softly over her body, ending at the tops of her thighs. At the beige raw silk slacks that were pencil thin all the way down to the ankles, where they covered her brand-new beige boots with the three-inch heels.

She raised a hand to grab the tortoiseshell pendant that hung to her waist from a thick gold chain and turned to confront Ian. "Don't say a word," she warned him.

And, for once in his life, the man was obedient, because he stood there, looking at her. And looking at her. And looking at her.

"Oh, for crying out loud, Ian!" she complained when he couldn't stand it anymore. "*Say* something."

He shook his head, spread his arms. "I can't. I don't know what to say." He used the sweep of one hand to encompass her hair, her face, her new clothing. "What happened?"

Madeline threw up her hands. "I knew it. I just knew that would be your reaction! I look ridiculous. Stay here, I'm going to go wash my face."

His hand snaked out, capturing her elbow. "Oh, no, you're not. Come here, Maddie," he said, half dragging her toward the mirror hanging over a table beside the front door. "Look at yourself. Your hair looks great, all pulled away from your face and curly and everything. And those eyes! Maddie, when did your eyes get so big?"

"Makeup," she told him tightly. "My eyes didn't grow, Ian. It's just makeup."

"I know that, Maddie," Ian said, giving her a quick hug as she faced the mirror. "And I love this color," he said, rubbing a bit of the fabric of her shirt between his fingers. "Silk. I'm crazy about silk."

Madeline shivered, knowing it wasn't cold in the apartment, and stepped away from the mirror, wrapping her arms around herself. "Then you don't think I look ridiculous? It's why we went back to the mall today, Annabelle and I. To have my hair and makeup done."

And then her shoulders slumped. "Oh, Ian, I can't believe I let people *do* this to me. Makeup, a new hairstyle, enough new clothing that I doubt my charge card will cool down for at least a year."

"You mean there's more?" Ian said, waggling his eyebrows at her. "You bought more than just this one outfit?"

"Oh, stop grinning," Madeline said testily. "And, yes, it's true. All your fondest dreams realized. I promised to get rid of my old wardrobe. Are you happy now?"

"Hey, I'm not brokenhearted," Ian said, shrugging. "You look good, Maddie, damn good. Except I never realized you're so skinny."

Madeline's mouth dropped open, and she blinked several times. "Skinny? You think I'm *skinny?*"

"Well, maybe not skinny-skinny, if you know what I mean. I just didn't realize you had any shape at all." He winced, obviously knowing he'd stuck his foot in it, badly. "That is, I know you've got legs. Great legs, Maddie, honest. It's just the rest of you that I didn't know was there. No! That's not right. I *know* you're here, Maddie. I've always known you're *here.* You're my girl, right? You've always been my girl. I just didn't realize you're also *a* girl. No! I don't mean that, either. Oh, dammit, Maddie, let's go eat, okay?"

"Sounds like a plan," Madeline said, grabbing her new purse—much smaller than a feed bag. "It's either that, or we stay here while you make a jerk of yourself. Come on, I'm starving."

Ian spread his arms, looking sheepish and silly at the same time. "Isn't that what I've been saying?"

Madeline rolled her eyes and headed for the door, hiding her smile. *Skinny.* Ian thought she was skinny. Did life get any better than this? Happy birthday, indeed!

IAN HAD ALWAYS gotten a big kick out of watching Maddie eat.

He'd learned long ago that Maddie compartmentalized her life. At work, neat and organized. In the kitchen, wildly creative and definitely sloppy. Meticulous about her checkbook, her drinking-glasses cabinet, her spice rack…while sometimes he teased her that the housekeeping police were going to come get her if she didn't stop using her floors and furniture as her personal clothes hamper.

So neat and orderly in some ways, so "oh, who cares?" in others.

Maddie's food fell into the "Who cares? I do!" category, definitely. It could take her, conservatively, five minutes to explain to the waiter exactly how she wanted her steak cooked, how well-done the onion rings should be, how crisp the spinach salad, how browned the garlic bread. And she'd watch, closely, to make sure the waiter wrote it all down. Ian had long ago learned to tip, heavily, if he planned on ever bringing Maddie back to the same restaurant and actually not have to watch the entire wait staff turn in their aprons and run for the doors.

Then she ate. Heartily. But it was a bite of meat, followed by a bite of potato, followed by a bite of salad. She saved her food, a bit of everything, making sure she got a taste of everything, and all the food got gone at the same time, all while she tsk-tsked at him because he ate his salad first, his potato second and his meat last—and had the nerve to call *him* compulsive.

Ian, having finished his steak, sat with his chin propped on his hand, his elbow on the table, and watched as Maddie enjoyed the remainder of her meal. Bite of salad. Bite of potato, scraping the inner skin to get all the best bits. Bite of steak. "Good to the last bite?" he asked, grinning at her.

"Delicious," she agreed, then glared at him. "You're watching me again, aren't you? Why do you do that?"

"Because it never ceases to amaze me that you don't, for instance, run out of potato before you run out of steak. How do you do that?"

"Planning," Maddie told him. "You should try it. Besides, I'm just naturally a very orderly person."

Ian sat back in his chair. "Sure, you are. Oh, by the way? If you're looking for your Rolling Stones CD, it's under my couch cushion, where you left it."

"It is?" Maddie leaned forward, her eyes wide—and still beautifully huge. He knew the makeup had something to do with this new look, but he didn't care. She was still Maddie—she was just, finally, living up to her potential as a woman. "I looked all over for that yesterday. What if I sat down? I could have broken it. Why did you leave it under the cushion?"

He shrugged. "Because you're such a neat and orderly person? I figured you put it there on purpose. Just like I left your gold signet ring on the bathroom sink. Because you're neat and orderly and probably want it there."

"But I wanted to wear that tonight, Ian. I looked all over for that, too." She closed her mouth, tipped her head as she looked at him. "Are we arguing?" she asked, narrowing those chocolate brown eyes of hers. "Are you trying to tell me I'm taking over your apartment with my *stuff* again?"

"I like your stuff," Ian answered, more honestly than he'd intended. "I like seeing it lying around. I may be crazy, but I'll probably miss it all if it ever goes away."

"Oh," Maddie said quietly. "That's…that's nice, Ian. Thank you."

"You're welcome," Ian said, trying to smile. Except he didn't really feel like smiling.

He knew why, too, which was really upsetting.

He wasn't smiling because Maddie had all but told him during that monologue of hers a few weeks ago that she was going husband hunting. That new hairdo, the makeup, the definitely interesting V-neck tangerine blouse and sexy slacks—they all subtly screamed, "Here I am, Bubba, come get me!"

He couldn't blame her. She wanted a husband, a home, a family of her own. At thirty-five, it was time, maybe more than time.

But what about *him,* dammit? What was he supposed to do without her? What *would* he do without her?

Could he do without her?

Ian protectively caught himself against the edge of the table as a sudden, hearty slap on his back sent his upper body forward.

"Ian, you devil, you! I haven't seen you in a while. How's it going?"

Using the arms of the chair to boost himself to his previous position on the seat, Ian turned his head, looked, then stood up, held out his hand. "Blake. Good to see you. I thought you were out of town this week."

"I was, I was, but I was able to take an early flight back from Phoenix this morning. I was going to call you later, so this is lucky. Are we still set for that meeting next Wednesday? You've definitely talked my board into taking you guys on for the Lattimer project. You're quite the salesman, Ian, although you might want to think about catching up on your social skills. For instance, who is this lovely lady? Aren't you going to introduce us?"

"Oh, sorry," Ian said. "Maddie, I'd like to introduce a business associate of mine, Blake Ritter. Blake, Dr. Madeline Sheppard."

"Doctor? No," Blake said, bending over the hand Maddie extended to him, making a total ass out of himself—in Ian's opinion—by kissing it. "You couldn't be a doctor. You're not old enough to be a doctor. Ian, it isn't like you to rob cradles."

"Down, boy," Ian grumbled, taking his seat. "Maddie is most definitely a doctor—a fertility specialist, as a matter of fact—and most definitely all grown up."